TRAVELLING WITH DJINNS

Jamal Mahjoub was born in London and brought up in Khartoum, Sudan. Originally trained as a geologist, he has worked at various times as a librarian, journalist and translator. He has published four previous novels, *Navigation of a Rainmaker*, *Wings of Dust*, *In the Hour of Signs* and *The Carrier*, which have been highly acclaimed and widely translated. *Travelling with Djinns* won the Prix de l'Astrolabe Etonnants Voyageurs. Jamal Mahjoub currently lives in Barcelona.

Jamal Mahjoub

TRAVELLING
WITH DJINNS

To Alec McInnes

With all best wishes

[signature]

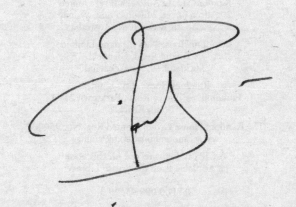

V
VINTAGE

Edinburgh

16-8.
2006

Published by Vintage 2004

2 4 6 8 10 9 7 5 3 1

First published in Great Britain in 2003 by
Chatto & Windus

Vintage
Random House, 20 Vauxhall Bridge Road,
London SW1V 2SA

Random House Australia (Pty) Limited
20 Alfred Street, Milsons Point, Sydney
New South Wales 2061, Australia

Random House New Zealand Limited
18 Poland Road, Glenfield,
Auckland 10, New Zealand

Random House (Pty) Limited
Endulini, 5A Jubilee Road, Parktown 2193,
South Africa

The Random House Group Limited Reg. No. 954009
www.randomhouse.co.uk/vintage

A CIP catalogue record for this book
is available from the British Library

ISBN 0 099 45529 3

Papers used by Random House are natural, recyclable
products made from wood grown in sustainable forests.
The manufacturing processes conform to the environ-
mental regulations of the country of origin

Printed and bound in Great Britain by
Cox & Wyman Limited, Reading, Berkshire

Author's Note

The quotations from Rimbaud's letters come from *Arthur Rimbaud: Complete Works*, translated by Paul Schmidt, Harper Colophon Books, 1976. The reference to Brueghel in Chapter 8 owes something to Richard Sennett's analysis of Pieter Brueghel's Landscape with the Fall of Icarus in *Flesh and Stone*, Faber and Faber, 1994. The Joseph Roth book referred to is a Spanish edition, *Las ciudades blancas*, published by Editorial Minúscula, 2000. A number of other books are mentioned in passing. All conclusions and confusions are mine alone.

My thanks to Rebecca Carter for restoring my faith in publishers generally, and in the editor's craft in particular. Also to Gillon, Sally Riley and all at G. Aitken Associates for their valiant efforts. A nod of acknowledgment goes to the late Ian Hamilton whose encouragement sparked off this book and whose company is sorely missed. Thanks to Lieve Joris for attentive reading and generous enthusiasm. Thanks also to Jean and Madeleine Sévry in France as well as Bernard Magnier, Evelyne Chanet and all at Actes Sud. In Spain; Enrique Murillo and Imma Espuñes at Alfaguara, and Robert Antoni for the final word. This book is dedicated to Aisha and Louis, as always, and to Rosa for her enduring patience.

Prologue

A tiny white sphere, arching high up into the air.

My father was hit on the head by a golf ball when he was nine years old. I was told this by Haboba, my grandmother. I wasn't around at the time.

I envisage the scene as follows: I see them all craning their necks to look upwards. I see my father, resting his chin on his hand, his elbow on the bulky leather bag that stands upright alongside him. That was his job, carrying the clubs for the *khawaja*, the English gentlemen. He was the native caddy. He shields his eyes with the flat brim of his hand as the ball vanishes into the wide, pale aureole of the sun. For a moment, I imagine, he is captivated by the idea of that ball soaring away freely, high above the earth – if anything, he was a daydreamer, my father. He would sit in class tapping his feet together and humming 'Twinkle, twinkle little star, how I wonder what you are' until the English teacher swatted him behind the ear, shouting, 'Wake up my little rhinoceros!' My mother gave me that detail – about the rhinoceros. All the stories that make any sense in my life have been given to me by women.

I wonder what that ball meant to him at that moment. Was it his soul soaring high above the planet, or was it a sense of purpose, a message being carried to him by an angel sent to whisper incantations and mystical spells in his ear? Whatever it was, the hard porcelain globe dropped out of the cloudless sky and struck him right between the eyes. He fell to the ground without so much as a whimper.

★

Everything has a beginning, a starting point, a place of departure, some moment of punctuation where the old story leaves off and the new begins. Life has a habit of doing that. You think you know how it is going to turn out and then bang. For me, that golf ball marks the beginning of my own family's curious trajectory, the one which led me to where I am today. In a sense, it was our combined fate, as a family, that was knocked off course that morning. We've been on an elliptical wobble ever since.

Haboba told me later that he stayed out cold for a week. That she went to sit by him night and day in the English military hospital in Khartoum where he was taken on account of the fact that he had gone down in the line of duty, as it were, acting as caddy for two officers of the Royal Air Force. Everyone thought he would never wake up, that he would simply stay like that until his heart stopped beating. Neighbours came and sat in the house all day rocking back and forth with scented handkerchiefs held to their mouths, fanning their necks with their fingers, anticipating the task of mourning that was to come. Three days went by, and there was no change; he was neither dead nor alive, but suspended somehow between this world and the next. The would-be mourners shook their heads in dismay. To have the agony drawn out like this. How could one woman suffer so much misfortune? Her only child, her husband's only son, and that poor man's heart went and stopped while he was in some place called Musmar – which nobody had ever heard of, let alone seen – working for the Railways & Steamers Department. That was run by the British, too, muttered the more radical among them.

Another three days went by, and still no change. Haboba seemed to be familiar with life's catalogue of dismay and had learned to resign herself to whatever was thrown her way. She said that she knew with certainty that he was not going to die. He might have woken up a complete idiot, or not woken up at all, but he wasn't going to die. She knew that. 'In our family,' she smiled, warm with the memory of that

2

far-off time, 'we have heads like rocks. It's our hearts that are soft.'

I used to sit with her and listen to her talk in that slow deliberate manner of hers which told you softly and firmly that rushing never got you anywhere, things have to be allowed to take their time. In the evenings she and I would carry our mattresses outside into the *hosh* to lay them on the rough, palm-fibre strings of the creaky old beds. She would recline on her side with her legs curled up underneath her, her head cradled in the palm of her hand. I would lie across from her and listen, entranced. I could not see her face, I would just hear the sound of her voice coming out of the darkness. Some evenings she was speaking just to me, sometimes there were others with us there in the yard; the house was always full of people, coming and going. Aunts and nieces who had lived there for a time and then moved on, or the odd neighbour dropping by.

It was a house filled with women. All the men were long gone, left for other women, other pastures, gone abroad for work and never heard of again. And they passed away with such alarming regularity that I am constantly promising myself to go for regular medical check-ups. Men vanished. They remained only as reference points in the ongoing narrative of these women's lives. They were there in that wedding shawl that had been carefully folded and stuck inside a battered suitcase decades earlier. Or in the black-and-white photographs tucked inside the cupboard where the nice plates and glasses were kept that were never used; pinned in one corner, a wrinkled and folded passport photograph of a young man whom I knew as my uncle or second cousin. In another the picture of the man I knew as my grandfather, whom I had never met but in whose features I could discern the faint traces of my father, even down to the moustache; lean, dark and slim, in a white shirt and wide trousers that looked as though they had been pressed just before the picture was taken, standing against a painted studio background that depicted a river and a moon. There he was, immortalised, gathering dust among the soup plates and painted teacups. This is what happens to men, I imagined, they end up in glass cupboards gathering dust.

The evening conversations crossed back and forth between the women in the *hosh* around me, busy working over the details of their worried lives, while above us the sky was crowded with stars, blinking in constant amazement, circling our theatre by miniscule increments.

Often, as my eyes struggled against sleep, I had the strange feeling that I was falling into a vast web; a complex net woven of an infinite number of stories – I had no idea how many there were, or which of them were true and which made up, which handed down over generations, and which picked up at the market that very morning, along with an armful of aubergines and curly cucumbers. Time seemed to flow, just in that moment, and everything was instantly terribly old and new at the very same time. I could not imagine what all those stories contained, but recall vividly the overwhelming conviction that they were there for me alone to discover. I also knew that no matter how long I lived I could never learn them all, although somehow that didn't matter.

As for my father, well, he suffered no permanent damage, not visibly in any case, but from that day on, as Haboba said, you never knew what was coming next. Something inside him had been shifted, permanently dislodged from its intended orbit. How else to explain everything that happened, in his, as indeed, in all our lives?

I sometimes think I envy those people who know where they belong; writers who have a language and a history that is granted them with no catches, no hooks. Theirs for the taking. Along with a nation of willing accomplices, compatriots who see their own fate and that of their nation's history and literary tradition reflected in the mirror of the writer's labour. It is all so neatly sewn up. Of course, I enjoy no such privilege. I belong to that nomad tribe, the great unwashed, those people born in the joins between continental shelves, in the unclaimed interstices between time zones, strung across latitudes. A tribe of no fixed locus, the homeless, the stateless. I have two passports and quite a variety of other documents to identify me, all of which tell the world where I have been, but not who I am, nor where I am going to. My language is a bastard tongue of necessity, improvisation, bad grammar and continual misunderstandings. I am a stranger wherever I go. My history is not given, but has to be taken, reclaimed, piece by solitary piece, snatched from among the pillars of centuries, the shelves of ivory scholarship. My flimsy words set against those lumbering tomes bound in leather and written in blood. My nation is a random list of places on the map that I have passed through, upon which I have no claim. Some might say that I have been assimilated, but they would be wrong. Others would say I am alienated and ought to be better integrated by now, but that too would be to miss the point. This is the way of things. Don't get me wrong, it's not sympathy I'm looking for, simply that I have never really been able to make sense of all this before, I never really had to. There was always time later, further on, up ahead, round the next bend. And that's how most of us go through life, until something comes along to change that. And in my case it wasn't so much a what as a who.

I

His name is Leo – his mother's choice, not mine. The name I proposed was met with blank smiles, frowns and other marks of dull incomprehension as friends and relatives duly accepted that this was me asserting my territory, pissing on the party cake. It was not a difficult name, I thought, but it was shunted slowly and surely out of the way, relegated to Second Division by mutual unspoken consent. Gradually, of course, he simply got used to being called Leo; his English mother, her parents, his schoolmates and teachers all called him Leo. I held out, stubbornly referring to him as Hamdi until gradually I gave in to the realisation that I was not only making a fool of myself, I was also causing him pain and embarrassment. 'Hamdi Damdi sat on a wall. Hamdi Damdi had a great fall.' He became Leo. It was as simple as that, and not much I could do about it. Names have their own resolve and this one has already attached itself to his growing awareness of himself. At the age of seven he has already embarked on the inevitable (and impossible) course of trying to create a complete person from the figure he sees when he looks in the mirror. Sometimes I catch him there in the bathroom, splashing water all over the place trying to comb his hair down to one side like a proper English schoolboy. The little person he sees in that reflection is a complete human being and the name of that person is Leo. As soon as the water starts to dry little curls pop up like coiled springs, ruining the effect.

He is the real reason for this trip, this flight, this *hejira*, if you like. I want him to find out that he is more than just

Leo, although how I am going to achieve this I don't really know. I cannot claim to have planned this with the kind of rationale that it deserves. There is no logic to it. It all just happened. What can you ever promise a child, after all, except that you will always be there, reliable and dependable, a sail for them to navigate with? But all of that has come undone, and I am no longer sure I can keep that promise. The fact that he was given two first names at all was a warning sign, a precursor of the turmoil that was to follow. When two new parents cannot agree on what to name their firstborn child, there is a fairly good chance that this is a hint, a pointer to other incompatibilities lurking just beneath the placid surface of family bliss.

So I am driving by instinct alone. I hardly have a destination in mind. The vast undulating sheet of time tends to shift suddenly and without warning whole worlds disappear. I am at the centre of a great divide, a line that cuts through the earth like a plough, or a tectonic feature, a deep-seated fissure which has the potential to shake continents, disturb centuries of order and uproot entire nations. I seem to be traversing this line without being entirely sure why. I am thirty-seven years old. This is the midway point of my life. From here on, I am told, it is all downhill.

We are in a car driving south through Germany. It is late August and already the evenings have begun to grow shorter, although this may also have something to do with moving south, the changing latitude. There is a sense of urgency in the lengthening shadows that stretch between the trees. Rich lagoons of deep green turf flow into the gaps between islets of pine trees that run, like an uncharted archipelago, alongside us.

The car is French, a silver-blue Peugeot 504, circa 1973. A growling, predatory machine with a glutinous appetite for petrol. This car has a story. It was put together by an amateur mechanic, one of those harmless fanatics whose idea of joy is to spend their Saturday afternoons in the garage with the radio tuned to a Golden Oldies hit show while polishing mechanical things with an oily rag. He spent two years putting this one together. 'It had been sitting out there in the driveway under a tarpaulin for ages before he got round to it.' This from his wife, a motionless creature with wooden eyes the colourless hue of smoke on water. She did not move. Most people do. No hand gestures, no nods, no nervous tics, no awkward smiles. Her stillness was disconcerting. It made you look twice to see if she was really there at all. She had a story too. He finished the car and then he left her, setting sail for the continent on a cross-channel ferry with a woman who had grown tired of stacking romantic novels in the local library. They fled in an Opel Astra – this detail being the final shred of evidence needed to confirm that he had taken leave not only of his loyal spouse, but also of his senses. She disposed of all evidence of his existence, threw out all his clothes. The Salvation Army. Oxfam. 'Funny to think that his leaving me could in some way ease the suffering of the world,' she smiled caustically. The cars, there were five of them, all in various states of disrepair, she was selling to pay for a holiday. 'After twelve years of marriage I think I deserve a break, don't you?' I looked underneath the chassis as though I knew what I was doing and tried to knock a hundred pounds off the price. She let me get away with fifty.

The 504 has a raised flat hump at the back and a gently dipping nose which gives it that long-limbed athletic look. It resembles a flying wedge. It looks like it is ready to go anywhere and for the most part it will – this is one of the most durable cars in the world. There is something about old cars which is honest – not the same thing as reliable, of course, but that they have a mechanical tangibility to them which is reassuring. Lift up the bonnet of a modern automobile and you see something that resembles a Lego kit; flat plastic modules that appear to snap together. You wonder if you have opened up the wrong end, it looks like you have a set of Samsonite suitcases in there. To repair a fault the mechanic hooks the car up to a computer which flashes up the digital code of the defective part. Cars nowadays are cleanly designed to make you forget there is anything as dirty as internal combustion involved; no burning of fossil fuels, no flattened rainforests and polluted rivers, no millions of square miles of devastated nature sacrificed so that you can travel in comfort. New cars deliver smooth, immaculate, inexplicable traction. It is the illusion of a perfect world which I object to. Face the facts: things break down, oil is spilled, consequences have to be paid. Having said that, however, there is a rather worrying whine coming from the Peugeot's clutch when I engage first gear and this tells me that we may have problems ahead of us.

In this part of the world it really is like riding in a dinosaur. I tell Leo that it is like the car in the Flintstones and he finds this amusing, starts pedalling with his feet. But it's true; people nod as they pass by, craning their necks to catch a glimpse of us. Kids point fingers and laugh out loud, thumbing their noses as they pull ahead. But if this car is a relic, it is also a reminder of the world you can still see if you cross to the other side of the Mediterranean. It's a Third World car. A relic of another age. The Peugeot 504 is a legend anywhere in Africa or the Middle East. It is prized above any one of a number of competitors because it is as tough as a tank. The only factory in the world where they still make them is in Nigeria. Everywhere else they are recycled and restored endlessly with loving care. Here, among all those lightweight sleek machines, which are about as robust as waxed paper, there is something about this car which strikes a note with some people. They wander over in service stations to have a look. They seem to see in it a symbol of their own past, a sense of continuity, a memory perhaps, of sitting on Grandpa's knee and learning to drive one summer. A reminder of when the world had a fundament beneath it that you could feel, before everything began growing light and hard to hold on to. This car is what

I need right now, something solid around me, something that feels like it is in touch with the ground.

We crossed the German border just before midday and immediately it seemed to me the road and the air became heavy with industrial dirt. The border guards wore eagles on their tunics. They asked me to pull over and switch off the engine while they checked my name against the list of internationally wanted suspects. Is it the car, I wonder, or my face? The borders are now open, but these guards hadn't heard of the Schengen Agreement, or didn't care either way what those clever gentlemen in Brussels and Strasburg decide. I told them that if I were smuggling people or drugs I would do so in a large touring Mercedes-Benz with a white couple at the wheel, but they didn't have much sense of humour. It is obvious, though: no self-respecting contra-bandist would attempt to run the barricade with someone looking like me behind the wheel of a rusty old heap like this.

So we sat there and waited while the *Polizei* checked my particulars against any known act of terrorism perpetrated over the last thirty years, any crime or misdemeanour committed in the western hemisphere by anyone with a name similar to mine. This was a depressing start. The traffic rumbled past us and the bushes alongside the road where we waited were thickly leaden with carbonised, bituminous grime. Perhaps I am biased about the Germans, but why did I have the feeling that I was more likely to be victimised here than anywhere else? No doubt the product of all those war films and Biggles novels that came my way as a child. Stricken with guilt, I tried to smile amiably when they brought my passport back and in return got a strange look from the guard.

We drive on through the marshy northern lowlands. When the ice-caps melt this will be one of the first places you will get your feet wet. It is dairy country, dirty fields of grass inhabited by cattle that watch the endless stream of vehicles flying past them with morose interest.

'What do you suppose they think about when they see us?'

'It must be like watching television.'

Leo waves to the cows. 'Did you see that?' He jerks up in his seat to crane his neck round.

'What? What?' The car swerves. I am not a great driver. I am too easily distracted.

'One of them waved back.'

'Waved back? How?'

'With its tail, of course. I waved my hand and she waved her tail back.'

'That's very good.' I nod. 'The cow waved back.'

'Its true! You didn't see it.'

'I believe you. Look, there's one riding a bicycle.'

'Oh, Baba!' he folds his arms gruffly, offended.

He sees things. I don't know if this is the product of an over-active imagination, or a sign of more deep-seated distress. A reaction to the domestic turmoil he has been subjected to recently, perhaps, and which I am not alleviating in the least with my current behaviour.

For a moment I envisage this journey in the tradition of all the great journeys of literature; in the romantic tradition of reeling Taoists, wandering Buddhist monks searching for enlightenment. Bāsho's *Records of a Travel Worn Satchel*, or *Narrow Road to the Deep North*. Like the Sufis condemned to forever tramp the roads of the world. Ibn Arabi's restless search for the *kashf*, the discovery. Both Taoism and Sufism contain the idea of dualism, of opposites being in constant interaction with one another: being and non-being, the spirit and the body. The hidden and the revealed; the veiled and the unveiled – the *mahjoub* and the *zahir*. This idea of being between two such opposites seems to make sense to me at this point in time.

World War II is still lodged in my head and I recall

someone once told me that Eva Braun's house was somewhere along here. The family house it must have been. I am
looking for a ruined farmhouse, the wooden beams collapsed
and the thatched roof fallen in. But I have no exact reference.
How do you pinpoint a spot on a motorway? It all looks the
same. That is the nature of travelling by autobahn, life is
suspended. You never really know precisely where you are at
any given point. Your life is ahead of you, behind you,
waiting to catch up.

'Who is Eva Braun?'

'Well, she was the mistress of someone who once ruled
Germany.'

'What's a mistress?'

'Ah, well, sort of like a girlfriend.'

'I know who you mean. Hitler.'

The innocence of my son's childhood has already been
breached. I feel offended that such things have been passed
on without my being informed. Didn't the school have to
ask the parents' permission before they exposed your
children to such sensitive material? How much does he
know? I wonder.

'I know how to draw his sign.' He draws a swastika with
his finger in the dust on the dashboard.

'Where did you see that?'

'At school. They draw it on the back of the buildings at
school where no one can see it.' My son is attending a school
overrun by Neo-Nazis. How could this have happened?
Why did I not know about this sooner?

'You know the people who do this?'

'Come on, Dad, everybody knows.'

Perhaps this is not the wisest subject to be sharing with a
seven-year-old. When are you supposed to begin tackling
awkward subject matters, like sex and death? The sex part I
am not too worried about. People always find out about sex,
one way or another, and, besides, discovering it is part of
growing up, isn't it? I am more concerned about the darker
side of life. Who is going to explain to him about mortality,

12

that we don't live for ever; about failure, rejection, the whole existential doom and gloom of it all?

'How did she die?' he asks.

'Some sort of suicide pact, I think.' I am regretting ever bringing up the subject. 'I think they shot themselves.'

'Shot! really, with a gun! Where, Dad, where?'

'In Berlin.'

'No, I mean, *where*?'

I turn to stare at him, wondering if I have a psychopath in the making sitting beside me. He still looks just like a curious child. 'In the head, I think,' I mumble finally, relieved to see a healthy grimace of repulsion on his face.

'Yucckk!'

The house is long gone. I have missed it. I have no intention of going back, either. Perhaps it has been bought up and repaired. I was told that no one would live in it, but perhaps that has changed. Perhaps it has been turned into a shrine of some kind.

'How about some lunch?' I suggest.

He pulls a face. 'You don't expect me to eat after that story, do you?'

2

We eat fishcakes and potato salad that tastes of vinegar. Outside the toilets a man with two fingers missing is playing a sad tune on a worn harmonica. There is a strong smell of disinfectant. Inside a truck driver is combing his hair in the mirror. He punches the condom dispenser with his fist on the way out.

I should make it clear that I actually hate driving. Well, not driving as such, but the things that go along with it, such as roads, other road users, fast-moving vehicles. I am generally terrified of most forms of transport. My basic feeling is that if you are living and breathing well enough in one place why risk all that by moving somewhere else? How many people drop dead by staying in one place? Far fewer than die trying to get somewhere else is the answer. Flying, of course, is the most absurd of all: that entire pantomime you have to endure so as to make it seem a perfectly sane, perfectly normal thing to do — strap yourself inside a thin-skinned aluminium sheath pumped full of high-octane fuel to be projected at high velocity into the air. The perfumed towelettes, the boiled sweets. The little trays of food with the plastic cutlery and the breadrolls that require a machete to get through. The charade of explaining how the safety system works, where the exits are: 'Four over the wings, two at the rear and two at the front of the aircraft.' If the cabin loses pressure, pull the mask towards you and place it over your mouth and nose and breathe normally. *Breathe normally*? What is normal about gasping for air through a thin plastic mask while plummeting to the earth from thirty thousand feet in a burning metal coffin? All that business of the life-jacket under your seat (or is it the seat in front of you?) and pull sharply down on the toggle – wait! – after you have left the plane. When was the last time you heard of a plane coming down and everyone getting out neatly in their life-jackets? It never happens. There would be no problem finding the exits as they would be blocked with screaming people. People get aggressive enough just finding space in the overhead lockers when trying to stow their hand luggage (which they can often barely lift). Normal, rational people start to stampede when the flight is called, as though the plane might just leave them stranded in the departure lounge with a boarding pass clutched in their sweaty palm – out of spite. People cut in front of you, they stand on your toes, thrust their rucksacks into your face while in the midst of a last minute telephone conversation. So if the plane were to be plunging towards the ground, are we really supposed to assume that these selfsame people would behave calmly and not trample one another to death in the aisles? That someone would be level-headed enough to open one of those emergency exits? That the plane would not sink like a bullet into the dark ocean? Maybe, but I am not in a hurry to find out.

There are alternatives to flying. There are trains – but they overcharge, overbook and get delayed; a two-hour journey turns into eight hours of torture, trying to sidestep the overflow from the toilets swilling around the corridors upon a tide of discarded newspapers and empty beer cans.

And while train travel might be the most unpleasant, the most dangerous means of travel is still the road. All too easily I see visions of tangled metal, sparks flying and severed limbs. Any kind of road scares me, but the *Autobahnen* induce heart palpitations at regular intervals. The cars either crawl by or else shoot past at the speed of light. There is no in-between. You check in the rearview mirror, twice, and then indicate to pull out and suddenly there are lights flashing all over the place and a huge Porsche is trying to mount your tailpipe.

They don't believe in slowing down in this country, it is against some natural law. I tell myself it is legislation, not genetic heritage.

Talking helps to keep my mind off the fear, and we go back to a popular subject; my son's age. Leo is actually almost eight. A year makes a big difference, he tells me. One year is a much larger fraction of his life than of mine. Time means less when you are old. In some way he has a point, things happen much faster when you are a child. The first fifteen years of your life stay with you for ever, as a time primed with all the mystery and wonder of life's changes. Later on, when we get over all the acne and angst, we settle into docile steady-state existence and development is replaced by the demon of all demons: all-knowing worldliness. And time does move more swiftly without us noticing. We bump into an old acquaintance and say, 'Oh, is it really ten years?' A decade gone, slipped past almost without notice. It becomes more precious as we realise how it constantly eludes our efforts to make use of it. What have we achieved? What happened to all that time? Only childhood stands out as fixed in our memory. Our sense of who we are remains rooted in those first precious fifteen years.

Leo is right in the middle of that time. Whatever happens to him now, in the coming years will be determining. Whether he develops as a complete, rounded person, or alternatively, turns out a broken wreck who blames his failures on his childhood, his selfish parents, all depends on how he emerges from these years.

'It's like dogs,' Leo says, breaking into my thoughts again.

'Dogs?'

'Dog years are shorter than ours. A fifteen-year-old dog is like, well, ancient, like Grandma.'

'Please don't tell Grandma she's ancient,' I beg him. 'Or compare her with a dog, for that matter.'

'Ba*baa*.' He pulls that withering look which asks how I could take him for somebody dense enough to commit such an insensitive blunder. He has learned to take responsibility for others, a fact which surprises me for some reason. Anyway, six months in the life of a seven-and-a-half-year-old is one-fifteenth of their life. Six months in the life of a thirty-seven-year-old is one-seventy-fourth – his time is five times more precious than mine. We work this out slowly between us, and then wonder what this means. Can one person's time actually be considered to be more precious than another's?

'Everybody has their own perception of time and value. And life is never fair in the sense that the good, or those destined to achieve great things, say, are spared hardship or tragedy. All we can do is try to put our time to good use.'

He thinks about this for a second. Leaning forward, one hand on the dashboard, staring straight ahead. 'But doesn't everyone do that?'

'Well, maybe not everyone, but the point is that what I think is a worthy occupation you might think was a waste of time. Plato said that our true purpose in life was the meditation of perfection.'

'Who was Plato?'

'Greek man, very clever, long time ago.'

I am not sure why I am thinking of Plato, but it occurs to me that this was what we ought to be doing; what Montaigne did, re-examining the past, looking back at what had gone before. I want Leo to know the things I never knew. I want him to be prepared for the world.

Between the car and my son, there is nothing else in the world at this moment which matters to me. And so the wheel has taken on a kind of magic power, as though I have something quite precious passing through my hands. This is what is keeping me alive, I think. This child. This car. This road.

We reach Hamburg in the late afternoon. Luckily, the traffic is all going the other way. It is rush hour and everyone is making their way home. Home to the family heart, to husbands and partners and wives and all the complex permutations of modern living. All around us houses are coming alive, kitchens lighting up, filling with warmth and the sounds and smells of cooking. Television sets are snapping on, shoes being kicked off. And here we are, gliding along the long steel and concrete arch that is the Elbe bridge, with no bed for the night. A shower of rain stops as abruptly as it started and the sinking sun hurls a rainbow across the industrial skyline. Hard blue sapphires of rain cling to the windscreen. Neon signs buzz from the rooftops, their colours livid with mineral warmth. Below us lies a vast labyrinth of canals and countless rows of rusty iron teeth that turn out to be freight containers. One of the largest ports in the world. We reach the end of the bridge and begin the long curl up the hillside, into the winged darkness, and not a word spoken between us.

Flip open one of those self-help manuals on pocket psychology and they will tell you that I am over-compensating for feelings of failure and guilt towards my son. I am trying to make up for not being a good father, for not being there when I should have been. They might have a point. I wasn't even there on the day he was born. I was away in London. I was supposed to be back that afternoon, but I wasn't, and I couldn't be reached. I wasn't where I was meant to be. Ellen's mother left a note on the kitchen table to say they couldn't wait any longer. They were on their way and I should meet them at the hospital. By the time I got there Ellen had decided that enough was enough. She didn't want me there, didn't need me there; she would do it alone.

'Are you coming into the delivery room?' her mother, Claire, enquired.

'Yes, of course,' I replied. I was a modern man. My own father stayed at home when I was born. He sent my mother off in an ambulance and waited by the telephone. But I had read the books. I even attended a pre-natal class, once.

'No,' grunted Ellen from the corner of the room set aside for mothers going into the first stages of labour, groping, even as she spoke, for an orange plastic bin into which she was vomiting, or trying to, nothing more than a trickle of yellow bile was coming up by now. Pragmatically, the nurse held out a gown and asked me to put it on, just in case.

'Come along, dear,' said her mother, pleading for harmony. 'Let him.'

'Over my dead body,' groaned Ellen, hair plastered to her face, racked by another contraction; she still made a grab for the gown.

'Come on, Ellen, I said I was sorry.'

'Where were you? Your own funeral? No, worse than that, the birth of your own child and you were late!'

'I'm here now. Look, I'm sorry.'

She waited for another spasm to subside. 'No, it's not that, nothing to do with any of that.' She was mumbling, growing incoherent. I tried to soothe her.

'Ellen, it's our child. Let's not argue. You need your strength.'

'Hypocrite! Now you want me to be reasonable?'

I turned to her mother, who was shaking her head. The nurse was looking back and forth between the two of us, trying to work out which of us was the least insane. I tried to look reasonable.

When I look back, all the good times seem to have been edited out of my memory. All I remember are the conflicts. The very qualities which attracted me to Ellen, that high-spirited impulsiveness, were what drove me away from her in the end. And she would probably say the same thing. But when did it all start to go awry? When did we stop forgiving one another and start simply trying to inflict pain?

'Will it be long?' clucked Claire with a sigh, as though waiting for an overdue train, sitting down to pluck knitting needles and a ball of wool from her bag. Claire was pleasant enough, but it was rather disconcerting how she had managed to forget everything she had ever learned about the business of having children in the thirty-odd years since Ellen had been born. The few times we tried to get her to babysit in the early years ended in howling disaster. She went to pieces and needed written instructions for everything – where the refrigerator was, what time her favourite series came on. It took so long to get out of the house that we would inevitably arrive late, to find the only two seats left in the cinema were on the front row, one at either end. We could just about wave to one another as the lights went down. And when we arrived home she would be distraught, pacing up and down on the doorstep with a policeman for company, holding a soiled, tired, hungry and very unhappy child at arm's length.

The helpful nurse took her cue, looked at her watch and promptly informed us that she was going off duty. Ellen, who had been crawling around the floor trying to find a comfortable position, now collapsed, snarling and spitting expletives about the medical profession between waves of pain while I struggled to get my arms into the green gown and the bathcap on my head at the same time, but I had no idea what to do after that.

'Now what?'

'Perhaps if you had bothered with the pre-natal classes,' murmured Claire, who seemed always to be better informed about what went on between us than I expected.

But then an upright, square-hipped midwife swept in and took charge, and it was just as well. I can't imagine that it is often expectant parents actually come to blows in the delivery room, but we were close. The contractions increased in intensity and frequency and Ellen finally became incapable of preventing me from witnessing the birth of our child. I held out my hand, and limply she took it. There were still another two and a half hours to go, although I remember it as having happened very quickly, much faster than I had imagined. I did what I had prepared myself to do, I mopped her brow, I held her hand, I whispered encouragement. Her eyes were popping and her face was contorted with what could easily have been mistaken for fury rather than excruciating effort. By the end she was so far gone that the nurse turned to me and dumped the slippery creature into my arms so as to attend to her.

He was tiny, and covered in a white fatty substance that seemed to cake around his brows and chin, which made him appear incredibly small and old and wrinkled. This, I realised, was the kind of thing that made people turn to religion. The inexplicable mystery revealed. Rigid with fear, I held him motionless while they cut the umbilical cord and tidied everything up. I was afraid to drop him, or squash him. I was quite helpless. Then, all too soon, he was plucked from my arms and taken to be weighed and placed under a red heating lamp in a transparent plastic crib.

'Maybe you ought to sit down,' breezed the midwife. 'You look as though you're about to faint.'

I sat down. Ellen was delirious; the pain had receded and now she seemed to be floating in a hazy, drugged state of exhaustion. She looked at me and for a moment I think we both shared whatever it was that we had once felt for one another, and which had ultimately given rise to this particular miracle. I smiled and she smiled back. A humble, wordless moment. And then it was gone and she was talking to her mother on the other side of the bed, and the nurses were moving about and chatting away as if they had all just run into one another by accident at the bus stop. I stood poised motionless within that turmoil, gazing down at the squashed face, the smooth flattened hairs, the wrinkles around the wrists, the tiny fingernails, and I realised that, in an instant, my life had changed for ever.

We drive on for about an hour after passing Hamburg and then decide it is time to stop again. We have sung all of the Beatles' greatest hits at least twice and are in need of refreshment. We pass the blue modernist structure of the *tankstelle* to reach the parking area, cluttered with huge sixteen-wheelers. We find a large empty space between two camper vans settling down for the night, complete with dogs and children. I grab Leo, who has a tendency to stop still and stare at whatever his eye fastens on, and pull him along with me.

'We need to stretch our legs,' I say.

'This is a service station.' He frowns with the conviction of one who has absorbed the logic of the world and now questions the mind of his trusted guide. 'There is nowhere to go.'

'There,' I point. 'The trees.'

As we walk, he turns to ask me where we are going. I expected this question; he doesn't mean right now, he doesn't mean here. I don't have an answer for him.

'Let's just see what there is,' I say.

The place where we left the car is soon out of sight. I am surprised that we could get this far. I expected us to hit an electric fence, or a ditch loaded with rusty metal, but there is nothing to hinder our progress and so we press on without difficulty, pulled deeper and deeper into the trees. The air is slightly damp and an evening mist is gathering just beyond the edge of the woods.

Clutching the boy's hand in mine and tramping deeper into the gloom is like treading into the opening lines of a fairy tale. And it hits me with the slow, dull weight of a falling stone that this doesn't have to be a dire Odyssean epic, this journey; a series of tests and trials. No, this is an opportunity, a marvellous chance to travel through the world together, alone. We don't have to be anywhere at any time. I want him to learn about this place, this continent where so much of our fate has been forged, one way or another. Love it or loathe it he would have to learn to deal with it, this thing we call Europe. To assemble the facts into his own sense of who he is and where he comes from. Whether he decides to live his life here or not, this is where he was born. I was not. I came here, and my fate is tied to the soil of this continent in ways that I have never entirely understood. I want him to learn, to be equipped, to have power over things that I have never been able to master. I wander about with the mental framework of a transient, an outsider, not seeing myself anywhere. He belongs. He has a place, in as much as any of us have a place in the world. He needs to know the history in order to see beyond the glass towers and the steel and concrete. He needs to know how we came to be where we are today. I am trying to prepare him for the future, and for that he needs to know the past.

Only I am not sure what exactly I have to give him. He might be too young. I shall do my best, there is nothing more I can do; this opportunity will not present itself again. And as for him, well, even if he does not understand everything that he sees here and now, it will stay with him, precisely because it is out of the ordinary, an adventure. It will remain, form a part of his life. He might look back, perhaps long after I am gone, and realise that he discovered something important, about himself, about the world, some tiny insignificant thing, and that will make it worth it.

He holds his hands out from his sides as though playing a tree. Where? Where are we going to? He still trusts me, implicitly. I remember the look of utter abandon and delight when I used to toss him up into the air when he was small. Knowing, trusting me not to drop him. I never did. I don't want to drop him now.

'Let's try and see what there is on the other side,' I say. The muscles in my legs ache and I am sweating lightly. He nods resignedly, as though he had not expected to get an answer out of me that easily. Together we walk forwards. The uneven ground steepens and we find ourselves climbing, our feet sinking into the soft dark soil out of which tiny spots of white tumble. Small calcitic stones, or mushroom spores perhaps. The ridge is covered with springy moss. Beads of silvery moisture glint from among the blades of grass.

'Maybe we should go back. It's dark. We might get lost.'

'I know.' I nod. 'But I just want to get to the top of this and see.'

'See what?'

'Whatever there is to see.'

He hesitates again. I press him on a few more paces.

'Come on. It won't take long.' I know that if I keep going he will catch up. I can see a thin band of light now between the straight limbs of the pines. I am breathing heavily and my heart is beating as though it is about to fail. He has to run a little to catch up. I reach the top. A breeze flicks through the trees, tugging at the undergrowth around our feet. We are not very high up, but the view is rewarding. There is a glow in the sky that at first I think might be some kind of atmospheric phenomenon but then realise it must be coming from one of those giant greenhouses, ablaze with artificial light twenty-four hours a day. The light filtering through the trees lends the landscape an unreal quality. It resembles a dimmed stage waiting for the drama to begin. The stillness seems laden with the shadowy bulk of possibility. An undiscovered country. Behind us the burr of engines in the distance is like pebbles tumbling through waves onto a beach.

He can feel it too and we stand there for a while in silence. I have the sudden sense of time passing, of the frailty of this moment and of us, and, also, the timelessness of it all. Then I feel the tug of anxiety again and the moment is past. I turn and look back the way we have come. The interior of the little patch of wood is thick and black. In the faint light I can just make out the sketchy outlines of his features, and I see how much he resembles my father. It is like looking at one of those crumpled photographs that my mother always used to carry in her purse, that Haboba had wedged in her glass cupboard.

I put out my hand to find his. 'Ready?'

'Ready.'

We take a deep breath and together let out a yell as we begin running down the incline. It seems steeper and longer than I had anticipated. But somehow, trusting blindly, we stay in balance, and with arms held out wide we plunge onwards, screaming wildly, straight down into darkness.

3

It was Ellen's paternal grandfather, Sophus Mikkelbak, who provided the reason for the trip to Denmark in the first place. It was his one hundredth birthday party and the entire family, well, almost the entire country so far as I could tell, had been invited to celebrate. There were cousins and uncles and great-nieces, people flown in from as far away as Australia and South America.

One of the things that first drew me to Ellen was the fact that she, like me, was incompletely English. However slightly, that fraction of her broke the mythical mould of national uniformity, albeit more in my mind than in the real scheme of things, where it probably mattered a lot less than I thought. Still, it gave me that sense that here was something we shared. A mixed-up sense of belonging and not belonging, of having another space into which she fitted. The fact was that England was more or less all she knew. She grew up in Leeds where her father was teaching at the time and then in Oxford when he transferred to the Pitt-Rivers museum. Denmark, she told me, she recalled as a remote rural environment where they went to spend their summer holidays. She talked about the windblown beaches and the wild North Sea where they plunged and swam as children. She didn't even look Danish, well, not how I had imagined. She was dark and had thick black hair, all of which came from her father. Her mother was blonde, but she was Irish, so none of any of this really added up. I felt instantly at home with all of this displaced genetic soup. But in all the years we were together, first living casually and then hastily married when we realised that Leo was on the way, I never met any of her Danish family. She and I had travelled together before, to Italy, to Greece once, to France, but never to Denmark. In the early years especially I loved travelling with her. Ellen spoke half a dozen languages with casual ease and this made me feel as though I had acquired a layer of worldly sophistication. Of course it was probably more the kind of naïve, twenty-something belief in universal brotherhood which makes you think that you are welcome wherever you go, so long as you can manage to say 'please' and 'thank you' and smile a lot. I did the smiling. But I remember feeling as though with Ellen's help I could finally penetrate the mystery of what Europe was. I immersed myself in books on history and language. The Middle Ages, the Renaissance, Flemish painting, Gothic architecture, Edward Gibbon. Things I felt I needed to span the yawning gap in my knowledge of how the world worked.

When you come from a place that no one knows anything about you end up delivering a three-hour lecture to anyone who asks. You can't understand why their eyes begin to glaze over. The other extreme is pretending it doesn't matter, that we're all the same underneath anyway. There is a tendency to absorb difference, to diffuse it, to strip away the essentials and leave it denuded, hairless and irrelevant. And so where you come from develops into a vast unwieldy entity as you struggle to convey yourself in a series of confused signals and awkward silences, geographical short cuts that whittle away continents. I wasn't looking forward to having to explain myself to a stack of Ellen's eager Nordic relatives. The only person I had to go by was her father, Claus, who was either too clumsy or too old-fashioned to care about stepping on toes, or perhaps it had something to do with being an archaeologist by profession.

'Bedouins,' he would declare, as though providing the answer to the winning question on an afternoon quiz show. Sitting in their house in Oxford on a typical Sunday lunchtime visit, Ellen and her mother having disappeared somewhere leaving him and me facing one another across an afghan carpet thick enough to lose a medium-size lapdog in, wondering what to do with one another.

'Bedouins?' I repeated. We had these unnerving, elliptical conversations where no matter how hard we tried we never quite managed to grasp one another's exact meaning. Sentences would ricochet off into the air around us, just out of reach. We would sit glumly waiting for lunch, hoping for any kind of interruption. He developed the habit of suddenly remembering something he had forgotten to do and I would be spared, allowed to sit in silence and contemplate the yucca plants and the curious circumstances which had led me to this wicker armchair in this room in this particular family.

I always felt small in that room. They had extended the basement through the outer wall into the garden and put in a glass roof so you looked up at the sky and the apple tree and you felt a little like a garden gnome. There was a large brass tray in the middle of the room that Claus had brought back from an expedition to Yemen thirty years ago. He had some authority in these matters.

'They eat the liver of the camel raw.'

'Some Bedouins do, I believe,' I agreed without much conviction. I hated to disappoint him. When the telephone didn't draw him away, and his list of things to do had run out, we would be obliged to resort to conversation, and both of our efforts were usually pretty dire. I would find myself describing ancient rituals of long-forgotten tribes, often having to make up the details as I went along, not being schooled in such matters. Whatever hopes or ambitions he envisaged for our relationship, all of them were somehow centred on my being a ready source of accurate and precise information on the lifestyles and habits of every ethnic group living east of Suez. I did my best, not wishing to disappoint, and besides, it passed the time. I had a sympathetic spot for Claus, who was a large, gentle man and always reminded me for some reason of the giant invisible rabbit James Stewart talks to in the film *Harvey*. A quiet, unassuming, but

27

persistent presence. In all the years of our time together I could not bring myself to break the news to him that I was an urban child, that I couldn't with any certainty tell one end of a camel from the other. I grew up in a suburban environment where the problems of survival involved power cuts that lasted for days and water pipes choking to a trickle one minute and gushing reddish-brown river water the next.

'They also cook the meat on hot stones.'

'Really?' He appreciated this. He leaned back in his chair and propped his hands up in a steeple, pressing the tips of his fingers together in a contemplative attitude which I saw him adopt many times. 'I never saw that, but when we were in Aden . . .' And then, thankfully, he would launch into one of his lengthy anecdotes, most of which I became intimately familiar with over the years. I could relax my toes which were scrunched up inside my shoes in painful awkwardness.

I had always been curious to meet Claus's father, if only because of the infamous split between father and son some thirty years ago. Ironic, then, that it should come now as we were poised on the verge of permanently dividing paths. And so the curtain went up on the final act to find Ellen and me floating out in the middle of the North Sea, trapped on a weathered overnight ferry from Harwich, agreed that the only solution to our problems was separation. In a bar awash with beer sops and holiday-makers crooning along to Engelbert Humperdinck on the jukebox, I listened to her trying to make sense after three vodka and tonics. Ellen did not normally drink, but had decided for both our sakes to make an exception. We had reached the end of something, she said, and was having a hard time explaining what it was. I listened with the resigned sense of there being an inevitability about this conversation, and feeling something vaguely akin to relief.

'We've lost it, whatever trust there was between us. It's gone completely. Trust.' She slammed her fist down on the table so hard that the rather plump man snoring contentedly away at the next table actually jumped. 'That's what we don't have any more. No no no.' She wagged a finger under my nose. Ferries impose a hypnotic spell on their passengers which allows people to indulge themselves in ways they might refrain from on dry land. At sea all rules are off until harbour comes into sight. It is a kind of suspension of reality, or maybe it was just the holiday spirit, but in any case, the place was soaked in a kind of wringing desperation. I imagined all the children sleeping below (including, I hoped, Leo. Not wandering the decks tearfully in his pyjamas) and wondered how that sober procession of respectable families filing aboard that afternoon had turned into this wild scenario. People were thumping their boots on tables and others were staggering sideways fumbling for handrails that simply weren't there, as though we were in a Force Ten gale when the sea was steady as a duck pond. The music went on and on. 'A Whiter Shade of Pale' was the high point with thirty or so adults warbling out of tune. Locked together in a corner, Ellen was bowed in concentration trying to find the words that formulated her frustration.

'Trust. That's what this is all about. And you never, ever trusted me.' She was angry. Deeply angry. This was a marriage, things go wrong all the time, but most people manage to patch things up. 'Patch things up? Hah!' she exclaimed, so loudly that a group of young men at the bar cheered and raised their glasses to her.

'Maybe we should continue this chat somewhere else.'

'What for? I like it here, and I want another drink.'

'Maybe you ought to take it easy.'

She stabbed a finger at me. 'That's the thing about you. You're so pious. You know that? So bloody pious. Don't do this. Don't do that.'

I got to my feet. 'I'm going to bed,' I said.

'I've worked it all out, you know. All of it.'

I sat down again. She was weaving about, circling like a punch-drunk shark. But I knew what she wanted me to tell her and so, eventually, I did. I watched as she got to her feet and then lurched towards the bar. 'You go on to bed. I'm fine here.' I lingered for a moment, contemplating dragging her back to the cabin, but it seemed pointless. It was no longer enough to care for one another. The rocky shore was now in sight and we were headed for it at full speed.

We drove in silence the next morning (apart from the litany of groans coming from Ellen, and a couple of stops for her to throw up by the roadside) the two grey hours it took us to find her grandfather's house, somewhere in the middle of the Jutland peninsula. A windy place of blue sky, grassy meadows and creaky pines. Bertolt Brecht wrote some of his best plays looking at this landscape: *Mother Courage, The Life of Galileo*. He took refuge from Hitler and Stalin at Svendborg, an hour away from where we were, and only left when the war broke out in 1939. He also wrote some of his best poetry, including 'The Legend of the Origin of the Book Tao Te Ching during Lao Tzu's Journey into Exile'. I draw confidence from this thought as we drive into the unknown.

The house was miles from the road and with nothing but gentle flat meadows and forest all around. It was a flat-roofed modernist structure that looked as though it might have been whittled by Mies Van der Rohe in his spare time. A great deal of pine lumber had gone into it. Long glass windows ran the length of the house on the riverside and olive-green stone slabs along the other. I was very impressed and found myself in conversation with an odd-looking fellow who appeared impishly at my elbow. He also happened to be called Klaus – with a K. That was one thing I was to learn during my short stay, everyone in Denmark had the same name. Lars, Jens, Jens, Lars. On the whole, I suppose, it kept things simple. We stood staring at the idyllic scene, the little house in the copse in the woods above a stream.

'This is the new house,' explained my informant eagerly. 'The old one burned down years ago.' He had round little apple cheeks and one eye much larger than the other, as though he were peering at you through a magnifying glass.

He was a mine of sordid details. First he told me why Claus was not going to be there. He had sharp yellow teeth which at several key points were missing. I noticed this because his mouth was fixed in what could best be described as a manic grin: 'They don't talk, father and son, not for forty years. Not since the old man seduced his girlfriend. Claus was just a young man at the time and she was a gorgeous actress of nineteen summers.'

I wasn't sure I ought to be hearing all the slavering details. On the dappled green lawn underneath the trees a wide horseshoe of tables had been laid out, covered in white cloth and decked with fine porcelain and cut glass. I felt as though I had stepped into a scene from Chekhov or, more appropriately perhaps, Strindberg, who was Swedish of course, but the closest I could get. There were yellow roses arranged along the table and little wreaths of blue corn-flowers appeared here and there. The guests were standing around in clumps chatting as waitresses in uniform circulated with trays of glasses filled with kir. The Danes, I was rapidly discovering, like a drink.

The family was more wealthy than I had realised. On the verge of divorce I learned that my soon to be ex-wife was part heir to a vast fortune. The great-grandfather had invented a machine for putting meatballs into cans. When World War I came along he was transformed into a very wealthy man, meatballs in tins (I think they diversified, but it was the tinning part that was the catch) being indispensable in the trenches. Most of the money was soon squandered, however, what with the end of the war and the rest of the great man's devices being apparently useless. He also had a talent for throwing good money after bad and through a series of unwise investments would have lost the remainder of the family's dwindling fortune if his wife had not secretly invested some of it herself. He went to the grave believing himself a pauper, but his son grew up never wanting for anything and indeed Sophus Mikkelbak was said never to have done a day's work in his life, which might have gone some way to explaining his dapper condition at the end of a century. By the time the Third Reich came along the firm was a respectable investor in German industry and rumour had it that Ellen's grandfather had attended one or two high-level galas in Berlin in his time, but nobody talked about that. He had a particular fondness for actresses it seems, and not only the ones his son was besotted with. On that fateful occasion Claus apparently came after him with a rifle and there are those who say he ought to have done it and spared himself a life of regret.

Sophus Mikkelbak was a spritely figure of a man with liver spots everywhere and an expensive cigar soldered to his left hand, defiantly angled at death, daring it to come after him. Looking at the old man now it was difficult to imagine him having been such a nuisance. During our initial intro-duction I had caught a glimpse of the gristly knuckle that lurked beneath that doddering surface of centenarian docility:

'*Henderson the Rain King.*'

'Saul Bellow?' I raised my voice, unsure whether I had heard correctly, whether this was a test. I was also concerned about his hearing. He had been staring at me for several minutes in a disconcerting kind of way, as though a thought, making its way from some high unseen place to his trembling lips, had been unaccountably delayed. We were in the living room and had just gone through the introductions. The closest he had managed to get to my name was 'Safari'. At least, that's what I think he said. It turned out that he had travelled to Upper Egypt as a young man in the 1930s. When I looked at the old photographs of ragged little children on a riverbank waving at the visitors from Europe I found myself wondering if one of those scruffy little barefoot urchins might have been my father.

'Have you read it?'

I said I had read Bellow's book and immediately wished I had lied. It was my least favourite of his novels. Better to plead ignorance than have to find something nice to say about something I had never been able to see the funny side of. But I couldn't follow the line of his questioning and was starting to feel uncomfortable. I was beginning to wonder what I was really doing here.

'What did he say?' Sophus Mikkelbak quizzed the person sitting next to him – his fourth wife, a stout former pastry chef from a nearby town, the last point on a downward curve of succession, following rather dowdily on the more glamorous heels of the dazzling socialites and svelte nymphs of former times. He nodded at me, with a smile that might have been mistaken for a sneer. He didn't believe I had read the book at all. There was more whispering between the old man and his doughy wife.

'He doesn't look like an oil sheikh, to me.'

'Not oil sheikh, his father was a political candidate, I think.'

'I didn't know they had elections.'

I felt I understood Ellen's father a little better now. He had renounced the family business, and set out on his own. And what little I knew of his writing made more sense. He wrote poetry in his spare time. 'Just a hobby,' he told me. But I had not realised how highly respected he was, as my informant (Klaus with a K) explained, puffing his cheeks out as he chuckled and clucked. How could I *not* have heard of him? The world, it seemed, was determined to prove me an ignoramus today of all days.

'I know very little about Scandinavian literature,' I confessed feebly.

There were societies devoted to Claus's work. He was considered to be among the top handful of living poets not just in the country, in Scandinavia as a whole. And I hadn't realised. As none of his work had been translated, I had really nothing to go on, but now, meeting his family and seeing the landscape he grew up in, I imagined that I could see where a child might have chosen to escape the presence of his father by wandering off into the woods on his own, and finding himself in solitude.

33

Klaus pointed to a wide grassy meadow on the opposite bank. In 1959 the old family house had burned to the ground along with a great deal of the surrounding woodland. Nobody knew how the fire had started although there was some suggestion that it was not an accident. In his younger days our birthday boy had been quite the wild thing, living the life of the idle rich. He had inherited his father's talent for losing money, and although he did a little speculating on the market it mostly went on the gaming tables. Otherwise he did nothing. He travelled the world and invested in a collection of sports cars with which he raced about the continent from Monte Carlo to Paris and everywhere in between. When he was home he generally made a nuisance of himself and spent his spare time seducing every female who came within pawing range. They went through a list of maids and house staff that would have made Buckingham Palace look crowded. He seduced his wife's female friends as well as his son's, and then, as the years passed, most of their daughters. None of this made for much harmony in the home. On the night of the fire the groundsman who lived nearby was woken by screams in the early hours of the morning. He stepped out of his house to see flames flickering through the trees. He wasted no time summoning help. When they arrived they found Mrs Mikkelbak standing in her dressing gown calmly watching her home burn down. The men set about digging firebreaks and fetching water up from the stream to try and douse the flames.

'Where's the master? Where's the master?' the groundsman demanded, assuming that her inability to answer was a symptom of her being in shock. But he was astute enough to realise that the master might still be inside. Throwing a wet coat over his head he charged in and found Sophus Mikkelbak lying on the carpet in the bedroom, out cold. The shattered remains of a chamberpot lay suspiciously close to his head. They managed to drag him out into the open air and turned back to the blaze. But again they were obstructed. The lady of the house insisted they save her piano first.

'But the fire, Mrs Mikkelbak, we must tend to the fire.'

'I don't care about the fire, I want my piano. Fetch it out for me now.'

They say that people behave strangely in the face of catastrophe, and the groundsman decided that it was best to humour her. It took all hands to manoeuvre the huge Rönisch out through the study window, and a safe distance from the house. By then the flames were out of control and had spread to the roof thatching. There was nothing left to do but stand out of the way and watch it burn. Ellen's grandmother sat down at the grand piano and played Chopin until dawn rose up over the smoking timbers of her home.

We were being asked to be seated at the big table outside, so I took my leave of my informant who, thankfully, had been placed out of earshot. The seating plan had been meticulously constructed to avoid conflict and encourage festivity. We all had little place names. Ellen had been elected to the head table among the guests of honour. I assumed this was somehow a sign of her new-found devotion to her grandfather, probably much to the chagrin of her father. This was her family, and it seemed she was here to reclaim them.

I remember thinking at that moment how beautiful she looked. The light reflecting from the bright tablecloth and the flowers made her seem to radiate. The soft breeze brushed through the trees and a tiny white speck of elderberry blossom had become trapped in her hair. The sadness took root then. I waved to Leo who was sitting to one side at a table set up for the children. He looked a little nonplussed by all this sudden formality outside among the trees. He sat quietly with his hands in his lap and surveyed the cutlery in front of him and the children around him. He gave a quick wave back and dropped his hands back under the table. He had been watching me looking at his mother. Probably he saw the way things were much clearer than I ever could.

The meal was an interminable affair, where the business of eating came in third place, after the drinking and the

35

speeches. Plates came and went, glasses were filled and emptied. The conversation grew louder and louder. Speeches were made and then more speeches. They liked making speeches. I had trouble making head or tail of anything. The starchy woman to my left stared at me for some time when she thought I wasn't looking and then leaned forwards and offered to translate for me. It was a generous offer, except that she kept getting stuck and flustered and I ended up more confused than ever. Klaus, my impish informant, gave an extremely long oration that appeared to start out well but soon had people yawning and looking at their watches. He was oblivious. One of those showmen you have to shoot to get them off the stage.

And then, to my surprise, as we turned towards the glass being clinked gently, I realised that the next speaker was to be Ellen. She spoke in English:

'I want to tell you how happy I am to be here, among you all. I feel as though I have found a new family, a home I never really knew I had.' I looked past her to where the children, who had long since given up the idea of eating or listening to more of this, were now chasing one another in circles between the trees. Leo seemed to be in his element. Ellen seemed fluttery and not quite there somehow. The champagne, or was there something else disturbing her?

'A hundred years is a long time for any one person to witness and it makes this person,' she rested her hand on her grandfather's shoulder, 'even more special. I came here not knowing what to expect. I suppose that I have always been curious to know the part of me which belongs here, among you.' She paused and her head dropped until she was looking down at the table. Perhaps I wasn't the only one to suspect that the tremor in her voice was not fuelled only by emotion. I probably wasn't the only one thinking that this would be a good point for her to tie up her little speech and sit down. I certainly wasn't the only one to be a little disappointed to hear her continue. I was, however, the only person present who could possibly have had any inkling of where this was leading. I listened with that sinking feeling of impending doom.

'I have always believed in the importance of family and being here only confirms that.' She was staring straight ahead now, in a glazed fashion, at a spot somewhere up in the trees where the pine cones bobbed innocently in the breeze. This would be a very good time to stop, I was thinking. The tension was palpable, everyone now sensed that we were headed into choppy waters. I recalled our exchange on the ferry the night before.

'It's sad, really, isn't it? Or maybe it's just one of those strange coincidences.' She gave a slight giggle, which sounded alarmingly out of place. 'Just when I have found this great big family — all of you wonderful people, my own little family is on the verge of disintegration.' She nodded to assure those who thought they might not have heard correctly. 'My husband and I are to be divorced'. All eyes now swivelled in my direction. Guilty as charged. I knew, of course, where this was leading. I suppose I had known it for months, years even. I knew what she was about to say. It was one of those slow uncoiling convictions that stirs deep down in the abdomen. This was what the scene on the ferry was all about.

'I tried to put it behind me. I thought it best to just ignore it.' Nobody was breathing by this time. Ellen sniffed and lifted her head. 'But some things you can't forget, or forgive. And now, here, looking at all of you, I feel I must make a new start, a clean slate.' She wouldn't, I said to myself. In front of all of these people, surely she couldn't go that far? She could and she did. I listened. I heard her say the words, and it still didn't seem quite real. She was smiling at me as though she had just slit her wrists: 'You see, for some time now I have known that my husband has had an affair with my best friend.'

The woman to my left gave an audible gasp and uttered something that sounded very much like a filthy expletive in any one of a dozen languages you might care to choose.

4

After nearly three more hours of driving we are somewhere north of Kassel and quite exhausted. I am so tired I can barely take my eyes from the mesmerising red strip of tail lights running ahead of us. On the other side, the oncoming cars float down towards us like fireflies out of the dark. The inside of the car is cold and in the back Leo is flicking a flashlight on and off in boredom. He has given up asking when we are going to stop.

The road is a long straight incline that cuts down through the wooded hillside. I need to find somewhere to sleep. At the very bottom of the bowl there is an exit, beyond which I glimpse the yellow sign of one of those spooky, automated motels, completely unmanned. You use a credit card to get in and never need to see a soul. They have as much homely charm as a coffee dispenser, but if that was the only option I would take it. As I take my foot off the pedal a wave of fatigue hits me. You can drive for hours on automatic pilot, rigid with concentration and fear. The moment you turn off the road the tension drains away and you need to find a bed very quickly.

The orange indicator blinks back off the crash barriers as we come off the ramp. At the bottom I hesitate, too weary to make a simple decision. Left or right? Finally, I simply pull the wheel and we turn to cut under the bridge away from the automaton. We will take our chances and see what else there is.

In minutes the motorway becomes a distant memory. It fades with each curve in the unlit road. And as luck would have it we soon run into a small village, no more than a handful of houses secluded in the trees. There is a hotel, too, marked by a long white wall and a row of chestnut trees. I draw up to this and switch off the engine. For a moment we just sit there. I decide then that if they don't have a room we shall be sleeping in the car. I lead a yawning Leo into a *bierstube* that doubles as reception area and negotiate the room in sign language. They have plenty, the man says, no problem. I suspect, from the number of keys on the board behind him, that apart from us the hotel is empty. Our arrival is of no interest to anyone. All eyes are focused on the enormous screen fixed high up in one corner of the room. Between the cheering and ribaldry – much beer drinking, too, by the look of it – expert analysis is being offered on the tactical strategy of Bayern München. The place is crowded with unathletic-looking figures clad in sports garb. The local amateur football team's social get-together following the exertions of their weekly match. We order supper and Leo stares open-mouthed at the spectacle, accidentally stabbing himself in the cheek a couple of times with a ketchup-tipped potato chip.

We eat in numbed silence. The boisterous mood makes conversation impossible and, besides, both of us are too tired to utter more than monosyllabic grunts. As soon as we manage to clear our plates we climb to the second floor to find that the noise from below does not reach us. Not that I think either of us would notice if it did. While I unpack my things I notice how Leo, without being told to, folds his clothes neatly onto a chair, puts on his pyjamas and brushes his teeth. He is quiet and I have a feeling that he is a little uncertain about what we are doing here. I have no answers to his questions and hope that he will fall straight to sleep and stay that way. There is nothing more heart-wrenching than the sound of a child crying in the night. He turns on his side, but five minutes later he says:

'Will you tell me a story?'

'A story?' I have my eyes closed and no intention of opening them. 'I can't think of a story.'

'You remember the one about the bear in the cave filled with leaves?'

'I told you a story about a bear in a cave?'

'Yes, you remember.' He snaps on the bedside light and sits up to look over at me. I shrug. 'You told it to me,' he insists. 'A little bear who lives in a cave and wakes up after a long winter and starts going through his pile of leaves, because for every leaf he has made up a story in his head to help pass the time on all those long winter nights.'

'I don't remember that story.'

'Well, it's your story,' he declares adamantly, as though it were something I had left lying on the floor and I should really get up and fetch it.

'Wait,' I say. 'Hold on.' I clear my throat, trying to think of how to recuperate my standing. 'OK, I'll tell you a different one.'

'Any good?'

I frown in his direction. 'Good enough.'

'All right.' He settles himself down, puts out the light over his bed and pulls the blankets up to his chin ready for a story.

'OK,' I begin. 'It's about some birds.'

'Birds?' He turns this over in his mind trying to decide whether it is a good omen or not.

'It's the best I have at short notice.'

'OK, OK, I'm ready.'

'Right, then. Well, it happened that all the birds in the world gathered together to hold a meeting. They did this every year. Anyway, this time one of the birds, a hoopoe, stepped forwards and announced in a loud voice that there was little point in holding such a meeting when they did not have a leader, or a king, to bow down to. Everybody else, after all, had a king. The others conceded that he had a point. Well, he told the assembly, he was happy to inform them that actually they did in fact have a king, a very special bird whose name was Simurgh. All the other birds immediately began chattering excitedly, many of them claimed to have heard of this Simurgh, although none of them knew more than the name. The Simurgh was a mysterious bird whose existence was known of only by accident when one of its feathers fell down from the sky.

'Well, all the birds were really excited about this idea and wanted to know how they could get hold of this Simurgh; where did he live? So, the hoopoe explained that the only way of seeing him was to make the long and very arduous journey through the Seven Valleys. The other birds, all very excited, agreed instantly. They were prepared to do whatever was necessary, go to the ends of the earth if need be. They began to ask the hoopoe lots of questions about the journey ahead. And then a strange thing happened: the more the hoopoe told them about how long and hard the journey was, the more they all began to find reasons why they couldn't go along. One by one, they made their excuses. Some of them had problems with their feathers, others were not feeling very well, or had a bad wing. The hoopoe tried to persuade them that the journey would be worth it. That nothing they knew of could possibly compare with the experience of meeting the great king of all the birds, their king, the Simurgh. It was an opportunity that came only once in a bird's lifetime. He knew the way and he would lead them. Few of them seemed convinced, however, and despite his efforts to encourage them only a much smaller group of birds remained who were prepared to go.

'And so they set out across the Seven Valleys. And it was a hard journey. Many of the birds proved to be too weak to make the journey. Some fell by the wayside, and others gave up and turned back. Finally there were only thirty birds left. And when these thirty birds made it through the last valley they saw before them a great glittering palace. When they got there they made their way to the chamber of the King. All the walls were made of shiny gold that gleamed with a bright light, so it was like being in a room of mirrors. But, to their disappointment there was no sight of any king anywhere. They were alone. They turned on the hoopoe: "OK," they said, "so where is this great Simurgh of yours?"

' "Here. He must be here," said the hoopoe, pointing at the walls around them.

' "Where?" asked the other birds, mystified.

' "Look around you and tell me what you see."

' "We see our reflection on the walls, but that's us, not the Simurgh."

'The hoopoe had never actually seen the King himself, but now he suddenly understood. "But look, don't you see? It is because *we* are the Simurgh. The meaning of the word Simurgh is thirty birds, the same number as we are." And the birds looked around and realised that they were indeed what they had been searching for all along.'

It wasn't my story, of course. It was a classic of Sufi literature, attributed to one Farid al Din Attar, the Perfume Maker as he was known. And it wasn't really a bedtime story and I wasn't sure it would make much sense to Leo. Attar lived in Persia in the eleventh century. His reputation is often eclipsed by that of another poet, born in the same town of Neishapour – Omar Khayyám. Perhaps that is why it came to mind. I have been thinking about Khayyám recently.

'That's a pretty nice story,' Leo murmured in a dreamy voice. He was asleep in thirty seconds.

Haboba first told me that story years ago. I don't think she even knew who Attar was. It was just a story she had heard as a little girl, the same way she learned most of the stories in the *One Thousand and One Nights*; she knew them as stories, but she had never read them. She couldn't read. Years later I picked up an English translation of Attar's *Conference of the Birds*. As I read it I realised that I already knew the story. What was far suddenly became near in one of those curious moments when the two halves of your life come together and everything fits and the world makes perfect sense.

I look at my watch and see that it is almost midnight. Leo is sound asleep. The last cars have tailed off into the night and I have been awake for hours, despite being exhausted. How silent it is. I can hear nothing but a gentle trickle of water, which I work out, after a time, must be the sound of the stream which runs through the woods behind the hotel. I lie there staring at the ceiling, wondering what it is that has led me and my son to be sleeping in this hotel in a strange village in the middle of Germany.

5

The reaction of the guests to Ellen's revelations was less virulent than might have been expected. Perhaps people were always getting to their feet announcing incest, family mayhem and adultery. Perhaps this went some way to explaining the heavy drinking. Maybe the Nordic family gathering functioned as a kind of ritual group therapy session where everyone threw the worst they had at everybody else and they all left hating one another more than ever. In which case our wretched problems would be forgotten before we got to the cheese and biscuits.

I was sitting there with a rather silly smile on my face, not sure how to proceed. The stern-faced woman to my left cut me off without so much as a glare and I found myself turning to the long-haired lout to my right. He seemed determined to get himself voted the most badly behaved guest at this function and was sprawled in his chair chuckling to himself. He was some kind of boy genius, I had gathered, heir to a firm that designed furniture and the outside parts of electronic equipment. They had a distinctive style that was apparently very popular with those wealthy enough to afford the exorbitant prices they charged for what was, once you got over the shape of the thing, a fairly standard-quality stereo system. Cold clean lines, all the surfaces brushed aluminium and smoked glass. This was modernism taken to the extreme and it had all the charm of a pair of shiny jackboots. The same could be said of the person seated next to me. In reaction to Ellen's announcement he made a kind of chortling noise and knocked his glass against mine so heartily that it toppled over on the table.

'We all get up to it, you know. It's nothing new.' There was a rather opaque glint in his glassy eye. I had the feeling he could be very unpleasant without even setting his mind to it. But the fact was that I felt bad. The coming apart of two people is a sticky, complicated business with every sentiment pulled out of shape. The last thing you wanted was to throw it open to the public. I felt as though I were suspended from a series of wires pulling in every direction.

I looked around for Leo, but he was off in the grass, thankfully, chasing around with the other children. He had looked up, in that perceptive way of his, when Ellen had been helped away from the table in tears and into the house, and then, tellingly, he looked away again. I wanted to go in to her, but something told me that this would only make things worse. I thought about going for a walk in the woods, and staying there until darkness fell. But I didn't see why I should run away. It was none of their business, no matter what Ellen might think.

People were making a good job of avoiding looking in my direction. All except the Boy Wonder, the whizzkid who was pouring the wine down his throat so fast that he didn't even notice that he had just drained his companion's glass, a thin blonde with translucent bones who reminded me of a carp for some reason. It occurred to me that he had done this on purpose. He took pleasure in annoying people. Still, when he managed to get to his feet I allowed him to sweep me away from the table as he staggered off, trawling up another almost full bottle as he did so. It was a good enough excuse for me to go and so I went. We circled around the house, him turning to giggle from time to time, and me not sure why I was following him. There was a small conservatory on the other side of the house overlooking the little stream. He soon revealed his real reason for wanting to get away when he produced a ziploc bag which appeared to contain the refined harvest of a small Colombian rainforest.

He was half a dozen years younger than I was and already a multi-millionaire. Along with running the company he had also inherited a few other family traits. His father, I later learned, was something of a reprobate who would go on notorious drinking binges that often lasted a week, during the course of which he would usually smash up a few cars, threaten various innocent bystanders with hunting rifles and machetes and generally run amok. The local inhabitants would lock up their wives and daughters, bar and bolt their windows whenever they heard that this modern-day Dracula was in town for a little fun. The rumour was that he had abused his daughter and run away to Greece with her best friend who was then just fifteen years old. There was something of an outcry, but the matter was settled amicably, money changed hands and the girl was apparently willing, so no lawsuits pending. This was the kind of marriage they devote horrified documentaries to, when it happens in Kyrgyzstan.

I sat with him for the moment, trying to collect my thoughts. It struck me as being terribly sad that with all the troubles of the world, Ellen and I could not make our tiny little family work. He, meanwhile, was snorting white powder up his nose noisily and talking very quickly at the same time.

'So what do you do?'

'I work for a radio programme.'

'Doing what?'

'I read books and interview writers.'

He began to giggle again. I wondered what would happen if I hit him with the chair I was sitting on and whether, if he had designed it, that might be considered poetic justice. He began telling me about his recent trip to Thailand, about how you could buy anything you wanted out there. 'You can have a baby, two-year-old, three-year-old, whatever you want.' It took me a moment to realise that he wasn't talking about adoption. I glared at him. He stared malevolently back, eyes hooded, nostrils flared and lips thin and blistered with red wine, daring me to go for him. I started to get up. 'I'd better get back.' But when I tried the door it seemed to be jammed. I shook it a couple of times. He sniggered behind me.

'Why go back? You think they miss you?' I hesitated, if only because I had never encountered such pure malevolence before. I was fascinated, the way you stare at a coiled snake. He relaxed a touch and smiled. 'You ought to do what I did. I had this girl who was crazy about me, let me do anything to her. I even stuck a gun up her snatch once. Made no difference, she still loved me. Finally I took her on holiday to the Caribbean and I went to a bar and found a guy, a big black guy. I took him back to the hotel and told them that I wanted to watch her and this guy going at it. So she did it and afterwards I paid the guy off and then I told her she was a whore, that I would never touch a woman who had been with a black man, never. I left her there, stranded with no money!' He slapped his knee, chortling away.

I was locked into a glass house with evil on a par with Mengele, or Ivan the Terrible. I shook the door harder and it came free. As I turned the corner of the house I bumped into the carp-girl who had been sitting next to him.

'Turn around and go back,' I said to her, 'if you value your sanity.' She looked at me as though I had made an obscene suggestion and continued on her way. I heard his laughter again as the door opened. I needed to get out of here, out of this house, this crazy party and out of this country, before something really bad happened. Night was falling already, the sky was growing dim and wisps of cloud were etched above the tall pinetops. Leo was in one of the rooms in the main house, watching television with some other children. I found Ellen in the long empty kitchen. People came in and went out, fetching bottles and ice. Sounds of laughter came from elsewhere in the house and somewhere mariachi music was playing.

'I think we handled that very nicely.'

'I feel abused,' she said, slumping down at the table.

'Well, you did a good job of getting even out there. Did you ever stop to consider Leo's feelings?'

'It's a little late to be concerned about his welfare, isn't it?'

'Why bring all that up again? It happened ages ago. It was a mistake. It started, it ended, that was it.'

She shook her head. 'That makes it sound very tidy. You are always looking for the easy way out.'

'That's what you think this was?'

'There's more to it than that.'

'There's nothing more to it. We were both looking for sympathy and we thought we had found it together.'

'I think I'm going to puke.'

I looked up. Someone had come into the kitchen, seen us and vanished again without a word, but it gave Ellen time to compose herself.

'There is more to it than that,' she said, thoughtfully.

'You mean you and me?'

'I mean everything. This is the end of it, but it's been dying for a long time.' Ellen got to her feet and went towards the bathroom. The guests had come in from outside and were now assembled in the living room. Voices cracked into laughter and then fell back into the foaming swell. Ellen returned, wiping a hand across her drawn face. She was right of course, there was no point in going on. Why was I determined to keep arguing for another chance?

'We owe it to one another to just end it, cleanly, right here and now.'

'What about Leo?' I asked.

'What about Leo? What do you think people do when they get divorced, split the kid down the middle like a peach?' She leaned against the doorway and looked over her shoulder. I had lost everything. I had no case. Leo would live with his mother. I would see him every second weekend, if I behaved myself. But I wasn't thinking about that. I was thinking there was something about the way she was standing in the doorway which took me instantly back to the

48

time we first met, years ago. The first time I knew I was in love with her she was standing just like that, in a doorway.

We were both working part-time at a place called Borsalino's in Oxford. I was doing a course at an undistinguished school of journalism and Ellen had just finished university and was trying to decide whether to carry on with social anthropology or to get a job in the real world. While she tried to make up her mind she thought she might make some money and travel. We talked about the dread of following in our parents' footsteps. Her father was an archaeologist and she was reluctant to make a career as an academic. And I had ended up doing exactly what I had sworn I never would do – journalism, like my father.

That was all it was, a few late-night conversations, usually in the company of the chef and one or two others after we had put the chairs on the tables and turned down the lights. Then she went off to see the world and I landed my first job at a small local paper in the far north. Well, not exactly the icy wastes, but for someone like me, who knew next to nothing of Britain, Sheffield was far enough. We did not exchange addresses, or make any plans to meet up; what for, nothing had happened? So that made it seem as though something more than just coincidence was at work when we met the second time, two years later, at a party in London.

I hardly recognised her then; she looked wilder somehow, having just returned from a trip to the Far East. It was one of those long summer evenings that seem to stretch out endlessly. The air thick with the earthen chemistry of flowers in bloom and the smell of cut grass mingled with smoke from a dwindling barbecue. The sun was stuck somewhere between the row of chimney pots and saw-toothed rooftops.

And people talked hazily as though they had plenty of time. The air was full of unfinished conversations and it was how you imagined life in the leafy suburbs at its best. Ellen and I had talked briefly earlier on, in the thick of the mêlée, but now that things had calmed down and everyone was drifting around, we found a moment together again. She was full of energy, full of life. I remember an old Van Morrison song was floating out from the house behind us and she was saying how much there was to learn. She wanted to go back to studying.

'Everything else is a waste of time,' she said. She was now set on doing a Ph.D. on the identity of displaced communities. It sounded, not vague, but ambitious and brave, as though she were preparing to take on the world. This is what attracted me, her conviction. This is what I wanted. So the party fell away from us and we dropped into a little conversation of our own. She was wearing blue denim overalls with the buckle of one side of the bib carelessly unhooked. The white strap of her brassière luminous against her tanned shoulder.

Love, ultimately, is a conspiracy of two people trying to take on the logic of the world. We reinvent ourselves, because love gives us the belief that we can become what we appear in someone else's eyes. So we wrap ourselves tightly around the axis of another person's existence. This is what shifts planets, what holds the universe from flying apart. It is a kind of gravitational pull. And when it goes, when it slips its hold, then you are disorientated for a moment, not quite sure which way to turn, daunted by the sudden awareness of that great dark void that was there around you all the time.

When the final guests had staggered off into darkest Jutland, collapsed into the back seats of taxi cabs and cooed their cheerful goodbyes, Ellen came walking home from the main house. I had left them all there to their partying and used Leo's bedtime as an alibi. Ellen's grandfather had in his possession acre upon acre of undisturbed woodland, dotted here and there with fine little cottages that looked as though they had stepped out of a book of Grimms' fairy tales; low thatched roofs with tiny little windows peeking out from underneath the eaves. We had been lent one for our stay.

The inside smelt of old wood and stone and the furniture looked as though it had been installed in the fifties.

After I put Leo to bed I found a blanket and sat out on the little porch. The sky seemed to expand in the night air and the stars over the trees pulsated with the squandered energy of a dwindling universe. The faint strains of music and laughter drifted over the open ground of a grassy clearing and through the band of pines the lights of the main house could be glimpsed.

'What are you doing out here?' she asked. I said I couldn't sleep.

'Look,' she said, taking a deep breath. 'We need to talk this over seriously.'

'You mean rather than throw ourselves on the mercy of a houseful of strangers?'

'I'm sorry, I just needed to say it. To get it out of that place in my head where it has been driving me crazy.'

'Neither of us is going to win this.'

'That's right, everyone comes out a loser.' I suppose the same thought went through her head as it went through mine, and she sat down beside me.

'Leo is going to be the real loser,' she said, speaking aloud for both of us. For the first time in months we were actually having a conversation. There were no plates flying or doors slamming, or threats being yelled. Just a normal conversation.

'I want to stay here for a while. Maybe you should go home with Leo. I'll join you later.'

'Join us later? Join us where, how? When?' There was a degree of trust necessary to float this offer of hers and neither of us had any left to spare. I was not the only guilty party. Had she found her true match here among her Nordic ancestors, one of those blue-eyed, blond types?

'What do you need to stay here for?'

'Don't start, all right? Just don't. I just need time by myself, that's all.'

'I'm not trying to start anything. I'm just trying to understand why you need to be here to think this out.'

'What difference does it make where I am?'

'Well, it makes a difference to Leo to begin with.'

'This is not about Leo.' She slipped off her party shoes and rubbed her feet. 'I'm not doing this, Yasin, not now. I need to sleep.' She turned to look at me from the doorway. 'Spend time with your son,' she said. 'He needs you. And goodness knows he is going to see precious little of you over the next few years.'

The door closed behind her and for a time I heard her moving about the house, to the bathroom, the kitchen for a glass of water and then the snap of the lights and the squeak of the old springs as she got into bed. I listened attentively to every move, every tiny gesture. I needed to be sure that this was not a truce, that there was no possibility for reconciliation. I had pulled a couch out onto the porch from the living room. A piece of furniture which, although I am sure it was a masterpiece of Nordic design, was also hard, wooden and uncomfortable. Their loyalty to their architects was touching.

The house fell silent and I was alone again. The moon had vanished and the stars looked different to the ones I knew. Flung up there like granules of broken glass in a bowl of indigo dye. I sat there watching them slowly slip across the opening in the trees until I fell asleep and awoke shivering with a crick in my neck. Birds were chirping cheerfully as I went inside and made myself a cup of coffee and drank it standing in the kitchen staring at a shelf of old utensils: a colander, a funnel, a coffee pot, all in the same uniform blue metal. Then I went to rouse Leo, told him to get dressed, and packed his things, which meant throwing them into a small holdall with Taz the Tasmanian Devil on the side. He watched me, yawning.

'What are we doing?'

'We're going on a trip.' I had an idea about going to look for Brecht's old farmhouse, but I wasn't sure this would kindle much interest. Also, I had read about a fourteenth-century church nearby which had a frieze of interspliced arches supposedly inspired by Arab architecture, but this, too, seemed a little pallid.

'Where are we going? What about Mum?'

'I talked to her last night. She wants to stay here for a while. So we two are going exploring.' He realised I was serious and stared at me for a moment. He wanted to go and ask her. 'She's asleep. She came home really late. Come on,' I said. 'It'll be fun. Just the two of us for a change.'

Leo looked sceptical and I didn't blame him. He had no idea where we were supposed to be going. I put my hands on his shoulders. 'Listen to me – this is a wonderful opportunity. You and me. A father-and-son thing. How many boys do you know who ever did something like that? How many of your friends in class do you think went on an adventure like this?'

'An adventure?'

'An adventure, that's it, exactly. A real all-time, once in a lifetime, never to be repeated, fully guaranteed adventure.' I held out my hands for an answer. 'Well?'

He jumped to the floor and began to dress hurriedly. We were almost out the door when he said, 'Wait. I have to say goodbye to Mummy.'

'OK.'

I waited on the porch outside. It seemed to take him an awfully long time to make up his mind. If he came out, I thought, then we would manage somehow. If he didn't, I had no idea what came next.

And suddenly there he was again, smiling, racing me to the car, and I knew that everything would be all right, after all.

6

The *bierstube* is dark and gloomy in the morning. There are
antlers on the opposite wall. The head of a wild boar hangs
over our table. No trace of the cheery spirits from the
previous evening. The room is chilly and stale with tobacco.
Leo is silent and unresponsive. A change has come over him.
Earlier I had made him take a shower. He was up and dressed
before me, gripped, it seemed by a kind of travel fever. I
insisted, trying to convince him that these were the rules a
traveller has to go by; take the hot water when you've got it,
because you never know when next you are going to have a
bathroom at your disposal.

He didn't exactly swallow the idea whole, but recognised
that there was a logic to it for which he had no counter-
argument. One of these days, I thought to myself, he is going
to be smarter than me. But for now I have the edge. He, after
all, had no idea where we were going to sleep tonight.
Neither did I, but he didn't know that. I watched as he
slipped off his clothes, dropping them in a pile where he
stood. Underpants inside the trousers, shirt on top of the
whole heap. I stared at the heap of clothes on the floor,
the abandoned shoes, as though a little boy had just been
abducted by aliens. I found myself thinking morbid thoughts
about death. I sat there for a long time trying to decide what
to do next. He was singing to himself in the shower. The
bathroom was clean and the water was hot and I had to tell
him several times to get out or we would miss breakfast. As I
rubbed him down with the towel he flicked on the television

and asked, 'Did you and Mummy used to travel a lot together?'

'Sometimes.' They were showing a cartoon, *Tom and Jerry*, his favourites. In German, but that made no difference. He sat down to put his clothes on while I went into the bathroom. The conversation stretched out over long gaps, interspersed by flurries of violence, the sound of blows being administered and taken. Wooden doors splintered, glass shattered, little birds sang.

'Before I was born?'

'Before you were born.'

But by the time we are eating breakfast a dark mood has descended over him. I try to distract him by talking about the decor, but he doesn't even raise his head to look at the wild boar looming over us. My attempts at humour only make it worse. I am trying too hard. My efforts to make our situation seem normal accentuate the oddity of our being here.

The morning air is surprisingly cold when we emerge. The sunlight forms a band of honey-coloured light high on the northern side of the valley. Down at the bottom where we are it is green and stony grey. In a few months there will be frost here in the mornings. In the river that runs alongside where the car is parked the water wells up in beautiful glassy plates that go sliding over mottled olivine stones. The car feels damp, cold and forbidding and the engine is not happy and proves sluggish to start. I convince myself there is an odd rattling noise that shouldn't be there. Leo has no patience for my twittering trepidation.

'It sounds all right to me,' he declares.

'Nevertheless, we ought to keep our eyes open for a garage.'

Once back on the road we fall into our own thoughts as we join the procession of vehicles on their way to or from the places that make sense of their lives. The road rises and falls in grand sweeps and the traffic moves in strange kinetic formations, rather like shoals of fish. For a long while there is no one around, and then suddenly a swarm descends out of nowhere and you are wrapped up in a flurry of urgent movement for a few minutes. And then, just as easily, they disperse and the road is calm again. We are driving at a speed which I (and the car) find reasonable, but which to most of our fellow travellers is positively geriatric. I catch glimpses of people steering their way confidently past me at what I estimate must be around 180 kilometres an hour. I expound on my theory that in the long run they don't gain all that much time. The pressure of driving that fast means that they have to stop more often.

'Their nerves, from concentrating so hard, make their bloodsugar drop and also, they need to go to the toilet.' I nod knowingly.

Leo listens but is not, I sense, convinced. I point out a yellow Volkswagen with an unhappy-looking family aboard. We have seen the tiger clinging to one of the back windows by its plastic paws before.

'You see, there's that one again.'

'Baba, they probably give those things away.'

I disagree. I am convinced that the same cars keep overtaking us. You watch a car pass you and then you watch it pass you again, and the reason is that they have stopped somewhere in between which means that on average they are doing the same speed as we are. Leo sighs.

We turn to a conversation about forests.

'People used to worship trees,' I say. He sits up and takes a closer look out the window. 'They used to think they had spirits inside them.' I am not making this up. The pines we see along the sides of the road are the scant remains of what was once a vast ocean of trees. In the days of Julius Caesar it was said that you could wander through the forests that covered Europe for two whole months without seeing the sun once. This kind of scale awes both of us into contemplative silence. The first temples were trees and forests. According to Plutarch, one of the most sacred objects in ancient Rome was a cornell tree. If ever it appeared to be wilting, people would rush up with buckets of water to try and revive it, believing that if it died their fortune would turn.

'Before they cut down a tree they used to have to ask the tree-spirit for forgiveness. When a child was born they used to plant a tree to protect it.'

And there is a connection between the neem trees of my childhood and the forests of ancient Europe. Neem derives from the Latin word *nemus*, meaning a wooded grove. The druids used the same word to mean sanctuary. My parents planted a neem tree in our garden when Leo was born. Now both house and tree have been sold.

We are entering the Rhineland, I tell him, a place not only of tree-spirits, but also of mystics and visionaries. I read to him from the guidebook when we stop for a break. Hildegard von Bingen, a nun in the twelfth century: 'She had visions when she was your age.'

He tilted his head to one side trying to recall if anything he had ever experienced might fall into the category of visions. I read on: 'She was locked into a room in a convent for thirty years.'

'Why?' he asks with alarm. I turn the pages in the guidebook looking for a suitable answer. They don't provide one.

'To devote herself to God, I suppose. They had to be dead to the world physically. In fact they were given the last rites before they went in, just as if they were actually being buried.' He frowns. He is right, it is pretty strange stuff. 'They passed her food in through a little window, and that was it.'

'Doesn't sound like much of a life.'

We sit on a wooden bench attached to a picnic table. The grass around our feet is littered with crushed cans and bright plastic wrappers, abandoned by hasty travellers before us. Leo sits kicking at the stones under his feet, rocking his leg back and forth restlessly. I turn the page and show him a photograph. It is a portrait of Hildegard with her hands clasped in prayer and her face raised towards the sky.

'It says she was devoted to music as well, and composed a fair number of spiritual chants. She opposed the Church's call for the Second Crusade. She didn't think they should have anything to do with swords and fighting.' As I recalled, the First Crusade began with a massacre of Jews somewhere near where we are sitting, in the Rhineland area. Hildegard knew what the Church was up to and she didn't like it.

The mention of war and swords makes Leo perk up. 'The Crusades was when they had all those knights in armour, wasn't it?'

'Pope Urban X called on all Christians to fight for the Holy Lands which were in the hands of the Saracens.'

'Who were the Saracens?'

'Well, they were . . . us.' He looks at me in a strange way and I decide to go back to the swordplay. 'It lasted around four hundred years altogether and actually it was nothing to do with religion but was about money and controlling trade routes. How about some chocolate for dessert?' His eyes light up and he jogs over to the car to start monkeying around in the boot where we have our provisions. I throw the guidebook aside. History is not the easiest of subjects at the best of times. Leo returns loaded down with biscuits and raisins and some chocolate. History is forgotten.

'Did you ever do that?'

He is pointing to a curious-looking man standing by the exit holding a sign on which the word 'Paris' is scrawled in thick letters.

'A long time ago,' I say. 'I hated it. But you meet some interesting people, the kind you would not otherwise meet. I don't know whether I would try to nowadays.'

'Maybe we should give him a lift.'

'Maybe.'

We don't. A lorry pulls up while we are watching. Part of me, I am ashamed to say, is relieved, although the hitchhiker didn't look like a mad axe maniac. Maybe we get too cautious as we get older, we lose our trust in people. As we drive on I find myself thinking about him, and about the sign he was holding. How far away is Paris?

According to the guidebook Trier is unmissable. We turn to the west and drive for another hour or so. I was once told that many of the older German roads running east–west were laid down during the war, when they were in a hurry to get fast supply lines in place. This explains how roughly made they are. The gaps between the slabs of cement tick noisily by under the wheels.

I feel as though I have been sucked along in the relentless flow of a dream, for seven years. Now, suddenly, I was wondering why. I realise that up until this moment I have simply improvised my life, hopping from one plan to the next with no real idea of where it was all leading. Now, for the first time in my life it becomes plain to me that I have no idea what I am doing. I do not have another dream to latch on to. I feel no ambition, no burning desire. I have nothing, not even this road. All I have is the boy.

The light is a soft, loamy yellow that makes the air smell of moist earth. Unlike Henderson, the character in Bellow's novel, I don't have an Africa to run away to when my life turns sour. Europe is my dark continent, and I am searching for the heart of it.

7

I was born between duelling histories: The history that
forged the empire and the counter-history that defied it.
Both halves formed opposed and yet essential parts of the
same whole. My father, when he had graduated from chasing
golfballs to being a junior filing clerk in the Steamers &
Railways Department, joined the nationalist movement early
on. A young man of principle, moving furtively through the
night ferrying communist propaganda (copied on the office
stencil machine) to fertilise the growing awareness of the
movement for change, for independence. The activists put
aside their concerns about Stalin and what evil he might have
perpetrated, about pogroms, gulags and long cold trains to
Siberia. They knew that if you want to take on anything as
big and powerful as the Union Jack you needed something
tangible on your side. So there it was, two world powers face
to face in the form of a bundle of inky papers wrapped in
newspaper and tucked under the arm of a young man's
tightly fitting jacket. Already his political allegiance compro-
mised by the fact of that suit, picked out from Lombard's
mail-order catalogue, ordered from London to keep up with
fashions. His head, too, showed signs of diverging from the
nationalist cause: long strands of crinkly hair drenched in
Brylcreem and combed into geological striations on a
diagonal course away from his high forehead. He preferred
his office in the Steamers & Railways Department (the very
same which had sent his father to meet his fate at an obscure
distant junction a quarter of a century before), with the fan
blades spinning above his churning mind, and which he

abandoned only with reluctance every afternoon to catch the tram across the river, home where he stripped off western duds and hung his suit on a hanger for the next day, emerging like a dusky Clark Kent blinking myopically in the sun. In the late afternoons he would sprinkle water over the yard in a creased gellabiya and the smell of moist dust rising to the nostrils would send a tingle up his spine. This was where he belonged, in this dust, with those bleating goats. But the following morning he would be Brylcreemed and stiff-necked in his collar and tie, heading for his office across the river in search of the modern world.

The Sudanese nationalist movement needed a voice. It needed to be able to formulate itself in such a way that the world understood what it wanted to achieve and why. And the only way of getting a voice was to learn how to speak. So he conducted himself in exemplary fashion, completed a correspondence course and won a grant to go abroad to learn about the business of newspapers.

England was an enigma to him. He knew nothing of fried breakfasts and landladies and sleet and rainshowers that last a week, and the damp that gets into your bones, and the loneliness of bedsits. He knew it as the country of Ruskin, John Stuart Mill and Keats; everything he knew he had gleaned from the pages of books. He arrived to discover himself adrift in an alien country where people sneered at your Lombard's mail-order catalogue outfit.

'What made him want to go there?' Haboba asked me years later. 'I'll tell you. I asked him what he thought he was going to do there. Who asked him to change the world? Why go and live there? What for? Things are the way they are because Allah put them that way. He never had an answer. What made him decide to go? How did he get those ideas into his head? I'll tell you how, that accursed golf ball knocked his brains silly, that's how.' There it was, the course of the family line had been permanently kinked by my father's errant wanderings. Except that if he hadn't gone to England he would not have met my mother and I would not be around, and we would not be having this conversation, would we? Haboba clicked her tongue. Smart-aleck grandchildren Allah sends her. I would have turned up somehow, she said. A little different, maybe, without that wild bush of hair on my head, perhaps, but I would have come along.

I was a thirteen-year-old child, still in school. I was trying to make sense of the whole scheme of things. The problem was that the world out there was a mystery, and part of that mystery stemmed from the fact that we didn't seem to have a history. We had stories, but we didn't really have museums or books to put them in. How we came to be assembled here at this confluence of streams seemed to be a question no one was particularly interested in asking. What went before? History, the hard stuff, the earth-shattering events, all involved other people, other places. What strange concatenation of forces had given rise to this mixture of peoples which we called a nation? In class we learned that history consisted of foreign words like Verdun and the Treaty of Versailles, Auschwitz, Pearl Harbor, Hiroshima, Dien Bien Phu. Those distant lawns and pavilions, those men in wide hats and breeches. We memorised words like Realpolitik and Von Bismarck, the Scramble for Africa, without really understanding how they had affected us.

We gazed out of the classroom window at the stony sun, a piece of discarded newspaper blowing across the dusty yard and wondered what exactly they might have been scrambling to get here for. That all of these strange men wearing rows of medals and huge moustaches had something to do with our present situation seemed curiously absurd. 'England Needs You' read the caption. And the man in the picture with the big moustache was pointing at me. Fashoda was another important name we learned, the place where that same mustachioed man, Lord Kitchener, attended an important meeting with a Frenchman named Marchand. There was a photograph of the two sitting on the deck of a Nile steamer at dusk, deciding *our* future.

Our history was never going to be a straightforward, linear narrative, but rather a series of contortions, disjointed incidents, haphazard circumstances that eventually led down to us, a group of noisy kids with unsavoury habits. Not even the teacher had much time for it. He would stand there facing the window with his back to us so that he could pick his nose without us bothering him.

'And so Emperor Franz Josef wanted to protect his Habsburg empire by marrying Elisabeth, the sister of Johann Strauss. Yes, what is it?' My hand, despite my reluctance to draw attention to myself, had gone up of its own accord. 'Stand up! What is it?' He finished digging his little finger into his nose and carefully examined the results of this excavation, while waiting for me to explain why I had broken his rhythm and dragged his attention away from the window, and back to forty-seven nasty little creatures.

'Sir, Johann Strauss was a composer. The wife of Emperor Franz Josef was the sister of Ludwig of Bavaria.' At home I had read on in the textbook, impatient for answers. For a brief second I felt very pleased with myself. Then a pellet of well-masticated paper moulded into an arrowhead and catapulted from an elastic band struck the back of my neck with the sharp stabbing impact of a wasp sting. I must have looked as though I were having an attack of some kind, my shoulders up, scrunching up my face and clapping a hand to my neck. The teacher frowned. It was plain that I was intent on making a fool of him. Whether I was mentally retarded or not was irrelevant. He picked up the board rubber, a piece of wood the size and shape of a small brick onto which a strip of felt had been lamely nailed, handy for anything but wiping the board, and hurled it at me. Instinctively, I ducked and felt a surge of guilty satisfaction as it rammed home, hitting the person sitting behind me, a boy named Girgis whom I suspected had fired the paper pellet. But my career as an eminent historian folded before my eyes.

'What difference does it make to you whose sister she was anyway?' asked Girgis when he cornered me later, rubbing his bruised eye, inspecting my sandwich which he had confiscated in compensation for the pain I had caused him. He had a point. History was not a priority. Maths was a priority. Algebra and Faraday's Law were priorities. We were a developing country, so we studied Civics; we memorised how many tons of fish had been pulled out of the river every year over the last ten years, along with similar statistics for sorghum crops, groundnuts, sugar cane, sesame and cotton. We learned about the importance of bridges, railways and dams. The message was clear; we were to become engineers and doctors and help this country onto its feet, to turn it, as the slogan went, into the 'breadbasket of Africa'. What was the point of looking backwards? By the time we got to secondary school all the humanities had been dropped, including geography. So we had no real idea, not only of how we got here, but *where* we were to begin with.

The place where we really got our education about the world was a source of flickering light that played on a whitewashed wall in the open-air theatre down on the river road. My mother did not smoke, drink or do drugs as far as I know, nor was she known to gamble at the roulette wheel or play a cool hand of poker – her only known vice was the movies.

By day the Blue Nile Cinema was a whitewashed brick quadrangle inhabited by dead leaves, lizards and dozens of metal chairs strung with plastic cords once bright with colour but long since faded and distended by the sun into cracked loops of hardened spaghetti. At night it was transformed into a well of magic and thrills, shimmering in the leafy shadows, hidden beneath the brooding neem trees. Compared to the rowdy establishments downtown, this theatre was quiet and fairly respectable, the sort of place you could take your children. It drew in a select audience: students who wandered over from the sleepy university hostels nearby, educated professionals with their families, all dressed up in their Friday best, even the odd expatriate, eager to mix with the locals, clutching aerosol tins of mosquito repellent.

My mother knew all the staff by sight, and many by name. They would enquire politely after her husband every time, improvising theatrically to accommodate this English woman who turned up every week with her three long-haired and unruly children: myself, my sister Yasmina, and Muk (rhymes with book, his real name was Mohammed, but we never called him that).

'*Ma'shallah*. Good evening, Mrs Zahir. Mr Zahir not joining you?'

'Not today, I'm afraid.'

'Working hard, as always. Not a moment of leisure for him.'

She would smile and say maybe next time. She never ever told them he was in prison, although in all likelihood they knew as well as she did where he was. That too was part of the charade. The only time I can actually recall my father going along with us, the film – *El Dorado* starring John Wayne and Dean Martin – was interrupted by a sandstorm hurled down upon us from on high, sending us all coughing and gasping out of the cinema. You couldn't even see the screen, the coloured beams from the projector were trapped in the swirling dust like writhing djinns.

At the slightest hope of something new being shown (new was a relative term as most films would arrive with a good five-year headstart on us) my mother would bundle the three of us into the back of that battered old Volkswagen beetle of hers – a sun-faded hibiscus-red – and we would scuttle off in an airy clatter of shuddering baffles. Innocent times. Nobody really worried that these films might contain something we ought not to see, or – more to the point – that we might not understand. There was no parental advisory board – there were just parents, and ours decided that anything that managed to get into the country must be harmless enough. There was a national censor to judge whether the film was coming in at all and, added to that, the prints had usually done the rounds of most of the Middle East beforehand. By the time they reached us they would be so cut up and jagged that you often staggered out nauseous at the end, as though you had watched the whole thing while clinging to the bar of a roller-coaster ride.

There was an element of anarchical dissent to my mother's madness. She had missed out on the hippy movement. She had missed Woodstock. She had missed experimenting with sex, psychedelic drugs, Jimi Hendrix and whatever else, partly by age and partly by being too far away. I don't think she really wanted to roll about in the mud naked, I don't think she really understood what was going on, but she empathised with the breaking down of convention. Khartoum was a long way from California, but she did what she could. She tie-dyed all our clothes. She once stood outside the American embassy with a placard that read 'Leave Vietnam to the Vietnamese!'. A crowd of curious onlookers formed around her wondering why this crazy white woman was concerned with something happening in the jungles of South-East Asia. Burning your bra just wasn't an issue in East Africa in the 1970s.

'People who are afraid of God are afraid of life,' she once said, although I was never sure what she meant exactly. It was one of the rare occasions when I heard her refer to anything of a religious nature. The cinema was her church, that was where the real contest of life was happening. People were imperfect. They had doubts. They made ambiguous decisions, were weak-willed and lived in an unjust world. God had a lot to answer for, including a husband who was in jail for speaking his mind. 'An idea never killed anyone, it's people who are afraid of ideas that do the killing.'

And there was no better place for expanding the mind than in the cinema. So there we saw Paris for the first time, and Venice and Rome and Sophia Loren pouting at us (we never imagined that Fellini had awoken the wrath of Catholic Italy by making such daring films). There were the streets of London with their double-decker buses and black cabs. We cruised San Francisco's hills with Steve McQueen in *Bullit*, and wandered New York with Woody Allen. The

Americans were obsessed with disasters, earthquakes, burning towers, falling aeroplanes. The British provided cumbersome dramas loaded down with bizarre costumes and reams of medieval history. Too many gloomy castles and not enough swordplay. We wanted *Captain Blood* (the Italian remake), and what we would get was Richard Harris as a demented *Cromwell* (the screening of which was notable for the party of English expats sitting on the balcony above us who all stood up and sang 'God Save The Queen' as the credits rolled) or Peter O'Toole in the dreary *The Lion in Winter*. We cracked roasted watermelon seeds between our teeth, stuffed peanuts into the long necks of our Al Kola bottles and prayed for a battle. We would quiz one another on the plot: where was it going, was there a plot at all?

'She's not his wife, idiot. She's married to the other one.'

'No, she isn't!'

The French flicks were different. Truffaut's strange and familiar characters who seemed to talk for hours without making any sense. The ever stylish Alain Delon in *Borsalino*, or *The Red Circle*. We all walked around with hunched shoulders and hands in our pockets and wished we had an excuse to wear raincoats. Slick cobblestones and pavements that echoed to a pair of sharp heels running in the dark. Pistols stuck in the pockets of trenchcoats and people jumping on or off the running boards of a speeding black Citroën, knocking back glasses of funny-looking stuff at the bar that was later explained as being made of liquorice – which none of us believed. These were exciting films, which formed around a dark existential twist, although it was a long time before I could even spell a word like 'existential'. They were moody and full of complex motives and left us emerging blinking into the neon-lit forecourt muttering, 'Why did he do it, why did he kill her?'

'Who knows, but it was good, wasn't it?'

'Yasin, don't pretend you understood what it was about.'

Perhaps we didn't understand everything we saw, somehow it didn't matter.

The cinema was also the closest we could get to observing the greatest mystery of all, SEX, in action. Not so much graphically, on the screen, since these were the choppy bits, flayed mercilessly to shreds by the snappy scissors of every film censor board from Tehran to Timbuktu (actor approaches actress. She closes her eyes and offers her lips. He moves closer. CLOSE UP and . . . KLUNK! We are back to the speedboat chase), but all around us. The cinema was a respectable place to go in those days. Well turned-out bachelors took a whole box of four seats when they were only going to use two. Cheapskates only paid for two seats and risked being joined by two strangers – or worse – two noisy kids slurping Fanta noisily through straws. We watched these big spenders avidly, as they clicked their fingers and the waiter came skidding along the aisle in his long white gellabiya to unsnap the soft drinks in the crate on his shoulder and place the bottles on the wobbly little table between them. This sometimes in the middle of a crucial scene, which made it clear that the main purpose was not to see the film at all but to sit together in the dark! We would crane our necks, fascinated. They would talk softly and from time to time, they would lean towards one another to whisper, which was distracting in the middle of a film. They were obviously not married. Mum and Dad were married and they never got up to any business of whispering and giggling. My parents' preferred means of communication was yelling, loudly, usually when the person being addressed was on the other side of the house. No, these women were definitely not *wives*. They dressed in transparent *tobes*, layers of sheer cloth that wafted about them like clouds, elegantly falling from their hair around their shoulders. Underneath they wore dresses the colour of mangoes and pomegranates, and when they approached the night air was filled with a powerful burst of intoxicating scent.

'Stop staring, Yasin,' my mother used to mutter, nudging me with her sandalled toe through the plastic strands of my chair.

'Gas attack!' Muk would shout when a perfumed cloud wafted by, clasping his hands over his nose and mouth until everyone in the cinema turned around to look at him. He always thought he was terribly funny. Yasmina would turn to the woman with an apologetic smile while I punched my brother sharply in the arm. Muk had no tact. He was always trying to draw attention to himself. He also had a strange habit of running away. He would do this any time things went against him. The slightest reprimand and he would be gone, bounding from the house into the street, whatever time of day or night it might happen to be. He would start running at the drop of a hat. One night when we came out of the cinema and he was told that he was definitely not having another ice cream cone, he didn't hesitate for a second – he was gone. There were no streetlights on that road. Beyond the cinema there was nothing but a few trees and lots of puff-fruit plants. The next stop, so far as any of us knew, was Ethiopia. Still, we had to chase him for half a mile in the car, just this skinny figure in baggy shorts and long bushy hair jogging along in the bouncing beam of the headlights, with my mother swearing through clenched teeth that she was going to strangle him when she got her hands on him. I have often wondered where he thought he was going.

Whatever images we had of what lay beyond the world we lived in came to us through the prism of a projector lens. The swiftly running celluloid showed us life as it was lived by other people far away. We identified with all of them. That was where we belonged, up there alongside Jack Nicholson and the oil derricks, or paddling downriver with Jon Voight and Burt Reynolds (and what exactly did they do to that one with his trousers down on the log?). We would play a game, The Classic Moments Game, trying to outdo one another by remembering particular scenes.

'Where the hand comes up out of the water in *Deliverance*.'

'Uggh! I had nightmares for weeks after that.'

'Where the head floats into the porthole in *Jaws*.' We saw the shark-terror film long before we should have done and it was lucky we were not traumatised for life. That was one of the few films my mother regretted – she sat through the entire film muttering to herself, 'I knew we shouldn't have come. I *knew* we shouldn't have come!'

'*Play it Again Sam*, where he throws the record across the room.'

'*Butch Cassidy* where she takes her clothes off.'

'Yasin, don't be disgusting!'

Nowadays, when I see those refugees clinging to their life rafts in the cold sea, or hanging from the sides of some rusty sinking trawler in the Adriatic, or being helped, shivering, ashore on the beaches of southern Spain, I know that it is not just the lure of a better life which makes people take their lives into their hands. What sends people careering off into the world like human cannonballs with no safety net is the Technicolor dream that was lodged in all of our heads long before we had even learned to write our own names.

8

In Trier, I tell Leo about Attila and his Huns sacking this, the oldest Roman town in Europe, some fifteen hundred years ago. Attila he has heard of. We sit and eat ice cream. Emperor Valentian's disgraced sister Honoria, upset with her brother for having locked her up (this on account of his discovering that she had taken a common servant for a lover, but I didn't go into details on this point) sent a ring to their most feared and dangerous enemy, Attila, betrothing herself to him. Attila eagerly rode across the Rhine, gleefully exclaiming that he was only coming to take what had been promised him, and going on to sack most of Western Europe while he was at it.

But apart from that nothing much is happening in Trier. We wander through the streets looking for diversion. We pause outside a shop window and look at the posters. They are reproductions of art works and seem to cover everything, from Andy Warhol to the Impressionists. Inside, I flip idly through the plastic leaves which are placed like enormous open books in the middle of the gallery. Leo is looking at pictures of robots and spaceships. I find myself staring at a Cézanne; *La Montagne Sainte-Victoire*. The landscape is dotted with facets of colour that somehow make coherent sense. Cézanne was trying to paint what he perceived of a landscape, rather than depicting what was simply there. But he did this by imposing a subtle sense of order. The trick is the way he puts the patchwork of colour together. At first glance it looks as though he has just thrown dabs of paint on the canvas, but you barely realise you are looking at anything but a complete picture. There is something about the way in which all the little pieces add up which holds me there until Leo tugs my arm.

'She's staring at us!' he hisses, nodding over his shoulder in the direction of the woman behind the counter. She was. I flip forwards a couple of pictures and stop again.

'Brueghel's *Icarus*.'

Leo twists his head to one side to get a better look. 'The one whose wings melted? I don't see him anywhere.'

'All you can see are his feet,' I say, pointing to the right-hand corner of the painting where there is a little splash. Leo almost crawls onto the book stand to get a closer look and I decide it is time to leave.

'But why was it named after Icarus, then, if you can hardly see him?'

'Well.' I take his hand and start leading him towards the door. 'The title of a painting tells us what the artist was thinking.' I manage to smile at the shop assistant as we pass, but she pretends not to notice. 'Maybe the point is that we are all so busy with what we are doing that we don't even notice something so remarkable as a man falling out of the sky.'

'That's pretty strange.'

'Well, exactly. But supposing it wasn't that they didn't notice, but that they didn't *want* to see him?'

'Why wouldn't they want to see him?'

'Because they had everything they needed. The shepherd looks at the sky, the farmer ploughs his land, there is even a man fishing, I think. When you are comfortable, when you have everything you need, you don't want to know about other people's problems. It is easier to look away.'

He thinks about this for a while and then he turns to me. 'How can you know what a painter was thinking hundreds of years ago?'

'I don't,' I laugh. 'Nobody does. But the point is that after all those years we are still thinking about it. So there must be something there.'

We decide we don't want to stay in Trier and after looking at the map together I suggest Luxembourg.

'I've never been there,' I say.

'Neither have I,' says Leo. So it is decided.

No sooner are we on the road than it begins to rain. Clouds sink heavily over us and the road is narrow and winding so that although it is not far to drive, by the time we get there I have decided we ought to find a hotel.

There is a yawning cleft in the earth in the centre of town. There are caves in the cliff sides where in ancient times the inhabitants used to kindle fires. These have since been transformed into restaurants and swinging nightclubs. Tables and chairs line a railed terrace above a huge sign bolted to the rockface. We shelter from the drizzle under a tree to eat our sandwiches, staring at the gloomy weather and the chasm below us. There must have been something mystical about living in a cave in the Stone Age. A man stops to let his dog pee next to our bench.

'Just think,' Leo whispers, his face aglow within the fluorescent halo of his orange cagoule. 'If dogs could fly like birds, it would get pretty stinky.'

Our legs are stiff and clumsy as stilts from the car. After lunch we stagger woodenly along, drooling at the displays of delicate pastries until finally I give way and we dive inside to emerge with one each the size of a man's shoe, stuffed with enough vanilla cream to choke a horse. As we walk along, laughing at each other's efforts to avoid getting cream on his face, Leo turns to me.

'Maybe we should call Mummy and tell her what fun we are having.'

'Hmm.' I nod. 'But first we ought to think about where we are going to sleep.'

By the time we have found a place to stay and moved our things into the room evening is falling and we are hungry again. Around the corner from the hotel there is a pancake restaurant and it is Leo's turn to choose, so pancakes it is. They are supposed to be Dutch but they taste plain enough and Leo rouses himself to devour a large plateful covered in a variety of gooey sauces. Nutritionally speaking, probably not recommended, but he looks happy and tired as we leave, so I suppose a little indulgence has its merits.

As we walk back to the hotel, Leo observes that the toyshops have the same toys he knows at home. I am cynical, however, and see it as more evidence of the voraciousness of multinationals bidding to rule the world. Trying to get all the children in the world to want the same toys.

'Not all of them, Dad. Some can't afford it.'

'Right.' I stand corrected. 'Not all of them.' I feel a glow of pride; I have a son with a conscience. I can't really claim any responsibility for it, but it is good to know he has one. The toys I remember as a child were produced by another conformity, that of the People's Republic of China. We had painted aeroplanes and locomotives, all rudely stamped 'Made in China'. Metal police cars with rubber policemen who looked like aliens, not even vaguely oriental. The sirens wailed like the ones in *The Untouchables* (The 1950s series. Everything we watched, on television or at the cinema, was out of date. We were still watching *Run For Your Life* long after Ben Gazzara had stopped running and the series had become history elsewhere on the planet).

These metal toys could be dismantled into lethal sheets of tin within a matter of minutes by bending back the spikes that held the frame together. They could be adapted to all kinds of use. Inside there was a friction engine with a revolving flint wheel that gave off sparks and which made quite an impressive instrument of torture when held close to somebody's face; a younger brother, say, or that kid down the street who was always throwing stones from behind the safety of his front door. The simplicity and incongruity of those toys lent them to our imaginative tinkerings.

'The best toys are the ones you make yourself,' Haboba used to warn sternly, shaking her head in disgust at such frivolous use of money.

Yasmina, Muk and I grew up with a longing for all kinds

74

of things that were out of reach. We hoarded catalogues and drooled over brochures. We longed for our father to go away on one of his trips so that he could bring us back something different (of course, his 'trips' usually took him closer to the interior of a prison than out of the country). Western toys were such a rarity that they became something of an obsession. Yasmina even developed a fetish for a doll she was once given. It stayed in its box on a shelf in the wardrobe for seven years. She would dig it out every so often and stroke the packet. The packaging was in tatters by the end of it, but still she refused to succumb and unwrap the thing. There was a hole through which she could poke a finger and perversely stroke the acrylic fabric.

Now, however, looking at the prices of the objects Leo has his eye on, I begin to see the beauty of Haboba's logic: knocking a few nails through a bit of wood to construct a Sten gun or an aeroplane is much more satisfying than anything those brainy people at the toy factory could come up with in moulded plastic. The closer they strive for perfection the more likely they are to disappoint. After all, they are trying to sell you their dream, why should it fit yours? Leo listens patiently but doesn't seem entirely convinced.

We sleep in lumpy beds to the tune of running water. At first I take it to be the rain, but it turns out to be a toilet cistern down the hall. Pipes gurgle discontentedly and I miss the soothing effect of the stream of the night before as I lie awake watching the spidery orange pattern of rain and street light through the chintzy lace curtains wondering how many other people have looked at exactly the same view and where they might be now.

The following morning sightseeing is vetoed due to the weather – we are both edgy and keen to be on the move. Leo walks around the outside of the car, drawing patterns in the moisture that he is supposed to be clearing from the windows while I curse and mutter as the starter whines ineffectually. Finally, all the moving parts manage to find one another at the right moment and the motor splutters to life. I feel an almost religious sense of gratitude. Leo punches the air triumphantly and shouts, 'Yes!' which is a gesture he has picked up from television.

By day the town looks hungover and grey. The light wells up like sea brine between the brooding ancient buildings, hinting at a better life elsewhere. We wind through birchwood forest to flat straight motorway· and I begin to relax. The rain stops and starts. The sun breaks through in blinding fits and the road is slick with the hiss of wet tyres.

It is a short stretch to the town of Metz. The St Étienne cathedral is famous for its stained glass windows − 6,500 square metres of them. It has been dubbed 'God's Lantern'. Leo endures my tourist guide chatter in silence.

'You're not really interested, are you?' He shrugs his shoulders. 'I don't blame you. But this is the kind of education you can't pay for. This is about the way we look at the world.' Talking is difficult as I have to concentrate on finding my way through a traffic system which seems to involve several pointless circumnavigations of the city to reach where we want to be. When we are finally parked I realise something else is bothering him.

'I just don't understand why we couldn't call Mummy from the hotel.'

'I told you, hotel telephones are expensive. We'll call later on. I promise.'

Consoled by this thought, he clutches my hand as we run across the square. The first thing that grabs his attention are the gargoyles. Monsters. This is an unexpected treat and we spend a long time walking around the cathedral with our heads craned back (bumping into people with cameras) looking up at the curious figures.

'It is as though they are meant to scare people away, but why?'

'The word gargoyle comes from gurgle,' I venture. He gives me a nasty look, but I stick to my guns. 'That's one theory, anyway. That's the noise they make when the water drains through them off the roof. But these are more like *chimères*, which were believed to keep evil spirits at bay.' By now he is beginning to suspect that perhaps I am not making this up, which I am not. ' "Dernières ressources des malheureux!" Rousseau called them. Chimères were mythological monsters that were hybrids, composed of different kinds of creatures.'

'Like us,' says Leo suddenly.

'Like us how?'

'You know, different kinds of mothers and fathers.'

I need time to think about this. Are we unhappy monsters? In an essay on DW Griffith's film, *Birth of a Nation*, James Baldwin tells us that mulatto comes from the Spanish *mulo* and was used to describe the mixed race progeny of Caucasians (usually men) and Negros (their women slaves). The emergence of the word in the 16th century tells us something about racial theory in those days. The mule, a cross between a horse and a female donkey, is usually sterile. The Christian slave owners, stricken with guilt at their savage, lustful behaviour towards their pagan property, who usually had no choice in the matter, sought to wash away their sin and discredit the outcome of their transgression of nature's and God's laws, and so depicted their offspring as misnomers, half breeds, sterile freaks who could never reproduce, which of course they could. The mulattos in Griffith's film are rather sorry creatures who lust after white people and whose existence is a threat to the entire social order. They must be put down. Race is the last great taboo, the myth of sacred purity that unites Klansmen and the Nation of Islam in unholy alliance. The one thing that overcomes their hatred for one another is their hatred of the mongrel nation growing all around them.

'There is a great deal of superstition mixed up in religion,' I say. 'Even though most people in the Church, or the mosque, would rather deny it. These mythical monsters, or chimères, derive from an earlier fear.'

77

'Give me another example.'

I rack my brains and tell him something I recalled from a visit to Avignon with Ellen. The *probar* was a kind of testing stick the Pope used to check his food had not been poisoned. It would be placed on the table where he sat. It consisted of a piece of coral on a golden stand from which there hung bits of flint, ivory, a couple of shark's teeth and a piece of unicorn horn, which actually came from a narwhal whale. When it came to eating and drinking, all the crosses and prayers were just not enough to safeguard you from your enemies.

It strikes me that this cathedral, like so many churches, was probably built on Roman ruins. We are standing right at the hub of the ancient world, where the decline of Roman civilisation gave way to Christian Europe. Until the early fourth century practising Christianity was a subversive activity – meetings took place underground, in the subterranean chambers of Roman circuses. What made it catch on? Probably because the very things which symbolised all that was wrong with the Roman way of life were denounced by Christian doctrine: sin, excess, evil. There were no sacrifices in Christianity, because its god had taken human form and had been sacrificed for all the sins of mankind.

In the fifth century the Empire was foundering in a squalid mire of decadence and disease. Rome had overstretched herself. The borders which kept out the Barbarians had been pushed back continually as the growing population increased the demand for raw materials and food. A series of shrewd plots and political intrigues had been instigated to keep the provinces at each other's throats; it was the Romans not the British who invented the tactic of Divide and Rule. But within the Empire the rot had already set in; widespread exploitation was bolstered by corruption. The tenant farmers could no longer meet the demands of their landlords; to maintain equilibrium the army had to be bribed to keep providing more and more of everything. As a result they were constantly trying to expand the Empire, to find more slaves, more food, and so on, to sustain the centre.

The circus was to keep everyone's minds off the trouble-some stuff going on out there. Entertainment was required to soothe the idle masses and keep them occupied. Things were not, in fact, so different from today.

The baths were the Roman equivalent of the shopping mall; people spent all day there in search of diversion. The circuses had gladiators, sex shows, chariot races, torture. Everything imaginable was provided for the audience's delight. They were mesmerised by their daily dose of the horror of the world. So much so that even when things were getting out of hand and people were warning of degener-ation, no emperor could put a stop to the circuses. When the Vandals were battering down the gates of Hippo, it is said, nobody could distinguish the cries of the soldiers dying in defence of the city from the screams of delight coming from the arena. During the reign of Emperor Claudius there were more than a hundred and fifty days of the year marked as public holidays, and on nearly a hundred of these public games were staged. Everyone thought they were safe because the Barbarians were far away, and being kept at bay by the wall that was the border of the Empire, but they were wrong; the real malaise was eating away at them from within.

The rain lifts as we drive west out of town, into the pale soft hills of Moselle. The sky is a rosy shade struck by bands of blue, and Leo manages to dig the Beatles tape out from under the seat, so we can start going through the whole repertoire again, beginning with 'Nowhere Man'. It is hard to imagine war and mud and death in this placid setting, but I read in yesterday's paper that a town nearby is sinking into the earth. The whole area is honeycombed with tunnels dug during World War I and never filled in properly. Farmers are still dredging up fragments of human bone with the blades of their tractor ploughs. With your foot down on the motorway it takes less than fifteen minutes to traverse the entire width of the front line, every metre of which was hard won at a cost that ran into millions of lives between 1914 and 1918.

We are passing through time; across the face of the continent and down through the centuries. As we drive we spy a sign marking a vantage point. We pull off the road and climb up the small hill with our bag of food and settle down to eat an early lunch.

It is a fine balmy day with a slight haze over the fields. There are picnic benches and a chart showing where the jagged defenses once stretched away to the west, towards Verdun and Saint-Mihiel. If we had X-ray vision we would see through the placid surface of these dewy fields to the muddy wasteland below. Terrified men huddled shivering in waterlogged trenches, their feet so swollen from constant immersion that they could barely walk. Leo wrestles with a large unwieldy sandwich as he tries to envisage it. He looks thoughtful. To him it seems as far away as the Romans.

'Why did it happen?' he asks. I scout through my frail grasp of events and come up with the assassination of Archduke Ferdinand in Sarajevo. I can still recall a photograph of him riding in an open car moments before he was shot by a Serb nationalist who believed he was striking a blow for freedom. The day chosen for the assassination, 28 June, was the date the Ottomans had conquered the Serbs in 1389. The name Sarajevo has become familiar to Leo from more recent events. We sit there on the picnic bench crunching our apples and listening to the birds over the roar of the motorway behind us, enjoying the tranquillity of it.

Back on the road the traffic seems to be moving with more purpose and it is easy to sense that we are approaching a large metropolis. I am still thinking of the placard held by that hitch-hiker we saw yesterday and wonder if it was some kind of message. Paris doesn't seem such a bad idea.

We push on through the flat Argonne region, the landscape either side of the road rather like a bruised forehead protruding from the ground. The stark silhouette of a charred tree looks as though it simply burst miraculously into flame one day without explanation, a brooding, ossified sentinel watching over the road. It would be harder to turn off now than to just keep going straight. A row of electric pylons resembles the tail ends of giant stitches against the sky, suturing the earth together.

By now Ellen will be wondering where we are. She might have gone further than just wondering. She might already have enlisted the services of a group of trained killers, mercenaries, to find me. With her grandfather to support her I imagine she could offer quite a hefty sum to anyone willing to wrest her son back from the arms of his lunatic father. I can just see the headlines: 'Muslim Fanatic Kidnaps Own Son', or 'Arab Extremist Gunned Down in Race for Border'. Perhaps I am getting carried away. She might just be sitting by the telephone waiting, not unreasonably, for me to call.

But I can't call, not just yet. What would I say? She might not have bothered to call home yet to see if we were back there. Do I even owe her an explanation? Of what? I took my son for a drive. I have a right to do that, haven't I? But that's not the real reason. The real reason I can't call Ellen is because I am still not sure I can explain what I am doing, or why. I feel as though, after years of being lodged in a swollen river, unable to move, growing resigned to my own drowning, I have finally broken free.

Why have I never been able to escape, to really escape, to just get up and go? All of those other stirrings, straying across fences, flirting with the idea of breaking free − I mean the affair with Dru and the other, lesser adventures − none of them led anywhere, except to the incontrovertible fact that nothing *could* change. And now here I am, drifting along on the surface, not quite able to believe it. How long will it last? How long can it last?

'Maybe you have the wrong number?'

Leo leans across the table and waves a hand in front of my face. I must have been sitting there for quite some time just staring into space.

'The wrong number?'

He is looking at me in such a concerned fashion that I stop

stirring my coffee and take a sip, only to discover it is cold. The cafeteria is almost empty. There is a row of tables lined up alongside the window. Below us we can look down into the parking area and beyond to the motorway, humming angrily with moving vehicles. People come and go, rolling slowly along until they find a space. They climb from their cars, stretch and begin looking around to see what there is to do in this port of call. They run energetically up and down a few yards to summon the blood back into circulation. Some bounce balls, others light cigarettes. Children yawn, mothers reach for Thermos flasks and bottles. Fathers flip open hatchbacks, flailing wildly to field the cascade of objects that tumble out. All kinds of people and vehicles: old, young; families; couples; smart coupés, messy campers. Watching them passes the time and I am in no hurry to leave.

Leo is drawing the view in his sketchbook. It is a nice big sketchbook that I bought him for the trip before we left England. It has good thick paper and he has his pencil case unzipped and crayons and pencils now comfortably strewn all over the table cloth. The drawing so far consists of a few trees and a lot of blurred lines that signify the passing traffic. He keeps becoming distracted by the arrival of another car down below. He watches and then tries to guess who is inside and what relationship exists between the various people who emerge. But now he wants to know why he can't speak to his mother.

'The number is all right,' I say. 'It must be the connection.' I have tried about half a dozen times. Each time it is the same thing: I go out to the stairwell, look at the telephone for a while and then come back. He looks at me for a moment and then looks away again without saying a word.

'Unhappy family,' he declares with world-weary confidence, staring out of the window, pencil poised in distraction. 'The boy wishes he had stayed at home with his friends, and the mother and father can't stop arguing. Oh, look, they have a dog!'

Below us a man opens the rear of the car to ruffle the head of a large St Bernard. An enormous pink tongue flops out of its jaws to hang down almost to its paws. The dog drops ponderously to the ground and starts lapping away at the water the man has just poured into a bowl. From time to time the dog glances round as though wondering what on earth they are doing *here* of all places. Leo sketches furiously to try and catch dog, car and man; they look out of proportion to the rest of the world, but never mind.

Over his shoulder I see a woman moving along the tables towards us. She seems to pause as though in search of someone and is clearly not looking for a place to sit. She is listless and distracted, glancing around, sizing up everyone in the place.

'Do you think Pluto would like it if we kidnapped him and took him with us?'

'Who is Pluto?' I ask, watching the woman drawing nearer.

'That dog.' He seizes my jaw and points me in the right direction. 'Baba, down there. Look, he's getting locked up again. Bye-bye, Pluto!'

'Hey, what a great picture!'

We both look up. Leo casts a look of suspicion at her attire and says nothing.

'Hi there. I'm Angela? I saw your car down there? UK numberplates? Are you going home?' She is talking so fast that she barely gives me time to nod.

'I saw you outside,' Leo says. 'Did you follow us?'

'Follow you?' she laughs, but her smile is forced. 'No, I just saw you walking in so I thought I'd come and say, you know, hello.' She glances over her shoulder. I notice the women over by the cash desk nodding in our direction.

'You don't mind, do you?' she asks as she sits down.

Leo looks at me, and then goes back to his drawing again.

Angela leans her elbows on the table and pulls the hat from her head. She is older than her clothes at first suggested, and visibly tired; her face has a strained, weather-beaten look

83

about it. I notice a leaf stuck to the sleeve of her suede jacket.

'Do you have a cigarette?'

'Sorry.' I shake my head. I look around to see if anyone else in there is smoking, when I turn back I catch her examining me again.

She leans forwards urgently: 'You are English, no?' I look at her. There is the long version and the short version, and I am familiar with that look of scepticism. 'Do you think you can take me to London?' Although her accent is uneven, she speaks English well, which suggests that perhaps she might have lived in Britain for a time. Now, it seems, she is trying to get back there.

'We're going to Paris,' I say, ignoring the way Leo glares at me. He has not been consulted on this decision yet, mainly because I have only just made it.

'Oh, that's great! You'll love the Louvre. There are so many great pictures.' Leaning close to Leo, she says, 'You like drawing, don't you?'

Leo twirls his crayon in his hand but says nothing.

'Then Paris is the best city in the world for you.' She is already getting to her feet, impatient to be off. 'How old are you?'

'Nearly eight,' replies Leo.

'The same age as my son.'

'Look,' I say, feeling guilty. 'We can take you as far as we can.'

'No,' she shakes her head curtly. I was no use to her. Paris is a detour – she has to get to England. Already the hope has faded from her face, the smile has vanished. She turns on her heel and walks away, barely managing to murmur goodbye.

We sit in silence. I am struck by the awesome good fortune which has provided me with passport and car, with a son who is sitting with me looking at the world, trying to take it all in, put it all down on paper.

As we drive towards the exit slipway Leo spots them, over by the trees. Standing by a collection of bundles is the woman who said her name was Angela. A girl of twelve stands beside her cradling a baby. A forlorn, snapped twig of a family.

'I don't see a boy,' says Leo. 'Do you think she was lying about her son?'

'Maybe,' or maybe something happened to him. 'Wave,' I say. And so he waves. They don't wave back.

9

Life is a dream, said Ibn Arabi, the archetype of the eternal Sufi wanderer, who devoted much of his life to travelling the world in search of knowledge. From Murcia in Spain where he was born in the twelfth century, to Damascus where he passed away. He maintained that the true world was too vast for any cartographer to map: 'The earth is not the true form of being, but something illusory.' The world we live in is a 'realm of signs' in which spirits, angels and djinns are made flesh. In dreams we pass beyond this physical realm into the real world, which otherwise cannot be seen. Ibn Arabi set off around the world hoping to awaken himself, to 'die' in a metaphorical sense so as to be able to see.

There are numerous theories about the origin of the word 'dervish' or 'darwish'. One of these is that it derives from the Persian and means simply, 'the seeker of doors'. As though the physical world were a dark room and the Sufi mystic blindly trying to find a way out. All of these images have preceded us along the open road looking for answers. They suggest the importance of movement, of insight gained through motion. But is this a mystical quest or am I just running away?

My first encounter with Sufi mysticism coincided with a bout of teenage angst. I read Idries Shah's *Tales of the Dervishes* while trying to decide who I was and what I wanted to do with my life. I immediately perceived a link between the dervishes (I had seen our local version dancing in the dust across the river in Omdurman), and Taoism, which I had come to by way of a fascination with kung fu –

the Hong Kong film industry having made big inroads into Africa around then.

The Taoist idea of dual, intertwined opposites which are complementary and at the same time inseparable seemed irresistible. My sense of being divided, split, incomplete, went back to an early recollection of my parents leaning over my crib as a baby – one dark and the other pale. At least, I think I remember. But the image remained, whether it floated up from the buried subconscious, or was an early flash of inspiration.

It is an attractive thesis, that the world is made up of opposites: day and night, hard and soft, water and sand, black and white, all constantly seeking harmony. Life is made up of a constant barrage of contradictory impulses and doubts, out of which we strive to achieve a balance. We try to convince ourselves that we are in control of our lives, and yet we eat things we know are bad for us, we fall in love with the wrong people. Instead of staying put where we know we are safe and loved, we set off into the unknown expecting to find something better. It's all about contradiction. Admittedly, all of this didn't really help solve the question of what I wanted to do with my life. I seemed to float through the world in a daze. My lack of resolve was only enhanced when contrasted with the conviction and dedication that I saw embodied in my father.

From the day he came back from England he had only one real god: journalism. He believed in the sacred value of truth, and not in any mystical sense, either. His chosen mission in life was to seek it out and then print it. He didn't believe in compromise or keeping his mouth shut, no matter how many times they threw him in prison. When we were young they used to say he had 'gone away'. Gone where? Why? I can recall the confusion I felt when I discovered he was in a place where they send bad people like criminals and murderers and things like that. What had he really done? I wondered.

'They locked me up to silence me, but you can't put a gag on the truth.'

'Why can't he just keep his mouth shut?' Haboba would groan. 'Who asked him to have an opinion?'

But he was a man with a mission. When it came to seeking out the facts he would pursue his goal with the tenacity of John Wayne looking for Natalie Wood in *The Searchers*. Prison did not weaken his resolve, it simply confirmed that he was on the right track. Who was he after? Everybody. Every petty dictator, every corrupt minister, every dishonest judge, every dictatorial imam.

'You can't suppress the truth,' he would say. 'No matter where you hide it, it finds its way out. Whether it takes a lifetime, or even longer, sooner or later, it will out.' His face would widen, as though he were in the grip of a feverish calling: 'Truth is like a boomerang, the harder you throw it, the harder it comes back at you, and it *always* comes back.' One of my earliest memories is of visiting the newspaper and seeing him poring over that huge old manual typewriter, beads of sweat crowding his brow. The power had been cut and everyone else had long since gone home, but we had to wait until he was finished.

The Boomerang of Truth
Let those concerned about recent evasive tactics by that person currently occupying the office of the Minister of Roads and Public Works not be too worried. Rumours of lavish trips abroad are confirmed by sightings of said *public servant* dancing in Paris nightspots with glamorous 'hostesses'. These accusations are too substantial to be dismissed as hearsay. The feeble attempts by certain junior officials to swat away the accusations like so many flies are only helping to fan the flames under the Minister's *hotseat*. The Boomerang of Truth always comes back, dear reader, and as we know, many a Minister has, in his time, lived to regret not making a clean slate of it from the start!

Such earnest campaigns against corruption made him unpopular. Drinking champagne and engaging 'hostesses' were seen by many as the legitimate perks of public office. And while such behaviour was not exactly evidence of political corruption, he saw it as a sign of the moral decay that was eating away at the very core of the independence project.

It was like having a stranger coming to live in your house every time he came back. You had to get used to the sound of him snoring in the afternoons, wandering about the house in his shorts, or calling you in from playing football in the street to do your homework. The spells in prison wore him out physically. And he would emerge leaner each time but with his resolve firmer than ever.

They never broke him, but they almost killed him a couple of times. My mother resigned herself to her fate and drove across the river to Koba prison every day carrying baskets of food to keep him alive. You could die of a lot of things in prison – prison food being one of them.

The last thing I ever wanted to do was follow in his footsteps. How could anyone follow an act like that? The devotion, the dedication, the sheer conviction of it all. At the age of twelve I convinced myself that I would become an athlete, a world-class Olympic swimmer like my hero at the time, Mark Spitz.

'Spitz?' my father exclaimed. 'You worship a Jew?'

I looked up at the huge Olympics poster on the wall. I had been given it by some kind soul at the American cultural centre where they had a library that stocked movie magazines and they were always giving things away free, although it was years before I suspected that I might have been a willing pawn in a hearts-and-minds campaign. It was matched on the other side of the room by a picture of a Palestinian Fedayeen fighter leaping over a barbed-wire fence with a Kalashnikov across his chest. I peered at the figure plunging through the blue water.

'How can you be sure he's Jewish?'

'His name is Spitz. Spitz is a Jewish name.'

89

It wasn't that he had anything against Jews, as such, but in 1976 the memory of the last Arab-Israeli war was still fresh. Sadat had retaken the Sinai but Golda Meir had been about to nuke us all. This was no time to be sitting on fences.

I had just joined the Sea Scouts. They weren't actually 'sea scouts' in the literal sense as there wasn't any sea anywhere in the vicinity. They were more like 'river scouts'. We had two rivers, the Blue Nile and the White, both of them muddy and wide. The Sea Scouts were a rough, boisterous lot. You had to swim across the river to pass the initiation test. My mother objected. She carefully fed me stories about water snakes and electric fish that could stun you for just long enough for you to drown, along with treacherous undercurrents, and even crocodiles, though none had been seen in the region for decades. The truth was that I preferred swimming pools with clear water and no suspicious-looking floating objects. Why was I pushing myself back and forth across that muddy river, jumping at the mere touch of a dead twig? What was I trying to get away from? My father decided that I was going through a difficult time and needed guidance. Time to make up for all those long months of absence.

'Come and have a chat with me,' he said. A father-and-son chat. I didn't like the idea but I went along, invited to enter his private study, a little room of its own propped up between the garden wall and the main house. I watched while he poured himself a gin. I didn't like him when he drank. I didn't like the change in his voice. I looked around my surroundings and saw further evidence of what I had always known – that there was a centre of gravity to my father's life, a firm sense of direction which told him what was important and what wasn't. The books, the thick wedges of box files and piles of newspaper cuttings, the maps, the photographs of African statesmen on the walls – Nkrumah, Kaunda, Nasser. All spoke of a sense of purpose. The fate of the country gave his life meaning – the absurd conviction that the curious collection of ethnicities, races and creeds fenced in together by colonial rule could be turned into a cohesive nation. As I watched him fishing ice cubes from a plastic cooler shaped like a pineapple I had an idea what was coming. I had heard this sermon before.

'We live in difficult times, Yasin. When I was your age I didn't have the opportunities you have. I did not have the privilege of being able to study, though I dearly wanted to. I had to work. I had to feed a family. My father was gone. I was the head of the house at your age.'

At that moment he seemed suddenly old to me. A tall figure, slightly hunched at the shoulders and slim as a slice of lime, and with that little moustache that trailed white fur across the upper lip as though he had just downed a glass of milk and forgotten to wipe his mouth. As always he was on his way out, off to talk politics with his friends until the early hours, as he did most nights. And as always, immaculately dressed in a navy-blue suit, double-breasted, and a tie. During the day he wore a short-sleeved safari suit, and the white gellabiya was reserved for bed and for Fridays when he went to visit his mother.

'Do you have any thoughts on what you want to do with your life?'

'Swim,' I answered, with all the confidence of a man who knows the world has great plans in store for him. I saw medals, saw myself atop podiums in far-off places, raising a clenched fist in a Black Panther salute.

'Apart from swimming. Swimming you can do in your spare time, as a hobby.' He was talking to me as a man again, and that worried me. I half expected him to inform me that I was about to be married to my second cousin and shipped off to grow dates in Kassala to learn about the land. I think it struck me then, for the first time, that he was going to die. Not right at that moment, not immediately, but one day, and that I would inherit all these heaps of paper and books and would be incapable of carrying on where he left off.

'Professional athletes last a very short time. You must accumulate possibilities. You never know when they might come in useful. It takes people years to find out what they want to do in life. But I can tell you one thing, worshipping Jewish swimmers is not going to get you anywhere.' And he was off, making his own plans for the life he would have dreamed of: 'You need to learn about the world before you can be of any use to us here. There is still so much to do. Let me talk to a few people. We can find you a scholarship. A university or a college of further education. Maybe . . .' I just sat there and listened to my life being sent off on its way into the future. This was his idea: go away, get trained and come back to help with building the nation. I was twelve. All of this seemed a long way off. I barely knew who I was let alone what I wanted to do with my life. I wanted to be Bruce Lee and François Truffaut rolled into one. I wanted to stroll the streets of Paris with a scarf around my neck and the collar of my raincoat up with Cleopatra Jones, the black karate-kicking heroine, on my arm.

He got to his feet and drained his glass. 'Time waits for no one, my boy. In a blink of an eye it will all be over.'

I looked up at him and nodded in agreement. I didn't believe a word of it.

I could never have imagined that fifteen years later I would find myself shivering in thick November mist on a hillside in northern England interviewing senior citizens about why they were afraid to go out of their homes in broad daylight. I could barely understand their Yorkshire accents. On a bleak ridge of a housing estate perched like a furrowed brow above the gritstone and chimneystacks of the city of Sheffield. Painted yellow boxes on the ground marked the spots where it was safer not to tread; places where a clear drop meant that you could end up with a television falling on you from a great height. The lifts were ripped up, grilled with wire and scarred with anger. Swastikas made as much sense as anything in an environment like that. The stairwells reeked of piss, murder, drugs and delinquency – it would have made a fine theme park for Viking holiday-makers out for a spot of rape and pillage. The place was ruled by roving tribes of juveniles, wild adolescents high on sniffing lighter fuel and amyl nitrate. This was not the England my father imagined he was sending me to:

'You must start at the bottom, the ordinary people, the workers, the voiceless ones. You will never regret it.' I wasn't entirely sure I agreed with him, but I wound up working on the *Daily Crow*, as I shall refer to it. The editor, a man named Harvey Greenbow, took one look at me, fresh from a journalist training college in Oxford, and put me on 'local colour' stories. So I went about town interviewing Pakistani restauranteurs about life in general and the loutishness of their Friday night customers. I tackled rap bands who thought talent was proportional to the size and number of earrings they wore. And then pandemonium struck: Saddam Hussein sent his troops rolling into Kuwait. The *Daily Crow* did not, needless to say, have a Middle East correspondent on hand.

'Invaded what?' Panic on the editorial floor. 'Well, where is it? Somebody? *Anybody!*' A map was produced. 'Local angle,' declared Harvey Greenbow decisively, stabbing the air in a characteristic gesture: 'Harvey Greenbow: a Decisive Man for Decisive Times' ran the caption on the advertisement that was plastered along the sides of buses throughout South Yorkshire. Harvey was running in the local council elections. When he stood on the floor of the editorial room and announced something that way then it 'were as good as writ in stone', one seasoned hand informed me.

So we went looking for the local angle on a war taking place three thousand miles away. Photographers rushed out to take pictures of fighter bombers through the chainlink fences of US airforce bases. Mothers were interviewed on doorsteps about how proud they were to have a son serving. On page 3, they ran a series of photographs of young women in military uniforms (half-dressed, or -undressed, depending on which way you look at it) whose affiliation with the armed forces was tenuous, to say the least. More important, a large television set was installed in the editorial room so that we could all keep abreast of things by watching CNN. I sought out irate Kuwaitis living in the area, thinking I could bring in a scoop, and discovered there were precisely none, either that or they were keeping a very low profile. I did manage to locate a Yemeni who ran a newsagent's shop in Rotherham and had a brother who once worked in Kuwait. This brother had unfortunately passed away years ago and, besides, the grey beard trembled with regret, they had not spoken since they were children. He didn't want me to mention his name as he had relatives in Salford and was worried they might think he was doing well and venture across the Pennines to ask him for money.

The war began on television, one otherwise unremarkable Thursday night, at a late hour which coincided with prime time in the Eastern seaboard of the United States. The picture on the screen was quite hypnotic. Necklaces of dotted light arched slowly upwards into the Baghdad sky. It was like a fireworks display, only more serene, as though it were all happening underwater. It was hard to believe that those graceful sprites were burning-hot pieces of sharp metal, tracer shells capable of killing and maiming. Years later I met an Iraqi painter who had been there that night. During the bombing, he said, it was like being in a dream from which you could never wake. Light travels faster than sound. You saw the explosion before you heard or felt it. Buildings, cars, walls, people would vanish in front of your eyes in a flash of light and smoke, and then the shock wave would hit you. He said horror was a physical thing. It gripped your entire body; some people froze, others could not stop moving. Gradually you got used to it, the air raids became part of life, like powercuts, he said. He lost his five-year-old daughter one night when the ceiling of their flat caved in.

'The world is illusion,' wrote Ibn Arabi. 'It does not really exist.' I remembered these words as I watched it happening on television. It was a cruel joke being played out on the world. For the first time in my life I began to wonder about the integrity of the British press, which I had always been led to believe was second to none (my father, of course). It was open season on Arabs, and anything, anywhere, was a legitimate target. Some days it began to get to me. I was told by a man in a pub that I ought to be grateful that Britain had put its troops' lives at risk to save the likes of me and mine. It got worse when casualties came in, the first planes went down, and people started to call me to say that their shops had been daubed with grafitti, or their daughters were being harassed for wearing the veil. I became angry and defensive. I wanted to be in the thick of it. I begged Harvey Greenbow to transfer me to the foreign desk. I could be useful, I said. He squinted dubiously ('Harvey Greenbow: a Dubious Man for Dubious Times'). I could read the foreign press, I said, give the lowdown on what the Arab world is thinking about all this.

Harvey was incredulous: 'But nobody cares what *they* think.' He looked around him for inspiration. 'Think about it from the angle of our boys. What's the desert like, eh?'

'Hot,' came a helpful voice from across the room.

'Exactly. Hot.' He slipped his arm around my shoulders. 'Tell us what it would be like out there, sweat burning your backside to butter.'

For a newspaper man he certainly had a way with words. 'But, er, Harvey, we're a long way from there.'

'Right, exactly my point. We're not there. So what do we do?'

I looked at him stupidly. 'I don't know – what *do* we do?'

'Come on, somebody,' he called over my head. 'Anybody? What do we do?'

'We make it up, you bastard.'

Harvey Greenbow swivelled back to me. 'See what I mean? We *make* the news. Get it? Look around you, son. It's not the friggin' *Telegraph*. People want to know how close this war is to their own lives. I want them to wake up with the screaming heebie-jeebies thinking Saddam bloody Hussein is coming down the bleeding chimney.' He gave me a wink. 'Try to think like your average reader and you won't go far wrong.'

But the more people I talked to the more I realised I did not understand the average *Daily Crow* reader as outlined by editorial policy. I sensed a morbid fascination with those militarised images: the planes in the desert, the aircraft carriers, the slow inevitable puff of smoke as a building disintegrated beneath another 'smart' bomb. It wasn't real. It was a movie. It wasn't really happening. I filed stories, Harvey Greenbow spiked them. He suggested I use a pseudonym.

'The problem is,' he sighed, 'with a name like yours nobody can be sure which side you're on, if you get my drift.' Harvey Greenbow resembled a bruise, big and swollen and sore to the touch. He always had one side of his shirt hanging out; he came back from the bathroom buttoning his flies; he smelled of sweat and stale talcum powder. He was likeable in an earthy sort of way. Harvey Greenbow was one of the lads. He had been born and brought up in Steeltown, went to the local school, supported Sheffield Wednesday. Harvey Greenbow once spent a year in Australia shooting kangaroos and drinking lager (a terrible sacrifice according to him, having been weaned on Tetley's Best Bitter). The year abroad made him something of an expert on foreign affairs; he knew how the world out there ticked. Everything about me, my accent, my manners, my education, all of it suggested to him that I was a jumped-up ponce with a funny name. 'Let's face it, you are at least halfway across the line to their side.'

'Whose side?' I asked.

'Them, the Iraqis, the towel heads.' Harvey surveyed me carefully as he reached into a creased pocket of his grey suit, polished with wear to a glowing sheen. He lit another Regal. 'Keep it close to the ground, son. Keep it local.'

So I went back to filing stories about the small domestic items that had been steam-rollered out of the way by the war drums: little old ladies who were afraid to go out of their flats after dark, or even before dark; charity fundraisers, a murder once, a student sleep-in at the university library, a protest against the closing of a school, etc. etc. It was, just as my father had assured me, an experience I would never forget. I didn't feel enlightened, or enriched. This mission, this sojourn, was also part of a personal quest for the world in general, and more specifically, for a Britain I had never really known and yet felt bound to explore. I developed some affection for the place, despite the haunted old factories and the smell of pickling vinegar that hung over the city. The countryside was serene. I often went out into the Peaks when I had a free afternoon, or at the weekend. I rambled along the rounded gritstone ridges, propped in the air like pieces of primeval sculpture. Down below, thin plumes of smoke could be seen rising from tiny villages hidden within the narrow winding valleys that snaked through the limestone.

I did file one story on the war, although ironically it was all over by then. I dug up a family living in Mansfield whose son had just returned from fighting on the wrong side. We sat in the living room of a small terraced house. It was a big family. I couldn't imagine how all of them could fit into that small house. The father ran a halal butcher's shop on the high street. The boy was a plump twenty-year-old with a shaven head and protruding ears. His mother hovered in the doorway and his father stood by the gas fire. Ranged along the sofa were five sisters, all of various size and shape. The boy's ears were red with the heat of the crowded little room, and the excitement of having to recount what he had been through yet again, this time to an outsider. He was the centre of attention.

'I only went there on 'oliday, like.'

'What happened?'

'They friggin' – sorry, Mam. They put me in the army, dint they.'

'They did it. They did it!' said the father, shaking his head. '*Wallahi*, bloody Foreign Office wash their hand of whole

97

bloody affair.' He gestured at the boy. 'Look him. British passport an' all. Show him your passport.' They switched back and forth from Arabic to English in a way that sounded familiar to me. The father struggled to use English when he wanted to impress the importance of some detail on me. The boy had the passport stuffed in his back pocket. The father frowned disapprovingly as he smoothed out the creases before handing it over for inspection. He was, I thought, a little put out that they hadn't sent a 'proper' English journalist. The father had emigrated here in 1979 he told me and been in full-time employment ever since.

'I never slacker. No matter what I find for working. I work like a . . . a . . . *'abid*?'

'A slave?' I proffered cautiously. He nodded gratefully. He meant a black person, any black person, an African. 'Hard-working Mr Shafiq,' I wrote in my notes.

The boy had been sent to visit his father's family in Baghdad. Unfortunately, his visit had coincided with the outbreak of hostilities and he was rounded up along with all the other men in the neighbourhood aged between fifteen and fifty. Two weeks later he found himself sitting in a bunker on the Saudi–Kuwait border wearing a uniform and carrying a rifle he could barely lift. Everyone in the bunker was terrified, even the officers. It wasn't strong enough to piss on, said the boy with a quick glance at his mother. Still, they had no choice; hardened units of Republican Guards were roaming about outside looking to shoot anyone trying to surrender, or run away. The Allies bombed them every night. Some went mad and took to screaming their heads off. No one paid them any notice. Sleep was impossible. They took a heavy pounding the night the ground offensive started. The following morning found them sitting around the remains of the caved-in shelter in a stunned heap, their ears still ringing when the American troops rolled up some hours later.

'You took your friggin' time,' was his first comment to a rather astonished soldier from the 24th US Infantry Division.

'Sorry, Mam.' He chuckled, and so did his father. 'They couldn't believe I spoke proper English, like.'

'He speak good English,' the father reassured me as he showed me out. 'Is a good boy, and we are glad he is back home. We don' like that Saddam.' I shook his hand at the door. There were giggles from within as the sisters, who had remained utterly silent in my presence, began discussing my visit. 'His mother spoil him,' the father said to me. 'She cook him all the day food he like. He get fat if he don' watch his step. He just a boy.'

'He was very lucky.'

'No luck. Allah brought him back to us for a reason. Maybe the reason is you write that story and tell them English people. Not all Iraqi people is bad people.'

I wrote it the way it had to be written. Harvey Greenbow liked the title:

'Mansfield Lad defies Baghdad Butcher.' He nodded approvingly. 'You're getting there.'

But when summer rolled along they decided they no longer needed my services and that marked the end of my career as a newspaper man. I don't swim any more either. I dropped all of that when I came to England. The damp weather. The chlorinated pool. It wasn't a river, and I wasn't Mark Spitz. So I stopped, and after a while I forgot about it. Time has a habit of turning the facts of your life around until you no longer remember where it was you started out from, or why.

10

The nearer Paris looms the less certain I feel about why we are going there. I don't really know it very well. I have a vague romantic image of the city as a metropolis of artistic expression, seething with ideas; a meeting place for writers, artists and musicians, but no real plan of what we are going to do there. My memory of the city also proves to be less accurate than I thought. Within fifteen minutes someone has clipped the front of the car, and a roller-blader, having narrowly escaped being mown down, has skated off with one of my wing mirrors under her arm. Completely disorientated and in a state of rising panic I steer blindly left and right following the flow of the fast-moving traffic. After the sedate rural pastures we have just left behind it comes as something of a shock to be in the thick of this furious voltage which makes everything snap and hum around us.

I finally manage to pull into a clearing and park the car. I climb from behind the wheel feeling stiff, drained and trembling with nervous energy. I have no idea which part of the city we are in but have no intention of moving unless a gun is put to my head.

'Where are we going to stay?' Leo asks, looking around him.

'This doesn't look like a bad area,' I suggest. My son looks sceptical. We start walking and after forty minutes of going round in circles I drag him, grumbling and muttering, into the lobby of a modest-looking hotel. It is small, narrow and dark. The heavy drapes look as if they would go up if you waved a book of matches at them. But I suspect that the price is as low as we are going to find and the room is clean, if musty.

'It looks like Dracula's cave,' is Leo's verdict. I am not sure if this is good or bad. The toilet is at the end of the hall and the door of the wardrobe comes off in your hand if you are not careful. We leave our bags there and retire to the nearest café.

'So, here we are,' he says. 'Now what?'

'Well,' I begin, 'you are already having one of the most important experiences of Paris; sitting in a café watching the world go by.' He looks around him, then back at me and frowns.

'OK, OK.' I unfold the map I had picked up at reception. We are near the Place de la République. 'The only way to see a city properly is to walk around it.' The frown deepens. 'Only walking gives you a real feel for a place. Otherwise you rush from one place to the next and get no sense of how it fits together.'

'Baba, what is the point of walking when we have a car?'

'You don't drive in cities. Too much trouble and liability. You spend the whole time trying to find somewhere to park and picking up fines.' Leo stares at me for a long time, and seems to be wondering who exactly it is he is travelling with.

'All right,' he concedes finally, 'let's walk.'

Within a few blocks, however, he is lagging behind, taking a long time to study mannequins in shop windows or charts affixed to bus shelters. I flag down a cab and bundle him inside.

'Paris is big and there's a lot to see. No time to waste.'

'Good thinking, Dad.' He pats my shoulder – I am showing promise.

We reach the river and sit on the embankment in the sun with our legs dangling over the water, waving to the people going by in the glass-sided tour boats.

'Let's make a set of rules,' I say. 'We take turns choosing where we go.'

'No bookshops.'

'Nothing with a queue waiting to get in.'

'Ice cream stops every hour.'

We wander over towards Notre-Dame to find crowds of people milling about outside trying to get in. We crane our necks upwards to look at the building, the façade has been newly sanded to the colour of bleached bone. All around us cameras are going off like rapid-fire weapons. A stately-looking gent comes up to stand next to us. He sighs deeply before blowing his nose loudly into a vast handkerchief, and then starts waving a striped umbrella in the air. 'To me, to me!' Herds of checkered-trousered people begin converging on us. I grasp Leo by the elbow and steer him firmly through the thickening mob and down a side street. It is easy to see how tourism would have put an end to the storming of the Bastille.

'*The Hunchback of Notre Dame*, you remember?' I ask as we pass a café with a sign, written in English, proclaiming it *The Hunchback*. 'And *The Three Musketeers*?'

His eyes widen theatrically. 'They live here?'

I let him have his little chuckle before going on. 'The man who wrote them did. Alexandre Dumas. Dumas was the name of his grandmother, a slave on the island of Santo Domingo.'

'His grandmother was a slave?' Leo has heard about slaves, knows it was a bad thing, but that is about all he does know.

'His father led Napoleon's troops in the famous Battle of the Pyramids. The Egyptians saw this huge man bearing down on them and they called him the Black Angel of Death.' We come to a halt. I notice that his jeans are beginning to look worn and there is a hole in the top of one of his running shoes. I make a mental note to look out for discount signs in the windows of clothing stores.

'You made all that up, didn't you?'

'No.' I shake my head. 'But I haven't thought about it for years.' He nods understandingly and then takes my hand and leads me on. I know where it comes from, of course; my father and his empathy for the Civil Rights movement in the United States. I am not sure how much this was due to sincere political conviction and how much to the fact that he claimed to have once caught a glimpse of Sammy Davis Jr. waltzing along a platform at Paddington Station in a mauve silk dressing-gown, trailed by a waiter clutching a bottle of champagne in an ice bucket (a story he repeated at the first hint of the proverbial hat being dropped). My father's entire record collection consisted of two long-playing albums. The first was Paul Robeson (he used to sing 'Ol' Man River' to himself when he thought no one was listening). The second was *The Immortal Speeches of Dr Martin Luther King Jr.* The one time I tried, out of curiosity, to set it on the portable Sanyo, the vinyl turned out to be so badly warped by the heat that it swerved up and down on the turntable like a UFO wobbling alarmingly out of control and I immediately took it off, afraid it would fly away. Dumas somehow fitted into my father's private gallery of exploitation and deceit:

'They let you go on thinking he's like them, a European. Nobody ever says, actually he was African, a slave.'

'Half a slave.'

'No such thing,' my father claimed. 'Once a slave, always a slave. It runs in the blood, you see.' Dumas was one of the few novelists I ever saw him read. His personal favourite was *The Count of Monte Cristo*, an obvious choice perhaps. 'You can tell he's African,' he enthused, 'just by reading it. It's the way he can hold a tale.'

'What about Dickens?' I, the objectionable teenager, was not going to swallow all this lying down; whatever he said, I knew better. I also knew that Dad's claims of Afrocentric allegiance only went so far; prod him with your finger gently and there was a thick, chalky streak of Anglophilia. He loved the language, adored Dickens, Shakespeare, and W. B. Yeats, whom he called Yeets, even though my mother corrected him every time he said it aloud – invariably in the presence of some rubber-faced British Council type and his dipsomaniac wife, who no doubt went off into that good night chortling at the natives and their quaint love of their former masters.

'Ah, Dickens, now there was a storyteller.'

This inconsistency I put down to the fatal golf ball. He hated them, he loved them. Why, he even married one of them, although this might have been defended as a means of usurping their superiority, slipping like the Arab raiders of yore under the tent flaps to seduce the enemy's womenfolk. In the early years, according to Mum, nothing could deflect him from the great British breakfast – bacon rashers and pork chipolatas notwithstanding, although he would never admit this in later life. He arrived in London in 1955 as a young man of twenty-five, granted a scholarship to the Yardarm School of Journalism in Holborn. He met my mother in a tea shop in Chancery Lane. She was working for a barrister nearby there.

In those halcyon days, with independence in sight, London was awash with Africans feeling the constriction of suits and ties. Among them were a number of men who would one day emerge as illustrious heads of state in their own countries: such as Dr Hastings Banda GP, president for life and notorious demagogue of Malawi, whose clinic was then just around the corner from my father's lodgings in Paddington. His compatriots hailed from respectable families and would return home as Bachelored and Doctored Sudanese; groomed, as it were, for the day the British handed over the reins. Together they were busy learning to negotiate the high and the low of British culture all at the same time. The high being the learning; the struggle with a language that defied their tongues ('Lie-cester Square'), and the literature (what exactly did Shakespeare mean when he wrote, 'Out, damned spot! out, I say!'?). The low was in the quirky aspects of daily life in Britain. The dour climate of landlords and student digs, sharing the bathwater with strangers. The use of the water closet. The signs proclaiming 'No Blacks or Irish' in the windows of boarding houses (why pick on the Irish?). The sexual morals of landladies. The importance of pubs where you could warm yourself by the fire instead of freezing to death in a dark, cold and lonely bedsit. This was where his love for the proletariat was born, in the dingy saloons and cheery hellos of lounge bars. Wrapped in a heavy overcoat, hair oiled and fiercely combed into a parting on one side (his own mother would have had trouble recognising him). Standing shoulder to shoulder with the workers on a frosty afternoon at a trade union rally in Hyde Park. The British Labour movement. Nye Bevan, Clement Attlee, Harold Wilson, these were the English (*sic*) you could take your hat off to.

Leo and I continue our jaunt. In the Rue du Temple we discover you can buy every kind of global knicknack you might need to make your life complete: lizards and crocodiles made of ebony. Dogon hats. Fetish masks from the Ivory Coast next door to latex ones of someone that looks suspiciously like Monica Lewinsky (open-mouthed). Plump-cheeked Buddhas sit alongside SM vixens in leather thongs and whips. A knife shop displays katanas and kukris alongside sinuous Balinese krises. Mounds of unfamiliar vegetables, strange powders, earthy roots, malanga, igname, manioc. Everywhere we go in Paris we are reminded that the world is becoming more closely knitted together.

Outside the glass pyramids of the Louvre stands a row of young men, tall and lean. They have come from places like Dakar and Conakry, from Lomé, Abidjan and Bamako. Each has a square of cloth spread out before him on which there are arrayed a selection of compact discs and sunglasses. I wonder if any of them have ever been inside the museum to look at the art work on display, but I know the answer. Paying to stand and gaze at old paintings comes low on the list of priorities when you are trying to eke out a living from the pavements. In a moment of weakness I pay an exorbitant sum to purchase a car twisted out of an old sardine tin for Leo. I do this partly for nostalgic reasons, because it reminds me of the cars we used to make when we were kids, and partly for other reasons.

There are signs announcing a special exhibition entitled 'The Lost Art of Memory' – about the different ways in which, from palaeolithic art onwards, man has recorded his presence: the outline of a hand painted on a wall; the bulls in the Lascaux Caves; the curious silhouettes of mysterious creatures found at Tamrit and Yabbaren in the Sahara. I am sorely tempted but when the queue finally shuffles us inside I feel rising contempt as I catch a glimpse of the prices they charge. This is culture as a fashion accoutrement and I refuse to go along. So much for the universality of art and the heritage of mankind. Society is fragmenting along deep fissures in the human fundament. From now on only an increasingly privileged minority will be able to afford to see these works. Perhaps this is the way it has always been, somehow we just thought that things were getting better.

We go straight to see the *Mona Lisa* and find it surrounded by a small tribe of teenagers chattering irreverently in half a dozen languages. A teacher is droning on pedantically while they are more interested in pointing at the other visitors and having a giggle. We carry on around the museum, trying to avoid the guided shoals. Mass culture has become a huge global industry, I realise. The same franchise chains, bars, shops, restaurants, films, fashion trends, records, loves, hates, hopes, dreams. It's like one enormous theme park called the world, where everything is a reproduction of somewhere else. If you miss the Rembrandt retrospective in Rotterdam you can catch it in Madrid or Prague. The cities of Europe have begun to fuse into one unbroken metropolitan space, divided no longer by distance but into vertical strata according to the access your wealth will buy you.

By the time we emerge back into daylight we have both had enough of museums and so go for lunch in a noisy, busy restaurant full of plenty of things and people to watch. Leo is fascinated by people and I take this as a good sign. We have seen enough monuments and decide to go back to doing what we feel like. So for the next couple of hours we simply walk in whatever direction appeals most to us. We eat ice cream. We stop to sit on benches and watch the people walking by. We buy crêpes smothered in warm chocolate sauce, and we lie on the sunny grass in the park and doze.

Tired out, we opt for the Métro that afternoon, and I regret it almost as soon as we are in the train. I feel light-headed, and my anxieties about what we are doing here return. In front of us sits an elderly couple, dressed in matching sweatshirts, blue denims and tennis shoes. On the opposite side is a fashionable young black man in a linen suit and purple shirt who stares at his own reflection in the window. His spectacles glow with reflected light. The close physical proximity makes us all strangers rather than a crowd. It highlights our individuality instead of our belonging. The fluorescent glow strips the nerve endings of society bare, revealing the loneliness, the fear, obsession, love, desire, hatred. It all comes to the surface. A dishevelled man clutching a can of beer steps into the car and spits out a stream of indecipherable rancour, aimed at all of us. We pretend he's not there, and somehow his presence lends us a sense of unity. No one pays him any heed. A couple of musicians appear and play a very fast version of 'Those Were The Days'. They go straight into something that sounds like gypsy music, even faster, trying to finish before the doors open in the next station. They might be father and son. I decide we can walk the rest of the way. We step off the train and start for the exit. Then I change my mind and run back, managing to throw a coin into the older man's hand as the doors are closing.

We emerge to find evening is falling as we start back to the hotel. We turn into a street to discover it is bizarrely crowded with women, most of them plump and thickly made up. One looks as though she has stepped out of a picture by Toulouse-Lautrec, thick rouge on her cheeks. A giant of a woman standing in a doorway smiles at me, oblivious of the fact that I have a seven-year-old child clutching my hand. 'Bonsoir, m'sieu,' she says, in such a genteel fashion that we might have been neighbours exchanging pleasantries in a hallway, except that she was clad in some kind of flimsy lace corset, and nothing else.

'Bonsoir,' I murmur in reply. Leo is tugging me along, walking fast. The women are strolling about in next to nothing. Some are in fancy dress, but all are wearing outfits that lack substantial vital sections.

'Look, that one's dressed as a policeman, and there's a nurse!' Leo doesn't know whether to laugh or cover his eyes; neither do I. But it is curiously grotesque and thus theatrical. There is a blonde girl wearing big round glasses and what appears to be a traffic warden's outfit. For a second, I actually take her for a real traffic warden, but then she turns around and I realise that the skirt has been cut away to reveal a huge wobbly pink bottom. There is an air of pageantry to the whole thing, like a carnival, or fancy dress parade, except that they are open for business. When I was Leo's age, I find myself trying to recall, what did I know of such things?

In the street where we used to live there was a run-down house down at the end of the next road where there was a party every night. They had strips of coloured bulbs draped around the top of the walls and loud music playing all the time. The people at the corner shop talked to the girls with a kind of familiarity that also hinted at some shared hidden knowledge. During the daytime when things were very quiet, it resembled an ordinary house. But we knew that there was a secret world behind its walls. A steady stream of strange men passed through those doors in the afternoon. There were used prophylactics scattered in the dusty square opposite the house where the rubbish was thrown, which could be quite effective weapons when flicked at somebody on the end of a stick.

We find ourselves in the thick of a crowd of men congregating around a large battered wooden door. A small sign explains that it is a mosque.

'Let's go in,' I suggest; me, the unbeliever. I have not been inside a mosque since the day of my father's funeral.

Leo can tell this is not normal. 'What for?' he asks. He finds the group of men intimidating. They are all ages: older men with grey whiskers stuck to their hollowed-out cheeks. Younger men with their hair neatly combed backwards. They appear to come from all walks of life, some in suits and ties, others in overalls, parkas, kurtas, gellàbiyas, or combinations of old and new, one man with a huge beard is wearing beige pyjamas underneath a threadbare overcoat.

'Just to take a look.'

'No,' he shakes his head, adamant, backing away. 'You go. I'll wait here.'

'I can't leave you out here. Supposing something happens?'

Impatiently, he rolls his eyes. 'What can happen? I'll wait right here. I won't go anywhere. I promise.' I don't move. 'Just go,' he says, pushing me away. 'I'll be here when you get back.'

There is no excuse for leaving a seven-year-old child alone on a street in a foreign city, even for five minutes. But still. 'You promise you won't wander off? Stay right here in the doorway, don't talk to anyone, OK? I'll just take a quick look. If anything strange happens, you come straight in here to find me, right?'

He nods wearily and waves me away, turning to tuck his hands into his pockets and gaze around him as though he has been standing on street corners all his life.

This is part of the business of letting go; allowing your child to be out of your sight for periods of time. It is a progression which began years ago when we took him to the crèche for the first time and left him in the care of strangers.

'They're not strangers!' exclaimed Ellen. 'They get paid to do this. They're qualified.'

'They're strangers to me, and I don't like leaving my son with them.' All of this took place in the front yard of a harmless-looking semi-detached house with cut-out cardboard animals hung along the windows and the faces of a dozen children and several concerned adults staring at us through the window as we tugged the child back and forth between us.

'He's not ready.'

'*He*'s not the problem.'

She had a point. All around us parents were arriving and leaving their loved ones without even a glance over their shoulders. In years to come we too would find ourselves waving goodbye as he set off for three days away at summer camp, but at that moment I just stood there, unable to go through with it. I wanted this. I wanted to be a part of that society of rational parents who could deliver and collect their child and have their day to concentrate on their careers, but I couldn't do it. Inside, staff were dragging children away from the windows, to stop them staring at the two funny-looking people fighting over a pushchair outside. Car doors slammed around us as mothers snapped themselves efficiently into driving seats to speed away to board meetings or whatever. I was condemned to remain a social cripple. That world would stay closed to me because I couldn't bring myself to leave my son with a group of trained people for a few hours.

And now here I am preparing to abandon him on a street corner surrounded by strange men with a parade of hookers marching up and down in an assortment of kinky garments designed to lure a very strange type of clientele. But I feel compelled to go inside. I am not sure why.

So I walk through the gate which, apart from the little sign on the wall, is indistinguishable from any other nondescript warehouse in the street and is indeed in bad need of a touch of paint. There is a dirty, rusty old factory door through which I push my way against the crowds that are congregating around the stairwell, or on their way out. On the second floor I discover a hallway and a set of simple shelves set on the wall for people to leave their shoes. I kick mine off hurriedly before I can change my mind and step in through the doorway.

Instantly, I feel a sublime sense of contentment and harmony washing over me, almost a kind of relief, of being in the protective embrace of something much larger than myself, something that recognises me. The interior decoration seems at first glance to be at odds with the building. The brickwork of arches, which not so many years ago housed a clothing sweatshop and hummed to the sound of sewing machines and steam presses, now lends itself rather well to the industry of prayer. Along the walls between the old steam pipes a series of black silk banners have been hung. These are embroidered in gold with passages from the Koran in Arabic calligraphy. At the far end of the room an intricately carved wooden portal, the *mihrab*, marks the direction of Mecca. The floor is covered by intersecting Persian rugs.

This sense of belonging catches me off balance. I am not sure what I had been expecting. Churches I am clear about. I visit them for the architecture, for the feeling of history one gains from the stone walls and steepled arches, not so much for spiritual consolation. But I didn't come in here for the nineteenth-century industrial architecture, and religious sentiment has never been a great conviction of mine. So what am I doing here?

Prayers must have just finished. A handful of people are lingering, sitting around the floor in small groups, or in solitary contemplation. Taking a few more steps I move further towards the centre of the room. It is a long time since I have tried praying. Over a year ago at the mosque in Regent's Park I knelt down with the others, but then it had come back easily. I was in among a crowd of relatives and old friends, minus my brother Muk whose whereabouts were anybody's guess. Yasmina was behind me, out of sight up in the women's gallery. It took some effort of the imagination to believe that my father was really inside that plain wooden box they had just wheeled in through a side door. I found myself moving with the crowd that stood shoulder to shoulder with me. It was like being within a human wave. When it bowed, I bowed with it. When they knelt, I knelt. A vast organism that lived, breathed and thought as one. Suddenly you were in the embrace of all these men, in their stockinged feet with the occasional stray toe sticking out. There was a creak of limbs and ageing joints as they knelt to touch their foreheads to the floor. The smell of bodies and perspiration was all around. These were people in the midst of their existence, between birth and eternity. For a few minutes that was what it felt like to be part of humanity.

A man appears at my side. He is small and neat in his long cream-coloured Moroccan burnous with gold embroidery down the lapels and a trim little beard. From his rather elegant clothes and manner I assume that he holds some measure of authority. He murmurs something which I have to lean forwards to catch. He repeats it for me.

'C'est interdit, m'sieu. Pas de touristes ici.'

'No, no, I just wanted to take a look.' I indicate my eye.

'Pas de photos. Pas de touristes.' He wags his head from side to side. Sensing something is amiss, a large burly man with a thick beard and a smoothly shaved head gets to his feet over by the door, and begins to lumber over. His legs bow outwards under his weight, like the roots of a heavy tree.

'No, wait. Look . . . you don't understand. I am a Muslim. Je suis musulman.'

'Musulman?' His tone rises a pitch. Now he sounds offended. The big lunk's small eyes are darting back and forth between us. 'You wish to pray? Vous voulez faire le prière de *magrib*?'

Do I want to pray? And if I do, do I want to do it in front of them, scrutinising me for any telltale signs of lapsed irreverence? I begin to panic.

'No. I mean, yes. I just want to stay here for a while. You understand?' The urge to be truthful is flushing out the culpable liar in me. The man in the burnous looks steadily at me as though he can see right though me. It is a sad, rather pitying look. A hand is held out, careful not to touch my shoulder, to guide me to the exit.

'Pas de touristes ici. S'il vous plaît.'

'Look, I told you, I'm not a tourist.'

His tone sharpens. 'Disrespect for religion. You don't want to pray. This place is for praying.' He is talking quickly now, and his vehemence conflicts with the benign look on his face that reminds me of my brother-in-law, Umar; a benevolence which is closed to me now. Over his shoulder I see the big man, whose muscular arms swell out from his plump chest. There is a rip visible in the backside of his tracksuit trousers as he turns and waddles away.

'OK,' I say finally. 'I'm leaving. Salaam aleikum.'

'Wa aleikum salaam wa rahmat allahu barakatu.'

He remains in the doorway watching me while I pull on my shoes. A couple of others come up to enquire what the problem is. He gestures at me and turns away. I descend the stairs feeling humiliated. He has no right to bar me from entering, even less to judge whether I am worthy of being a Muslim. I could have insisted. I didn't.

Leo is surprised to see me back so soon. He is where I had left him, examining a sheep's head which sits with its tongue lolling out in the window of a halal butcher's.

'Well, was it worth it?'

'I'm not sure. Perhaps in a different way than I expected.'

He shakes his head in wonder; 'Sometimes you say the strangest things.'

That evening we go out bowling. Leo's eyes grow round and shiny at the suggestion. We have never been bowling before. I have never been bowling in my life. It is one of those things I have just never thought of doing. But we are on holiday and this is the kind of frivolous thing people do on their holidays, isn't it? I study the sign across the street as we approach and realise that I have always felt intimidated by these places. Why? What is wrong with going to a bowling alley? Who goes to these places anyway? I seize Leo's hand

and guide him across the street and up the steps. Once inside I am surprised to find that it is much bigger than I envisaged. A whole world that I have never glimpsed before. Nobody pays us any attention. The loud music, the flashing lights, and the whoops of excitement coming from the bowling lanes, all make me wonder about the wisdom of this venture. I am not sure I can seriously go through with it. There is Country and Western music playing over the loudspeakers, interspersed by calls from a fast-food counter somewhere – girls on roller skates wearing Stetsons go whooshing by bearing trays loaded with fast-food orders. It is like being in a movie.

'Come on,' Leo says. 'This is going to be fun.'

For the most part, it is. We go through all the rituals: paying a deposit, receiving a lane number, changing our footwear. When we finally get our red and white shoes on we look at one another and immediately burst out laughing.

The actual business of rolling the ball down the lane and striking the pins turns out to be more difficult than it looks. Leo has trouble getting his momentum up and letting go of the ball in such a way that it doesn't drop onto his foot or fall into the escape chute along the side to trundle disappointingly past the pins with no chance of touching them. He can only lift the smaller balls to begin with and needs a lot of encouragement. It helps that I am barely able to launch a ball in the right direction myself, let alone hit anything. I manage to fling one with such vigour that it flies into the next lane, drawing laughter and derision from our fellow bowlers. Leo and I fall down about the same number of times, but, nevertheless, we are bowling. It feels like an achievement.

Towards the end I manage to throw a fluke curving shot that loops along the lane and knocks the three remaining pins out in one go. I turn towards Leo with a cry of satisfaction. He hasn't noticed my shot at all. I go over to find him sitting deathly still on the moulded plastic bench by the scoring console. When I ask him what the matter is he can't bring himself to speak. He shakes his head wordlessly and buries his face in my chest. I can feel the sobs pulsing through his body and for a moment I don't understand what is happening to him. And then I see it. The aisle to our right is deserted now, but beyond that there is a family. Two children. The boy is around Leo's age and the girl a little older, and they have the full complement of parents – one father and one mother.

11

Leo is asleep the moment his head touches the pillow and I am left once again to my thoughts. I switch off the lights and lie down on the bed fully dressed. The room feels like a cold void and I have to keep glancing over towards Leo to remind myself that I am not alone. Without him I am left at odds with the world. I gaze at the ceiling. I hear the sound of people going up the staircase. A door closes. Muffled voices float through the building.

When I open my eyes again nothing has changed except that it is much quieter. Nothing around me moves. I look at my watch and it is almost 1 a.m., which means that I must have slept for all of three hours. I remain there, lying in the dark staring into space. I can feel a great weight pressing down on my chest and my breathing becomes shorter. I wonder if this is a sign of an early heart attack or if I am just suffering acute anxiety. I feel constricted, as though I am suffocating and the air feels clammy. I stay where I am, rigidly exhaling in short gasps. I feel like a swimmer kicking towards a surface he is afraid he won't reach.

I try pacing the room, but there isn't much to pace. From the window I can look down into the narrow street below. The building opposite is calm and still. Behind each window there are people living their lives, sleeping their way towards another day. If I press my head to the glass I can make out a red-and-blue neon sign winking down the road. The light pulses in the dark windows opposite. I turn back to the room and see that Leo is still sleeping soundly. Nothing will stir him for the next eight hours, earthquakes notwithstanding.

On the chair by the window stands the large, battered canvas holdall in which I have been carrying all my books about. These are my favourite books, many of them I have had since I was a teenager. I drag the metal zipper open and dig out a random collection of reading matter. By the thin light from the window I go through them, looking for something that will catch my attention for long enough to dispel the welling despair: Dorothy Parker, Faulkner's *Sanctuary*, Blaise Cendrars, Kenzaburo Oe, and Homer. None of them hold much appeal, however. I deposit them on the bedside table and then I sit down for a time to watch Leo sleep. He appears to be completely at ease, his face tilted upwards, his mouth hanging open. After a while I manage to convince myself that unless he were to wake up suddenly from a bad dream nothing is likely to disturb him. So I pick up my coat and head for the door before my logic collapses around my ears like a house of cards. There are countries where they imprison you for leaving a child alone, but I have a feeling this isn't one of them.

Once outside in the street I immediately feel the tension subside. I walk slowly up towards the main road. Cars glitter darkly under the streetlights. The occasional thumping rhythm of a stereo system slides by. I pass the bar with the flashing light that I had glimpsed from the window of the hotel earlier. I take a look inside. It is almost empty. The interior is stained the murky colour of tobacco. A single pulse of white light over the bar illuminates a set of glass shelves where a collection of bottles is arrayed, testimony to the ingenuity that goes into producing alcohol in various parts of the world. The display contains labels in unfamiliar scripts, curious logos and indeed creatures: a Mexican worm lies suspended in golden tequila, and alongside that two medium-sized geckos with long spidery toes are curled up inside a bottle of clear liquid covered in Chinese characters. I am about to go on when I feel the tiny hairs on my spine stand up. The song that is playing in the bar, 'Yellow River', is a song I have not heard for decades, not since I was about eleven years old and dancing on the back veranda of Iman Khalifa's house, with Iman Khalifa herself in person.

Iman was a couple of years older than me. A tall, willowy girl to whom I could normally not speak a straight sentence without my tongue tripping itself up. But there I was dancing with her. To dance with Iman Khalifa was to attain a high-altitude state of karmic bliss. I had pursued her for months with cryptic (and unsent) letters of devotion, and longing glances delivered from great distances on the rare occasions when we had met socially. In the intervening time I had thought about her, repeated her name to myself in half sleep, like a mantra, half expecting her to materialise out of the night beside my bed. Now, on the occasion of her thirteenth birthday, I had managed to pluck up the courage to ask her to dance and she had accepted. No conversation was necessary. We communed wordlessly with meaningful glances and smiles. She could continue to chat quite easily with the people around her, I didn't mind, I had enough to do concentrating on holding the pattern of my irresistible and outrageously cool dance technique. This involved putting the right foot behind the left heel, bobbing down before bringing it forwards again, and then repeating the movement on the other side, left behind right in the same way, hands swinging independently in time with the music. This I could keep up for as long as an hour, even more, without variation. Between records I would take a moment to rest my burning calves while standing to one side, hands in pockets, discreetly fanning my cheesecloth shirt to let the sweat dry, displaying an air of aloof confidence while waiting for her to finish chatting to her friends. For such an important occasion my long unruly hair had been dragged free of curls with a steel brush, then combed over to one side so that it resembled a frozen wave, or a beehive in a force-ten gale. I wore my hair long and my shorts short. Hipsters were in, according to my mother's hippy informants. Maybe so in Haight Ashbury, but I had to endure the taunts of my school friends whose baggy shorts often came down to below their knees ('Hey, did you forget to put something on this morning?' followed by peals of laughter). But it was all right. I knew Iman would find her way back to me across that veranda, which must have been all of seven square metres, just as I knew that she and I would never part. Clearly, our fates having finally crossed nothing could possibly break us apart now. Inevitably, I was proved wrong. She married a knuckle-headed officer from a tank regiment and spawned half a dozen little militia boys for him to train. Later, I heard she got divorced and moved to Nevada with a US Marine. How and why this happened remains a mystery to me.

So I push open the door and step inside before anything can change my mind. A group of young men in the corner are talking animatedly about something which might be football. At the far end of the bar there is a man with long hair talking to a young girl wearing a miniskirt and a leather jacket. When he comes over I order a beer. One beer and then I will go back to the hotel and sleep.

As I reach into the pocket of my coat for some money I find Muk's card. It is ripped and worn, having been folded and refolded for quite some time now. I turn it over in my hands and read the cryptic lines which, apart from an address, are all it has on it:

> The Moving Finger writes; and, having writ,
> Moves on: nor all your Piety nor Wit
> Shall lure it back to cancel half a Line,
> Nor all your Tears wash out a Word of it.

'Poetry!' I turn to find the girl in the leather jacket has moved down from the end of the bar. She points at the card in my hand: 'It's poetry, right?'

'Omar Khayyám.' I nod.

She taps her chest urgently and says, 'Wallada.'

'Wallada?' I look at her blankly.

'You know Wallada?'

I'm afraid I don't. I shrug my shoulders. 'Wallada. Wallada,' she repeats impatiently. Then she turns to the group of men in the far corner and calls out, 'Djemel! Tu connais Wallada?'

One of them breaks off his conversation and looks over: 'Wallada? C'est la salope qui vend couscous au Château Rouge?' The table breaks into laughter. The girl dismisses them and turns back to me.

'Idiots. "Wallada". It's a poem about the most beautiful woman in Andalus.'

'In Spain?'

'No, before Spain, with the Arabs.' She leans on the bar and twirls her fingers through her hair, staring at the brightly lit shelves above the bar. 'I heard that someone in China once died by swallowing one of those snakes they keep in those bottles.' She shudders. 'It wasn't really dead. Imagine that. It woke up and bit him. Uugh!'

'That's your name, Wallada?'

'No.' She shakes her head and turns to examine me. 'My mother's name. My name is Haya.' She holds out her hand.

'Yasin,' I say, taking her hand.

'So, you live here?'

'No,' I say.

'Where do you live?'

She must be about nineteen I imagine. She is leaning very close to me, so that her thigh is pushing against mine and her perfume is strong and very flowery in a rather overpowering way. A long veil of dark hair hangs down the side of her face. She makes a point of giving me a chance to study her as she fishes in her handbag for cigarettes and a lighter, pushing a strand of hair back behind her ear like an actress in a very self-conscious fashion.

'I lived in England.'

'In England?' She blows smoke over my head. 'You don't live there any more?'

I'm not sure why I used the past tense. 'I'm on holiday.'

'So, you like to dance?'

'I don't really dance,' I say.

'No?' she shrugs, and puts her hand on my arm. 'You

want to go somewhere quiet?' I look at her. She is nice, but I have a feeling this is not the time.

'You are nervous. Why? You're catching a plane, perhaps? Or your wife is waiting for you?' Her hip juts out provocatively. There is a scar on the tip of her jaw, and her nose looks like it has been broken at least once, but she still has a striking face.

'I left my wife three days ago.'

'Really?' The news makes her a little concerned and she examines me carefully as though wondering if this means she is looking at a serious case of mental unbalance: 'So you are alone?'

'I am with my son.'

'Your son?' She looks around the bar. 'Where is he?'

'I left him sleeping in the hotel.'

'Ah.' She nods understandingly. This, I realise, is her profession – reading people. Sorting out the lost from the lonely, the madmen from the merely meek. Like a therapist, she handles people whose lives are out of joint. She could detect loneliness by instinct and knew exactly how to nurse it, fondle it, until the pain went away, not for ever, nobody could do that, but for a while, for an hour or so. The physical part came afterwards. She calls the bartender over and asks him to put a record on, leaning far over the counter to give me time to study her short skirt. He obliges.

'Who is it?'

Haya frowns and holds out the CD for me to examine. Celine Dion, apparently. 'Some people say I look a little like her.'

'Really?' I peer at the picture on the cover. 'I don't see the resemblance.'

She shakes her hair out. 'You have to look carefully. The light in here isn't so good. In here, you put the lights up and everyone vanishes, like cockroaches.'

I ask where she is from and she says Paris. Of course, she might well be from Paris, but I am looking for something else. 'No, I meant before that.'

She picks at the corners of her cigarette packet, tearing tiny strips off as she begins to talk. She is from Western Sahara. She grew up in a refugee camp in the desert. She didn't know her father. He was away fighting the Moroccans. 'That's what men are good for, making war.'

I look at my watch. I should be getting back. I am about to make my excuses when the man she called Djemel comes over to lean on the bar next to us.

'So, you like my sister?' he says to me.

'Your sister?' There is an unmistakable menace in his smile. I get to my feet slowly. 'I'm sorry,' I say. 'I didn't realise.'

'No. No. Sit down.' Sliding an arm around the girl's waist he pulls her tightly to him. 'It can be taken care of.' When I don't say anything he runs his hands over her a little more. 'She is beautiful, no? And young?' I turn towards the door and Djemel steps in front of me to block the way. 'Hey, what's your hurry?' I am aware that his friends over in the corner are observing all this. It's a stalemate. Then, to everyone's surprise, the girl, Haya, makes a decision for all of us. She steps between us and turns on him.

'Why do you always have to go and spoil things? We were getting along fine. Now leave us alone, will you? And what's this about a sister? Didn't you sell her along with your grandmother?' Laughter erupts from the table in the corner and Djemel throws up an arm in resignation. He goes over to his friends and Haya walks out the door with me.

'Look,' I say, turning to her. 'It's late and I really don't want to . . .'

'Don't want to what?' she asks, lighting another cigarette. 'It's OK. I'll just walk with you for a while until he forgets.'

'He won't make trouble for you?' I nod towards the interior of the bar.

'No,' she laughs. Her smile reminds me of girls I used to know, girls like Iman Khalifa. 'So,' she says, after a time, 'you ran away from your wife, and then you run away from your son?'

'I didn't run away. I just left him in the hotel asleep.'

'OK, you didn't run away from him.' She looks at me in a strange way. 'Tell me about your holiday.' She hooks her arm through mine. 'Where are you going?'

'I don't really know.'

'You don't know?' Her eyes widen. 'North? South? East? No idea?'

'South maybe.' I shake my head. 'I'm not sure.'

'South is better. I have friends in Aix-en-Provence. You could solve both our problems and take me there.' Outside the hotel she steps away from me.

'Thanks,' I say.

'For what?' she laughs. 'I didn't get a chance to show you what I can do.' Then she waves and I watch her walk away, swinging her hips at the oncoming headlights.

Leo is still sleeping soundly. I silently promise myself never to leave him alone again. I rummage through my bag until I find the anthology I am looking for.

Wallada was a princess and the famous poem that bears her name was written by Ibn Zaydun (born 1003 in Cordoba). He fell out of favour with her when he declared his love for one of her African slave girls and was thrown into prison for his troubles. He managed to escape from gaol but died destitute in Seville. I tuck my brother's card into the book and crawl into bed, exhausted, and fall into a long and dreamless sleep.

12

Difficult as it now seems to imagine, there was a time when Ellen and I believed we would never be anything but happy together. We didn't waste any time giving it much thought. So long as we had one another, we could deal with whatever came along. What happened, then? She said it herself, people get divorced all the time. They part amicably, they come to civilised agreements. They sit down with marriage counsellors and divorce solicitors and they come to terms, rationally. But there was never anything rational or amicable about our relationship. Right from the start it was founded on the opposite of rational. But isn't love always like that? Isn't that exactly what people are looking for, someone to knock their tedious life straight out of its frame? Isn't that what all the songs are about? What we couldn't get to was that gentle, doting love that comes with time. That graceful acceptance of dependency and trust. My parents spent their lives snapping at one another and yet one could not live without the other. Ellen and I were locked together in a passionate embrace from start to finish. From the moment of our first coupling, falling on one another like squabbling marsupials on a mohair rug, to the final act – like two battered prizefighters, barely able to stand, yet still trying to raise their fists – it was all flying fur and fury. We had it all, the crashing plates and slamming doors, screaming child in the background. Like an awful tragedy, like something by Strindberg – we were bound together and couldn't let go. And so we pushed one another, step by step slowly towards the crumbling edge.

In the beginning we needed nobody else, and so we locked ourselves away from the world in a draughty old farmhouse on the outskirts of Thame. The owners had retired to South Africa and were letting it out. I had a suspicion they were involved in some unsavoury business, like arms dealing or diamonds, but it was cheap. We barely paid a pittance. They wanted someone there to put off squatters from moving in until they decided what to do with it, or waited for the market to rise before selling. It may have had something to do with evading taxes. I tried not to ask too many questions. In any case, they certainly didn't care much about the house. The roof leaked and the place was bitterly cold. The first winter we had to seal off one side of the upstairs floor with plastic sheeting. There was no central heating, so we made do with a combination of a small wood-burning stove and electric heaters. It was a primitive existence, as though we had been sent back through a time tunnel to the stone age to see how we would fare. It was also isolated: those of our friends who knew where we were found it a bother to come all the way out there, which it was if you didn't have a car. There were buses, but they were infrequent, especially at night, and the taxi drivers were like roving freebooters on wheels – they took you for everything you had.

In retrospect it was a fairly insane thing to do, to cut ourselves off like that. To begin with I was a town dweller, I had never lived in the countryside before. It took me months before I could even sleep at night and I never realised why until it finally struck me that it was simply too quiet. I need noise around me, the sound of voices coming from the house next door, people going by in the street.

Any sane person would have stopped to consider the situation first, but two people with their minds apparently in good working order did not. Both of us, I think, took it as a challenge. There we were, a child on the way, no visible means of support, just us. Could we do it? It all went very quickly. And it wasn't as if everything between us was blissful. Differences were already starting to show, even before Leo's birth.

We hadn't planned on having a child. It happened, and we weren't ready to back away from it. So there was the plan. Lock ourselves away. Prove to the world that we could handle it, that we would overcome. Ellen was going to go back to her studies. She had plans to write a doctorate on Urban Manifestations of Kinship Loyalty Among Tamil Refugees. Every three weeks or so she would take the train to Birmingham and interview a few more informants. Why Birmingham? Why Tamils? I have no clue, but it was her idea, and she believed in it enough for it to seem plausible that we could build our lives around her being able to deliver a completed thesis on the subject.

Once Leo had made his appearance I found myself spending long periods of time alone with him, Ellen locked into the spare room that had become her study. I went for long walks along footpaths and country roads, finding myself coming to terms with rural England for the first time. I got used to the twitch of lace curtains as the locals squinted out at this odd-looking man pushing a pram. My hair grew long and unruly and I wore a wool-lined leather pilot's jacket I was rather proud of: picked up at a parish fair for next to nothing, and patched with strips of adhesive tape. I had, more than likely, deprived some poor mutt of a warm lining for its basket that winter.

Ellen's parents were not far away and they would drive over with stoical enthusiasm and supplies of food which they guessed, rightly, we might appreciate. But I would see them on the way back towards the car, shaking their heads in wonder at the mess their daughter had managed to get herself into. Ellen's mother would smile and say, 'It's very brave of you.' It was more than brave, it was downright foolish. Left to its solitary self, love has a habit of wearing itself thin. We might as well have moved to a frontier post in the great northern wastes of Alaska. Cabin fever, that's what we had.

Even the novelty of visitors soon wore off. Frivolous tales

of the single life, free of responsibility, obligation, children, became rather pesky. I suppose we were rather proud of what we were doing, in our own way. Our visitors' enervating accounts of nocturnal adventures and who was doing what behind so and so's back acquired a puerile, superfluous quality that left us yawning and thinking about how many hours of sleep were left to us. Knowing that anyone you invited to dinner would end up staying the night makes you more choosy. So our new friends tended to be people Ellen had met in her prenatal classes, or at the hospital. New parents. There were two categories, the completely distraught mothers who would burst into tears at the prospect of having to change another nappy – their male partners patting them understandingly on the shoulders, while not actually reaching for the baby wipes themselves – and those who went into raptures at the first hint that another bowel movement had occurred.

Linda Royle was a case in point. She was a single mother, which is to say that she had decided she wanted a child without the encumberance of having a man along for the ride. She had picked her target, and gone after him. She did a very thorough job of it, you had to give her that. Her prey was married, fairly good-looking in an upright, square-jawed, Caucasian kind of way, excellent tennis player, and on his way to an early vice-presidency of the insurance company where they both worked. She checked up on his university results. She even went to visit his old school, posing as a television researcher for a programme that was about to do an in-depth profile, and came away with copies of his test results back to age ten, as well as photographs of his triumph in the school athletics championship age thirteen, winning an egg-and-spoon race, and so on and so forth. She set her plan into motion and began timing her lunch breaks to coincide with his – all of this took well over a year. She would bump into him outside sandwich bars and this led to long lunches. She would casually enquire about his family, where his parents came from, his blood type, whether there was any history of mental or physical disability. She made her move at the big Christmas party, traditionally an occasion when everyone in the firm became incoherent with drink and then unleashed whatever lustful desires had been welling in the building over the past year. Linda got her man, in a toilet cubicle on the third floor of the Mariott Hotel on Park Lane where the party was being held. It was nothing more than a brief and undignified clinch, after which the man of her dreams, the father to be of her child, vomited in ungainly fashion all over her new shoes. Come the following autumn Linda was on maternity leave with her new son, Algernon. She requested a transfer to the Oxford branch and had no further contact with the father, who apparently had no recollection of the affair in the toilet and absolutely no knowledge of the existence of little Algy.

Ellen and Linda had become firm friends. Linda became a regular guest, as did Algernon. Linda didn't need a husband, just as Algy, she assured us confidently, did not need a father. Men were aggressive, impatient, brutal. They missed out on all of the finer things in life. They were driven by testosterone and peer pressure. Algy would not be subject to such manipulation, he would grow up in a male-less environment, free to experience the world without prejudice and without acquiring the desire to conquer everything, and everyone, his eye fell upon. I looked at Algy, with his twitchy little nose, his myopic eyes (the father wore contacts), and felt immense male sympathy for him. It wasn't that I disagreed as such. I disliked aggression, brutality and all the rest of it as much as Linda did. What I wasn't sure about was whether the absence of a father was going to help him. Didn't the Khmer Rouge evolve out of an absence of father figures thanks to the war in South-East Asia? And besides, what kind of female qualities was he going to acquire from a woman who went after sperm the way a roving shark pursued blood? Linda and I did not get on very well. For a while I entertained the idea that she was after Ellen, that she wanted us to form a ménage à trois. I admit I gave some consideration to the possibilities of this at first, but then I began to wonder if she didn't just want me out of the way so that she could have Ellen to herself. Eventually I settled on the idea that she was simply aggressive – she liked to pick a fight.

'So where do you stand on Zionism, Yasin?' Far back in the primordial mists of her parentage there was some Jewish blood, although as I understood things, it was on her father's side, which would have broken the maternal lineage and excluded her. There was a certain poetic touch to this, it seemed to me. Nevertheless, this drop of Yiddish blood back in the ancestral pool was sufficient for her to see herself as a defender of the Jewish faith and, indeed, state. She took on all comers, I was just one of them. Israel was one of her favourite subjects, the other being female circumcision.

'Well, in principle, I'm against any kind of -ism that involves inflicting pain on others.'

'That's an evasive answer.' She leered at me from the sofa where she was reclined, with Algernon beside her on the floor tearing her address book to shreds with his year-old fists. She did not believe in telling Algernon off, because discipline was a 'fascist' thing. In practice this meant that she waited for him to stop by himself and then, when he didn't, she lost her temper and hit him.

'What kind of Zionist state do you have in mind?' I asked. 'An ethnically pure homeland? A remote European outpost, with sunshine and perfect beaches, good diving and all those pesky Arabs under control selling trinkets in the bazaar, like the Navaho reservations? Look at what the Americans did to the Native Americans. All that's left of them are the names of football teams and helicopter gunships. Hawks. Apache.'

'Are you mocking me, you bastard?'

'Linda, relax, put your Amazonian poison darts away. This is not about soothing anti-Semitic guilt, it's about inflicting pain and suffering. It's not a fair fight.'

'What's fair? You think bombing civilians is fair? Those people are terrorists.'

'So were David Ben-Gurion and Shimon Peres. Don't

you see? That's all you have, an argument based on the actions of fanatics. You exclude the moderates and persecute the majority, who are, by the way, innocent civilians.'

'I can't believe how aggressive you are. You are so aggressive. That's so typical male. As soon as you start to feel threatened you attack.'

Algernon was staring at me with those big round eyes of his while chewing his way through the letter K. I wondered whether an anonymous note to his biological father would be immoral. It was long past his bedtime but his mother didn't believe in constricting his sense of time by imposing such babarities on the creature. He looked wide awake, spitting flecks of paper and drooling on the carpet. He was turning into a nocturnal animal, left gnawing electric cables long after the rest of us had passed out exhausted. Ellen was asleep upstairs with Leo. I could barely keep my eyes open.

'It's sexual power, isn't it?'

'What is?' I asked.

'That aggression. I bet you fantasise about me. Come on, admit it.'

'I'm sorry, Linda, much as I'd love to continue this conversation, I have to sleep. My ears are beginning to play tricks on me.' Algy gazed up at me from the floor. Perhaps just a cryptic missive, or an anonymous photograph?

'Run away, go on, get out of here. I'll tell her you tried to assault me.'

'You can tell her whatever you want,' I yawned. 'In the morning.'

People change when they have children, women change, men change. There are tiny chemical alterations in character. Some women mature with the contentment of having fulfilled their natural potential. Others wobble unnervingly about in every direction, trying to do what most of us do most of the time: avoid the fact that time can have any effect on us at all. Men, who do not experience either the pain of childbirth or the fatigue of having to carry another living creature inside them for nine months, throw themselves into the business of parenthood with all the enthusiastic pride of a boy seeing the ship he has just constructed out of two bits of old wood go sailing away down a stream. They punch the air, they wave their football scarves and cheer, no doubt proud of having achieved so much from so little (ninety seconds of puffing and panting according to the statistics).

The fact is that nobody's life becomes more interesting just because they have had a child, they just think it does. Couples metamorphose overnight. From easygoing, funny and relaxed people with a range of interests, they become nervous, twitchy individuals who are fixated on one thing – the existence of their child. They arrive with enough equipment to mount a lengthy military assault; they have collapsible tables, folding chairs, bags of sterilised utensils, tupperware boxes containing yesterday's supper put through a food processor, jars of banana purée, sackloads of cuddly toys, a bumper pack of disposable nappies, and fifteen changes of clothes. You could manage with one lot of all these things, but with two or more sets you start to lose your orientation. As for conversation, it rarely rises above nappy level for long. People argue. That's the thing about parenthood, nobody has tried it before but suddenly everyone is an expert.

Those first years of marriage went by in a kind of blur that is evoked by a particularly malodorous combination of sour milk and pungent nappies. The atmosphere of organic decay was all over us. The house itself suffered from chronic humidity; swampy mushroom growths pushed their way through loose joints in the panelling and floorboards. Because we were not connected to the local sewage system, the toilet was a monstrous chemical pit at the end of the garden. It reminded me of my grandmother's old house. At home we had toilets that flushed, but at Haboba's house you had to squat over a hole beneath which lurked a bucket that was emptied every night. Somehow this was not what I had expected to find myself dealing with in England.

I tried calling the owners to press them to resolve the most urgent problems, such as the leaking roof. I had the feeling though, that lying on their beach deck in Durban, they were not overly concerned. I could hear the surf rolling in behind them when I managed to get through on the telephone.

'Darling, it's those . . . you know, the ones in the house.' More crashing waves.

'What on earth do *they* want?'

'It's about the house.' I was being drowned out by the Indian Ocean. I was talking to a deity perched on the shores of a distant paradise. He did not have time for my trivial problems in leaky Oxfordshire.

Eventually, someone did turn up, a local handyman named Henry, driving an old transit van held together with knotted rope and sticky tape. He was about ninety and did not like the idea of climbing a ladder, he explained as we shook hands, and surveyed the problem from a safe distance.

'Not too keen on heights,' he hummed, 'not since me accident'. He did promise to provide some spare materials he had and some old tools I could borrow. The tools were indeed old and very rusty, but I had no choice.

It was a kind of pioneer existence. For the first time, I found myself concerned with the physical task of providing shelter and warmth for my family. And it felt rewarding for a few precious moments of the day, which is not to say that I was any good at it: I brought hammers down on thumbs, put ladders through window panes and so on. Tasks were left unfinished, abandoned in despair, or in urgent need of a first-aid kit.

Henry's real job was looking after the grounds of an estate over on the other side of the bypass. He wasn't sure who owned the place any more. It changed hands on a regular basis but used to belong to a pop star who was big 'not so long ago', by which Henry meant back in the late sixties. But regardless of who the proprietor was at any given time, none of them had any idea how much land they actually owned, nor how many acres of forest. They left Henry more or less in charge. It had been that way for half a century. He agreed that I could take away as much wood as I needed in return for clearing up and helping with chopping down a few dead trees here and there. The wood needed to be thinned out from time to time to stop it from starving itself of light and nutrients. He went through and tagged the ones that needed felling with a can of red paint. I had convinced him (and myself) that I was perfectly capable of using a chainsaw, and in restrospect I was lucky not to do myself a nasty injury. Admittedly, it is difficult to feel in control of your life when perched on a roof in a rising gale, a handful of nails in your teeth, plastic sheets flapping all around you, and the wail of a baby rising from below, but there is something tremendously satisfying about walking through the wood, with the wind in the treetops above your head, swinging an axe. This is how we make places our own, by inhabiting them, learning how to live with them. Besides, going amok with a chainsaw in your hands is a good way of getting rid of any pent-up primal aggression.

And while I was scatting about the English countryside, setting up like Swiss Family Robinson, three thousand miles away my own family was starting to unravel. My father was becoming distant, my mother wrote. 'He is up to something, I'm sure of it.' This last sentence underscored by two thick lines of ink. What could he get up to? He was supposed to be coming up to retirement. It was a question of which went first, the newspaper or his health. The government was continually threatening the paper with closure. I wrote that we would come and visit them as soon as the baby was old enough to travel. Mum wrote back the following week to say that she had already fixed up my old room which was now equipped with a baby bed and she had found someone to paint stars on the ceiling. The baby will love it, she assured me.

But underneath the light-hearted jabs and caustic asides about my father, there was, I began to suspect, something seriously amiss. On the telephone they spoke only of the day-to-day difficulties, of power cuts, water shortages, sugar riots, the hopeless plans of an inept government. I kept my eye on the news and watched the awful tragedies unfolding from afar. The place I came from, the country that would always be home in my mind had become a metaphor for human suffering on an unimaginable scale. In my absence the rainbow had come to an end, the flags came down, people were starving, children were turned into soldiers.

We were witnessing the final death throes of the bizarre dance with democracy. For half a century the country had struggled to make coherent sense of its post-colonial heritage. Throughout the turbulent years of the Cold War, the country had switched ideological sides on a regular basis, first right, then left, then right again, until suddenly neither option existed. Left to its own devices, nobody had any time for democracy any more. It was all a sham: political pluralism, multi-ethnic representation, religious and racial equality, none of it worked. There remained only one viable path to salvation and that was the one marked by the Almighty. Righteousness had come to stay with a vengeance. An unholy alliance was emerging between Allah and crude oil. The *jihad* was marching south into the pagan lands, turning godlessness into gold and trading prophets for profit. In the meantime, the government grew concerned with silencing all dissent, including the press.

In England these matters raised little alarm. The internecine complexities of distant backwaters merited only a few inches of a single column tucked into a back page. Unless a pop star or actress happened to take a passing interest, it wasn't news. An indifferent censorship, then, rather than the kind my father found himself up against. Inside the country, the only way to write about corruption, imprisonment, genocide and torture was to smuggle your articles out and publish them under a pseudonym somewhere else. He managed to do this for a while until they caught on. They couldn't prove it, but they knew it was him, and so they started harassing him. They watched him. They searched his office, and even staged a burglary at the house and searched that as well. Of course, they found nothing, but that didn't stop them.

I knew none of this, but I could tell from the tone of my mother's letters, and from the strange, disjointed conversations we had whenever we talked that things had changed, by tiny, significant and irreversible increments; the ways back to the world I had left behind me were going up in flames like so many paper bridges.

The first real inkling I had of impending crisis arrived with my sister, Yasmina, on an official family visit. In my absence, Yasmina had grown up. She was now a married woman and the mother of two bouncy boys. She was in London with husband Umar on holiday: 'Well, sort of holiday. He's sort of thinking of opening a business here.' Why would he want to do a thing like that, I wondered? At the time, of course, it didn't occur to me that this was a sign – that people were preparing to bail out, abandon ship.

Yasmina had married surprisingly early – surprising for everyone, who had never expected her to act so hastily, nor with such convention and conviction. It was a marriage of her choosing. Not that my parents would ever have dreamed of arranging anything like that. Yasmina had married the Sardine King, or rather, his son. The sardines in question were not locally produced, but came in tins with Chinese characters stamped on them. When we were growing up, those tins, with the big key inside the waxed-paper wrapping were a familiar sight in every grocer's shop in town. They were one of those rare things, a manufactured foodstuff that could dependably be found stacked on the box shelves of every street-corner shop, piled up alongside packets of soap powder, matches and pink cubes of carbolic soap big enough to wash a horse with. The sardines were covered in gooey tomato sauce and could only be eaten (in my humble opinion) when properly doused in lime juice and sprinkled with chilli pepper – even then the fishy memory would linger on your breath for days like a guilty secret. They had been broadly adopted as a staple necessity and in every house there was a little cache of tins that had been packed away in case of a flood or something. All three of us hated them when we were small, even Yasmina, but we still had enough tins in Mum's Emergency Cupboard to keep a flock of penguins happy for months. The Emergency Cupboard was where she hoarded everything, 'just in case'. She had bags of rice and flour (all infested with weevils, we later discovered), tins of instant coffee – which none of us drank, but anyway – jars of orange Tang, enough torch batteries to light up a small village, boxes of candles with little mice toothmarks in them, tinned pineapple chunks (also Chinese) and walls of carbolic soap stacked like giant mah-jong bricks along the back of the cupboard. We might starve to death, but they would find some very clean skeletons when the time came. What was my mother imagining? The droughts and famine hit people far away, far enough away for people in the capital to think it was happening in another country. Or was it something left over from the war, that 'other' war of her childhood in London that we knew so little about?

Of course, the Sardine King didn't make his fortune simply by importing finned creatures in tins, but his name would forever be associated with the first product he ever brought in. That was the cruel side of success – you might make your millions on enamel bowls, plastic slippers, sweet factories, even a luxury motorcar dealership. Your empire might stretch to a couple of thousand acres of sugar cane, sesame and gum trees and you might have a fleet of trucks to your name, but the one thing that stuck in people's minds was the one you started out with – the little slimy things in tins.

Yasmina had married into an empire, according to Muk, who told me all about it on the telephone: 'She's going to live in *Dallas*, or *Dynasty*, I don't know which, one of the two.' He was not happy about the situation, he thought it horrifying that someone would actually want to marry her. 'She's our sister for god's sake,' was his main objection, as though this placed her firmly out of reach of any man's desire.

But the one who was really taken aback by this love match, the one who was knocked squarely between the eyes, so to speak, was my father. He, after all, had spent his life running down people who devoted themselves to the crude task of simply accumulating vast sums of money. What had happened to integrity? What about those principles he had tried to instil in his children since the moment they could be made to stand still long enough to listen to him telling us about the great leaders, Franz Fanon, and Gamal Abdel Nasser? And didn't we remember the fate of Uriah Heep? And Jafaar? And what about Ali Baba's brother who had to be sewn back together by the blindfolded tailor because he was so greedy? Later on these bedtime tales had grown up into bitter stories of corruption in high places and government officials trading their authority for multi-million-dollar commissions on aircraft sales and weapons of every calibre.

'They all come unstuck in the end,' he would declare, nodding his head with satisfaction whenever someone was caught with their fingers in the till. He had done his share of uncovering the culprits, following in the tracks of hapless envoys clutching suitcases full of cash, trailing them across Europe, North America and the Middle East – even as far as Japan once, to unmask the guilty party in a hotel elevator, wearing a wig for disguise, in the company of a pair of geishas. Of course, nobody ever got caught, not really. No one ever came to trial. They had friends who tipped them off. They turned their backs on politics. They fled the country. They had mansions in Hampshire and numbered accounts in Zurich. They had all the dancing girls they wanted.

It had all gone terribly wrong. The great age of national independence had proved to be nothing more than a neo-colonial mirage. It was easy to see why he took it so personally, when the ideals he had founded his adult life on, from the dark pre-independence days, to those Labour rallies on foggy days in London town, stamping his feet against the cold – all of it was gone, defunct, old hat. And so, in a manner of speaking, was he. The pluralists and the securalists, the ones who preached Pan-African unity and a nation of equals, regardless of race or creed, or who your father was and how many franchises he owned, were now just a gang of toothless old grumps who mumbled nostalgically about things nobody remembered. Nobody had any patience for any of that any more.

So the marriage of his daughter, through choice, to a man who represented everything that he had spent his life trying to combat, was as good as knocking the proverbial nail into the proverbial coffin, as he put it himself.

'Just put me in the ground now, why not? Nobody respects me any more.'

'Oh, come on, Baba, stop being so melodramatic,' protested Yasmina, barely out of her teens, hands on hips, still wearing the pink headband in homage of her outmoded idol, Olivia Newton-John; unaware that ahead of her lay that pious rebirth which would deliver her to my cottage door all those years later clad from head to toe in the drab greys of a Muslim feminist of the late twentieth century; emancipated and devout in one breath. No contradiction there as far as she was concerned, and no sweatbands either – she wouldn't even uncover her hair in my presence.

Umar, the Sardine King's son, was not a bad fellow. He was large, clumsy and well meaning. He had a plump face that broke easily into a smile and a rather silly moustache that refused to develop beyond adolescent fluff. He drove a huge car and he worshipped Yasmina. What more could any prospective father-in-law ask for?

The wedding went ahead like a badly plotted farce, as Muk described in a long letter. The Sardine King insisted on paying for the whole thing, lock stock and barrel, which was just as well, since Dad was almost broke by this time, the newspaper having long since run out of funds to pay its staff. Some days they didn't even have the paper to print on and would cut the issue down until eventually it all fitted onto a single sheet of foolscap. That was one way to censor your press, starve it into silence. According to Muk, my father spent the entire evening muttering – in increasingly slurred tones, as he ventured time and again out to the dusty square where the cars were parked – 'These are not our people. We don't belong here.' The ban on serving alcohol at the wedding had been imposed for religious reasons by Umar's family. Dad had been warned in no uncertain terms (by Yasmina and her soon-to-be mother-in-law) to let his 'communist cronies' know that any sneaking out of the house for a quick snifter in the car park would be severely frowned upon. Obviously, they had decided not to heed the request. They turned the boot of someone's car into a makeshift bar, with a selection of spirits and glasses propped up alongside a large block of ice on a piece of sacking. Was this the kind of civil disobedience that revolutions were made of? Whatever they tell you not to do, you do twice as hard and twice as long? Sneaking about in the dark they resembled a bunch of naughty schoolboys more than revolutionaries. But you could see where his pain came from: people were languishing in gaol. People were being vanished. This was not the time, nor the place for him to be playing father of the bride at a fancy wedding modelled on some second-rate Hollywood production.

But fate had its mind made up and in a bizarre scramble of traditions, bride and bridegroom paraded through the garden. Umar dressed in a grey dress suit complete with tails and a top hat while Yasmina, transformed into the princess in the fairy tale, stood in a flowing white dress that had been specially created for her in London. The wedding march was played on a Yamaha synthesizer and there was even a cake, up to which they stepped, holding the knife together to cut it.

At this moment my father's relatives arrived, herded in on the back of a truck normally used for transporting bleating sheep or sacks of grain. Whistling and wailing, their ululations could be heard four streets away as the lorry came lumbering out of the darkness of an unlit road. The enormous pink mansion was visible from miles off, strung with neon lights all around the garden walls, the railings, and up the three floors of the main building like a tiered cake.

There were only women left on my father's side. Haboba and her sisters, cousins, second cousins, unmarried aunts and nieces, all those who never managed to find a husband, or whose spouse had passed away, or never returned. They all lived together in the rambling old mud wattle house where my father spent his childhood and where I used to listen to my grandmother's stories.

'The women in our family never had much luck in marriage,' my father ruefully observed to Muk, as he watched them trample across the lawn, still whooping in that high-pitched wavering tone which accompanies such celebrations, to clutch an embarrassed Yasmina to their heaving sweaty bosoms.

A table had been set aside for them – a long way aside, in the shadows under the brooding carob trees, where the fleet of Mercedes were usually parked, away from the honoured guests, away from the lights. But they were having none of that. They broke the banks and chaos flooded before them. In their wake, a crowd of uninvited guests swept in. Pandemonium ensued. Waiters bearing huge trays loaded with food and cold drinks went down in the mêlée, plates and cups went flying. Gasps of outrage issued all around as the street children who had been skirting around the periphery hoping for a few scraps now rushed in to grab what they could in the onslaught.

'Was that why you never came back?' My father asked me, the year he died. 'I said to myself, perhaps he's like me, and cannot stand the sight of wealth being squandered before poverty. Those children scrabbling in the dust for a mouthful of food. I used to think that you should have been there with us, fighting to stop them taking it away, wasting it all, turning the country into a dustbowl for their empty-headed religious poppycock. Or perhaps you realised we were done for even before we knew it ourselves?'

And now here were Yasmina and Umar, the happy couple, coming down to rescue me from myself. They flew up the drive in a huge silver car.

'What are you doing?' demanded Yasmina with a heavy frown on her face as she stepped out. I was pushing a wheelbarrow full of dead leaves and mulch over to the compost barrel. Her eyes widened in horror as she peered at the heap of muck.

'It's good for the soil,' I said, indicating the patch where we grew vegetables.

'You mean you eat things that have been wallowing in that stuff?' She held a hand to her throat. Umar came around the car and swung my hand nervously up and down in his paw a few times. Every time I saw him he seemed to have grown, upwards, sideways. Only his head remained the same size, so that I imagined one day there would be this giant blimp with a peanut on the top where his head was supposed to be.

'All of this land is yours then?' he asked, surveying it with the eye of a man who knows to what profits empty spaces can be turned.

'We're renting,' I shrugged. 'It doesn't actually belong to us.'

'Too bad,' he lamented, not even trying to hide his disappointment. To Umar, renting was what children might do to practise for when they were old enough for the real thing. We walked around the side of the house to survey the long and rather pleasing sweep of high grass that dipped to meet a band of hawthorns marking the stream. It was muddy down there so I had no intention of going any further, but we stood and looked at it for a while.

'The air is very fresh, isn't it?' Umar beamed, pleased with his observation: outdoors, countryside, fresh air, it all went together. Yasmina was looking at the side of the house.

There was washing blowing back and forth on the drying frame, a red jumpsuit of Leo's whipped in the gusty wind.

'You have a fire,' she observed, pointing at the plume of smoke coming from the chimney. As I was somewhat proud of my ability as a gatherer of firewood and indeed a lighter of fires, I began to explain the whole business of Henry and the woods across the fields. The glazed looks told me they weren't too interested. They stared.

'All that smoke inside the house is not good for the baby,' surmised Yasmina.

'Perhaps we should go inside?' I suggested. I sensed that they weren't too keen on the idea, but we couldn't very well just stand outside as it was starting to rain. They walked through the back door with the trepidation of a papal delegation entering a house of iniquity.

'You've been away a long time,' Yasmina declared, in reply to my question about how things were at home. She peered at the cooker, opened drawers. It was not a modern kitchen. 'You don't remember what it is like. The heat, the smells.' I detected a sense of propriety in her voice, which seemed to say that I had no business asking or concerning myself; I had been absent too long to be really entitled to show concern.

The place was a mess, despite my frantic efforts to tidy up in anticipation of their arrival. When there is a small child in the house physical objects lose their ability to remain where they are placed. It is as though everything becomes infused with a form of telekinetic energy: blankets unfold and stretch themselves across the floor; cupboards come open and scatter their contents about the room. Cups, plates and spoons fly off tables in every direction. Anything that is not nailed down will move. Gaps appear which you never noticed before – between wall and cupboard, refrigerator and oven – to swallow spoons, pens and essential things like car keys. There was even, I realised, as Yasmina craned her neck back to look straight up, a ketchup stain on the ceiling. How it got there remained a mystery, but there it was, shaped like a finger pointing at my incompetence as a human being, a parent, a brother, a son. Leo was two at the time, big enough to be able to undo things but not do them up again, to take things apart but not put them back together. He was a restless spirit. A poltergeist whose purpose in life was to keep his parents in a state of perpetual exhaustion. Books were his favourite thing at that stage. He was fascinated by the way the pages came out when you pulled. Whenever he was silent for longer than five minutes you knew he had found a way of getting to the bookshelf again, despite the obstacle course constructed out of chairs and tables, bits of furniture, the webs of string and bungy cables improvised to fence him out.

A pool of milk was spread across the kitchen tiles like a cartoon bubble waiting to be filled with words. The cat was sniffing suspiciously at it which suggested the milk was probably off. Leo was inside the refrigerator. That is to say that somehow he had climbed onto a chair and managed to prise it open and was now busy climbing inside. I had left him with Ellen, but there was no sign of her now. I plucked him down just before he knocked over a bowl of eggs.

'How did you do that?' I asked.

He giggled and pointed to the cat. 'Faustus did it.'

'No, Leo, I don't think Faustus opened the fridge by himself.' I placed him in his chair and moved quickly round trying to right things. 'Look who's come to see us.' Yasmina and Umar looked dismayed.

'How are your two?' I asked. They had two boys, twins. Two miniature blimps, the same shape as Umar. They fought all the time when they weren't eating and they ate most of the time they weren't sleeping.

'They are staying with my mother in London,' explained Umar, as though this was the sensible thing to do with children.

'Would you like some tea?'

Yasmina said yes, but Umar murmured something very low and made a gesture with his head that I was not fast enough to catch. Then Yasmina said, 'Never mind. Don't bother.'

'Don't be silly, I have to feed him anyway,' I nodded at Leo, who was staring at them both. I made a space on the kitchen bench for them to sit down. Yasmina pulled a plastic dolphin out from under her and waved it at Leo as though she had never seen a child before.

'You really do all of this yourself, eh?' Umar was watching me prepare Leo's dinner. 'That's really very good, isn't it, Yasmina? It's very good that Yasin can do all of these things by himself.' He tossed his car keys on the table and folded his arms, all the better to survey me in action.

'You should learn from him.' She looked up at me. 'Umar is really quite hopeless, you know. He can't manage without people around the house to do his every bidding. The other day I had to go out, you remember? I left everything ready and still you managed to ruin the oven.'

Umar was tickled by this, he laughed in fits, rocking back and forth, trembling with mirth. They both began talking at once of the follies of life in London. They were renting a flat in Baker Street that cost an arm and a leg – or it would have done for most people. He turned to me to explain.

'Look, it was simple, I thought that it was for the oven, not for the microwave.'

I stood there with a tin of tomato soup and a can opener watching them like an idiot. They were talking that curious mixture whereby they borrowed words from English to put into Arabic sentences, and vice versa. It was a long time since I had heard that. I didn't care what they talked about, I was happy just to listen. Leo was silently transfixed.

'So he took the pot which was clearly marked "For Microwave Only" on it.'

'I didn't read it.'

'They are not idiots at Marks and Spencer, you know. What were you doing watching television at the same time?'

'It was *Mind Your Language*.' He broke into another long peal of laughter at having been found out. His favourite television programme apparently: a repeat of a series that should have been left dead and buried back in the seventies, about a group of people trying to learn English; it was racist, sexist, moronic stereotyping at its very worst. Umar loved it.

'It melted all over the oven. We had to buy a new one.' A new oven. They clucked away like this, like newlyweds chirpily going at one another. How wonderfully simple life could be, I remember thinking.

It was at this juncture that Ellen made an appearance. Deeply ensconced in Pierre Bourdieu and 'post-structural deconstruction of the Other' while investigating the merits of the Observer-Anthropologist's reflexive voice, she appeared to be finding herself severly challenged by the matter of simple communication with fellow human beings on a day-to-day basis. This had a dampening effect on normal conversation. Either she didn't talk or she went into fits of stream-of-consciousness gabble. The room went dead as she entered. We all just turned to look at her. She looked pale, distracted. Yasmina tugged her headscarf firmly forwards and Umar got to his feet politely.

I wonder now what Ellen saw when she walked into the kitchen that day: three foreigners and her son? An invasion? A curious assembly of unreliable informants the inconsistency of whose cultural capital was due to lengthy exposure to more than one set of traditions and therefore invalidated? Or maybe she just saw *his* family. In any case, she just about managed to mutter hello before plucking her son out of his high seat and sweeping from the room. I remained standing there with the now superfluous bowl in one hand and the spoon in the other, aware of their eyes on me.

'So,' said Umar, after a time. 'How cold does it get in winter?'

'Maybe,' I suggested, 'we should go for a walk.'

Their idea of a walk was straight back to the car; they had seen enough. As she was getting in Yasmina hesitated. 'Everyone is worried about you, Yasin. Mum and Dad are worried about you, and so am I.'

'Well, they shouldn't be, and neither should you.'

'But they are. What are you going to do with your life?'

'This is it, this is my life. I have a wife and son and a place to live.'

She fixed me with a firm stare. 'You don't really believe that, do you? You don't belong here, Yasin, with these people, with her. It's all wrong. Why are you doing this? Don't you know it hurts us to see you this way? You started out in journalism and you should have seen Baba's face. He was so proud. But now look at you.' She gestured around us as though it was self-evident – the decay, the fall from grace. 'It's as though you were doing it on purpose.'

'I could never live up to his expectations, and you know that. Nobody can. And besides I was no good at it.'

'He's your father. You have to try.'

'Why? When it's obviously not going to work?'

'Then what is your alternative? To live here like a peasant? You, Yasin? You know nothing about farming, about the countryside. You think life is about doing what you want, to please yourself. This is a game of some kind and it is . . . selfish. You know it is.'

'I am just trying to make the best of things.'

'Is that any way to go through life, trying to make the best of things? And how is that boy going to grow up? Did you think of that? Who is he going to be?' She turned and climbed into the car, slamming the door after her final, parting shot: 'You'll never belong here. You will wind up being a stranger to everyone, even your own children.'

The cruel truth of her words struck home and I was left motionless and silent long after the car had gone; a silver blur curling down the drive to slip through the trees and vanish with a flick of its tail. What had I actually done with my life, apart from turn my back on everything and everyone, every opportunity that had presented itself? Life does not reward you for trying to remake yourself, to escape the traps set by previous generations, to try and live your life as though it were your own. Not in a selfish way, but in a way that allows you to find your true potential, your real gift. I hadn't found mine yet, and until I did I would have nothing to offer Yasmina in compensation, nothing at all to offer anybody.

I was reminded of a book I once read avidly over the course of three days, unable to move. It was one summer when I was about fourteen and the novel was *Little Big Man* by Thomas Berger. Arthur Penn made a film of it which I never went to see because I hate seeing films of books I have read, and besides, *Dustin Hoffman*? But in that book the character, Jack Crabb, finds himself moving back and forth, switching sides, from life with the Cheyenne Indians, to life among the whites, the cowboys. He is most at home in the diminishing, dying world of teepees and roaming the plains, but he can't stay there, and besides, the Cheyenne universe is threatened by the encroaching world of the white man. Jack Crabb's life is confounded by those people on both sides who insist on reinforcing the lines which he is forced to cross and re-cross to keep himself alive.

13

'She is definitely waving at us,' insists Leo.

I look out of the dining room window at the rainy Paris street. Breakfast has turned out to be a joyless experience. Our room had been decorated entirely in a uniform shade of brown − curtains, coverlets, carpets, all the same colour, rendering everything somehow to an abstraction. And now the thin coffee and the rubbery croissants, even the flavourless jam has the same dull hue.

The figure on the other side of the street is wearing sunglasses, despite the rain, and a hat, probably because of it. 'She can't be waving at us,' I decide, turning back to him. 'Eat your breakfast.' But Leo remains where he is, watching her. The croissant in front of him has disintegrated into a handful of crumbs now evenly distributed over plate, tablecloth, him and floor. As if in response to my words, the woman, who is wearing a red leather jacket and a pair of elasticated pants with a leopard-spot pattern on them, walks over and raps on the window next to my face. Everyone in the dining room looks over at us. Actually, it is more of a dining 'area', being separated from the lobby and front door by only a flimsy screen. The man behind the reception desk is studying us. She knocks on the window again, insistently, then pulls off her sunglasses and waves frantically at me.

'I told you,' says Leo. 'Why did you pretend you didn't know her?'

'I wasn't pretending. Wait here.' I get to my feet and go out to meet Haya. She is studying an expensive set of Louis Vuitton luggage in the window display of a small boutique next door to the hotel. Her own luggage consists of a heavy-looking nylon holdall that keeps slipping from her shoulder awkwardly. The rain has stopped and she pulls off her hat, causing the bag to fall to the pavement.

'Voilá!' she smiles, throwing up her arms theatrically. 'I have decided to help you with your difficulties. I will guide you and you will take me to the south. We help each other.'

'I'm not sure this is a good idea.' I am aware that Leo is watching us carefully through the window.

'Why not? You are leaving today, no?'

'Well, yes. This is not the best weather for seeing Paris.' Which was true, and besides, Leo is not interested in seeing more. He is growing impatient with me, I suspect.

'And what is this?' Bowing over, Haya clasps her hands together in the manner of an ageing aunt presented with a new puppy. I look round to see that Leo has now emerged behind me.

'This is Leo,' I say, in English, ignoring his look. Haya doesn't seem quite sure how to handle children. Perhaps she is out of practice. I seem to recall her saying something about taking care of her younger brothers and sisters when she lived at home.

'Say hello to Haya.'

'Hi-ya, Haya,' he says flatly. The three of us stand there looking at one another. The hotel receptionist is hovering in the doorway pretending to study the street. He glances up and down both ways when I look over at him.

'How did you know we would leave today?' I ask, turning back to her.

'Aha! You see how clever I am. I look at the sky and see the rain. How sad, I say to myself, now Yasin and his son cannot see the city. So they will leave today and not tomorrow.'

'You might have been wrong.'

'It is my spirit which tells me to go,' she declares, punching the air triumphantly.

'Baba, are we leaving today, or what?' Leo, unable to follow the conversation, is growing impatient.

'We are leaving,' I assure him. 'Maybe you could put your rucksack in the car?'

'My rucksack?'

Our luggage is in the reception area, ready for an early start. I hand him the keys to the car. He looks at Haya and then at me, and then turns and without a word goes into the hotel. We cross the street and stand outside the doorway. It is starting to rain again.

'If you had arrived fifteen minutes later, you would have missed us.'

'C'est pas grave,' she says with a shrug, as though life were full of such hazardous uncertainty.

I watch Leo emerge from the hotel with his little bag over his shoulder and disappear down the ramp to the underground car park next door: a little man weighed down by a heavy burden. Haya pushes her hand through my arm.

'Don't worry about it. I will sit quietly and not make a sound.'

'Look, I'm not sure it's such a good idea. Leo . . .'

'Don't worry about the boy.' He appears at precisely that moment and sees her holding onto my arm. She reaches out to ruffle his hair as he passes. 'Mon petit lion.'

He gives me a dirty look, and goes inside again. He emerges with another bag and staggers past us towards the garage again. I am trying to think of a hundred reasons why I should say no, but I am hard pressed to come up with one single concrete one. 'We're not driving straight down. We might, you know, stop along the way.'

She steps back and gives me a firm look. 'If you don't want to take me along, all you have to do is say so.'

But I can't bring myself to do that, even though it all seems like a very bad idea. I ask her to give me a minute and walk down the ramp into the dark cavern of the garage to talk to Leo. He is leaning against the car, in no hurry to come back out, I suspect.

'Look, she needs a lift and so I've offered her one. It seems silly when we have so much space. You don't mind, do you?'

'When are we going to call Mummy?'

'Soon,' I say. 'When we get going. Once we get out of the city, away from the traffic.'

'When did you say you met her anyway?' he asks suspiciously, looking past me up the ramp to where Haya is standing, outlined against the grey light, smoking a cigarette.

'Yesterday. In the lobby,' I lie. He is still looking at the floor. 'We just started talking. Why? You don't believe me?'

He lifts his head and looks at me for a moment. 'It's all right, Dad,' he murmurs softly, 'I believe you.'

Maybe I am not thinking clearly. Maybe it is time to do someone a favour. Maybe it isn't my brain that is doing the thinking. Haya is, in any case, not exactly impressed by our means of transportation.

'This is it?' She gives a low whistle. 'This is what you want to drive to Aix in? This car is older than I am.' Which is true. 'Are you sure it can make it?'

'There's always the train.'

'What did she say, Dad?' asks Leo, a trifle indignant.

'She said it's a classic, ought to be in a museum.'

Haya holds up her hands in apology. 'I was just asking.' She runs a scarlet fingernail across the dashboard and smiles in a mischievous fashion. 'Don't be surprised if we get stopped by the cops. This will draw them like flies to warm shit.'

She was expecting something modern and zippy. This is certainly not that. It is hard to explain my attachment to this car. To someone like Haya it seems like a whimsical foolishness. What is the point of having a car that isn't smart and cool-looking? To me the Peugeot is a nostalgic reminder of my childhood, of the long-gone past, to her it is like stepping back into a world she has been trying to escape.

In any case, once back in the car I have other things to occupy me. The traffic for one, and I find myself listening attentively to the engine again in case some mechanical flaw might have developed in the time it had been resting idly in the hotel garage. Haya talks about herself as she guides us out of the city towards the road south.

'My family thinks I'm an actress,' she explains. 'I send them money. You know a little bit of money goes a long way over there.' Most of her family are still there, in the camp where she was born. All she had ever known of life was the desert and the war. She saw her father once, maybe twice a year when he came home from fighting. All she ever dreamed of was getting away as fast as she could. She met a Frenchman working with a charity organisation. He was twenty years older than her. He arranged for her to come back with him to France, promising to marry her. But after about six months in a small flat in Brittany he grew tired of her.

'I did everything wrong.' She wasn't interested in what was happening in the world. She did not share his outrage at the exploitation of coffee pickers in El Salvador, or the abuse of women's rights in Afghanistan. 'What do I care about those people so far away. I have my own problems.' She had common tastes. She dressed like a tart. She watched trash on television. She hated the theatre, especially that kind of avant-garde production where people spent three hours on the point of killing themselves and never got around to actually doing anything. 'Talk, talk, talk, that's all he wanted. No wonder he was half crazy.' Life was bad enough by itself without having to sit through that kind of thing for entertainment. She liked light-hearted frivolous Hollywood productions and did not understand why he got so upset about this. Who cared about cultural hegemony? Either it was a good film, or it was a waste of money. She wanted to eat proper French food, not badly cooked couscous in dingy places full of people with orange hair and pins through their lips. She wanted comfort and respectability, she was not a fashionable accoutrement for the alternative lifestyle he flirted with. And then he found someone else. 'An ugly woman. I tell you this in all honesty. She could make a bus look beautiful, and what did they do together? No, they talk talk talk. That is all. So let him have his proper French wife.' So she walked out one day, carrying only the clothes she was wearing, and headed for Paris. The only thing she was certain of was that she wasn't going home. She had no papers, so she couldn't find proper work. She had nowhere to stay. 'In the beginning it was difficult. But now I have things under control. I have my own place.' She didn't walk the streets, that was too dangerous, but when she needed money she knew where to find it. She had a string of regular 'friends' who paid her well. 'You know where you have a man if he has to pay for what he wants. That cuts out the usual amount of bullshit they come up with.' Now she is happy, she says. Occasional trouble, but so far nothing too serious. She goes kick-boxing in her spare time. Twice a week. She laughs and throws a couple of punches in my direction.

'I believe you, I believe you!'

She puffs her hair out of her face and sees that Leo is grinning. 'Listen to me. I never talked so much in my life. Where did you say his mother is?' I see his face stiffen. He realises we are talking about him. We are going to meet her down there, I explain, she didn't like driving. More lies.

'Ah,' Haya lowered her chin, which may have meant she believed me, or that she didn't. The question sets me thinking, however, about all kinds of things, but most of all about why things have turned out the way they have. I didn't want to leave Ellen. I knew that we couldn't stand being together, that we were probably inflicting more damage on Leo by staying together than if we were to part, but I didn't want to leave her. To leave would be to concede defeat, to give in to the Yasminas of this world.

It is only when Haya reaches out a hand that I realise I have been overdoing it. I am gripping the steering wheel. I glance in the mirror and see Leo's gaze is transfixed on the road ahead. I take my foot gently off the accelerator.

'Where were you?' she asks. 'You didn't hear me.'

Orphan boy, Ellen used to call me. 'You don't need anyone. You've spent so many years trying to live away from home you forget that we all need somebody.' This was in the early years, her face flushed with hormones, her body swollen with amniotic fluid within which, deep inside her belly, a tiny half-moon curl of flesh and blood was floating towards the world. All I have to hold on to now is the boy who is sitting behind me turning the arms of his super-nuclear-power-enhanced shark, confident that I shall deliver us safely to wherever it is we are going.

Haya, of all people, ought to understand all this. I glance across at her, suddenly grateful that she has come along. She turns back to face Leo and makes an effort to demonstrate her limited English.

'Good boy,' she says. Not, I imagine, a phrase that she is normally in the habit of addressing to little children.

14

I did manage to make myself a home of sorts in the English countryside. I came to love its oaks and beech trees and hedgerows and people who were always mowing their front lawns when you walked by and who would raise their heads to nod that brusque hello which said so little and spoke so much. I forced myself to forget the anonymity of the city with its averted eyes and hurried heels and the indifference of shop assistants who only ever worked there temporarily.

If I ever felt overcome by that sedentary feeling of domestic entrapment and wanted only to lose myself in the crowd, I took the car and headed for the shopping centre, a sprawling complex of garden centres, DIY stores and an enormous supermarket, all wrapped into one. The numbing, non-stop muzak was as intoxicating a tune as that of any pied piper. I would plough the fluorescent aisles like an old hand, immediately alert to any changes. I wanted order and stability. I resented all attempts on the part of the management to revise and update the set-up. As soon as you were familiar with the lay-out they would change it. Why? Sliced brown bread should be where it was meant to be, not replaced by tampax or condiments, or shifted down towards frozen goods. I loathed the obsequiousness that crept in with baseball caps and uniforms, as though everyone had some important role on the NASA space programme and were not employed just to stack jars of mayonnaise. I could buy fresh houmous and ciabatta bread with olives in it warm from the oven. What did I care if the neighbours gave me a funny look? The supermarket told me that variety had come to town and was here to stay.

I would trundle my trolley around with Leo propped up in the little seat squealing with delight as he recognised, like familiar streets, those aisles where his favourites were stored: chocolate biscuits, cornflakes, sweets. I took him with me whenever I could, partly to give Ellen free rein of the house, but also because somehow it was part of the deal. Single males are suspect. Single fathers, on the other hand, I discovered, are highly commendable persons. Perhaps I am oversensitive on this issue, but if my eyes ever happen, however innocently, to catch those of a member of the opposite sex, the usual reaction is for them to clutch their handbags more tightly to their sides. I am not sure what a mugger actually looks like. I probably wouldn't recognise one until he was halfway down the street with my wallet, but they certainly know, those women, and I fit the bill perfectly. When in the company of my son, however, I become a normal person. The girls on the checkout desk would gurgle, and chuck him under the chin, lone mothers would exchange knowing smiles with me across trolleys. I felt as though society had finally opened its doors to me.

I had a new job, too, which made life easier. I responded to an advertisement for proofreaders and found myself in Oxford one afternoon, outside a large Victorian house set back from the road. The house had been converted into offices and the sign beside the bell for Breen Gaze Publishing said: 'Ring and walk around the side.' I did as instructed and found myself standing outside a small door with steel-reinforced glass which, after a time, opened outwards to reveal a small neat woman dressed in a navy-blue suit and a carnation-red blouse. No handbag. She shot me a cheery hello and immediately turned to show me the way down a sloping corridor that seemed to lead under the house, the lagged heating pipes forcing me to duck my head. We came into a spacious basement area where three women were hard at work behind computer screens. Along one side of the room was a stack of cardboard boxes, presumably full of books. I was led into an office on the far side. The large man who came around the desk to shake my hand was Allan Wycliffe. He introduced himself as Managing Director, owner and general dogsbody, ending this with a kind of awkward laugh. He had long foppish blond hair and was putting on weight in that kind of chubby unconcerned midlife fashion. At first I thought he was older than me, by a good ten or fifteen years, but it was the way he dressed, I later realised, that made him look that much more staid. He surveyed me observantly for a few minutes while I talked about my journey, how I had found the place, then he seemed to make up his mind. He smiled over at Helen. She looked up, nodded and looked down again. This, I surmised later, was the mark of approval. Allan turned to me and said, 'Have you eaten? No? Well, why don't we go for lunch?' I suspected there had not been a great deal of response to the advertisement in the paper, but I didn't think it advisable to ask. I needed the job.

'Live in the area? Thame? That's good. Done this kind of thing before? No? Well, don't worry about it. Anyone who has even the faintest modicum of intelligence could manage. And you have done some writing, I see.'

'Journalism – does that count?'

'In this day and age anyone who can spell their name counts.'

'What kind of books do you actually produce?'

'Good question. We are actually expanding right now into a very interesting niche.' He beamed and held the door open for me.

Allan Wycliffe's idea of lunch was chicken and chips in a basket at the local pub. I stuck to Indian tonic water while he downed three pints of Best Bitter like a man who had just staggered out of the Kalahari. After that he began to expound on his business and the book business in general.

'Literature is dead. No, seriously. People say we still have the stuff, but open your eyes and take a look. What was the last good book you read, really good, something that stays in your mind? I'll take a guess, Kafka? Flaubert? Tolstoy? Do I detect a flicker? One of those anyway. The new stuff? Well, it comes and goes. The last great European novelist of worth was probably Kundera. Since then it's all a blur.'

'You don't make it sound like a very appealing business to be in.'

He squinted at me as though measuring me up for a suit. 'I was talking about literature, the book business is fine, couldn't be better. What people want today is entertainment. There's enough grief in the world, wouldn't you say? Real grief. Why would anyone want to read a novel about it? Fancy a game? Winner pays the next round.' He nodded towards the pool table at the far end of the room and got to his feet without waiting for an answer. He sauntered over as though he had never seen a table in his life and then beat me in three straight games. As I was watching him bend down over the green baize it struck me where the curious name of his company came from. He must have spent a lot of time in this place, I decided.

'You still haven't told me what kind of books you publish.'

'I'll get to that. Another round? How about raising the stakes?'

I looked at my watch and said I was a little worried about the trains, which wasn't far from the truth. If he won another couple of games I would be walking home.

He told me about himself as we walked back to the office.

'I was born in Zimbabwe – Rhodesia, as it used to be. My father had a farm and he lost everything. So we came over here and started all over again. Just as well, the way things are now. Anyway, you know what I am talking about. I've seen hardship. I just follow my nose. If I fall flat on my face I just get up and start again.'

'Who writes these things for you?'

'I have a veritable horde of scribes, women for the most part, happily married, middle-class, middle-aged, happy and content women. None of that neurotic stuff. They sit down and write these sappy romances, and they are perfect.'

Back in the basement I picked through a mound of paperbacks with titles like *The American Patient*, *The Season of Love*, *The Sailor's Return*, *Molly's Choice*. Suggestive titles, all of them on the right side of plagiarism, but only just.

'Who buys them?'

'The same people who write them, that's who,' laughed Allan. He was thirty-nine years old and he still lived with his mother upstairs, had done ever since his father died fifteen years ago. He had bought the house with the proceeds. He rented out a couple of rooms and the rest paid for itself. Breen Gaze published almost forty titles in a good year, a fraction of what their major competitor produced, but it was a fine balance. They pumped them out as fast as they could without saturating the market. They had a limited shelf life. If they sold, fine, if not there was always another one ready to go.

Mine was a curious job, and it paid well so long as I kept at it: Allan paid me by the book, not by the hour. 'That way it keeps you motivated. No sleeping or slacking on this ship.' I grew to like Allan. He was up and down, one minute you were his best friend and the next he was chewing your head off about some oversight you had warned him about a week ago when he wasn't listening. Helen was the one who kept everything afloat. She was the go-between and managed to maintain a harmonic balance between accounts, printers, writers, salesmen, distributors, shopkeepers, bank managers. Allan was the guiding hand. He knew instantly what was wrong with a manuscript and would harry the author in question until it came out the way he wanted it.

He was also lonely and often called round with the proofs himself, or told me to come in and get them over another of his pool-table lunches, when he would pour out his deeply melancholic heart for an hour or two before returning to work restored.

And so for a time everything seemed to be working out.

Ellen was locked away with her Post-Structural Theory and I was wrapped up all day with something like *His Pretty Woman*, while in the evening it would be *Tintin in Tibet* for Leo. I worried sometimes that my reading habits were turning my brains to peanut butter, but there was food on the table and the house spirit was at peace, for the moment.

15

'So what do your friends do?' Haya asks me, lighting up yet another cigarette. There appears to be no way of dissuading her. I have tried a couple of times, seeing Leo clutching at his throat and frantically crossing his eyes at me in the mirror. But the effect is the same: she apologises profusely, stubs it out, and then a while later absently reaches for another. It is easier to open the windows. By way of making conversation I have managed to convey the idea that we are planning to stay in Provence with Dru and Lucien, although this would be news to them. When I tell her that Lucien is a filmmaker she becomes quite excited. I disappoint her then by explaining that he does not make the glamorous kind of film she had in mind, but documentaries, which makes him sound dull, which of course he is not. Still, film is film and the floor is open on that vast subject. She used to watch Egyptian films on television. She knows of Abdel Halim Hafiz and Adel Emam. Her all-time favourite, however, is *Titanic*, which I have to confess to not having seen. This is her cue to recount the whole story, from start to finish, scene by excruciating scene. She has seen it something like twenty-seven times and even owns the video.

'That film is like my life,' she says wistfully. 'The moment of happiness, the couple brought together and then driven apart by fate. That's the story of my life.' She adores Leonardo DiCaprio and claims to have caught sight of him once in the back of a taxi stopped at a traffic light on the corner of Boulevard St-Michel.

'It was like seeing heaven driving by. I almost threw myself in through the window. Imagine.'

Conversation with Haya is not easy. My French is functional, but basic, and she speaks very quickly and with all kinds of slang thrown in. Her Arabic is also difficult to follow. We run out of films somewhere near Dijon. Politics is out. All politicians are crooked, she says. Leo is very quiet; I wonder if he is asleep. To the south it is starting to rain again. A band of cloud obscures the horizon ahead.

'You think somebody can clean up the mess this world is in?' Haya says. 'No chance. They take what they can get and thank their stars if they get out alive.' She asks me what I do for a living and when I tell her is astonished.

'You read books, and then the radio pays you just to talk about them?'

'Well, yes.'

'*Merde*,' she mutters, philosophically, as though this is another one the world has put over on her. I can't quite bring myself to tell her I actually wrote a book myself once. I have the feeling that claiming to have written a novel no one has ever heard of would not stand up very well alongside a sighting of Mr DiCaprio in a taxi.

'I did read one book,' she says after a time. 'Someone left it on the bus and I happened to sit down where it was so I just picked it up. It was by a young girl, in Holland, I think it was. Anyway, it's her diary. She tells you how they all live together hiding in this house, and then it stops because the Germans come to take her and her family away.'

'Oh,' I say, looking over at her. 'I think I know it.'

Haya is incredulous. 'You know it? You mean you've read it? The same book? I don't believe it.' I explain that Anne Frank's diary is very well known. But it still takes time to convince her that I am not pulling her leg. 'It was a good book,' she says, as bits of it come back. 'But you knew they were going to get her in the end. They always do.'

'What is it?' I ask. She is staring at me.

'Your job,' Haya shakes her head. 'That's truly funny.'

'It's not that funny,' I concede.

'It's better than lying on your back under some fat sweaty pig, I'll bet.'

I glance in the mirror, thinking that it was a good thing that Leo is not due to start taking French until next year. She notices and glances back to look at him. He isn't asleep, just sitting still.

'He's very quiet,' she says, looking at me. 'He is thinking about his mother.' She says this as though it were a certainty, and I wonder if she might not be right.

The rain starts to reach us and I switch the wipers on.

'Is she English?'

I know what she means. I nod. Yes, she is English-English.

Haya nods to herself. This is how things work out. Men like this (meaning me) don't marry our kind of women, they marry European women, English women, French-French women. White women. But it seems more like a lament coming from her, rather than the censorious disapproval of Yasmina. Although in retrospect my sister did, in a sense, see what was coming.

'Oh, Yasin,' she sighed. 'How I tried to warn you.'

'Warn me about what?' It was my own fault. I had asked for it, confessing that Ellen and I were having problems.

'You need to find yourself again, remember who you are, where you come from. I feel sorry for you, but to be honest, I never expected it to last.'

'Now that we have this thing out in the open,' I said. 'Perhaps you could tell me exactly what it is you disapproved of?'

'Yasin, you are my brother. I love you dearly. But you must know that you betrayed your faith and your culture by marrying someone like that.'

'You mean an infidel, a Christian? Like your mother, say?'

'Don't start looking at me like that. I'm not prejudiced, I'm just telling you the way things are.' The way things were was in her new kitchen on the estate outside Canterbury

163

where she and Umar had just bought a three-bedroomed semi on a housing estate in the middle of nowhere. England had certain advantages these days, but Yasmina was going through her own period of adjustment.

'What are you talking about, Yasmina? What culture are we talking about? What happened to tolerance, what happened to compassion?'

'Tolerance? You want tolerance?' she spat. Her nostrils flared. 'I have seen how they treat us in this country. We are lower than the low. Muslims, Pakistanis, Arabs, Africans, Bosnians. This is the bottom of the barrel and they want to scrape it clean. You see the filth they paint on our walls out there?' The wall of the underpass leading from the main road was daubed with graffiti: AREANS ARISE CLEAR ORF YU WOGGY SCUMM!!

'We weren't brought up this way, Yasmina.'

'Yasin, listen to me, you poor sucker. This is the way things are.' She leaned her elbows on the table and counted off the odds against us on her fingers one by one. 'We have been robbed of our cultural heritage. All that stuff and nonsense our heads were filled with as children – Charles Dickens, Wordsworth, Shakespeare. What was all that except brainwashing? What does Shakespeare tell us about the world we live in? It tells us that we are nothing.'

Why Yasmina and Umar had settled in England I had no idea. I was under the impression that recent political changes back home would not affect the Sardine King's enterprises – the new regime needed people like him; people who were open for business no matter who was on the throne. People without scruples, my father would mutter. In any case, Umar had decided that he needed a change and had come up with a scheme: importing coral-reef fish from the Red Sea – following in his father's footsteps, you might say. But he was being cautious about setting up, and wanted to keep his cash flow fluid. When I asked whether people actually ate them or kept them in tanks he laughed uproariously, as though this were the funniest thing on earth, but he never gave me a straight answer. Business acumen and caution had led him to move out of London. House prices were more reasonable. Umar was not fond of unnecessary expenditure. He had a warehouse filled with tanks nearby – plus the open air was better for the children.

The decor was straight out of one of those catalogues they push under your door. They didn't take the plastic covers off the furniture in case they decided to sell it again and instead threw some Indian cloth over the plastic. It actually looked rather nice until you sat down and it started squeaking. The only thing in there that was not wrapped in cellophane was the budgerigar in the cage by the kitchen door – a present from a client with a pet shop. That was very English, they explained, having a budgie.

Their habits were those of newly arrived immigrants, unsettled in their new home and sensing they were not yet part of a community. To deal with this they had arrived at a curious blend of the old and the new worlds, which a talented sociologist would have had difficulty disentangling. Some things they rejected, others not. The microwave oven was the new-found goddess of modern living, and they worshipped it like dizzy pagans. Not because they had never seen one before, but because now they could buy specially made meals to put into it. They filled their shopping trolley, car, refrigerator and kitchen with a thousand varieties of colourful packets with easy-to-follow instructions. Instant soup, frozen lasagne, popcorn, pizza. This was real affluence, the kind that knocked having a fleet of house servants at your beck and call out cold. This was the luxury of plenty. They ravenously ripped off carton tops, gleefully tore open cellophane wrappers and waited for the *ping!* of the timer with all the joy and anticipation of children expecting a birthday surprise. They steeped themselves in popular culture and read *Hello!* magazine with fervent dedication. They watched game shows and followed every twist and turn in the plots of half a dozen soaps. They knew the names of all the characters and chuckled at how badly the English spoke their own language. Modern society provided everything you needed at the distance of a remote control. They retreated joyfully into a comforting bubble of prepackaged existence as though they had never known any different.

Like one of Ellen's anthropologists, I tried to understand the curious psychology that informed their choices. They wanted to inhabit a typical English bungalow on a typical English housing estate. But they also seemed to despise their neighbours, the way they lived, the food they ate, the drink they drank, the god they prayed to, or didn't. They ate Marmite (I didn't have the heart to tell them it was originally made from the yeast scrapings from the bottom of beer vats) and baked beans on toast and worried about the garden not looking its best. They hired a gardener to mow the lawn and tidy up the hedges. When Umar tried to have a go by himself he managed to slice through the cable of the electric trimmer and put himself in casualty, with shock and a possible hip fracture when he fell off the stepladder.

'What is all this about?' I asked Yasmina. 'You sound like Malcolm X in drag.'

'Brother Malcolm was on the right track, Yasin. Cultural slavery, that's what they got us into. The big post-colonial trap. We want purchasing power, the freedom to shop where and when we choose, and that gives them the right to denigrate us. They've got us right where they want us.' She smashed her fist into her palm so hard the budgie actually skipped on its perch. 'Our parents betrayed us. Dad with his high ideas about Western civilisation. You call this civilisation?'

'You're confusing religion and culture, they are not the same thing.'

'You're the confused one, and don't waste your breath with all that clever talk. They may not profess to be practising Christians, but you pull out the drawer in any hotel in the country and what do you find? The Bible, that's what. It's like a secret society, like aliens in *The X-Files*. It's all there under the surface.'

'Yasmina, think about what you are saying.'

'You can mock all you like, but the fact is that your marriage will end in ruins and your child is going to be a no one, a non-person. He will not know who he is, where he belongs, or where he comes from.'

'What do you suggest – take him to the mosque and ask them to adopt him?'

'It's an idea.'

'An idea? You don't think that would confuse him, pretending there was nothing else to him?'

'At least he would have a centre of gravity.'

'He would have a headache. Why not let him grow up and decide who he is?'

'Because that's not how it works. I mean, look at you.'

Haya drifts into sleep. I drive on in silence. It is over a thousand kilometres from Paris to the Luberon mountains where Lucien and Dru have their house. I shall have to call them at some stage to let them know we are about to descend on them. I am not certain either of them will want to see me.

The petrol gauge is low and we are all feeling hungry, so we pull off the road and into a service station for lunch. I stretch my legs. Leo and I kick a football around for a bit. Haya sits on the bonnet of the car and watches us and then suggests we go inside and have something to eat.

'Baba, can I ask you a question?' Leo has his eyes fixed intently on the ground in front of him as we walk up the steps together.

'Of course you can.' I slip my arm about his shoulders.

He raises his face to look at me: 'You're not going to marry her, are you?'

'Who?'

'You know, *her*.' He lowers his voice and nods in the direction of Haya, striding ahead of us into the restaurant area, which is built like a spaceship for some reason, a circular disc of concrete raised on steel poles.

'No, Leo, I'm not going to marry her. I'm married to your mother, remember?'

'Oh,' he says softly, and runs ahead. I follow them upstairs to be met by oozing rock music, designed, I imagine, to waft away the nervous tension accumulated while driving. On the first floor we have a choice – to the right the stairwell opens onto a lobby that resembles something out of a Godard film, filled with mechanical units in orange and beige formica. No staff in sight, just a series of coffee machines and automats stuffed with cellophane-wrapped sandwiches, doughnuts and croissants. The French have a fascination with machines, things with buttons and slots and levers. To our left the vista is of an entirely different order. Through the swing doors a fleet of deserted tabletops can be glimpsed, stretching out towards the horizon, punctuated by atolls of plastic lianas and yucca plants. Not a customer in sight. A waiter with the pallor of wet cardboard glares through the glass porthole at us.

'Come, I am going to invite you,' says Haya, reaching for the door.

'Wait a second,' I say. 'Are you sure about this?' All my instincts tell me to steer clear of places that masquerade as the refined traveller's watering hole, complete with tuxedoed waiters and wine buckets. All of it calculated simply to entice the crisp bank notes out of your wallet. It has nothing to do with the quality of the food they serve. The kitchen is probably the same place they stuff the fromage into the baguettes for the machines across the hall. It has all the allure of a Venus flytrap. I hesitate but Haya tugs at my arm.

'No, come on. I insist.' She wants to pay us back for giving her a lift.

'You don't need to do this, really,' I say, but I can see that this means something to her. I give in and instead give a mock bow as I hold the door for her. Leo giggles.

'M'sieu, Madame, bonjour.' The waiter, like a badly wound-up tin soldier, snaps a couple of menus stiffly from a pocket on the wall and begins to lead the way across to a far corner at the rear of the wide empty room.

'Non, non,' protests Haya, waving her sunglasses in the air like a real actress. She points the other way, to the raised alcove in front of the big bay window. There are only two tables up there, but it is obviously a much better position than the place he was taking us to. The waiter hesitates. The restaurant, I can now see, is not actually empty – the only other people in the place are a couple, and they are sitting right beside the table Haya has set her sights on.

There is a moment of embarrassment. I can see it on the waiter's face. The distinguished-looking gentleman, who wears an expensive suntan that speaks of lengthy holidays on ski-slopes and yachts, glances over at us and then discreetly away. His companion, a robust blonde woman half his age, turns her horn-rimmed sunglasses in our direction and glares. The only person apparently oblivious to the awkwardness of this crowding of un-demarcated, communal space, is Haya. She steps up, sits down and calls Leo to her side, patting the seat next to her. Leo glances up at me, shrugs and goes forward to sit down. The other couple have been quietly contemplating the view, which is not altogether remarkable, but you can see over the motorway to the trees and valley beyond.

I edge into my seat past the other man's chair and sit down. Haya looks at me across the table and smiles. She has her table. As she turns to help Leo to settle down, making a show of arranging his napkin for him, it dawns on me that this is what she had in mind, playing families, if only for a short while.

'Isn't this great?' Haya squeals with delight. Leo grins. We order. They play a game of pointing at the cars driving by. Leo shows her his trick of turning toothpicks into vampire fangs and she dutifully squeals all over again. I feel myself begin to relax. We sit in silence for a while. Haya seems to become thoughtful. The food arrives suspiciously quickly and they have managed to mix the order up. I call the waiter back.

'One moment please. What is this?'

'Chicken fricassée.'

'There must be some mistake. I ordered the escalope milanese.'

He peers around our table slowly as though perhaps he has confused our table with one of the many other orders he was juggling in his head. He ticks off the plates on his fingers. Leo's hamburger, Haya's pasta salad and mine. Un, deux, trois. Then he gives a non-committal shrug. He seems to be waiting for us to say, never mind, it's all right. I look at him more carefully, and this time I notice the trace of something hard under the impassive dullness of his face. It is like looking over the side of a cliff and being momentarily startled at how far, how dark it is down there.

I look away instinctively. Perhaps he is one of those waiters whom life has short-changed. Perhaps he is having a bad day, the boss is on his back, his salary is lousy, his dog died. And perhaps he just didn't like North Africans.

'Never mind,' I say. 'This is fine.' I regret doing this the moment he turns away.

Haya's fork clatters to her plate. 'Wait a minute. Did you hear what he said?' He gives her a look of disdain. 'You have made a mistake. He ordered the escalope.'

'Mademoiselle, the order is here.' He reaches into his pocket, but he has already made his fatal mistake, addressing her that way. That 'mademoiselle' hit a nerve. She thumps the table with her fist so hard that the woman at the next table jumps. I jump.

'He ordered the escalope. We all heard him.'

The waiter is unperturbed. 'I don't make mistakes,' he smiles thinly. 'I write it down and the chef takes it and prepares it. That is how things work in a proper restaurant.' He holds out his chit of paper which is covered in illegible scrawl. His leer tells me that he is not afraid of physical violence. He has been there and done that. He is daring us, poking a finger through the membrane that maintains civil order to see if we would squirm. The thing about violence is that it is non-negotiable. You have to be ready to kill or be killed, to go all the way, to be prepared to lose everything. People are kicked to death in car parks, parents beat children senseless, arms are lopped off in churches, skulls are cracked, bullets are fired. Violence has no limits. Once invoked it carries on, until it burns itself out, until it meets its match. Our capacity for senseless violence is what separates us from most of the living world. It is also what makes us what we are. Without violence we would not have the music of Mahler, the paintings of Goya. We would not have Miles Davis, or Leadbelly. Haya has seen violent men before.

'I don't care what you call this place,' she says in a firm, low voice. 'If the customer says you are wrong then you should apologise and take it back.'

The waiter gives a snort at this. 'You want me to take it back to the kitchen and change it?' he sneers, looking away. The room is silent. I am aware of the people at the next table, turning in our direction.

Haya looks him in the eyes and smiles. 'I want you to get down on your knees, you stupid fuck, and carry that plate back to the kitchen on your head.'

I can hear the man behind me throw down his napkin and turn towards us.

'Baba?' Leo's eyes are wide. His mouth is full of hamburger which he has stopped chewing. 'What's wrong?'

'It's all right,' I say. 'Don't worry.' He doesn't look reassured. He puts down his hamburger and sits on his hands. The waiter meanwhile is beginning to realise what he is up against.

'I am afraid I will have to ask you to leave,' he says, tapping his feet.

'No, you don't have to ask,' I say, getting to my feet. 'We are leaving anyway.'

'I'm not leaving,' says Haya. We all stare at her. 'I'm not leaving until he apologises.' I sit down again. She nods at Leo to continue eating. He looks at me. As the waiter turns away I hear him mutter something under his breath. Haya hears him too.

'Hey!' she calls after him, and when he doesn't stop she lifts up a vase full of plastic roses and mouldy water and tosses it after him. It strikes a table and shatters. The man at the next table has had enough.

'This is too much! This is not the way to behave in public.'

'That's right,' Haya retorts, 'so why don't you go back to staring at those tits of hers that you paid so much for, eh?'

'Bitch!'

'It takes one to know one, chérie,' Haya replies. She has a slightly mad look on her face and I decide that this is a good time to make a move. Seizing her by the elbow I drag her towards the door.

'Baba?' Leo gestures at his plate.

'Just leave it. We'll go somewhere else. Come on now, we have to go. Quickly!'

'Don't leave it! We take it!' Haya grabs the plate as I steer her towards the door. She kicks and pulls at anything that comes within reach. Yucca plants, tablecloths, plates, cutlery, all crash down in our wake. Leo races for the door, which he holds for us. He knows all about getaways from television. I have one eye on the kitchen door from which I expect our waiter to emerge any second now with a sharp hatchet in hand. On the way down the stairs, with Haya yelling and swearing at anyone who looks her way, I think he might be calling for reinforcements. Had I seen any police cars nearby?

One of her heels breaks as she stamps to the car. I pick up the red shoes as she kicks them off. We drive off at high speed with me checking the mirror to see if anyone is chasing us or taking down the number.

'Voilá!' she says as she hands Leo his plate. 'Dinner is served.' He cackles and bounces up and down on the back seat and soon we are all laughing.

'You know what, Dad?' Leo catches my eye in the mirror.

'She's crazy!' He is laughing so hard there are tears coming from his eyes. Then Haya turns and touches her hand to his face and Leo falls quiet. I see him in the mirror, looking proud and just a little embarrassed.

We settle down. There are no blue flashing lights following us. Haya swears to herself in unbroken litany and reaches for her cigarettes. Most of what she is saying is unintelligible. She lapses into a vernacular mix of French and Arabic. After a while it begins to rain and Leo stretches out on the back seat and goes to sleep. Haya is staring straight ahead, as though mesmerised by the gentle pendulum of wipers and raindrops. She is silent for a long time and I notice her wipe something from her eye that might have been a tear.

The face of this continent is scarred by the passage of people. From east to west, north to south. From the earliest neolithic wanderers to the Mongol hordes, from the Huguenots to the Calvinists, pilgrims, refugees, gypsies. It is a history of railway tracks and roads. A history of transgression, of frontiers and border lines being crossed and recrossed. The Romans, the Visigoths, the Jews, Bosnians, Albanians, Kosovans, the blind, the sick, the old, the crippled. These are the people upon whose sacrifice the history of Europe is written, and our collective destiny is written in the course of those migrations.

We are part of that vast, nameless body of mongrel humanity with nothing to claim as their own, not even the road they are on. We could have been a family, the three of us. There is nothing odd about us really in that chaotic tumble, the cavalcade of road signs and service stations, the thin ribbon of insistence that cuts across fields and trees, down valleys and up hills, regardless of the constraints of nature. Nothing odd about us at all.

16

Of course the real Dervish was my great-grandfather, Zahir Abd al Nour. He was killed in the Battle of Omdurman on 2 September 1898. There was nothing remarkable or distinguished about his death. He was not a professional soldier. He was a follower of the Mahdi, the man who claimed he would lead the world to salvation and then died of natural causes, leaving the movement rudderless and exposed. Zahir was one of the *ansar* – which means follower – who were dubbed Dervishes by the British on account of their inscrutable religious fervour. According to one account of the battle, by a young officer of the 21st Lancers named Winston Churchill, the advancing enemy resembled the representation of the Crusaders in the Bayeux tapestry. An odd analogy, perhaps, but to the writer this was a medieval army, charging, quite hopelessly, against a modern one. The Dervishes, whose patched smocks signified poverty and a disdain for material possessions, acted, he wrote, 'with the instinctive knowledge of war which is the heritage of savage peoples', falling before the 'beautiful white devil' of the gunboats.

Somewhere on the Kerreri plains old Zahir's bones are scattered. The body, or what was left of it, was never recovered. When she was a child, Haboba said, she and her mother used to walk out to the battlefield and gather up the fragments of bone they found into little mounds as a kind of memorial.

Years later I told the story of my great-grandfather to Claus, Ellen's father, as we drove through the mountains of

North Wales. I had been enlisted to help him fetch a seventeenth-century oak chest he had purchased from an antique dealer in Cader Idris. If I didn't go with him, Claire said, he would try and drive up there by himself and do himself an injury. So there we were stuck together in a tiny Citroën 2CV for eight hours. To help pass the time I found myself delivering a lengthy sermon on Sufism and Dervishes in general. Claus was not entirely unfamiliar with the subject:

'Goethe, of course, was fascinated by all that, you know. He adored the Persian poet, Hafiz.'

The car was weaving a bit as the weight of the chest, which barely fitted into the back – even after we had removed the rear seat and tied down the boot with a piece of old rope – caused the nose of the car to lift alarmingly into the air. The traction of that particular model is in the front wheels and it was like trying to control a skittish pony, the wheels kept sliding around over the road. I wondered what kind of horses they had in the seventeenth century that could pull a weight like that. With its iron bands and corners, it looked like the kind of thing that would sink to the bottom of the sea with pirates, treasure and all.

Claus then deviated from Goethe by way of a detour into the comparative pastoral methods of the non-sedentary peoples of Central Asia, prompted by our observations through the tiny damp windows. The steep fields reminded him of Northern Iran, which he had once visited on an archaeological excavation in the 1960s.

'The nomads wander back and forth on the same difficult route over the mountains, following the seasons; up in the summer, down in winter. When they are too old to make the journey they just sit down and watch their families and herds going onwards, knowing they will never see them again.'

The gloomy Cambrian landscape reared up about us in waves of unkempt green punctured by slate fences from which strands of raw wool hung like ripped sailcloth. It was foggy as the car toiled upwards towards Llanberis Pass. I was crouched over the wheel while Claus chewed his way steadily through a pound of apples, tossing the cores out of the window at sheep that stared morosely back at him. He said he knew the way, and I trusted him. After several hours of backtracking and improvisations he still claimed to be right, it was just that the roads kept changing, he said.

When we reached the top of the pass we decided it was a good time to stop and stretch our legs. There was nobody else in the car park but a middle-aged couple eating sandwiches in their car. The woman rubbed the mist from her window and frowned intently out at us, no doubt wondering what devious mischief we were up to.

There was a path that seemed to wind its way up along the side of the ridge. Claus suggested we walk a little way along this.

'What about the chest?' I asked. It looked forlorn and abandoned, the string that held it bobbing lightly like a tail in the chill mountain air.

'Oh, goodness, nobody around here would be mad enough to take that.' He had walked all of these hills in his undergraduate days and was eager to renew his acquaintance, if only for a brief excursion. I couldn't really refuse, and besides anything provided a relief from the whining engine and wrestling with the steering wheel.

He bounded ahead of me on the track, talking full speed over his shoulder. These mountains had always reminded him of Goethe's minute scientific description of the Alps made during a journey to Italy in 1786. 'I was terribly keen to travel, to do like him, to describe exactly what I saw. When I grew up the world was thick with war.'

'But you travelled a good deal.'

'Later, yes. I travelled as much as I could. I left Ellen with Claire. She didn't like it. I think she still might bear a grudge.'

Which was not difficult to understand. She up to her ears in nappies while he was off gallivanting across Afghanistan and Turkey in search of Shangri-La. He was part of a pioneering group of archaeologists who found themselves welcome throughout the former colonies by postgraduate students who were now running their own departments and were glad to welcome their old professors, who arrived with foreign funds and equipment. I could see that the world Claus had lived in then was in some ways simpler than it was now. It seemed we had finally managed to overcome our awkwardness with each other. When we talked like this I felt closer to him in a strange way than I did to Ellen.

Kafka, Claus explained, once wrote of there being an indestructible element at our core, in which we trust. It might be belief. It might be creative talent. What it is matters little. The important thing is that it provides an immutable centre of gravity which gives us balance and helps us to orient ourselves, to know who we are and what we are. For Duke Ellington, that thing was jazz. Most people go through life looking and never finding it.

And perhaps, he said, it was this inner element, this instinct, to which Goethe trusted when he set out, in July 1814, on a journey of his own, down through the Rhineland of his childhood. He was sixty-five years old. Most of his friends and contemporaries were dead and gone. In the last decade he had not written anything of great worth. Instead he had polished up completed past works, edited his collected writings and picked up a lot of awards. He had even been given the legion of honour by Napoleon Bonaparte. Everywhere he went he was surrounded by admirers and students, a prisoner of his own fame. They would kiss me to death, he wrote, if given half a chance.

By then Bonaparte had gone, was living in exile on the island of Elba, and Europe was recovering from the havoc he had inflicted on it. Sixteen years earlier, Napoleon had invaded Egypt, in search of neither land nor wealth, but more than either or both. He took along the usual requisites of conquest, such as soldiers, ships and guns, but also an army of *savants*, scholars to catalogue precisely the mysteries of the East: botanists, biologists, chemists, physicians, astronomers, mathematicians, linguists. He didn't just want to see the Pyramids and the Sphinx, he was driven by the mystical belief that the secrets of the universe had been known to the ancient civilisations that had built them. He didn't care about the present occupants. He vowed to re-write the Koran if that was what it took to conquer them.

Goethe too, subscribed to the idea that hidden somewhere within those ruins of ancient temples and fallen palaces lay a clue to the substance at the core of human existence. Unlike Napoleon, however, Goethe felt the key to unlocking that source was to be found in poetry and mysticism rather than in physical conquest.

So, on his journey through the Rhineland, the Weimar poet, anatomist, painter, botanist, and Public Administrator of Roads and Mines, fleeing the pressures of public life and reputation, found inspiration in the great spiritual tradition of the Sufi poets. There he perceived a link that could prove his belief in the idea of a universal literature. It was a romantic notion, all the more so for the fact that the writers he discovered, starting with Ferdowsi's *Legend of Seyavash* from the eleventh century, belonged to an Orient that no longer existed. This, too, gave him a kind of freedom.

He wrote the poems of his *West-östlicher Diwan* leaning on café tables, in the corners of restaurants. It all came to him on the move. Within the space of a month he had amassed the bulk of the poems in his collection which renders homage to Hafiz, the fourteenth-century Persian master of the *ghazal*: the rising and falling ode that runs through endless permutations, never losing the thread of its essence − the word 'ghazal' means to spin, and Hafiz is recognised as the all-time master spinner.

Poets and prophets, Goethe wrote, were both possessed by the same spirit. The poet squandered his inspiration in spreading it out in all kinds of fanciful language to create his verse. The prophet whittles himself down to one truth, one banner round which his followers gather. The closest thing he could find to his definition of a poet who had not squandered his gift was Hafiz, the poet-prophet.

Through all of this Claus was climbing steadily up the narrow path through the sharp rocks. He was a tall man and could move with surprising speed. I was out of breath and felt light-headed.

'Travel is also a way of evading the world,' he said, turning to look back at me. 'It never solves anything. Not really.' We came to a halt. The mist was cold and blue and slipped like a diaphanous whim over the dark crags. I sat down on a flat-topped stone and thought how ominous it felt. 'There is an old expression in Danish, about your troubles going with you wherever you travel. Something called a *nisse*, which is an imp-like creature.'

'Like a djinn?'

'A djinn?' His face lifted. There was a bead of sweat rolling down his temple. 'Yes, I suppose so, perhaps that would do.' He paused. 'Anyway, the gist of it is that you can never really get away from the things that are troubling you. No matter how far you go, they go along with you. You see? The things that are pestering you are within. You can never get away from them.'

It was common belief, he explained, in the Middle Ages that the air was occupied by nimble spirits which had no souls. Hard to eradicate, they were usually mischievous and up to no good. Among their number were the souls of unbaptised babies, wolfmen, vampires and assorted ghouls. Every natural object contained supernatural powers. Eminent rational thinkers such as Erasmus and Thomas More believed in such things as well as in the existence of witchcraft.

We walked on a little further, the path began to level and crossed another which descended out of the cloud. High above us, somewhere in the mist, there was a spine of hard black granite that ran up to the summit of Mount Snowdon. We couldn't see it, but somehow we could feel it looming over us.

When my father died he took with him his corner of

history – the anecdotes, the stories of his childhood and parents. There was never enough time. He was always too busy thinking about the difficulties which lay ahead to worry about the past. The past could take care of itself, it would always be there – only now that didn't look so certain any more. In Africa, they say, when someone dies a library vanishes for ever.

We paused to catch our breath and then, at that very instant, the clouds in front of us drew apart like curtains on a stage, or a secret door opened by the murmer of a magical incantation. We saw the yellow and green landscape stretching away below us, the grey fins of stone walls and the rising mass of dark rock, and there in the distance, the warm glint of sunlight on the sea.

'Well,' said Claus. 'I think that marks the perfect end to a perfect little walk. We can start back now.' And without another word he turned and began jogging down the path. I stood there for a moment alone and then slowly turned and followed him down into the mist.

17

The house is set back from the road, some way up the
hillside behind the village. A narrow unpaved track winds its
way through lemon groves and almond trees. A bank of
leached yellow soil rises up beside the car. Above us are olive
trees like upturned hands, fingers crooked at the sky. We
emerge onto an open slope alongside a high stone wall and I
know instantly that this has to be the place. Over the top of
the wall rustic tiles in red and ochre mark the roof of a
farmhouse.

'Is it here?' asks Leo over my shoulder.

'I think so.'

I swing the wheel and edge the car in through the open
gate. Two heavy wooden doors lie on the ground, one on
either side, as though they have just fallen off their hinges,
although they may have been there for decades. The yard is
littered with rubble, broken tiles and bricks, bits of timber.
We roll to a halt in the middle of this and take a look at the
house. It is a simple old stone building, with low ceilings and
small windows, except at the far right-hand side, where it
looks as though a church has been added on. A tall window,
covered by flat wooden shutters, stretches up from ground
level almost to the roof of the two-storey building.

At the other end of the house the front terrace swerves
around the side of the building to vanish beneath a trellis
covered in vines. A wooden table painted in blue along with
a bench and a few weatherbeaten chairs can be seen. It
resembles an oil painting. Withered bunches of grapes hang
down over the table. The breeze gently trembles through the

leaves. Beyond this is a garden wall which is falling down in places. There is an open archway which frames a row of cypress trees that mark the edge of a pale meadow. In the distance a chestnut horse can be glimpsed flicking its tail in the tall dry grass. Looking up the hillside from there no other houses can be seen. The rough scrub and beige earth rises into a natural and very grand amphitheatre.

Leo comes up and takes my hand, 'It's like a castle!'

It isn't exactly that, but it is close enough. The wooden shutters are worn and in need of repair and the plaster has fallen away in plates to form strange geographies. The stone lintel of the front door is slumped on one side. The doorway is dark and shady compared to the bright sunlight and I get halfway towards this when a tall, slim figure emerges. With her head down she doesn't see me standing there at the edge of the terrace nor notice the car beyond. She has a tabby cat under one arm and a basket full of washing in the other. It is only as she turns that she catches sight of us. With a cry she drops cat and clothing to the ground and pulls the earphones of her Discman out, revealing the reason for her deafness.

'You made it!'

There was a word, you felt there had to be, one single word that could sum Dru up perfectly, I had just never come across it. She was smart and contained and kind and a long list of other things as well, all of which seemed perfectly encapsulated in her slightly uneven smile, enigmatic and disarming at the same time. She could be humming away while the walls around her were falling down, and she could be beside herself with rage over an injustice taking place on the other side of the world. The intensity and depth of her character was wrought into the fine bone structure of her face. She had one of the most disconcerting stares I have ever seen; she looked straight through you like the scanner of an X-ray machine.

She jumps down to us and slides an arm around my shoulders to give me an awkward squeeze, then she catches sight of Leo standing off to one side and knocks his Chicago

Bulls cap off as she sweeps him off the ground in a bear hug. When she lets go he steps back, looking a little lamefaced, but smiling gamely.

'How you've grown!'

'Is this really where you live?' he asks, putting his cap firmly back in place.

'It really is.' She nods. 'And you know what? We have a horse and three goats, and more chickens than I could count and there are pigeons too, and a couple of cats.' She breaks off with a laugh at the sight of his eyes widening and pulls him to her side again. They rock from side to side as though doing a funny dance. She looks at me over his head and I am not sure what she is thinking. I have never been quite sure what she meant when she looked at me like that.

'Oh, my, what have you brought along?'

We all turn to look at the car where Haya is bent over, her head in the boot, wrestling fiercely with the large unwieldy nylon bag. God knows what she has in there, but it writhes about like a goat destined for the slaughter. She manages to get it out and onto her shoulder but as she starts across the gravel towards us the strap breaks and the bag drops to the ground as though felled by a bullet. She stamps one high-heeled boot in frustration.

'That's Haya,' explains Leo. 'We're giving her a lift.'

'Really?' Dru flashes me a smile, this time the meaning is patently clear. It is almost three years now since Dru and I embarked on our doomed and messy affair, half that time since we called it off. A bond has been formed out of the sharing of secrets and the deception, which I am glad seems to still be there. She was part of the emotional turmoil from which I have only recently begun to find my way out. Seeing her again makes me wonder whether it is that bond, those subliminal forces of attraction which have drawn me here, like a strange undercurrent.

Lucien appears out of nowhere to come to Haya's rescue. He is wearing a blue boilersuit smeared with multi-coloured dabs of paint. Cigarette in his mouth, he starts berating her for trying to carry such a heavy thing, and doesn't she know what she could do to her spine? She looks at him as though he is mad and for a second I can see her considering taking a swing at him. But after much waving of arms they are soon deep in conversation, the subject of which I can hardly begin to imagine, but they seem in no hurry to join us. When I turn towards Dru, I see that she too is watching them. Her grey eyes meet mine and seem to read what is best left unspoken. I am not even sure what words I would have used.

'Hello everybody,' greets Lucien, ambling up to tousle Leo's hair and reverse his cap. 'Welcome to the house of madness.' He reaches out towards me and smiles, giving my shoulder a friendly squeeze as he goes by. A manly squeeze – he, too, seems to assume that Haya and I are an item.

'It used to be a mental asylum in the forties,' explains Dru. 'Lucien claims it is full of unharnessed creative energy.' They moved here just over a year ago, to escape the hectic pace of city life, and perhaps also to try and make a new start.

'Come up here out of the sun,' he calls. 'Are you hungry? Of course, you are. It is lunchtime. What would you like?'

Everyone is talking at once. They want to know how the journey was, where we stayed last night. Leo seems happy and content, perhaps relieved to be among people that he at least knows. Lucien soon has him chopping onions with a huge knife. I try not to look, but Lucien coaches him carefully, holding his fingers out of the way. He believes that children should be treated as what they are, small people.

In no time we are installed on the shady side of the terrace underneath the trellis. Haya has her sunglasses on and her head tilted back, letting the sunlight that twists through the vines play on her face. Lucien and Dru wander in and out of the kitchen through a side door, setting us little tasks, bringing out plates and glasses, and chatting all the while, about the journey, about the house, about everything and nothing.

Ellen and Dru met at university. They came from similar

backgrounds, Dru's father was an academic. They had similar interests. When Leo was still a baby we all went to Paris to visit them. They lived in a small chaotic flat in Montmartre. With thoughts of the damp, leaky house awaiting our return, I remember how springtime in Paris seemed so much more pleasant. But it was not just the city and the good weather they were experiencing at the time which made an impression, it was also how well they were suited. Ellen and I would snap at each other over every minute detail, every expectation undelivered, while Lucien and Dru complemented one another. Their life seemed uncomplicated by domestic order and yet somehow it all worked – bills were paid, clothes were washed, meals were cooked. The narrow space and the chaos made them more dependent on each other and brought them closer together if anything.

Seeing them like this again now only reinforced the sense of how right they were for each other, a reminder to me of how Dru and I would never have fitted together. They had that same quirky humour. The smile of feigned boredom on her face when he made some absurd observation was more intimate than anything nakedness could ever reveal. Lucien standing in the doorway, corkscrew in hand and Dru brushing by him with an armful of fruit and cheese. A couple. A more perfectly matched pair of people it was impossible to imagine.

Lunch is a simple business of cold chicken and salad and something Lucien threw together with haricot beans and red peppers. We eat outside and the conversation at the table divides two ways, with Dru and Leo talking about the eagles that can be seen in the hills above the house, and Haya and Lucien chatting away in fast French. He seems fascinated by her, as he is about everybody, and within the space of five minutes appears to have extracted more than I have in two days and one night (in separate hotel rooms) alone with her. He fills us in on the history of the Western Sahara.

'The Moroccans built a wall a thousand miles long across the desert, to keep the Saharawis out of their own land. It is the only man-made feature you can see from space, apart from the Great Wall of China.

'The region was first colonised by the Spanish and the French. When the Spanish pulled out in 1975 the Moroccans moved in, spurred on by visions of their own vastness, and the lure of phosphate deposits. The first part of the wall stretched from Cape Bojador on the Atlantic coast (the point beyond which European sailors once believed you would turn black or be swallowed by the Sea of Darkness) inland to Samara, whose legendary library was destroyed by the French in 1912.'

As Lucien draws to a halt, Haya, who is either impressed by his knowledge of her country, or impatient at having to listen to his account, gets to her feet and announces that she would like to see his 'studio'. Lucien is delighted. Leo is curious.

'Go ahead.' I nod. Leaping from the terrace he races off after them. He has been cooped up inside the car for too long, he needs to run.

Then Dru disappears inside and suddenly I am left alone for the first time in days. I feel the silence around me growing deeper. I can hear the wind blowing through the trees behind the house. There are birds chirping somewhere close by. A sense of ease comes over me. I don't want to move from this spot, I realise. I want things to stay this way, incomplete, and full of possibility. I can feel the hard surface of the road leaving me, the grind of the engine, everything just falling away. And then, no doubt stuffed full of too much food and wine, I fall asleep.

The others must have decided to let me sleep on. I wake up with a stiff neck. Evening is falling, the light of the setting sun draining through the olive trees that mark the rim of the valley below us. The table has been quietly cleared and the house is silent. I get to my feet and stretch. When I turn around Dru is standing there, squinting her eyes against the low sun. Without a word she puts her hand through my arm and leads me down away from the house, through the arch in the crumbling wall and out into the wide meadow where the horse is grazing.

'I can't get over how Leo seems so much older.' Her head is bowed and she appears to be studying the ground. The waning light hardens the lines of her face, picking out the jut of her jaw and the little crinkles around her eyes. What is missing from this country idyll is, of course, the sound of children's laughter.

The last time we were alone together we were sitting in a miserable little cafeteria in Waterloo. She on her way back to Paris for good and I to my mother's funeral. For a week we had been trying to make the decision we knew was inevitable. Dru was pregnant. After years of trying with Lucien without success, suddenly it was so easy. She wanted a child, had always blamed herself, thinking the problem was on her side, and perhaps that was what allowed us to be so reckless.

We talked beneath the dull boom of loudspeaker announcements, drinking coffee that neither of us wanted. A man in a shabby state came up to demand aggressively that we buy his magazine, and he remained there insistently, staring at us when we said no, until Dru finally threw some coins at him to make him go away. It was a hateful world, she said. The cold light, the waxed cups and the trampled sheets of abandoned newspapers, all spoke of a pathetic finality. The brutality of our surroundings echoing that of the decision we had to take. We both knew that we had been caught out; that whatever we had together, it would not be strong enough to hold a child, that each of us was wrapped up with other people, other stories. It was the moment of truth and we couldn't do it. Losing her was a certainty I had been aware of for some time, perhaps even from the start, but losing her like this seemed unnecessarily cruel.

She smiles wistfully now, remembering herself at that moment. 'I thought about having it, about pretending it was his, but, above all else, I wanted an end to the lies, the deception. I couldn't stand the thought of a life starting out on a lie. How foolish we are to think that living by our principles is so important.' She is looking at me and I see her face has changed, there is a resignation there which I have not seen before. 'I would have that child now if it wasn't for those fine principles.'

Who is to say there was no other way? But we lacked the courage, or the conviction, to run off. It was plain to both of us that it wasn't love which had sustained us, but something of an altogether lesser magnitude. So I returned to my life with Ellen, suitably chastened and morose. For weeks after that I was unresponsive and numb. I was useless to all intents and purposes. It wasn't that I didn't want to talk, it was that I couldn't. I didn't have anything to say. I found myself crying for no apparent reason, or lapsing into hours of silence. I had just lost my mother, so perhaps it was understandable, but on top of that, it seemed as though losing Dru had closed the one avenue of escape open to me.

A gust of dry wind sweeps through the olive trees and the silvery white leaves flutter frantically, like a cloud of butterflies.

Dru squeezes my arm as we reach a stone bench and sit down. Below us the land dips away southwards and keeps dipping. Far off beyond the gathering clouds must be the sea. Behind us the sinuous curl of the Luberon mountains rises up in pale rocky steps bathed in pink light and dotted with tufts of wild rosemary and thyme.

'So, that's quite an entourage you have brought along.'

She means Haya, or maybe she is trying to get me to talk about why I am here, what I am doing. I relate the story of the incident in the restaurant, how Haya dealt with the waiter. Dru is astonished: 'She did that? How did Leo feel?'

'Well, he was a little surprised at first; we all were.'

'I'll bet.'

For the first time I feel resentful. Not because of her concern for Leo, or the implied suggestion that it was irresponsible of me in some way to be wrecking restaurants and then running away. It is that in that moment I have the impression that Dru somehow disapproves of Haya being with us.

'She called here.'

'Ellen?'

'You told her about us, didn't you? I thought you might eventually,' she says. 'Anyway, she's pretty upset, understandably. She was going to report you for kidnapping. There might be a warrant out for your arrest already.' Her eyes widen theatrically: 'You could be a wanted man.'

'She would never do it,' I say.

'I wouldn't be too sure of that. Why did you run away?'

'I didn't run away. Is that what she told you?'

'If you're not running away, where are you going?'

'Well, as it happens we are on a little tour of Europe. An educational trip, that's what this is. I mean, it's a wonderful opportunity, and we have already seen a huge amount of stuff.'

'An educational trip? To where?'

Where? I look down at the hillside below, the slow gathering of dusk. 'You remember my brother, Muk?' I ask. 'Well, he's in Spain now.'

'That's where you are going? To Spain? To visit your brother?' She has a strange look in her eyes, as though not sure whether I am telling the truth or not. 'I didn't know you were in touch with him.'

'I got a postcard,' I say. I am not sure how long this idea has been growing in my head. It must have been nurturing for some time, but up until this moment it had never really struck me as being feasible. I see now how perfect it would be, just to carry on, to drive south to the Costa Brava.

Dru is silent for a time, then she says, 'What about Haya?'

'Oh, she has friends near here. I offered to give her a lift.'

'Where did you meet her?'

'In Paris. Dru, please, this sounds like an interrogation.'

'I'm sorry. I'm just a little confused. Why didn't you tell Ellen you were going to Spain?'

'Things are not good between us. You know how it is.

189

And besides she wanted to spend time getting to know her Nordic cousins.' The evening air is closing in. The trees are flickering shadows around us. 'Why the sudden concern for Ellen?' I ask.

Dru takes a deep breath and looks off into the distance. 'Why did you tell her now, after all this time?'

'She already knew. She had worked it out herself.' When I gave in on the ferry over from Harwich, I was simply confirming what she had been working out in her head for quite some time.

'I suppose the moral of the story is never choose your lovers from among your friends' husbands,' she sighs.

I get to my feet. It isn't quite dark yet. Perhaps it would have been better to find a place to stay, a hotel in town. 'Maybe this was a mistake. I mean Lucien. I thought it would be all right, but I can't look him in the eye.'

'Wait, just slow down a minute. What are you planning to do, run off again with your child and your teenage bride? Yasin, listen to me. I am happy you came and you are welcome to stay for as long as you want. And don't worry about Lucien. He is fine about this. Now sit down and stop being so dramatic.'

'He's fine about this? Then he's stranger than either me or you.'

'He's stranger than both of us put together and I love him dearly.'

'And he knows it?'

'And he knows it. OK?'

Finally, she takes my arm and leads me along the bottom of the meadow in the failing light. 'I'm sorry about your father, you know. I never told you. That must have been hard in the middle of everything else.' I can't see very well and am afraid to fall. Things feel as though they are getting out of hand. If I am not careful I shall be sobbing like a baby before long.

'I'm going to lose him, Dru. If we get divorced she will get custody and that will be it. I will see him once in a while, at the weekends maybe. When I think about everything, all the years, all the pain that went into trying to make the marriage work, I ask myself why, and the answer is simple: for him, to be with him. To wake him up in the morning and watch him eat his cornflakes and to tuck him up again at night. This is all I want.'

We have reached the archway again. The faint sound of voices reaches us from inside the house. They will be wondering where we are. Dru's face is just a shadow now in the darkness.

'He's your son. He loves you. He'll be all right. He has his own life, Yasin, let him live it.'

She leaves me there to go into the house and I turn to gaze down over the valley. Only a thin band of orange light still holds out on the horizon. We tend to think of our lives as following some kind of linear progression, from birth to death. We expect to continue to grow and learn, to keep rising. Time is a ticking clock, a counter that keeps running, and yet time is the greatest illusion of them all. We invented it, picked a convenient beginning and then divided it up into tiny increments. So we had weeks and months and bank holidays and Ramadan. And it made perfect sense, and so we assume that progress follows with the passage of time. We strive individually to better ourselves and we search for evidence of collective advancement, finding it in science and technology, wonderous advances in medicine. And from that we assume humanity is growing, learning, becoming more civilised. But the medical miracles are restricted, to the majority of people on the planet they are further away than a prayer. Time is not linear at all. It turns like the universe around a spiral we cannot hold onto. The answer is staring down at us from the stars above. The light which reaches us from those distant winking stars comes from gaseous clouds that burned out millions of light years ago. We look at the night sky and we see time flowing backwards. An illusion created by the speed of light and the enormous distances involved. But still we draw comfort from their constancy.

As a child I envisaged the rest of the world as a vast, nebulous mass floating beyond the stars. Life, the world, it was all going on somewhere else. Somewhere beyond that distant point in the sky, from which, sometimes, in the still moments of a quiet evening, say, a light would detach itself and begin its dreamy descent towards us. We lived right under the airport flight path and, at a distance, the sudden appearance of the steady pulse of blinking lights marking the approach of an airliner was evidence of a world not seen, hidden out there beyond the boundaries of our sleepy suburban existence; a signal seen only by us, a message from the great yonder, beckoning, always beckoning.

'What are your plans?' my father asked me when we were sitting out in the yard alone, just the two of us one evening. This was the time we went to stay with them, Ellen and I. For a moment I felt like a child again, looking for answers in an Olympics poster and knowing that I would probably never feel the sense of purpose that my father wanted me to feel.

'Well,' I said. 'We get by. We're surviving.'

'Surviving? What are you, a bushman? I don't understand this. Did I bring you up to survive? Don't you have any ambition? Don't you want to achieve anything in life?'

'We're managing,' I maintained. He could barely contain his irritation.

'Managing? Listen to yourself, please. Things, this life, the world . . . I mean, it's not easy.' He lit another cigarette and puffed away for a few minutes. 'I'm sorry. I promised I would not lecture you. It's good you came, anyway. Your mother is very happy you came.'

After that we sat there in the dark together, in silence. And then over the high wall behind us a neon light erupted, flickering, desperately trying to come on. The power was back. Sighs of delight came over the walls around us as people rushed to switch on their televisions and radios. A harsh gush of music came from somewhere nearby followed by a peal of laughter. The spell was broken and with a sigh he got up, pushed his feet into his leather slippers and wandered off through the house to get ready for his next meeting.

18

Leo was not yet two years old when Ellen and I went to visit my parents for the first and only time. My strategy was to avoid Christmas, that awful season of jollity, plastic reindeer and wrapping paper with mistletoe on. I can get through birthdays fine, but Christmas depresses me.

'Why don't we go away this year?' Ellen's suggestion. Yes, I thought, away, somewhere where the idea of cheery fat men on sledges seems just as absurd to everyone else as it does to me. Seized by the energy this thought gave me, I went straight to the building society and drained the account.

'We'll go home,' I said, waving the tickets in the air.

'Home where?' she asked, blankly, spoon in mid-air, Leo with his mouth open.

'Home where?' I echoed, stumped. 'Home, my parents. Home.'

'Oh.' We all stood there looking at one another as though waiting for our cue. Then Ellen put down the spoon and wiped Leo's face. Some things are just not suited to being big surprises.

The seven-hour flight turned into a nightmare. We went through the entire scenario: Leo threw up; he got earache; he screamed non-stop for hours; he insisted on wandering around the plane and then he tripped over and hurt his nose; he stood up and someone promptly tripped over him. He refused to cooperate. Sit down, stand up, move, sleep, eat; whatever you asked him to do he would insist on doing the exact opposite. He kicked the folding table, spilling hot beef stew over the poor man sitting on the other side of Ellen. I am convinced that nobody on the aircraft enjoyed that journey.

But the moment we touched down, and the three of us stepped out through the door of the plane, the heat struck me with the warm intimacy of a sleep-drenched blanket. I felt the stirrings of nostalgia, for my lost childhood, for my youth cut short by departure. As the gentle whine of jet engines died out, the smell of aviation fuel gave way to an evening breeze that smelt of sand and stars. I was home.

I pushed aside the vague concerns I had about my passport. I have two. The Sudanese one had expired years ago, but somehow I didn't want to lose it, which I would if I tried to present the British one; dual nationality being a non-starter as far as the junta in Khartoum was concerned.

'Are you sure you don't need to renew it?' Ellen had enquired before we set out.

'Don't worry. They will be only too glad to welcome me back with open arms, believe me. They can't give these things away.'

So I clattered eagerly down the steps, and walked quickly across the concourse towards the airport building without a worry in the world. It was after midnight and the immigration section looked like a still life, as though nothing had moved in years. Two wobbly fans gyrated indifferently in opposite directions. A young soldier sitting on a chair with a rifle on his knees rested his head against the wall and slept, his mouth yawning open. The walled desks stood unmanned in the middle of the room; glass islands like fishtanks waiting to be filled with water. We lined up patiently. On the far side a pair of double doors marked Exit separated us from the arrivals hall and my waiting parents. Alongside this another soldier, this time in blue fatigues, was leaning against the wall, a small sub-machine gun hung from his shoulder like an empty stirrup. Along one wall there was a shelf of laminated wood strewn with forms and papers which fluttered in the light breeze stirred by the fans.

'This passport has expired,' declared the immigration

195

officer after flipping back and forth through the document several times. He held it out towards me with two fingers. It was no longer worthy of his attention. He was already signalling for the next passenger to come forward.

'Wait a minute.' Wrong tone. He looked up at me sharply. I smiled hopefully; 'I'm going to renew it. That's what I'm going to do tomorrow.'

He tilted his head to take a better look at me. He heard my rusty Arabic, saw my Western clothes, my English wife, my child, now peacefully sleeping like a dead weight in Ellen's arms. He saw a young man who was probably earning more money than he was, probably living a comfortable life over there in England. He saw a turncoat, a rat come to sniff at the sinking ship. He thought my uncertain smile was a badly concealed sneer. He saw a young man who thought he was immune to the law, to the restrictions that normal people are subject to. He shook his head and reached for a stamp.

'Access denied.' He sent the passport spinning across the counter for me to catch before it landed on the floor.

'Wait a minute.' I tried bluffing. 'Wait. I was told by the embassy in London that it would be all right. I was told there would be no problem. Otherwise why?'

He had a squat, fleshy face heavy with fatigue, and bloodshot eyes. He probably had enough of his own troubles. He had bills that needed paying, ailing parents, children that didn't see the point in going to school (and neither, if truth be told, did he any more), a salary that didn't reach halfway towards where it ought to and which he hadn't seen a penny of in months anyway. What did he care about the problems of a privileged son of the middle classes who had never learned enough to know that laws are what make people equal?

He crooked a finger to reel in a police officer lurking over by the wall. Ellen was juggling the sleeping child from one arm to the other, frantically demanding to know what was going on while I tried to explain to this second man what the problem was. This man was different. He was tall and thin, with a bony unshaven chin and his lower front teeth discoloured from tucking tobacco under his lip. Everything about him spelled uncertainty, even the uniform he wore looked as though it had been meant for someone with shorter legs and longer arms than he. I followed him over to the wooden shelf along the wall and watched as he took off his cap and started shuffling through a heap of forms, as though straightening a pack of playing cards. Sweat was popping from Ellen's brow. She was jogging Leo up and down so frantically that he woke up and began crying.

'What are we going to do? What are we going to *do*?' She kept repeating. 'I told you. I begged you. I *warned* you.'

'Please, Ellen, listen,' I pleaded. 'This is my passport, OK? There's nothing wrong with it. I expect that I have to pay something and they stamp it and it's valid for another ten years, OK?' I repeated this to the policeman. He hitched up his trousers and shrugged, obviously not entirely in tune with my theory. He reached for my passport and turned it over in his hands a couple of times as though he had never set eyes on such an object in his life before.

'Oh my God!' Ellen's eyes shot up and off she went again, juggling Leo up and down like a basketball.

'Please, sir,' I went back over to the brute in the glass box, imploring him, trying to strike a tone somewhere between pitiful and respectful. 'My poor parents are waiting outside, they don't know anything. At least let me tell them what has happened.'

It was clear that more than anything I was an inconvenience. He wanted to get rid of me as much as I wanted to leave. He leaned an arm on the top of the glass booth and waved a hand at the tall officer. 'Don't let them out of your sight, and bring them back here.' By now we were the centre of attention. Everyone in the room was watching us, wondering what we had been trying to pull, even the soldier against the wall had woken up as we filed through the exit doors.

'Oh my God!' wailed Ellen. 'What are we going to do? What are we going to *do*?' I had no answers, no ideas. I couldn't really believe this was happening. We walked out to be met by the waiting crowd. They surveyed us, hopefully at first, and then with idle, picking-your-teeth curiosity. I saw nobody I had ever seen in my life before; not a father or mother, not a brother, sister, not a friend, not a distant forgotten relative, or second cousin, or lost uncle, or friendly neighbour, or anything, just a row of strangers whose expressions varied from complete lack of interest to wild amusement at the plight of this odd couple who had obviously just realised they were in the wrong country.

The police officer stood aside. He too was perusing the crowd, although I have no idea what for. Finally I saw a small hand waving above the heads over to one side and then an arm appeared and finally my father struggled through the crowd, white hair sticking all over the place, like an owl emerging from a sack. My mother just visible behind him.

'Where are your bags?' he demanded, gruffly. Short-tempered. No hello, or welcome home, or how are you, or anything. I was conscious of the faces of the onlookers all around us. Everyone seemed to have taken a sudden interest in the matter: yes, where is your luggage exactly? I explained what had happened and stood back as this triggered off a litany of appeals to the Almighty to ask how he could have fathered such a bone-ignorant son.

'How could you do that? You set off with a passport that is invalid? Are you out of your mind?' He thrust me aside and entered into conversation with our keeper, the officer looming over us from behind. Watching my father work, the energetic gestures, the gentle coaxing, I could see that I was a million miles away from where I thought I was. He had the touch, knew exactly how to turn this goofy-looking fellow from a reluctant guardian of the law into a willing accomplice in less than thirty seconds. I was out of touch. An essential piece of my genetic make-up had been lost somewhere. We prepared to go back. The officer purpose-fully straightened his beret, he would sort this out. No money had been promised or exchanged. It was remarkable.

My mother was still nagging at my father's sleeve, trying to tell him something while he tried to brush her off. 'What is it?' he demanded, finally turning to her. They both fell into a very animated conversation. The officer shifted nervously. He took my arm and I braced myself. The whole trip was turning out a disaster, a brief, heartbreaking glimpse of my parents and them of their grandchild and then off again, back to London.

'Wait a moment.' My father grabbed my other arm, I was being wrenched apart. He was beaming from ear to ear. His prayers had been answered: we had a friend.

'Who?'

'Ali Hadeed, you remember? He is now head of Airport Security.' He turned to the officer who had stiffened perceptibly at the mention of the name and was now nodding in a very efficient manner.

'You know Mr Hadeed?'

Oh, he knew him all right. A sobriety came over him and he turned to begin beating back the crowd who, sensing a turn in events, were pressing forward with all the excitement of loyal fans anticipating the outcome of the next episode of their favourite serial.

We didn't have a headmaster at school, we had a warden, and almost twenty years ago I had been sent to his office for fighting with Ali Hadeed. I had been eating a sandwich in class. The way to get through a tedious lesson and have a snack at the same time was to use the wooden lid of your desk as a shield, holding it in place with your head so as to leave your hands free to unwrap your sandwich and munch away. The inside of those heavy old desks was rarely used for books; you would not dare to put anything of value in there as it might never come out again. It might be ferried away by the trails of ants that mined those desks like coal seams. People used them as spitoons. There were crusts of bread as hard as cast iron; you needed carbon dating to find out how old they were. There were fava beans and onions and tomato seeds and reams of oily newspaper that people had wiped their noses and god knows what else on. People had graduated and brought children into the world, *their* children had had children, and still the remains of a bean sandwich they had eaten thirty years earlier would be sitting in one of those desks.

Ali Hadeed's father owned a watchmaker's shop. He made a fortune selling fake Seiko watches as the genuine article. He brought them in from Dubai wrapped around his waist inside an elastic girdle. Ali wore one himself and we knew it was a fake because he told us so:

'People will pay anything for a Seiko, even more for a Rolex.'

Fake or not, this watch was accurate enough to tell him exactly when the school bell for the lunch break was about to go off. He held a countdown for his audience in the seats behind him: Five . . . four . . . three . . . two . . . one! Then he launched himself forwards to flip my desk lid forwards, hitting the boy in front of me in the back of the head. Like a bather caught changing on a beach with his towel ripped away, I instinctively reached for the desk lid to cover myself, still chewing, but my attention was distracted from the sandwich and by then Ali was racing towards the door with it as the bell began to chime.

I didn't like Ali Hadeed. I never did. He was an arrogant bully who enjoyed hurting people smaller than him, or cleaner than him (he had a hygiene problem), anyone, so long as he could get away with it. His was that brand of malicious humour which knew no fear. He was scared of no-body, armed or unarmed, except perhaps his father. And lately he had taken to picking on me. I'm not sure what it was, but at that moment, seeing my sandwich fast disappearing in his grubby hand some primitive instinct unleashed itself from my psyche and surged through my eleven-year-old veins. I leapt across two tables to crash into him and bring him down. The heavy old school bell was still ringing as the two of us went skidding across the front of the classroom past a surprised Father Bernadini, our diminutive English teacher, with his prim little pointed beard and his white gown. The sandwich disappeared out of the window. The cheering gave way to moans as the teacher announced that the class was to be detained throughout the break. And the two of us found ourselves being marched by our ears (twisted in Bernadini's surprisingly firm grip) down the stairs to the warden's office.

It is true that from that moment on Ali Hadeed showed me a grudging sort of respect. I had brought him to the ground rather spectacularly in front of the entire class, an impulsive act which won me a number of new friends and admirers. But it was also true that I had not seen nor heard of him since we graduated from school and went our separate ways. My father was convinced that he was our saviour.

'He's here! In this airport. We must find him.'

I remained where I was, hearing the news go through the crowd of onlookers. I was less convinced than my father that Ali Hadeed would be any help. What if he still held a grudge? I did recall hearing that he had joined the national security forces, a viable career for anyone with a penchant for violence and a lack of scruples. There was not only the assurance of steady employment, a salary that arrived on time, a car and a gun, there was also the awesome power that attached itself to that feared service.

A few years after the sandwich incident, Ali Hadeed's nickname at school had become 'Carlos', on account of a scruffy growth on his face which he fancied was the beginning of a grown-up beard. In fact it lent him a certain resemblance to the most notorious terrorist in the world, familiar to us all from the smudged, inky image which appeared regularly in the newspapers. A real live wanted man. He was sought by every major law enforcement agency in the world and yet nobody knew where he was.

I was to watch in astonishment the following year when they announced on the evening news that the real man known as Carlos the Jackal (Ilich Ramirez Sanchez) had been arrested in Khartoum where he was apparently living the high life. Real life drawing towards the fiction of our schoolyard imagination (and a murky deal involving French intelligence and satellite photographs of the camps of the armed resistance in Southern Sudan – which were mysteriously bombed shortly afterwards, with remarkable accuracy). On the rather shaky home video shown in the news report the once notorious celebrity of the terror circuit, now grown somewhat plump, could be seen jiggling his flesh at a local wedding. And there, sitting beside him in the next shot, was none other than our very own 'Carlos', security chief Ali Hadeed.

But there he was coming to my rescue, striding through the crowd flanked by two very large security men. The human tide parted in front of him. People simply fell away. He was dressed in a light-blue suit and carried a walkie-talkie. On his wrist, I noted with a thrill of recognition, he still wore a large watch with a metal band. Fake? I wondered. Probably not; nowadays he could afford the real thing. He shook hands with me, briefly, turned to examine Ellen without speaking to her, and then spoke for a time with my father. He seemed mature and respectful and comfortable with his authority. He snapped his fingers and said a few words here and there as he led me back through to the immigration desk. Ellen looked as though she were about to faint.

Everything was taken care of in a matter of minutes. The brute in the immigration booth looked peeved, grumbling as he stamped all the necessary papers and avoiding my eyes as he handed back my passport. He didn't like doing it, but he knew how things worked. I now felt intense sympathy for him. He was, after all, only doing his job. I was the one who had caused him to commit an infringement of the rules. He turned away and resumed his seat to continue with his work. I never saw his face again, but I could feel his resentment; I still can. He was right – this is how the world works; those who don't deserve it get all the lucky breaks. Those better-off flaunt the rules that we are made to enforce. They pass unhindered through channels because they have friends in high places. They make a mockery of all of us. I was silent on the drive home, no longer overjoyed to see familiar streets. I was glad to be out of the airport but unhappy that I had bent the law to do so. My mother was more pragmatic.

'There was no alternative. You were very lucky he was there.'

'That doesn't make it right, Mum.'

'He's been living in England for too long,' Ali Hadeed had said to Ellen as he walked us out, only half joking. 'He forgets how things are.' After twenty years he had managed to get back at me; I was in debt to him now.

We drove slowly home. I saw houses I recognised from years ago and new ones I had never seen. There was a powercut just as we approached and the whole neighbourhood vanished for a moment. The darkness was broken only by the eerie spectre of floating headlights passing by, the glow of an oil lamp, the flare of a match, or a candle, shakily being lit. A bicycle slid out of nowhere to cross our path and disappear again. No sign of where it came from or where it was going. A small open fire burned in the entrance of a round hut made of palm-reed mats – home for a night-watchman and his family.

'Here, in this country you need friends. You get nowhere without them. It's not like in England, you see.' My father was talking in that ponderous manner of his which he slipped into when he had an audience ready to listen to the voice of experience. But Ellen was not listening. The business at the airport seemed to have unnerved her. She was wrapped up in the corner murmuring comforting words to her child, as though neither of them was here at all. Leo sat with a rubber dummy in his mouth looking out of the window. He seemed unconcerned by the change in his surroundings.

'Everyone needs friends.'

Coming back was not just a matter of physically returning,

there were other adjustments to be made, gaps that had to be compensated for. You are no longer one person, I remember thinking that night, but two – both of them strangers.

It was odd staying in the old house. It looked different. Everything that was left from our childhood looked smaller and less significant than I had imagined in my absence.

It was clear to me then that, gradually, our little family tree was growing into a strange and contorted shape. The dense foliage had begun to thin out and the branches were diverging on increasingly estranged paths. Yasmina, married to her fishy magnate, was busy providing a line of suitable heirs for their empire. She ceased effectively to be part of our family. She belonged to them. She felt sorry for us, my mother told me once. Since the change of government in 1989 the future had become more uncertain than ever. They had closed down the newspaper and my parents were in trouble. Yasmina offered to help them out financially. Dad muttered, predictably, 'Over my dead body' – another high-ranking hit on his list of quaint English expressions.

And then there was Muk, my errant brother who was apparently wandering Britain in the unlikely search for rock stardom. If it was true that I had not seen Muk for years, it was equally true that I had made little effort to see him. I was the eldest boy. Muk was the charmer, unable to do anything wrong in my father's eyes, and Yasmina, the eldest, was a princess as far as both were concerned. Perhaps that was why I spent so much time staying with my grandmother. I was an only child when I went to stay there. In school, too, Muk could do no wrong. Everyone thought he was a riot. He was regularly to be found outside the warden's office awaiting punishment for some stunt he had pulled. The teachers loved him even though they would regularly throw him out of class, send him off for punishment with the whole class cheering him on. The warden would be wiping tears of laughter from his eyes as he reached for the camel whip and asked him to bend over. Five minutes later they could be seen clowning around together on the steps outside his office – my brother and the warden!

Everybody loved Muk. After decades of absence, distant friends and relatives would regularly mistake me for him. Not that we looked alike, just that his was the first name that sprung to mind. He was the witty, funny one, the cheeky little imp who had that frightening ability to speak his mind without fear of the consequences. I was the blurred grey figure in the background. And now he was gone. We were staying in his old room, redecorated for our benefit. His things had been stowed inside an old wardrobe, heaps of curled, dusty sheet music left behind in his wake, along with a forlorn-looking guitar.

It wasn't just the house and the family that had changed – the country, too, seemed to be bound on a new course, and it still wasn't clear whether we were included in that future. I saw the shanty towns that had sprung up on the outskirts of the capital to absorb the refugees from the war in the south. And I heard the stories of people being arrested and tortured. My father tried to impress on me the urgency of the situation.

'We don't have political freedom, you understand?' He leaned forwards, his elbows on his knees, and his face took on an intensity that I had known only as an expression of anger. Now, I felt, he was talking to me as an adult.

It was late in the evening. We sat in the garden under the big lime tree. The only light that reached us came from the night sky, the electricity having been cut an hour before. There were powercuts every day. Sometimes it went away for only a short time, sometimes you went to bed and in the morning you found all the lights on.

'These people don't read,' he said. 'They want everyone to sit clutching their holy books all day. They want to blind people to the truth. They are doing for Islam what the Stalinists did for socialism.' He was tired. His eyes were swollen and puffed up. He slept less than he used to and long before dawn I would hear him shuffling around the house, sitting at the table on the front veranda with an oil lamp to save waking the whole house up. He worked better at night, he said, it reminded him of when he was young and used to read outside by the streetlights, as the house had no electricity. 'We were not unhappy, you know. Not at all. We had clean streets and standing pipes for water on each one. Those basics used to be a national priority. Give people a home, give them a way of making a living. Give them an education. Not any more. Now it's put them in the army and let them fight for the Jihad. Jihad? When did protecting your oilfields become cause for a holy war? We have to speak out.'

'But you have spoken out, you've been speaking out for years. It's time to let someone else have a chance.'

'There is no one else about.'

For two weeks we were spoilt rotten. We visited friends and relatives, Leo had his chin chucked and his cheeks pulled so many times that his face started to change shape. My mother took Ellen on tours of the town, to see the river, the whirling dervishes in Omdurman, the camel market, to buy old trading beads in the market. Ellen returned looking dazed and drained.

'She has so much energy,' she gasped, slumping backwards onto the bed. 'I don't understand how she does it. I'm half her age and I can't keep up.'

'It's practice,' I said. 'She's been doing this for forty years.' But even as I said this I realised Ellen was right, something was amiss. She *was* more active than I remembered. In fact, we hardly saw her due to the fact that she was constantly on the move, running from one thing to another.

She was making papaya jam in the kitchen when I cornered her alone a few days later, enough jars already lined up on the counter to last a decade.

'You'll take some back with you when you go?'

'Sure, sure.' I surveyed the steaming pots she was stirring carefully. She was barefoot, as usual, dressed in the simple and rather faded kaftan that she wore around the house. Her jet black hair was streaked with grey and when she wasn't conscious of being watched her jaw set itself into a pout of nagging preoccupation. 'We're having a great time, Mum,' I said. 'Ellen loves the house and Leo is enjoying the warmth.'

'Oh good, I'm so glad.' She glanced up and then returned to her stirring. 'If there's anything she needs from the shops let me know in good time. Sometimes you have to try several places. There are always shortages.'

'There's nothing we need.'

Something made her look over at me. She smiled when she saw that I was watching her. 'I'm sorry you couldn't stay longer. We'll miss you. The house is going to be so quiet and I said to your father yesterday . . .'

'Are you all right, Mum? I mean, is everything all right?'

She was silent for a moment as though trying to make up her mind about something before speaking. 'I'm not supposed to worry, you see. Stress is not good for you. And this thing with your father and his politics . . . Well, he never listens to what I tell him anyway.'

'Who told you not to worry?'

'The doctor, Zaki al Hajj. You remember him – he took your appendix out when you were a child. He says it's all in the mind. Oh, it's too early to tell yet, but they were doing research. He showed me an article about Holland or somewhere, perhaps it was Sweden. Anyway. They are doing research into how stress can wear away your immune system.'

'Immunity against what?'

'It doesn't look like much, does it? Just a little lump. It's been there for years, and I never paid it any attention.' She turned her head to show me the lump at the base of her neck. 'Maybe it would be better if I didn't know.'

'Know what?'

'Whether it has spread to the inside, you see? Into the glands? Once it's done that there's not much you can do, really.'

'You've got cancer?'

'Melanoma, it's called, actually.'

'And you didn't tell me?'

'We wanted you to come here and have a holiday. And for Ellen and the baby to see where you lived.'

'Please, Mum, stop that. Just leave the jam alone and tell me.'

'No, no. I have to keep busy, you see. I have to keep myself occupied.' She lifted the sieve and began dragging the surface of the liquid. The room was thick with the cloying smell of sugar and fruit. It was a smell that would lodge in my senses and I would never eat another papaya again.

'They are doing tests, then?'

She nodded. 'I may have to go to England for treatment.'

I could hear the sound of Leo crying over on the other side of the house where our room was. Leo was crying in that insistent worrying manner which said he was alone and in need of something. I walked quickly across the yard. He had fallen and hurt his knee. Nothing serious. Ellen emerged from the shower rubbing her hair with a towel. 'Where were you?' she asked sharply, a reminder that we had not left all our problems behind us in England.

I looked at her for a moment, then I sat down and I said: 'I think my mother is dying.'

19

A journey can help to heal a rift, they say. In our case it was the opposite. After Ellen and I returned from the Sudan the gap between us seemed to be all the more apparent. I returned full of resolve and a new determination. I managed to do what I realised I had been wanting to do for a long time: write a book. It was stimulated no doubt by what I had seen on our holiday, or rather, what I had not seen. All those details locked away in my head suddenly came to the fore as I tried to find myself in the city I had grown up in and which was no longer there. I wrote it, I think, as a record, afraid that my memories would desert me as easily as the place I remembered had fled the world. I wrote it quickly, at night, when the house was quiet and Leo and Ellen were asleep upstairs. I sat at the kitchen table, opened up a cheap cardboard-backed notebook and began to write in silence. Perhaps it was the fact that Ellen and I no longer talked the way we used to, about anything and everything. It began as a kind of conversation with someone I felt I knew. Anyway, I filled one notebook after another in a state of feverish release. It would probably have gone no further than that had Allan Wycliffe not happened to pick it up in his usual nosy way and start leafing through it.

'What's this, then?' When I told him he gave me a wink. 'Might be able to sell this for you. What do you say to that?'

'Sell it how, to a publisher?'

'You never know your luck. Let me get it typed up for you and we'll see what we can do.' He held the notebook under his nose and grinned. 'I smell money.'

If he did, it was a very faint scent. But he did manage to find someone willing to publish it. I not only found a publisher, I actually won a prize: the Natchford Blanch Memorial Prize to be exact, for a first novel written by someone under the age of thirty-five (only just), 'whose work reflects the unique ethnic heritage of contemporary Britain'. Thankfully it didn't last long, all the hullabaloo. I was presented my award and given a nice dinner by the judges. Natchford Blanch was a wealthy eccentric who had died young, just before his thirty-fifth birthday, in fact. He had always dreamed of becoming a novelist and had indeed completed his masterpiece when his plane (he was a keen amateur pilot into the bargain) struck an electric pylon in the Bahamas and both man and manus were charred to a crisp. I later heard that there was some talk of suicide. He had been undergoing treatment for manic depression apparently and was on medication. He should not have been allowed near a pair of roller skates, let alone put behind the controls of a twin-engined Cessna. He left instructions about the prize in his will.

The book, *Tamarind Days*, came out, sold marginally and soon vanished from the shelves. I still wonder sometimes whether I imagined the whole thing.

Everything else, meanwhile, was falling apart all around us. A year went by and things between Ellen and me simply grew worse. A deep resentment grew in the house as it seemed to each of us that the other was becoming a hindrance, a burden that was the root cause of every frustration, every setback, every unpaid bill and bounced cheque that came our way. A long damp summer gave way to an even wetter autumn, which was followed by a frosty winter, complete with burst pipes, persistent bouts of influenza and a sprained wrist on my part from chopping wood. In early spring Allan Wycliffe called to say his days in romantic fiction were numbered. He was selling out. Breen Gaze Publications was over. He sounded despondent on the phone.

'This is silly really, getting all emotional. I mean, it's not as though I ever got into this business for anything but the money.'

'Independence.'

'There's that.'

'Satisfied customers.'

'Thousands of them. You're not making me feel any better, you know?'

'Sorry,' I said. 'I was only trying to be helpful.'

'We've been out-trashed, I'm afraid. Too many competitors on the market.'

'But how can that happen? I mean there are millions of people out there buying these things, hungry for the next instalment.' It took him a while to come out with it, but the truth of the matter was that he had been made an offer by a large conglomerate. It sounded like a generous offer, but Allan was not in a generous mood: 'Breaks my heart. I have had scores of middle-aged women weeping down the telephone at me all week.'

'Distraught readers?'

'Writers. They are all worried they will be axed by the new people.'

'So what will you do?'

'An associate of mine in the States has come up with an interesting offer in pictures, and I shall take it.' Allan sighed. 'The other day I was in London and the tube was delayed and a man on the tannoy said, very earnestly, "This delay is due to earlier cancellations." Earlier cancellations? Well, what caused them? I'm telling you, this country is finished, and I never thought I'd hear myself saying that. Everyone is treading water, looking for someone else to take the blame. No more. Give me Los Angeles, a swimming pool, an open convertible.'

'They have smog, Allan, and drive-by shooters on the Freeway. Everyone has bulletproof windscreens and advanced paranoia. You don't want that.'

But Allan didn't seem to think he had a choice, this was

the move of a lifetime. The chance to pursue a dream of himself as being louche, outrageous, irreverent – everything, in fact, that a middle-class boy from middle England was not.

So I was out of a job. Not that I minded no longer having to trawl through the cloying sweetness of romantic novels, all those horses and doctors and nurses glancing coyly at one another over the vital organs of a dying patient. It was around then that I was offered a job at the BBC. They had heard of Natchford Blanch and were looking for someone just like me. I took the job. Ellen and I would both be glad, I thought, of the space the new arrangement would give us. I would be away two nights a week. When it came to finding somewhere to stay Ellen suggested calling Dru, who was apparently spending a year in London to do research for her book. She had a spare sofa. I would be welcome, she said.

Ellen herself had in the meantime arrived at something of a watershed, the momentum for her doctorate was dying away. She still went through the motions and locked herself up for hours in her room, hard at work, or so it appeared. I was often surprised to find she wasn't actually in there when I looked. And she no longer carted great boxes of books to and fro from the library. The trips to interrogate her subjects in Birmingham had ceased too, and the conversations with her supervisor on the telephone were replaced by extended chats to her friends, the sound of laughter ricocheting through the house like a death sentence. I think that she herself truly believed she would somehow complete it, that the dedication would return. Any enquiry inevitably unleashed a torrent of fury.

'Since when have you taken an interest in my work?'

'Well, there was a time when we used to talk about it.'

'Why do you always insist on going back over that?' She was incredulous. 'You know as well as I do that you never really took me seriously.' She folded her arms and leaned against the counter. She looked paler than normal, our holiday a distant memory after the long winter, spring having only just sent its first shoots pulsing through the frosty ground. She wore a black polo-neck sweater. She had recently taken to wearing only black: trousers, turtlenecks, shirts, long coats – all black, and no make-up. Leo sat behind us at the table, spooning cornflakes into his mouth while pretending to read the adventures of a mole in a red cape on the back of the packet. His ears were tuned towards us though. All our conversations took place in the kitchen, it was the only place we had any chance of bumping into one another. We were now two strangers sharing a house, no longer the same bed – that business was long gone – even the physical intimacy of just sleeping next to one another was unbearable.

'I've always taken an interest.'

She snorted derisively, turning towards the kettle. 'You've always looked down on my work, on my field even. You think it's a joke.'

'I never said that. I never used those words.'

'But that's what you think.'

'Look, I've read Lévi-Strauss. I know about the Yanomani. I just have my doubts about this thing, this self-reflexive trend.'

'Oh, I see,' she nodded, blowing on her coffee. 'Suddenly you're an expert.'

'I'm not saying that. I'm just explaining that if you ever sensed some scepticism on my part, then that is where it comes from. You know what I mean – all these ethnographers jet off into the great unknown and have an experience, and suddenly, they're not students, they're poets and writers and they're describing their feelings of living like a native. That's travel writing, not academic study.'

'It's a more honest reflection of the interaction between observer and informant.'

'It's easier!'

'Stop shouting!'

We both turned to look at the breakfast table. Leo was staring furiously at the pool of milk, thumping a spoon against the bowl. He got down with a clatter and marched from the room.

'There you are,' Ellen said. 'Are you happy now?' She slammed her mug down on the counter and ran out after him. 'Leo! Leo!'

More worryingly, she began to go absent without warning or explanation. I would come home and find the house empty. She would come back late, Leo inexplicably staying with her parents. The last vestiges of family life had started to fall away.

'Well, what is she going to do?' a worried Claus quizzed me when we were left to ourselves one Sunday. This was the last of the rituals to go: lunch with her parents, and even that was a rarity. Once we gave up on that there really would be nothing left. They already had a good idea of what was going on. Ellen and her mother talked, but Claus seemed to have been left in the dark and now turned his hairy eyebrows to me for an explanation.

I was trying to balance a fidgety Leo on my knee. He kept climbing down to play with the cat that was hiding under the low coffee table and then jumping back up when she spat and clawed at his attempts to catch her tail.

'Leave her alone, Leo. She doesn't want you to do that.'

'But, Grandpa, she's lonely.'

'Cats don't get lonely,' Claus reasoned with his grandson.

'She says she might drop the Ph.D. and join an NGO,' I said.

'Do they pay well?'

'I didn't think they paid at all.' We frowned at one another as though each hoping that the other had the missing part of the puzzle.

'Then what?' He crouched forwards in his chair, eyes arched like twin tunnels boring into a rocky mountainside looking for an answer. I had no answers. He was her father, for goodness' sakes. He ought to have a better idea. I realised then that I had actually given up all hope of reconciliation. I didn't say this out loud. I carried on, telling him that everything was going to be all right.

'What about your job? Ellen says you've lost your job. What will you do?'

'Well, I've been thinking about the radio.'

'The radio?' His face grew even more stark with concern. Where was this topsy-turvy ride leading to? 'The radio. I see.'

'It's a programme on the World Service.'

'World Service. BBC.' He nodded, repeating the words to himself as they came up.

'An arts review programme. I would come up with ideas, do the research, and, eventually, if I liked it and everything went OK, I could even present a few things myself.'

'On the radio.' He sat back and flung his big hands out, causing the cat to let out a screech and bolt for the living room. 'That's wonderful,' he said, not very convincingly. When I first published my book he shook my hand and gave me a warning: 'Don't ever think you can make a living out of it.' It was understandable, I suppose, that he was worried about us, but it was disheartening how little faith he had.

'I would have to commute to London. Twice a week at least, maybe more.'

'Ah.' The brows drew together like darkening clouds.

'But still, it's something.'

'Yes, it certainly is something.' Like two men who have spent too much time bound together on a life-raft we had nothing more to say. He reached out a hand to ruffle Leo's hair.

'Lunch!' called Claire from within. We were saved.

Into the gathering storm flew my parents, who settled into the Royal Marsden Hospital in London. My mother had finally been persuaded to make the journey, and the tests had revealed a situation so bad that my father did not dare tell me the whole truth. She was immediately put on a treatment of chemotherapy, her body shot through with a stream of heavy metals, highly toxic substances which all but kill the patient in the process of trying to cleanse them. I rushed to see them as soon as he called.

'Why didn't you tell me you were coming?'

'We didn't want to worry you.'

'Why are you treating me like a stranger?'

'You're a grown boy, you have your own life.'

Was this some kind of punishment? Had I been excluded from the inner circle of my own family? Was this what he was telling me? I marched through the hallways looking for the right ward, trying to follow directions. I found my father at his gregarious best, standing in a corridor engaging all the nurses in conversation. A tall man, stiff with age, impeccably dressed in a dark suit and bright yellow tie. He saw me approaching and introduced me to the nurse standing next to him.

'Ah, here you are. Gwen, look who's come to see us.'

'Hello.' Gwen had a wide face and a smile that pushed her round cheeks up into dimples. There were others, coming and going, passing around us, nodding hello, smiling to my father.

'Everything all right?'

'Fine, thank you.'

'Anything I can get you?'

'You work far too hard, my dear, I am going to put in a good word for you.'

'Oh, don't do that, they'll think I'm carrying on with the patients.'

'English nurses,' he said as he turned to lead me away. 'The best in the world. They have to work so hard and the government treats them like dogs, but the work they do . . .' The biting of the lip and gentle shake of the head. 'If we could have had that training, that discipline, what a medical service we would have had.'

He was back on his old stalking ground among the good working people of England. Salt of the earth. These were the people who had put the great in Great Britain. 'Humour, they have humour. The English can laugh at everything, but in a gentle way.'

'Tell me about Mum.'

He steered me by the arm out through the electric doors, reaching for his Craven A as we went. The air outside was chilly and we crossed the street to stand in a small geometric aperture of warmth where the sun fell between the buildings.

'The doctor – you know him, he took your appendix out – well, he called me to his clinic personally and told me that in his view we should come here for tests. I told him that this was a difficult time and that if it could wait a month or so it would be much better for all of us. He said no. He said she ought to have gone months ago, but she refused. This was the first I heard of it. He said, do it now, don't delay. Time is of the essence. Well, you can imagine. Devastated. I was shocked. I went home. She dismissed the whole thing and said it was just the doctor, an old friend making a fuss about nothing. That's when I knew how serious it was. She is a brave woman, much braver than me, but she didn't want to face this. I went the next morning and arranged the tickets. There was no time to warn anyone.' Within three days of arriving the specialist announced that she would be admitted immediately for treatment.

'The National Health System?'

He looked smaller, shrunken somehow, more frail. 'She tried to persuade me years ago. She said private health insurance is the thing of the future. I wouldn't hear a word of it. I said, let me die in my bed rather than break down public health care.' He puffed at his cigarette in silence. 'Of course I thought I was being noble. I thought it would be me to go first.' With a shake of his head he dropped his cigarette and ground it out. 'The doctor is a nice man, very young, but he knows what he is talking about, no question about that. No question at all.'

'And what does he say?'

'They are making ground-breaking progress at this hospital. You wouldn't believe it. Reputation of absolute highest world order. Doctor Marsh, the specialist, says that there have been huge advances in this kind of treatment in recent years. Big advances.'

'But she's going to die anyway.'

He flinched. I saw his eyes blink. We walked back the way we had come.

'You always think you have time,' he said.

Back inside, the hospital seemed absurdly frivolous and noisy. There was a red balloon tied to the medication trolley. The orderlies called cheerfully to one another as they passed. An old man shuffled by, pushing an intravenous stand before him: the human organism stretched out on a coat stand of a crucifix draped with plastic tubing. The air was rich with a cloying mix of bodily fluids and boiled cauliflower.

The verve had gone out of my father. He raised a hand and a light laugh in reply to a greeting from Gwen — who was stuffing a pillowcase with firm muscular stabs, like a Tuscan baker kneading dough — but his heels were dragging. She fixed me with a long look.

'Is he all right?' she mouthed.

'Yes, I think so.' I nodded back, feeling intense gratitude for the hint of concern. My father was standing by an open doorway beckoning impatiently.

'Here he is now,' he said, ushering me in.

From a distance she did not look all that different. Her eyes were dark and her head covered by a colourful silk scarf. Her hands rested on the top of the bed covers, a plastic tube was taped to her wrist.

'Well, you've heard my bad news, I expect,' were her first words.

'How do you feel?' I was scared to go near her, to touch her.

'Tired.' She was brusque and matter of fact, rearranging the bedclothes as she spoke, always moving. Even now, even here. 'Very tired. There's no pain, though, the morphine takes care of that.'

As I moved around to sit by her side I was watching the expression on my father's face. One I had never seen before. A look of dull surprise, as though someone had just hit him in the face. The spirit shifting shape. I thought of the golf ball and how the world seemed to turn in such skewed circles.

She had obviously taken some time to get herself ready for my visit. I was not supposed to see the make-up she had put on her cheeks, but it only emphasised the absence of natural colour in her skin. I had never thought of my mother as being a particularly vain person, but here, at the very edge of her existence, where the last vestiges of light were draining from her, she needed something. It was a sham, like face paint on a clown, a mockery of her former vivacity and appetite for life.

I sat with her as she drifted in and out of sleep. She could hardly keep her eyes open for longer than a few minutes. In sleep her face remained troubled, she would start, frown, mumble, but for a few brief moments a calm repose would return to her face, and she would snore lightly with careless abandon.

And so it went. He would stay there all day. I would join him as soon as I could. I was worried about him at first, tried to encourage him to do something else. But he just looked at me as though I were an idiot. I was underestimating his ability to make himself at home anywhere. He had been doing it all his life. He made friends easily with the other patients on the ward, wandered up and down, fetched them newspapers and bars of chocolate, cups of tea, sat with them and listened. I imagined people getting upset with this bothersome old man who kept chatting away, but in that frail, tenuous condition where the final outrage that is death has become urgently real, there were no barriers. And he was, ever the journalist, a good listener. He was a miracle worker, wandering about administering his healing.

'A really interesting man,' he would tell me and launch off into the life story of someone down the hall, or in the next ward whom he had discovered was the author of a great invention, or had once travelled the world on a bicycle, or a woman whose father was once stationed in Juba. He extracted all of these vivid lives from the frail and dying figures around us, their faces drawn and pale, their waning eyes lighting up for a brief moment as their lives were given meaning again. And what did they make of him, I wondered? With his funny accent and his bizarre ties. It didn't really matter. Everything had been stripped away, as life itself was being slowly drained from their bodies, all that was left was the urgent need to convey, to have someone to listen.

'He's a right character, your dad,' said Gwen one evening. 'Everybody loves having him here. He really cheers up the place.'

I felt a moment of pride, as I watched him walking down the hall, stopping to lean over an ancient woman sitting in an armchair by a door for a few words. He could lose himself in that tumult of lives and half-finished stories. But underneath it all he was scared. The driving force behind that loquaciousness, that endless reel of witty anecdotes was the simple fear of being left alone in the world.

One day I arrived at the hospital to find him pacing the hall in agitation. 'We must find your brother,' he said, standing up as soon as he saw me coming along the corridor. He didn't bother with a greeting. There had been a deterioration.

'Muk, but how?' I hardly knew where he was, had not heard from him for months. He wasn't listening to me. Instead he reached into his pocket and from his wallet extracted a pink slip of paper on which he had scrawled in that slanted higgledy-piggledy script of his that seemed to have no idea of left or right, but bobbed up and down like the graph of a heartbeat. His Arabic script, in contrast, was always neat and straight.

'Go and find him,' he said, handing me the slip. 'It's time.'

20

Dru and Leo are spending a lot of time together. She is teaching him how to ride. The chestnut horse we spied on the other side of the meadow the day we arrived turned out, on closer inspection, to be rather an old thing named, as it happens, Napoleon. He lumbers round only after a good deal of prodding on Dru's part. But as far as Leo is concerned this is a horse comparable to the great steeds of all-time adventure and he promptly renames him. He kicks his heels in avidly and 'Thunder' gamely plods a few more paces.

I sit on the terrace in the afternoons and watch him draw. An occasional breeze excites the slender green vines overhead and rustles the pages of the book that I am trying, without success, to read. The weather has grown even warmer. It is not unpleasant, this heat; it sinks into my body with pleasurable familiarity and settles in the meadow alongside us. It seems unusual for September.

Haya has left us. The night before she went we were all in high spirits, perhaps too high. Lucien had been in fine form, regaling us with dish after dish and hilarious anecdotes. We had eaten an excellent meal and sat out on the terrace until three in the morning talking and laughing. When we finally broke up and the plates and bottles had been piled up in the kitchen to wait for daylight we made our way upstairs. Haya was ahead of me. The others were elsewhere. We were alone. She stumbled and I put out a hand to catch her and suddenly she was in my arms. She stayed there a moment and then pulled herself away.

'What a strange person you are,' she said, holding me at arm's length.

'Why do you say that?' The dark eyes, the jagged interruption on the tip of her chin, the nose bent out of shape by the back of a brutish hand. A face that spoke of endurance and of kingdoms lost in the sand.

'Because everybody else here, even Leo, we all know what we are doing here, but not you.'

'I know where I am.' I tightened my arm around her waist.

She laughed lightly. She was standing barefoot on the step above me in a pair of flimsy shorts and a halter top. Her hair was pinned back, lifted away from her long slender neck. Without the make-up, without the leather jackets and the leopard skin pants, she was just a girl.

'So you think it was a good idea I had to join your caravan?'

'You seem to be enjoying yourself.'

She nodded, but her mood had changed.

'How long would it be before you got tired of me? We come from different parts of the same continent, but that doesn't mean the earth we walk is the same. You have your friends, your son, your life. I have mine.'

'Is it so different?' I asked.

'When he was talking before, Lucien, about his trip to Africa . . .'

'Look, it doesn't matter. Lucien is like that, he talks about the things he has seen with a lot of passion. I thought you liked him.'

'Sure, he makes me laugh. Great. But he spends his life studying people in places far away, and then he comes back here and talks about them. And while he was talking, I was thinking. Maybe he would have liked me to stay where I come from.'

'I don't think he sees it like that.'

'I tell you, in his world I belong on my knees in the desert churning milk in a goatskin.' Lucien had talked about his

222

recent trip to Mali, about the customs and beliefs of the Dogon people. 'Think about it, if you offered them this life, you think they would say no? They want televisions and video cameras and all the things he has. All the things that make him superior to them.'

'Why are we talking about Lucien?'

'Because you belong with them, not with me. How far do you think we would get with all the clever thoughts in your head? Are we going to eat those books you have in the back of the car? No, I have made enough mistakes to know I don't want to make any more.'

Haya looked down at me for a moment. She lifted my chin and put her lips softly to mine. Then she turned and was gone. The following morning she asked Lucien to drive her into town where she could catch a bus to Aix. She was restored to her former self, with miniskirt, boots and sunglasses all in place.

'I'm sorry you're going,' I said, when we had a moment. 'I'd like you to stay.'

'I have nothing to say to your friends. I don't have the words.' Now that she had made up her mind, she was impatient to leave.

'And, François, does he understand you?' François was her benefactor, her sugar daddy. They had met when he was a judge in Paris. Now he was retired and lived in a big house outside Aix-en-Provence with only a housekeeper for company. He spoiled her when she stayed with him. He took her to fancy restaurants, bought her fine dresses to wear. It was like being a princess while it lasted, which was sometimes a week, but never more. Then she would go back to Paris and wait and a few months later he would call and ask her when she was coming down again.

'He gives me what I need.' The way she said this seemed to imply more than one kind of pleasure. I was flattered she was trying to make me feel jealous. She stood up on her tiptoes to kiss me goodbye. I smelt her skin, freshly soaped and lightly perspiring. 'You will never know what you missed,' she whispered, giving me a wink, as she slipped her glasses back on. Then she was walking out into the sunlight, a slender waif, silhouetted against the doorway, off to take care of the world.

Haya's departure only underlines the temporary nature of our presence here. It reminds me of my discomfort in Lucien's presence. When he offered to drive her all the way to Aix, I was relieved. I am not sure how much Dru told him. She says everything, but I am not sure how much everything is. She said that she went through the abortion alone. As soon as she told Lucien whatever she told him, he left for the Bolivian highlands and stayed there for three months.

'I had no idea if I would ever see him again. I lived in the flat in Paris, but I heard nothing from him in all that time, not one letter. I called his father every week to find out whether he was still alive, but I had no idea what to expect. Then one day he just turned up again and it was all forgotten. It was as if nothing had ever happened.'

I am humbled by this man's capacity for forgiveness. It makes me feel small and shallow. This is the absolution of a saint, the generous understanding of a *wali*. The calibre of sage men and prophets. I slept with his wife, and here I am on his terrace, eating ravioli he has prepared with his own hands. I am fairly certain that I would not have been able to do the same in his place. In fact I know I wouldn't.

But I am sleeping better these days. Leo and I go for long walks in the hills, looking at rocks and plants and examining the tracks for signs of wildlife. Other days we meander down the stony path to the village. We trail around looking at the curiosities displayed in the shop windows: strange instruments to press garlic or shred lemons, and tin jugs with long spouts that come in thirty different sizes to pour your olive oil with. We examine folding knives and alarm clocks and hacksaws and plastic flowers and all manner of everyday objects that are interesting simply because they are different. Tools to take charge of your life. We go to the butcher's shop and watch him cutting up the lamb chops with an electric saw, or burning the feathers off a chicken with a blow torch like the kind you use for taking paint off a doorframe. It is all a far cry from the cellophane packets of the supermarket we are used to. There is even a tiny cinema in the village. Walking past it has become a ritual. We study the posters stuck behind iron grilles and try to guess the story of the film.

We always end up by the pond in the village square and Leo rushes over to stick his head under the thick brass tap of the water fountain to cool himself down. Then we retire to the café and I try to read the newspaper and drink my coffee while Leo wanders around looking for anything of interest. He can spend hours examining leaves, trapping lizards, or watching a trail of ants crawl up a wall. Finally, we pick up the shopping bag and start back up the path to the house.

After lunch Lucien and Dru disappear upstairs and the house acquires a certain sacred quality to it. I refuse to climb the stairs in the afternoon, even though our bedroom is at the other end of the house to theirs. I don't even like to hear them talking together in private. I prefer the terrace, which is common ground. So we spend the afternoons there; Leo drawing, and me dozing off while pretending to read. I still have the old canvas holdall full of books to occupy me.

'Do we really need to take all of those?' was Ellen's reaction when we were packing for the trip to Denmark.

'I need them.'

'Why?'

Why? For over a year we had been sinking towards the benthic depths beyond which all hope of being reached by sunlight was nil. We didn't even argue any more. We had stopped talking because anything more than an exchange of two syllables would invariably lead to war.

The books themselves were unremarkable. No first editions, no autographed copies. No antique irreplaceable gems. They were mostly old faded paperback editions of novels that I had read during my adolescence. Books that contained memories, not within their pages, but in remembering the time I was curled up on our back veranda at home, on that hard wooden sofa with the orange cushions that always smelled of dust, turning the yellowed pages for the first time. Many of them had once belonged to my parents. They had old prices on the back in shillings and pence, or inky stamps on the title page that gave the price in piastres: '*Nile Bookshop* – *35 pt.*'. Those faded covers spelt another era; the paper was brittle with age and it cracked and flaked like dry skin if you weren't careful. It was an odd assortment; *Lord Jim* with a picture on the front of Peter O'Toole, although I had never seen the film; *The Alexandria Quartet* by Lawrence Durrell, a novel which I carried with me only because I felt compelled to try and read the whole thing through in one go; a number of old Penguins, including Moravia's *The Conformist*, and Iris Murdoch's *The Sea, the Sea*. There were books by Kafka, Carpentier and also Camus, who I learn is buried nearby here in Lourmarin. Nothing of real worth. Nothing, indeed, to raise them from the level of well-thumbed, broken-backed, torn-paged, cheap and easy editions from half a century ago. This, however, was somehow significant to me. This ordinariness. It symbolised the kind of world into which I had been born – one in which our emotional attachments were hung on commonplace objects, things that to anyone else would have appeared quite worthless. The entire world was crowded with worthless objects invested with sentimental value. Our humanity was hung on the peg of a tide of useless junk.

But I have trouble concentrating today and am making little headway with *The Fall*, so instead I sit and watch Leo busy with his drawing. The big rough table is littered with paper and packets of crayons. He takes his time selecting precisely the one he is looking for. Colourful meanderings halted abruptly, abandoned for no apparent reason, for not fulfilling their author's purpose – the depiction of some shape or form he is trying to coax from the corners of his imagination.

The light, drained of its ferocity, slides up the wall of the house as afternoon folds into evening. The mottled plaster creates areas of light and dark which provide a semblance of character. In places it swells into blisters where rainwater has run down the brickwork underneath. Cracks spin spidery courses across the ravaged face. The wall resembles the map of a distant undiscovered country. When you lean back in one of the wicker chairs, the bumps become hills, the fissures rivers, the patchy white areas clouds drifting across a silent landscape.

Towards the end my mother began to talk to people she imagined were in the room with her. Her head would stir and she would begin talking about something that happened twenty years ago as though it were happening now, her voice by turn warm and then fierce as emotions from her past returned to her: 'Where on earth did she get that dress? It's so shoddy!' Time had begun to weave itself into spirals around her. She had begun to move freely between past and present, carried on a stream of morphine. It was as though her whole life were being played out at high speed. 'I think I shall ask for the bill, and then we can go.' And now she, too, is gone. Descended into silence. Tolerating, with that fathomless patience of hers, the noisy bypass, the hurtling traffic, the spinning electromagnetic waves from the high-tension pylons running overhead. A parody of a graveyard on a windy stretch of no man's land outside London. Where is the silent hill, the raindrops fresh on the rose petals? Gone, or else it never was. The one person to whom everything in your life is meant to make sense – your mother. Nobody else understood quite the way she did, no one ever would. She was the measure of the world, the good, the bad, and never indifferent. How to make sense of the world without a point of reference?

It is like the patterns of light and shadow on the wall of the house we sit beside: from a distance a complete landscape, but under closer examination simply chipped plaster and cracked brickwork. My life is a mosaic of juxtaposed opposites, fragments, flinty chips, all fitted together in such a way that it is only from afar that any kind of cohesion is discernible. Close up none of it makes much sense. Is that why I have been clinging to Ellen all these years, never wanting to let go? Without her I am afraid I shall make no sense — I will have lost all coherence.

Leo continues to work on, head bowed over the table and the sheet of paper. He saws away with an eraser. He adds lines, removes edges, gradually closing in on something in that blank sheet of paper, something which only he can see. This absorption is remarkable to watch. I have noticed how he refuses to give up when he is concentrating like this and so I let him go on, even if it is long after his bedtime. I sit there and watch him drawing and I think to myself: it's OK, he's going to be all right. He has something to guide him through life, an indestructible element.

He sits up and notices that I am watching him. He holds up the paper to show me a purple dinosaur.

21

All I had to go on was the slip of paper my father handed me in the hospital upon which was scrawled an unfamiliar address in North London. I hadn't seek Muk for ages. It was separation by mutual agreement. A muted interlude, a silence demanded by both sides. I assumed that when he had settled down, found himself again in this new life, this new country, we would resume where we had left off. But it never happened.

In the years after I left home I somehow imagined that things at home would remain as they had always been. That there would always be a home to come back to. Mum and Dad would always be there; the house would still be falling down in its own way; Haboba and her little bands of 'aunts' would be crouching over a charcoal stove frying discs of golden aubergine. I envisaged Muk and Yasmina, frozen in time, standing hand in hand in shorts and plaid skirt, just the way I remembered them.

None of that really squared with leather jackets and twanging guitars. Muk, it turned out, had something quite different in mind, determined to escape my fantasies. The first indication I got of this metamorphosis was when I arrived home one evening from a dreary day at the *Daily Crow* to find I had a visitation. The entrance to the old house in Hunters Bar was blocked: oddly shaped pods were docked like parts of an errant Russian space station that spread across the worn carpet and up the staircase towards my flat. On closer inspection these turned out to be instrument cases. Whose instrument cases? I myself had no musical talent, no musical friends of any kind. I had steered clear ever since that fateful day when my mother turned to a friend of hers who had kindly offered tuition – I was five at the time – and said: 'No amount of lessons would ever work with this lot. None of my children has the least musical talent. They're like me, tone deaf.' I have had an irrational dislike of musicians ever since.

I fought my way up the stairs and into my flat to find it strewn with a number of strangers wearing bizarre hairstyles and jangling earrings. Out of the dense cloud of smoke that now enveloped the middle of my home a figure arose. One of the druids was speaking to me.

'Oh, there you are! Hey everyone, it's my brother.'

There were heavy 'heys' and nods all round and several grunts and even a few smiles along with one or two glazed uncomprehending stares. Muk had risen to his feet from among the disciples. He looked taller and thinner than the last time I saw him. His hair had been shaved close to his head except for a kind of tail that hung down his neck, where it had been plaited with what looked like the feathers of a dead bird dipped in blood.

'How did you get in?'

'The landlord let us in. Nice guy.'

'What are you doing here?'

'We've got a gig, man!'

'A what?'

I took another look around the lost tribe. They did resemble a parody of what a rock band was supposed to look like. Where had he found them? I wondered. I led him to the kitchen and expelled something that was foraging through my refrigerator before closing the door.

'What happened to the telephone?'

'Oh, yeah . . . well, I lost the number.'

What had happened? If someone told me this creature was the lead actor in *Jesus Christ Superstar*, I would have believed them. But my brother? Where were the flares, the out-of-synch, peasant-from-the-sticks look that I had taken so long to grow out of? Me, the Man For All Seasons, learning that you needed a set of winter clothes for this new life. Trudging through snowdrifts in thin-soled tennis shoes, wondering how people lived with no feeling in their toes. It took me years to learn how to adapt. How did he manage this transformation so quickly?

He put his arms around me and hugged me to him. 'It's good to see you, man, really.' He even had a scruffy beard and two big earrings like a pirate.

'OK, they can stay, but I don't want any trouble.'

'Don't worry.' He lit a cigarette and smiled, 'I think you're going to like this.'

The gig was in a basement club so small and dark I hadn't even heard of the street it was on and Sheffield just wasn't that big. I remember I kept walking into the walls that were painted matt black, the lights were ordinary bulbs painted red and blue, the conveniences were mixed; men and women equally bent double, vomiting into the toilet bowls. The music was so loud you couldn't actually distinguish any notes. It was just an electric rush, like being caught in a storm. Perhaps Mum had been right after all. I had known that Muk owned a guitar. I could just never recall having heard him play anything all the way through. He would strum a few bars, lose the tune, stop, start another song, play a few bars, then stop again. My father always claimed that he had been a promising *oud* player as a young man, but the instrument never came down from the top of a wardrobe where it was gathering dust. Muk was apparently determined to bravely carry on the elusive family musical tradition, although the discordant playing suggested that he still hadn't quite shaken off his old habit of changing tunes in mid-flight.

After that I saw Muk only sporadically. He would call from one part of the country or another and I imagined this was all part of the business. I expected to find his face on the cover of a Sunday supplement: 'Kid from Back of Beyond Finds Rock Fame'. For a time he did actually do a fairly convincing job of making us believe he was, of all things, a rising pop star.

When Leo was still a toddler, Muk used to come and visit us at the cottage. Always in a hurry, on his way to or from some event of great importance. There would be no warning, just a call from a telephone box asking to be picked up from so and so station at such and such a time. Ellen objected. I objected. We said nothing. It never went well. He was restless, used to stay awake all night smoking and watching television. I had visions of a cigarette tumbling from his fingers in the early hours and the sofa catching light while he dozed away, the television blaring out some horror film from the nineteen-fifties while smoke crept stealthily up the stairs.

He would slouch around the kitchen listlessly, saying how much he enjoyed talking to me, but would never really say anything. Monosyllabic replies to requests for news about his life, about his plans. He changed jobs with such unpredictability it was as though he were afraid of missing out on any life-enriching experience on offer, no matter how minor: selling second-hand office equipment or shifting army surplus clothing in a warehouse with a forklift truck, or being quality-control manager on a video-duplication production line. He had all the drive and ambition of a somnambulist, sleepwalking through his own life.

The dreams of rock and roll stardom had been finally shelved. They remained in that shoebox in his head marked 'IF ONLY'. He hadn't sold out Wembley Arena. He hadn't even made a demo record. He came and went without ever giving any real idea of what was going on in his mind. He seemed to be waiting for something, as though one day someone would simply come up to him in the street and tap him on the shoulder and his problems would be solved. Perhaps it was celebrity he was waiting for, perhaps it was inspiration of some kind. In either case, our banal ordinary lives, our washing up and shopping and changing baby and that whole marital dirge, man, were pathetic to him. He would slouch around the house in a daze, leaving a trail of cigarette butts for Leo to munch away at, for forty hours or so and then give a yawn, lift up his rucksack, which often lay untouched by the front door where he had dropped it on his way in, and announce that he had to catch a bus. Eventually the occasional visits trickled out to nothing. He called after that, less and less often. I had a number but it had been disconnected.

'I move around a lot,' he would say.

'Have you thought about going back?'

'Hey, I just got here,' peering at his watch to make sure that a day and a night had not skipped him by unnoticed.

'No, I mean home, home. Back to live with Mum and Dad. You had a life then. You had friends.'

'Oh, home.' Nodding, jaw suddenly jutting out of place. 'No, no, there's nothing there for me.' He widened his eyes as though explaining something to an idiot. 'What am I going to go back with? I have nothing to show. No money, no wife, no family, no fancy car. Just me. Look at me. Send me packing back to the farm, eh? You'd like that, would you? Old muggins, the village idiot, out tending the sheep while big brother is living it up abroad.' His face took on a lopsided unbalanced look that resembled a sneer, an undigested grudge, something that he had been carrying about, festering inside him for years: 'You don't know how much you hurt them by leaving.'

'Who? Hurt who?'

'You know who. Dad said you had turned your back on him, on the country, on all of us. He never forgave you for that.'

'Everybody leaves home.'

'No. You were the eldest. The firstborn son.' He shook his head and pointed his smoking finger at me. 'You really hurt him.'

And so I found myself in Finsbury Park, squinting at an address on a slip of pink paper. A dreary building on a forgotten street, lined with cars that nobody could be bothered to tow away. Windows boarded up, broken bottles, cans of spray paint and lighter fuel kicking about. I walked up the steps and rang the bell, half hoping no one would answer. No one did. There was no name on the name plate, the glass was as murky as algae. Nothing moved inside. One of the windows was boarded up with plywood. It didn't look like anyone had lived there for a long time. I stepped back down to the street and stood there for a time. I was about to go on my way, duty done, when a man walked by. A black guy dressed in plastic waterproofs, flame-red trousers that flared out from his legs like riding chaps and a jacket that billowed off his back like a cape. His hair was beaded and braided and he carried a motorcycle helmet which had a sticker on one side with the words 'Snap On'. He slowed down when he saw me, flexing his knees and frowning. At first I took it as a menacing look, and then I realised what he had seen.

'Hey, hold on, wait a minute.'

His beads flew as he turned, rapping two fingers slowly to his chest, like a diver signalling deep underwater. 'You talking to me?' He was younger than he looked from a distance. The skin on his face was blemished by acne.

'I'm looking for my brother.'

'How's that?' Now he took his time to look me up and down. 'Do I look like your tribe?' He clicked his tongue impatiently and made to move on. I was certain that he had mistaken me for Muk when he first saw me. We don't exactly look alike, but it would be difficult to deny any family resemblance at all. I pointed at the building behind him.

'Taller than me, thinner, used to live here.'

'What is this, *Crimewatch*?' He looked over his shoulder as though expecting to see a television crew hiding somewhere behind a burned-out ice cream van.

'He used to have a band.'

'What kind of music?'

234

He had me there. 'I don't know.' I shrugged. 'Loud.'

'Your own brother, and you don't know what kind of music he play?' He sniffed and stepped back as though he had just caught a whiff of something that had died. 'No, man, I don't buy that.'

'But you do know him.'

'Do I?' He gave me a quizzical look worthy of a showman.

'He lives here, look.' I showed him the address I had. After examining the paper and my father's scrawled handwriting for a moment he looked up at the house as though he had just noticed it standing there. He seemed to be making up his mind.

'No longer, man.' He shook his head firmly. 'He's gone central.' He turned as if to go. I followed alongside him.

'Central?'

'West one. Central.'

'You know where exactly?'

He stopped walking to glare at me. 'I look like Moses, maybe? Gathering lost sheep in the wilderness?' He was shifting his helmet from one hand to the other. We had reached a much-dented Yamaha with a cracked headlight. The seat was patched with the same gaffer tape that had been used to repair his jacket. I guessed he was a despatch rider, or office messenger. A car rolled up to the kerb. For some reason, I have no real idea why, we both walked over. Three black men were sitting inside. It looked as though the car were powered by sound the way it reverberated with music. My courier friend leaned in the window. He said something I couldn't catch and then straightened up to face me.

'This his bruvver, innit.'

All three occupants immediately descended from the car. They were all different sizes. One short and messy in an overweight, baggy trousers and pimples sort of way, the next tall, hollow-cheeked and silent, and the third man, the leader, neat and muscular with a shaven head. He examined me as if I might have crawled out from beneath something.

'I'm looking for my brother. Do you know him?'

He put his hand to his crotch and said, 'I might do.'

'Look, I don't know about anything between you and him, all right?'

'I didn't say there was anything between us.' He turned to the others. 'Did I say there was anything between us?' Solemn shaking of heads all round. 'Did I even say I knew him?' More shakes. They looked as though I had just kicked their dog and ought to be considering paying.

'Brother seeking brother,' nodded the leader sagely. 'Sometimes you don't find what you're looking for.'

'My mother . . . his mother, is very ill. I have to find him.'

Mothers are the universal leveller among men. Walk into the hardest, meanest bar in the world and tell them your mother is dying and you will see grown men quake, choke back tears, wipe their eyes and show you a tattoo on their biceps that reads 'Mum'. After that those people would go into a burning building to pull you out with their bare hands. Friends for life. The Shaven-Headed One scratched his chin and consulted the others silently. They shrugged, this time presumably giving their consent. He stabbed a finger at my chest. 'All right, here it is. He *was* here. But he went downtown, and he can stay there. We don't want him back here, that much you can tell him from me.' He was moving back round the car. Doors were opening and slamming. Just as he got into the car he called out the name of a café in Berwick Street.

'He ain't heavy, man,' chimed the fat one, leaning out the back window to point his gun-finger at me as the car slid by, 'he's your brother.' The aqueous thrum of the stereo floated away down the road; the viscous sound of something bubbling away slow, dull and deep down.

In Berwick Street the stall keepers yell out like real Cockneys, even if they were born in Budapest, or Banjaluka. The street affects its inhabitants with a sense of loyalty, whether you are a hairstylist from Naples or a butcher from

236

Kabul. Tourists rub shoulders with pole dancers and 'models' who are nicotine-thin and pale as cellophane, or struggling with the weight problems of a sack of cantaloupes strapped inside stretch pants and bulging leather. 'Hello, dear,' they call from their spangled red booths. 'Live show, sir?' It has its own sad glamour, of the poky little crevices of human need, despair and solitary practices. The tourists come to gawp, and to walk away. I was here to find someone who had stayed.

I found the place I was looking for, pressed in behind a row of itinerant market stalls stacked with cheap jewellery, joss sticks, yin/yang carvings and dreamcatchers to protect your fragile soul. There were sellotaped boxes of vinyl records, old jeans and printed scarves fluttered from crocodile clips, along with hairdryers, camouflage netting, and steel-toe-capped boots. The air, damp with spidery rain, vibrated to a heavy bass line and idle chatter. The street was littered with spongy cardboard and foam chips. People wandered by munching sandwiches clutched in grubby hands, while the traders huddled under plastic sheeting, shuffling their feet to keep warm, blowing steam on styrofoam cups clutched in mittened fingers. And somewhere among all this was the thread of our story. We were part of the parade.

The café was the old-fashioned kind that had not yet succumbed to the franchising boom. The only thing you could be sure of in a place like this was that the coffee probably tasted like boiled toenails. The interior had been painted a bright tomato red and avocado green, which only made it look more forlorn. I sat there for three hours while the radio played the same songs over and over again. I read the newspaper and discovered that my old boss, Harvey Greenbow, had been accused of sexual harassment and was being asked to step down from his post as local councillor. 'A Devious Man for Devious Times', ran the headline.

I was right about the coffee, it was undrinkable, but then so was the tea, I later discovered. I went to the door from time to time to look out. The sky darkened, people shook the rain from their coats as they came in. The man behind the counter spoke in an accent I could not distinguish. In idle moments he watched me out of the corner of his eye. I went for a walk around the block and came back again. People were eating lunch. Somebody discovered a blonde hair in their lasagne. The guy behind the counter went to the kitchen door and started yelling in what might have been Serbo-Croat. By five o'clock I was bored out of my mind and couldn't bear another minute in there. The day had been a waste of time. I dropped a tip in the old margarine tub on the counter, and stepped gratefully out into the street. The lights were coming on and it looked as though it might rain again. I was glad that Muk had not turned up, I decided, as I began walking quickly in the direction of the tube station.

A tall, hunched figure with his hands in his pockets was walking towards me. He was close to the wall on the other side of the street. Something prevented me from calling out. Instead, I turned and began to follow him at a distance. The café where I had spent the day he passed by without even a glance. At the end of the street he crossed over the road and turned left, then right. I hurried forward and caught a glimpse of him entering a green doorway at the top of a narrow alleyway. I waited across the street. A light came on after a time on the third floor. I walked over and found that there were not one, but three buzzers marked '3rd'. I picked one and leaned on it. A voice erupted into abuse, some of which might have been English, and then it went dead. I tried the next two together. This time after a long pause a voice came on, deeper than I recalled, but nevertheless . . .

'Muk, is that you?'

'Yeah, who is this? Hello . . . Yasin, is that you?'

There was a long silence. After a long while the sound of a buzzer unlocked the door. I stepped into a narrow corridor heaped with rolled-up carpet, buckets of paint and a bicycle with a wheel missing. I walked up the creaking stairs. None of the doors had names on them. I waited while a series of locks and chains were undone; finally the door opened a crack and Muk looked me over.

'Hi.'

The final chain came off and I stepped inside. He remained standing by the door.

'How did you find me?'

'Some friends of yours in Finsbury Park.'

'Friends?' He looked taller and more gaunt than I remembered and there was something about his face, something which had stiffened as though the register of emotions had been reduced. His expression darkened as he stepped forwards into the room. 'They gave you this address?' he asked. I looked around while he put the kettle on. It was a small place, one room with a kitchenette and adjoining bathroom.

'Not exactly. Well, maybe not friends, then. But they seemed to know you.'

'Right,' he said, as he unscrewed the jar of instant coffee. 'Right. Coffee?'

'No, thanks.' I had had enough warm beverages to last me a week, and besides, I didn't like the look of the kitchen, with its heaps of unwashed plates and mugs in the sink. I didn't like the look of any of this.

'Where have you been, Muk? What have you been doing?'

He remained with his back to me, going through the collection of milk cartons arrayed on the counter, sniffing their contents and then putting them aside. It looked as though he was collecting them, or doing a school experiment. He finally turned up a tin of what looked like powdered milk and spooned it in.

'Nothing much,' he said. 'Everything is just . . . fine.' He smiled, or tried to. The result looked strained and showed his teeth were in a bad way: one eye tooth was missing and the rest were the colour of burnt molasses.

'So, to what do I owe this honour?' He was stirring his coffee, trying to sound a breezy note. I was suddenly unsure about what I was doing here. I could feel an awful hand clutching at the pit of my stomach.

'You've been keeping yourself to yourself. Where have you been hiding?'

'I'm not hiding. I'm right here.'

'I didn't exactly get an invitation.'

'You found the place, didn't you?'

I stirred the heap of magazines on the table, along with the packets of tobacco and torn-up Rizlas. I picked one up. 'Still keeping in on the music branch, then?'

'Fuck off.' He hadn't moved from the kitchenette, but the tension was visible in him now. I thought he might throw the mug at me. Instead, he turned away from me towards the wall. I looked out of the window for a while.

'This is what you wanted? For us to come and find you?'

'Dad knows where I am.'

'No.' I shook my head. 'He doesn't. He gave me the address in Finsbury Park.'

'He knows.' Muk sipped his coffee, stared at the mug on the counter. We stood there for a long time. There didn't seem to be much more for us to say. Then the intercom buzzed. Two short and one long, which sounded like a signal. Muk went over and spoke in a low voice: 'Yeah, no. Not right now, OK? Come back in half an hour.' He hung up and turned around, but I was ready to go. I'd seen enough.

'Five minutes, you should have said.'

'You're going? Already?' His smile was thin and mean, as though this was what he had expected all along, a token effort. I was part of the hypocrisy and indifference which had delivered him here, to this room, to this life. He sat up on the window sill, feet on the chair. The furniture didn't look too bad. Grimy with dirt, but not too bad.

'There's nothing more for me here. I'll leave you to get back to your clients.'

'Ah,' He laughed softly, his lip curling upwards. 'You really think you're some kind of genius, don't you?' I waited but I didn't expect what was coming. 'I read your book, you know.'

'Another ecstatic fan.' I went back to examining the room, the overflowing ashtrays, the newspapers, the heap of clothes, that rancid smell that made you wonder if there was a dead rodent stuck under the floorboards. The heap of paperbacks on his favourite subjects: alien abductions, gangland bosses, serial killers who took their victims to pieces with gardening shears and other household appliances. Diversionary interests. I was looking for bits of silver foil, burned spoons, syringes.

'Don't you want to know?'

'Know what?'

'What I thought of it?'

He had been waiting for this moment, I realised, for some time.

I took a deep breath. 'What did you think of it?'

'Shallow.'

'One word? That's all you can spare?'

'I expected more from you.'

'How did this happen? What are you on? How long has it been?'

'Don't start that. You think you're better than me?' He placed his mug safely on the counter beside him, which I was glad to see, and folded his arms. 'I'm no worse than people who drink. Look out the window and see them all throwing up. This country is filthy with people puking their guts out. It's disgusting.'

'What is it – heroin, cocaine, crack? I don't even know the names of these things.'

He made an impatient sound.

'What?' I asked. 'It's a waste of time talking to me?'

'Your whole life has been a walk in the park. You don't have any idea about pain. About real pain.'

'Tell me, then. Tell me about this pain that makes you want to throw your life away.'

He snorted. 'What's the point?'

What was the point of any of it, I no longer knew. He was in a place where nothing mattered any longer, not family, not friends, not even his own future – all had ceased to have meaning. I had no chance of reaching him. And there was something else. This was something to do with us, him and me. The family in whose matrix he now saw his fate as being the fall guy in a conspiracy. We put him here. We stuck the needle in his arm, or may as well have done.

I remembered the sight of him that night, years ago, outside the Blue Nile cinema, running ahead of the car down the river road. A little boy caught in the bouncing headlights, looking for a place to hide in the dark. Now he had found his way in life, or rather, life had found its way to pin him down. The world does not stand by, it does not leave you floating freely. It comes after you. It struck me that perhaps he had always been addicted to the idea of being above it all, clear of all the complex lies and deceit society uses to maintain itself. He thought the world owed him something when really it was indifferent, as it is to all of our endeavours. So now redemption held no attraction to him because he was beyond caring. The earth would freeze over and burn out. We live with the knowledge of our complicity. We tuck into three square meals a day knowing people are starving to death elsewhere on the planet. In Darfur, a child can be sold into slavery for less money than it takes to buy a pair of tennis shoes in Paris. They are sold for safekeeping, not for profit. There are earthquakes, tidal waves, freak ice storms, paedophile rings, oil spills and all kinds of toxic pollution, an expanding hole in the ozone layer that increases the incidence of skin cancer and so on and so forth. In all these things he saw not a reason to go on, but a reason not to.

In the doorway I paused, unable to walk out, for some reason.

'What are you going to do? I mean, where does this lead?'

A slight choking sound that might have been a laugh. 'Lighten up,' he said. 'You take things so seriously. I'm fine. Things are fine. Everything's OK.'

'You need help. You need to get your life back.' I saw flies buzzing in the air above the cluttered sink.

'You think what you have is a life? You call that a life,

living with that cold-hearted bitch in the English country-side? You think all those books make you better than the rest of us?'

The buzzer gnawed insistently again. His eyes found mine.

'This whole thing was fucked up from the start. We didn't have a chance. What did they think they were doing, having us? Where were we going to be at home? We don't fit in anywhere in the world. Neither there nor here.'

'Things have changed. The world is not like that any more. You ought to take a clear look at it sometime.'

'We never had a chance. Not ever. We are the lowest of the low. Maybe if you realised that you would have something to write about instead of that exotic crap about how magical and wonderful our childhood was. Maybe for you, but not for me. Next time you are standing in front of the mirror practising your acceptance speech, you ought to think about that, Mr Nobel Prize.' He plucked the intercom off the wall. 'All right, where's the fire?' I noticed how slow his movements were, like a man under water. He listened for a moment and then murmured something and pushed the buzzer.

He lit another cigarette and the door swung open before me. 'Go on,' he said. 'You did your bit. You found me, now go back to the world and forget what you've seen.'

'I'll call you,' I said.

He snorted. 'Yeah, do that. I'm in the Yellow Pages.' I heard the door slam behind me. On the stairs I met a girl coming up the other way. She was young, still in her teens I think, thin and shivering. Her face didn't lift as we passed. I stood to one side to let her by and heard her murmur, 'Thanks', very softly.

I crawled into the back of a taxi cab to take me back to the Royal Marsden, too numb to negotiate the tube. We stuttered along the Embankment at a snail's pace. It would have been faster to walk. A necklace of lights marked Chelsea Bridge. The dark water below glittered with diamonds.

Louis Armstrong was singing 'Hello, Dolly' as I walked

243

onto the ward. A whooping nurse was twirling one of the male orderlies around the corridor in a messy jig and a small audience was staring numbly at the spectacle.

My father was saying goodbye to an old friend, a man my parents had known since before I was born. Two doddery old men at the end of the road. I saw him find a handkerchief to wipe his eyes. He straightened up when he saw me, fixing me with a tight-lipped stare.

'Well, did you find him?'

I looked my father in the eyes and said, 'No. He seems to have moved.'

His gaze held me for a moment and then he folded the handkerchief carefully, the tension going out of his narrow shoulders. 'Ah well, nothing to be done.' He took my elbow and together we walked slowly back up the lighted corridor. 'Perhaps it's better this way.'

On the bus home that night I recalled reading Elias Canetti's description of a wretched figure that lived in Djema al-Fna square in Marrakesh. Nothing more than a dirty bundle on the ground, it consisted not of a voice but of a single sound. Canetti never caught a glimpse of what was actually beneath the sacking. But whatever it was, it was undoubtedly human. Perhaps it had no tongue, he writes, to utter the name of Allah. Instead, a wailing sound, the same unvaried note, came from underneath all day and long after the square had been deserted at night. Canetti was repulsed. He felt helpless because he was scared to touch it, but he also felt pride: In that plaintive, insistent cry Canetti recognised some essence of the human spirit, alive with diligence and persistence, despite the body having been withered and eaten away by an awful disease. Myself, I had once dismissed Canetti's observations as those of yet another European traveller seeking the grotesque to illuminate their own civilised condition. Now the story came back to me and I wondered what I would have felt had I been in Canetti's place.

22

Things began to happen very quickly after that. It was as though the seams holding my world together were slowly but surely becoming unstitched. All I could do was marvel as it unravelled in my hands, at the delicate weave of what I had always taken for granted. I was losing the protective cowl of immortality that signifies youth. I realised that people who mattered to me would no longer be there for ever. I was suddenly as vulnerable as everyone else.

I had started working at the World Service. Ellen's doctorate had been ditched by now and she had thrown her tremendous energies into a hundred different projects, each of which (calculated or not?) would take her further away from me. She taught for a while, running evening courses. She was also writing articles for journals. Most of all she wanted to travel, to write serious reportage for magazines like *National Geographic*. She was planning to make a documentary film on the diminishing environment of the Saami people in Northern Finland. They have twelve languages which are being drowned out as the young tune in to US satellite stations to watch insipid, barbituate soaps and real-life action dramas, cop chases in Los Angeles. They have television sets attached to their motorised sledges. She went into serious preparation and would empty everything out of the big chest freezer and climb inside to train herself to operate the camera in sub-zero temperatures. She took the cordless phone in there with her in case she got locked in by accident. I once lifted up the handset in the kitchen and inadvertently eavesdropped as she complained to her mother, teeth chattering, how awful I was to her, how I abused and made her life a misery. Was I that monster? How had everything become so poisoned between us?

The house was becoming stranger every day as her net of contacts widened. To come home was to find the place inhabited by strange people in chunky jumpers discussing the merits of Tarkovsky and Gurdjiev in convoluted abstractions. Chief among this band of earnest simpletons was a fellow with conch-shaped hairy ears who claimed to be Romanian. He said he came from the region of Transylvania and that he had left because the radioactive pollution was causing children to be born deformed. They were being born with paws, and people believed them to be throwbacks to werewolves. He was either very paranoid or in need of urgent psychiatric counselling, neither of which endeared me to his presence. But looking around the kitchen and seeing only gently nodding heads in the candlelight, I could see that I was the only one who noticed anything out of place. Ellen explained what was wrong with me:

'You are so cynical. You come here to try and humiliate me in front of my friends.'

'I do not humiliate you. I am just astonished. These people are supposed to be academically trained, intelligent people. Why do they swallow this stuff and nonsense?'

'You were laughing.'

'OK, I'm sorry. I just find it hard to keep a straight face when people start talking about deformed children being werewolves.'

'It's metaphorical.'

'Oh, I see. Sick children as a metaphor. For what, communists? Nationalists? Gypsies, Muslims?'

'You see? So cynical. Everything is a joke to you.'

'Look, I'm just tired. OK? The last thing I expect to deal with is a séance going on in the kitchen. I've had a long day, my mother is very ill. Tell the coven to find somewhere else for their meetings. Did Leo eat anything?'

She erupted. 'How dare you! You're sick, you know that!'

'I'm sick because I'm worried about whether my son is being fed?'

'You never ask about my family, never! You couldn't care less what my mother is going through and now you're accusing me of abusing my child.'

I was confused. 'What is your mother going through?'

'Not feeding my own child? Whatever next?' She was yelling by now. We were having this 'discussion' upstairs. I could hear chairs moving uncomfortably down below. Her friends were probably lighting a joss stick for her, or alternatively, plunging the bread knife into a wax effigy of her awful husband.

'Listen to me, Ellen, you need to talk to someone. Someone outside all of this, not family or friends.'

'Yes,' she sneered. 'Mad. That would suit you, wouldn't it? Have me committed?'

I sat down heavily on the bed. 'I just can't understand what is going on here.'

The door swung open and Leo appeared, wearing his pyjamas and rubbing his eyes. 'Mummy?'

Ellen rushed to him and swept him into her arms, turning on me, spitting bile.

'You hate us, don't you? You want to be rid of us both.'

'I didn't say that. I never used the plural.'

'Ellen?'

It was the vampire slayer down below, wooden stake in hand no doubt, ready to climb the stairs if his services were needed. She got to her feet and wiped the back of her hand across her eyes, already smeared with mascara.

'It's all right,' she called, taking the half-asleep Leo by the hand. 'Come along, I'll make you some hot chocolate.'

I slumped backwards and closed my eyes tightly. Where do you go from here? It was a never-ending stalemate. I spoke to her mother, Claire, one afternoon when she came by and Ellen was out.

'Has she ever had psychiatric treatment?' I didn't know her any more.

247

'My daughter? Psychiatric treatment. Whatever are you insinuating?'

'I'm worried about her, Claire. I'm trying to find out what is best for us.'

'I blame her father,' worried Claire, biting her lip. 'Always filling her head with big ideas, saving the world or doing something wonderful. Never a good idea. We all have limitations. We *need* limitations.'

This made a strange kind of sense. Ellen wanted to save the world. The Saamis, the rainforests, the Tamils. Perhaps even me. Was that what had drawn her to me in the beginning, a desire to help me? Was I a case study in her fascination with deserving ethnographic curiosities? Did she think she was saving me by marrying me? But then it all went wrong, the monster you have created is out of your control. It speaks! Nothing could be more disappointing, surely, than discovering that your subject can speak for itself. I was ungrateful, insensitive. Was that it? Whatever it was I got no more out of her mother; Claire became frantic whenever the subject of her daughter came up, and would pull away if she thought I was about to broach the subject. I would pursue her out to the car, hoping for a quiet word.

'Find a solution,' she wailed, waving me away, slamming the door on her coat while fumbling with the key, 'for my grandson's sake.' I watched the car speed away down the drive, swerving to narrowly miss colliding with an oncoming milk float. The sound of the car's horn vanishing like a soft ripple into the landscape.

I had a recurring dream around this time, of a yellow liferaft floating on a blue ocean. I have no idea what it meant, but the fact that it kept coming back to me seemed like a bad omen.

My mother died in the spring. Muk had vanished again and never turned up for the funeral. No one was expecting him to, except maybe Yasmina, who was draped very sombrely in black from head to toe. It was decided that she would be buried in London, city of her birth, in a newly opened cemetery off the North Circular Road devoted to the religion she had adopted when she got married, Islam. It was the only available option. We stood on a windy field, Yasmina's voice almost drowned out by passing traffic as she wiped a tear from her eye with a paper tissue and pronounced bitterly: 'This family has turned into a lost tribe wandering the earth.'

She stared at my father, but he was not listening. His eyes were on the newly filled-in patch of stony earth, being patted down enthusiastically by an Iraqi from Luton with a broken shovel.

'Well, she beat me to it,' he said. 'I always thought I would be the first to go, but she beat me to it.' He had nothing more to say. The world had struck him right between the eyes again. This time, though, it would take him more than a week to recover.

I was isolated out there in the wilderness, or else sitting on a train bound for London and back. I began to find excuses to stay away for longer each week. Two nights could easily be stretched to three, or even four. I enjoyed my work for the World Service. It was a connection to home, to the past. I recalled with uncanny familiarity the high-pitched rising and falling of the BBC World Service signature tune. The military march folding into an unearthly moan as the signal lost itself somewhere in the stratosphere and then swayed back to us, coming through the robust old Grundig that my mother used to lug around the house with her in the morning, from bedroom to bathroom to kitchen to living room, clinging to the old world for a precious fifteen minutes a day. The chimes of Big Ben at the top of every hour, clanging around the world. Could there be anything more English than that voice assuring us in the same sombre tones as one might announce the death of a beloved statesman or the imminence of nuclear apocalypse that 'This . . . is London'? The dramatic pause, the poise of it. There it was. All was well with the world, London was in its place. The flag was flying over the Houses of Parliament and there was that old bell chiming. Whitehall was still intact on yet another glorious morning.

Why did she listen to that every day? Was it more than just the need for reliable information about the possible coup d'état in Djakarta or Djibouti? The summit meeting in Geneva? How did any of that impinge on the life of an Englishwoman in middle age who had settled herself thousands of miles from friends and family, who had a husband who said he loved her and children to take care of and jam to make and sell – papaya and mango, tamarind and hibiscus. A little cottage industry of her own making in a flat-roofed sunbaked, cracked and lizard-overrun house in a semi-arid suburb. People dropped by in the afternoons to load up their cars with jars of pickled limes, guava and orange marmalade. Was there, in all of that, a suppressed longing that measured itself in the radio ritual? She didn't do afternoon tea. Christmas was no more than a few strands of tinsel that she kept in a shoebox at the back of her wardrobe. She had gone native to all intents and purposes. What, I wondered, would she make of her son being at the other end of that chiming bell?

I enjoyed the work, despite the fact that on my first day I certainly had doubts about my ability to fill the post. I was met in the lobby by Tara Reed whom I was to work with. Tara Reed was brown like me; she was also very small, pocket-sized, *concise*. She hummed with high-voltage energy and did not appear to stand still or pause for breath. A snapshot of her would have been blurred. In the space of thirty seconds she had shaken hands, signed me in, clipped on my pass, ushered me through security into the central vestibule of Bush House, turned towards the lifts, turned away again and now she was springing up the stairs ahead of me. I was out of breath.

'Lifts out of service *again*. Good to have you aboard. Loved your book.' She stopped then, which gave me a chance to catch my breath. Tapping the edge of a pencil to the rim of her glasses, she said, 'Just to get it straight – how do you prefer your name to be pronounced?'

'No preference. Just how it's written,' I said. 'Two syllables: Ya–sin.'

'OK.' She beamed with relief. 'One less mystery in the world.' And then she was off with me loping along behind. The great building loomed above us, heavy and dark with marble and age. It was like entering a large cavern dug into a mountainside and made me think of the Kremlin for some reason. The wide staircase wound its way up into the beast, turning this way and that to pause on deserted square ledges the size of tennis courts. Singly, in pairs, people appeared and disappeared mysteriously through the swing doors. Tara Reed was already halfway through one of these, while I was still climbing the stairs. I jogged over to find myself in a maze of corridors. I caught a glimpse of her down at the end, turning a corner. Soon, I was no longer just out of breath, I was also completely disoriented. I wandered back and forth for a while, looking into various offices, until she came back and found me.

'This is it,' Tara announced when we finally reached the right office. She pointed to a desk by a window too high to look out of. 'Your desk. Coffee?' There was an automat down the hall. A heap of plastic cups piled in the waste bins testified to this. A stuffed cat on the next desk. An aerial picture of an island set in emerald sea.

'St Kitts. Ancestral home. Milk?'

'Please.'

'Sugar?'

'Three?'

'Very bad for you.' She frowned disapprovingly, but gamely set down her clipboard on the desk and went to get the coffee. I put my hands in my pockets and looked around me.

'You must be the new guy?'

A slim white man with lank dark hair that hung over his

eyes and an unbuttoned denim shirt over a Newcastle Brown Ale T-shirt appeared in the doorway. He pushed the hair out of his eyes and slipped the headphone cups down to his shoulders.

'Hi, I'm Dave.' There had to be a Dave. Dave was a graduate in sociology from Hull University. He had been in radio since then – first local, then national, now global. He had a record collection that would be the envy of many a professional DJ. On Sundays he liked to light up a large joint and doze off to *Dark Side of the Moon* by Pink Floyd. He was easygoing and not in much of a hurry to get anywhere. He was content. He had a girlfriend named Sally. They were at university together. They had a baby due in September. That was all I ever learned about Dave.

Tara returned to announce that the machine was out of order and we would have to go down to the canteen in the basement. She handed me an empty white plastic cup and stirrer. 'Dave, Ya-sin. Ya-sin, Dave.'

'We just met.'

'Right, off we go. Ready?' I followed closely behind this time.

'Has a sort of Oriental feel to it, hasn't it, Ya-sin?' She smiled while slowly squeezing the life out of a raspberry-flavoured tea bag, strangling it efficiently with the little string. 'So, tell me where you stand?' The brightly lit cafeteria in the basement was silent and deserted. It put me in mind of the galley of an ice-breaker heading for Arctic waters.

'Where I stand?'

'What are your politics, culturally speaking?'

'I'm not sure, really. I mean, quality is the thing, isn't it?'

'Quality is subjective. No such thing as objectivity any more. What is good is a matter of who decides. History is about power. One history displaces another. You see what I mean? That is why we have to fight for our corner. This is an opportunity, this programme. That is why we have to be clear.'

I had come into this with the naïve assumption that I

would just have to read a few books and think of something interesting to say about them. Now I was being assigned a leading role in the emancipation of Western cultural awareness. Tara was staring at me intently over the rim of her cup. I was given the job because I had managed to patch together a novel that nobody had read, that was my sole claim to qualification. She was educated. A string of qualifications. Black Studies. Post–Colonial Studies. Race and the Media Studies. She was an erudite collegiate urbanite. I was a barely literate backwater bumpkin.

'I understood from the person who interviewed me . . .'

'Maggie. Our producer. A mid-life crisis in Pradas. Typical. Well-meaning. Liberal. Spends her life apologising for herself.'

'A little harsh, aren't you?'

'It's a harsh world, Ya-sin.' She sipped her tea and set down the cup. 'I'm not trying to give you a hard time. I worked hard to get here, and I don't see myself staying here for ever. We need to be clear about where we stand.'

'Right,' I said slowly. A grey man with grey hair, wearing a suit and overcoat, wandered past our table. He had a thick pile of newspapers under one arm and was balancing a cup of coffee in the other. He was smoking a cigarette, oblivious of the fact that only one small corner of the place was designated a smoking area, and he was not in it. He also appeared to be muttering in a low, intense fashion as though in the midst of an argument with himself.

Tara's gaze followed mine and she fixed me with an arched eyebrow. 'That's Troy Marchand. He's a *poet*. Old school. Steer clear of him if you value your life, he's pure poison.'

I watched the poison poet settle himself quietly in the corner of the room, patently ignoring the huge sign that read 'No Smoking Area' which hung over his head like a guillotine. He looked harmless enough as he carefully arranged his papers around him, and then folded his arms and looked up at the ceiling, puffing away.

'So tell me. If I was to say Yeats, Coleridge, Keats, what would your reaction be?' Tara laced her fingers together, hands on the table, and waited.

'Writers?' I ventured.

She shook her head. 'Dead, White and Male. His territory.' She jerked a thumb in the direction of the resident scribe who was now being told by a canteen lady, in no uncertain terms, that he was to move if he was going to carry on smoking. 'We are not here to promote those people. We have a struggle on our hands, to promote the Other. The unknown, the exploited, the disadvantaged, the silenced.'

'I imagine that's why they gave me the job.'

'Assume nothing. Unless you are clear about what you are doing here they will slowly but surely take control of the programme, and before you know it we'll be reviewing the latest Martin Amis.'

'Who are *they*?'

She didn't answer. She looked at me over the rim of her cup for a moment before setting it down on the table. 'So what did you do before this?'

'Well, I was a freelance editor for a publishing company.'

Tara seemed to relent. 'I'm sorry, you must think I'm terrible.'

'Its OK – good of you to take the time.'

'You don't mind?'

'Not at all.' I drank my tea.

'So you forgive me for the Grand Inquisition tactics?'

'Nothing to forgive.'

'Well, then, do you mind if I ask you one more question?'

'Fire away.'

'Do you stare at women's breasts?'

'Sorry?'

She leaned her elbows on the table. 'I just need to know,' she sighed. 'I need to be sure where you stand on this. Sexual politics is a life-and-death issue with me.'

'Breasts?'

'A woman is walking towards you: do you look at her face first or her chest?'

'It depends.'

'On what?' She peered at me carefully.

I had to think about this. 'Sometimes a person's clothing, the way they move, they draw your attention to certain aspects of their appearance. Like that man who just walked past us. The poet. His shoulders were hunched as though he were caught in the middle of a thought. We do it automatically; the mind acquires images in a kind of shorthand of the imagination, according to Calvino.'

'Interesting answer,' Tara said, reaching for the pencil behind her ear.

'The right one?'

'There is no right one. But all men stare at women, and at least you didn't try to deny it.' She got to her feet and held out her hand. 'Nice to have you with us. I have a feeling we are going to work well together. Take your time. I have some things to do before I can show you round.'

I apologised silently to the spirit of Italo Calvino and sat there wondering what I had managed to get myself into. I had a suspicion this was going to be more complicated than I thought. I looked up and saw Troy Marchand staring at me across the room with a malevolent look on his face. I nodded amiably and a shudder seemed to pass across his features. His gaze dropped down at his papers again.

In those difficult early days at the BBC I found in Dru welcome companionship. Those evenings when I came back to her place to sleep on her sofa, exhausted, unable to think, I found I was grateful only that I did not have to go home. Dru and I went out together to eat cheap meals in places filled with noise and people and laughter. We went to the cinema and talked all the way home about why the film was unconvincing, or where the director had made a huge mistake, and what an awful creep the leading actor was, and what could have been done had we received a phone call from Hollywood to fly out and save the day. We had long conversations about everything and nothing at all. Politics, books, and all the rest of it. Conversations that didn't have to add up to anything, that weren't cut short by domestic duties or tempers. It was as though the world came back to life again and I was still a part of it.

I suppose we both knew where it was leading, that the usual hindrances were not making an appearance. We knew what would happen, what was bound to happen eventually. We had a choice and we could have walked away from it. Put a stop to the foolish carefree running around, the fun, the confessional sessions that solved nothing and only got us deeper into mutual dependency. But neither of us seemed willing or able to do that. The reckless pursuit of oblivion, both of us determined to lose ourselves for a time. That doesn't produce happiness in the long run, but then I suppose neither of us was really thinking of the long run.

Dru had reached her own personal crossroads, both in terms of her work and also Lucien with whom she was no longer certain she shared a future. She had come to London ostensibly to work on a book she was thinking of writing, a popular history of medieval medicine. She had started out doing medicine years ago and then switched to history. But she was unhappy with the way the book was working out and was worried the whole idea would simply evaporate in her hands. She, like me, was in a state of flux, as though oscillating between two forms of existence, unable to decide which one she belonged to. During the course of our year together the book was eventually dropped only to be taken up again some years later and finally finished. In the beginning there was a period when she was in close touch with Ellen. The two of them would go out to the theatre together, or to an exhibition. Later, she would try to find excuses, which did not always work out; for a time it was a strange triangulation.

And so finally, one day, like actors who find themselves in a scene that isn't in the script, we stood there in the kitchen doorway unable to let go, our hands entwined inextricably, locked together for the first time in *that* way. The meal we had been going to such elaborate trouble to prepare now completely forgotten. Neither of us would have been able to say with certainty what it was we had been talking about a moment ago. Or what all those chopped green peppers, sliced onions, raw king prawns were doing strewn about, and water boiling on the stove. All was instantly eclipsed by that simple act, so long postponed, of our hands touching. In one of those brief, inexplicable moments. It didn't feel like just simple physical desire. It was more a longing which seeks a release from the solitary practice of life itself.

For a time everything was wonderful. The sex, the evenings out, the evenings in. Ellen and I argued less. She had her life and I seemed to have mine. In my work at the BBC I had finally found something which I enjoyed doing and enjoyed doing well. I took pride in what I did; I seemed to be able to do it with some degree of confidence. It might have been a small contribution in the great scheme of things, but it was satisfying work. I threw myself into the task with considerable dedication, in part because I felt I had a lot to catch up on. So I read books, lots and lots of books. I read novels, poetry, essays, journals, anthologies, travelogues, biographies. I took the whole thing very seriously. I actually believed you had to read someone's work before you interviewed them. Some authors were surprised by this and would regard me with a look of incredulity: 'You mean you've actually read it, the whole thing?'

I cared about the job. I enjoyed it, felt as though I were at the heart of a huge mystery that only I could resolve. Literature gave me something I could believe in. And I felt a responsibility to the listeners, those people living out there, wherever it was, with a little transistor and a coat hanger for an aerial, tuning in faithfully every week to hear what the world of letters had to say for itself. Perhaps because I had once been there myself. It was a function as necessary as medical supplies or fresh water.

257

Even Tara Reed turned out to be more amiable than our first encounter had led me to believe. We disagreed on certain points, but we learned to work together. She, Maggie and I made a good team. We looked after one another, learned each other's weaknesses and blind spots and all agreed that the programme came above all else. Dave did his own thing. Nobody knew where he was most of the time, but a tape would be there every week with his segment of the half-hour programme.

We reviewed books, interviewed authors who had just jetted in from the sprawling urban chaos of a city in West Africa, from Lahore, Calcutta, Manitoba, Ivory Coast. This was World Literature as Goethe never imagined it: we had Sikh poets from Quebec, Turkish dissidents in Turku, Punjabi novelists, dramatists fresh in from Guadaloupe, Mapuche storytellers from the Amazon, Potawatomi performance artists from Ottawa. These were people on the move. We had to grab them whenever and wherever we could. People who were in London for only a couple of days, a few hours between transit halls. I was a man with a mission. I would rush over to their hotel with a DAT machine and pin them into a corner of a deserted dining room (someone would invariably switch on a vacuum cleaner the minute you turned the recorder on) and try to find out what made them tick, what made them do what they did and how.

The technical side of it I picked up as I went along, mostly through trial and error. In the early days I used to sit there, eyes glued to the instrument panel until a rather elevated Somali snapped: 'Are you interviewing me, or that damn machine?' A year went by. On a day-to-day basis I began to listen more. I would close my eyes and just listen to the sounds around me. I learned to prepare the sequence in my head before I spoke, to lower the tone of my voice and speak evenly and clearly.

So this was my job, sitting across the table from a studious-looking type who stared moodily at the floor with drooping eyelids. Each one was different. One would have a degree in aerodynamics and a doctorate in creative writing from an East Coast university, the next be just out of prison for posting a poem on a government wall. One would divide his or her time between Simla and Seattle, the next would be a teacher running a drama project with no funding, and no facilities in Rwanda. Some talked fervently about politics, others talked earnestly about the influence of *Finnegans Wake* on the Caribbean novel. Some were deeply intellectual and others frivolous.

I learned a lot about writers that year, not just about writing. The best writers on paper were not always the most insightful when you held a microphone under their nose. Success and arrogance were surprisingly, although not always, linked. Quality and popularity rarely went together. Poets tended to be evasive. Political writers were often confused. Mediocre writers tied themselves into knots to prove they were not confused. The bad writers made you wish you'd taken up dentistry and could pull a few of their teeth instead of listen to them rabbit on about themselves.

I loved it all. The good, the bad and the tedious. I learned that people write novels for all kinds of reasons: because they are in the middle of something they think they understand, or don't; because they are outraged and indignant; because they are invisible, or because they are not; because they have loved and lost. There are a thousand other reasons, none better or worse than the next. Many were ordinary, unhappy people who had had one lucky break and were busy trying to turn this into a vocation. I couldn't really blame them. After all, I was very nearly one of them. But I was saved. If my experience taught me one thing, it was that I preferred talking about other people's books than writing my own. I was a radio man and had no intention of going back.

Which is not to say that I was perfectly suited to the job. There were lessons to be learned, and some of them came more easily than others. The most notable case in point was that of Shaka Baraka. His real name was Stanley Earlsfield and he was a rap poet somewhat in the style of Linton Kwesi Johnson, only light years behind. Shaka Baraka's thing was Africa, with a capital A. He had been around for longer than he cared to admit, claimed to be forty, but even the cobwebs had cobwebs on that claim. Eternally youthful, he dyed his hair with henna and wore it in short, spiky locks. He refused to remove his wraparound sunglasses in the studio and moved very slowly, probably to avoid bumping into the furniture. The African continent dangled like a hostage from around his neck on a wooden amulet. There was a cross in there as well, and something that looked like a chicken's foot. I held out my hand.

'How do you do, Shaka? My name is Yasin Zahir. I'm doing the interview.'

'Right, man.' He gave me a brother's handshake, flipping his hand over to clasp my thumb in his as he winked at the receptionist over my shoulder. His shirt was open to the waist. He liked women. Tara refused to go anywhere near him.

'He's old enough to be my father and he had his hands all over me last time.'

'He's quite the ladies' man,' agreed Maggie with a strange gleam in her eye.

Tara snorted. 'He's a walking cliché.'

'You're volunteered, Yasin.'

I didn't want to do the interview. I didn't like his poems, which were indulgent and portentous. In one of those curious flukes his new book had been given an award which meant we had to do something with him. I couldn't really blame him for winning a prize, but maybe it was the fact that the Africa he seemed to be talking about sounded more like a product of wishful thinking than real insight that bothered me. Maybe it was the fact that my mother was dying and my father was now, to all intents and purposes, in exile. He had been warned that if he went back to Khartoum he would be arrested. All this because in a rash moment he had published an article in a Cairo-based magazine on mass killings in the

Bahr al Ghazal province. The government was claiming he was a spy for the infidel West, paid to spread propaganda against his own people. I was in no mood for fashionable posturing.

'Now, Shaka. Can I call you Shaka?'

'Call me what you want, man. I'm right here in living Technicolor. Heh heh.'

'I imagine it must have been quite a surprise for you winning this prize.'

The eyebrows drew together over the shades. 'Well, of course one never really knows about these things. You never know with these things, you never know.'

'Right. So, after thirty-five years in Clapham how well do you know Africa?'

'I am Africa.'

'In other words, you don't write about the continent, but about yourself.'

'Of course I write about myself. I AM AFRICA. Whatever I write is about the true soul of the African continent. I'm not concerned with all that surface stuff. I am talking about the roots of the matter. The heart and soul.'

'I see. Well, let's talk about the work itself.'

'By all means.'

'You seem to be heavily influenced by a kind of writing that was popular in the United States at the height of the Civil Rights movement in the late sixties and seventies.'

'I'm not influenced by anyone, I'm an original.'

'Right.' I looked at my list of questions and couldn't see a single one worth asking. 'Original,' I repeated. He was waiting. In the darkened control room next door, Maggie and Tara and the engineer were all waiting. What was it that I couldn't respond to? Was it the notion that politics should never be placed above art? And yet here was a man who had been rewarded for doing just that. My father, who spent his life defending plurality, was being washed away by sectarians who saw secularism as treason. Can you fight dogma with aesthetics? Is it not immoral to oppose one set of prejudices with another? What about Yasmina?

'Yasin?' Maggie's voice came through the speaker behind me. I realised they were all looking at me. I glanced through the glass at her. She smiled and gave me the thumbs up. This was the last segment of the week's programme which was scheduled to go out this afternoon. There was no room for error.

'Mr Shaka, I am sure you are aware of the number of great literary works that deal with slavery. What did you feel you had to bring to this subject that was original?'

'What?' He was looking at me over the top of the sunglasses. 'What did he say?' he asked, turning towards the control room. 'He's taking the piss.'

'I can't do this,' I said quietly. Through the glass panel I could see waving and hand gestures. The intercom was off but there was a discussion going on. I picked up my papers and got ready to leave. I bumped into Maggie on the way out.

'Thanks a lot, Yasin.'

'Look, Maggie. I'm sorry. I just can't do this.'

'Later, Yasin. I don't have time for this now.' The door shut firmly behind her. I stood in the corridor for a moment. I could hear Stanley Earlsfield swearing about incompetence and insults.

Tara was standing there. She looked at me in a strange sort of way: 'I always wondered where your loyalties really lay.'

'Is that what it's all about? Loyalties? I thought it was about literature?'

'He's a well-respected and prized author, Yasin. Don't you get it? He is one of ours. No matter what you think of him, you have to play the game.'

'Even if that means suspending our critical faculties?'

'Oh, stop being so naïve for a moment. We have to stick together.'

'That's it? The great philosophical questions boil down to us and them?'

She folded her arms firmly. 'There are no in-betweens in life, Yasin. You ought to think about that.'

After that I wandered around the building with no real idea of what I was doing or where I was going. I stood in the lift for a while and rode up and down according to whoever got in. Finally I found myself in the cafeteria in the basement. Deserted as usual. I sat there for a long time staring at the ceiling when a deep voice boomed:

'*Bad day at Black Rock*?'

I turned to look over my shoulder. Troy Marchand, the grey poet. I took a sip of coffee, preparing my answer. 'Nineteen-fifty-five. John Sturges directing. Spencer Tracy plays a one-armed man who comes to town looking for . . .' My memory failed me.

'A Japanese man named Komoko who was taken to an internment camp.'

'Best line?'

'As Spencer Tracy gets down from the train the conductor says, "What a place, everyone looks so woebegone and far away." And Tracy says, "I'm only staying twenty-four hours." '

'And the conductor replies, "Around here, that could be a lifetime." '

Troy Marchand exhaled slowly: 'Good film.'

'They don't make 'em like that any more,' I quipped.

'They certainly don't. What happened, anyway? Why the long face?'

I sighed. Marchand knew more about English literature than I had any hope of learning, but we rarely talked about books. He was known for being belligerent and argumentative and had made a lot of enemies. People steered clear of him. A mystical lore surrounded his isolation. He was held with a mixture of reverence and revulsion. For some reason he had taken a liking to me. Our shared passion for the cinema had provided me with one of my closest and most unlikely allies in that building.

'I think I may have just made myself unpopular.'

'It happens.'

'What do you do, then?' I asked.

'Well, let's see. Basically it's the lifeboat principle.'

'Every man for himself?'

'There are times for self-deprecation and times for standing shoulder to shoulder.' He shrugged and got to his feet. 'Remember, "Resolve to be thyself; and know, that he, Who finds himself, loses his misery!" '

'Sounds like Confucius.'

'Matthew Arnold, "Self-Dependence", eighteen-fifty-two.'

I watched the grey poet retreating through the harshly lit cafeteria and I think then I understood how he had survived so long in this place.

Shaka Baraka had the last laugh though. The poet of such memorable lines as; 'Life! break my back, but never crush my balls', ended up in a hotel room off the M25 with my naked wife. She slurred this information to me in the company of a shipload of drunken passengers on the overnight ferry to Denmark. They met at a reading. She went there with no other purpose in mind but to get even – she didn't really know what for, but she had convinced herself I was seeing somebody. In her lonely, anguished bitterness she had decided that she was going to cause me pain. The strange thing is that it still hurts. Even when you can no longer abide the sight of someone, it still hurts.

23

A gentle ripple of strings, trickling up and down the scales, filters out through the window to the terrace – the sound of a *kora* being played. The warm breeze stirs the leaves that hang down behind me, and a fly is buzzing insistently about me.

There are idle moments in life when you are not trying to achieve anything, not chasing or running away from anything, when just being alive is enough, and you realise how fragile existence is. Elsewhere on the planet there are murders and car crashes and public executions and all manner of terrible acts, freak accidents and misfortunes, and here you are, sitting on a terrace waving a fly away. I am more preoccupied with death than I used to be. I think about Leo and what lies ahead of him. My dreams are full of disasters which I am helpless to stop. I wake up convinced it has already happened. In some cases it has.

The kora is an African version of the harp. There are eight strings on either side which rise up in architectonic symmetry to create a ridge, and intricate harmonies. With characteristic ingenuity, Lucien has rigged up a complex network of loudspeakers all over the house. He sets the music in motion from some undisclosed location, inside his studio, or upstairs in their bedroom perhaps, and the house, digitally wired, comes alive. Some days it is Stravinsky, others Verdi's *Aïda*, gnawa music, Indonesian gamelan or the Rolling Stones' *Exile on Main Street* album. This kora is the music he brought back with him from his last trip. The house is filled with curious objects, mementoes from his travels. A stuffed green mamba from Morocco which he found in the window of a junk shop in Paris on the day he returned from the Atlas mountains. A huge boat carved in jet-black ebony from Bali. A headless granite statue from Cambodia, which he bought in Thailand, illegally I suspect. Each piece has a story attached to it. He has bronze horsemen from West Africa and wooden masks the size of a table. There is a rounded creature with four legs, shaped like a headless hippopotamus, which he says is a *fetische* made from mud and dried sacrificial blood.

I give up my battle with the fly and throw my book aside. The music tugs me into the house, as seductive as any modern-day piper, down the narrow stone passageway that leads through the house, to emerge in Lucien's studio.

The huge room at the far end of the house is cool, dark and cavernous as a church. The windows are covered by long wooden shutters, which we noticed when we first arrived. It is two floors high, the walls of what must have been a stable once are now covered with shelves. Lucien has installed all manner of gadgets, screens, cameras, developing trays. Strips of celluloid hang down, stacks of video and tins of 8mm and 16mm film reels. There are mountainous piles of books, magazines and newspapers. There are bottles, some with various chemical substances in, others with candles stuffed into their necks. It is like an alchemist's cave. There is a tremendous amount of junk – half-dismantled optical instruments, cameras, old record players, hairdryers, food processors, all with bits of wire poking out of unlikely places, or with their electric motors removed to power some ingenious device he's invented.

Lucien is holding a screwdriver and a cigarette in one hand and staring at the ceiling. There are words between us which have yet to be spoken. A conversation pending that I am not sure how to tackle. Perhaps this is why I have wandered into his inner sanctuary with no particular purpose in mind.

'Ah,' he nods in greeting. 'Where is Leo?'

'Outside, playing with the kite.'

'Good. I have an idea to make it better.' He and Leo

constructed the kite a couple of nights ago, the old-fashioned way. They cut the wood to size and found an old shirt to make the sail and then they added a long tail with some red ribbon. And when it was all finished it actually worked. To Leo's astonishment it took off into the air and stayed there. Lucien has a natural talent with his hands, a mystical sense of the physical world containing its own magic which his fingers can unlock. Now he picks his teeth and looks down into the viewfinder of a monitor. He is editing his Mali footage and is a notoriously slow worker according to Dru.

'Is that your film?' I ask, awkwardly. He stands aside and motions for me to take a look. I lean over the viewfinder and he pushes the switch. The film clickety-clicks through and I watch the landscape jolting by as though we are in a moving car. Giant baobab trees climb into the sky like parts of an old and knotted Indian rope trick left still standing. A herd of lean, long-horned cattle stroll through a cloud of dust into the setting sun. There is a jump and then an entirely different scene, this one completely motionless: an indigo-blue lizard poised on top of a wall. The vivid orange head bobs once quickly, up and down. Its eyes swivel and it seems to look straight at the camera.

'Oh,' I say.

Lucien looks at me sideways. 'The lizard, it's quite amazing, isn't it? They are everywhere.' He motions me aside, rolls the film back and takes another look himself. 'They look at you and they seem to see right through you.'

'Yes.'

We stand there for a moment. I feel there is something I should say, but I'm not sure how to say it. The room is dark and gloomy, only thin cracks of light filter through the gaps in the long wooden panels of the door. Lucien's cigarette has gone out and so he sets about finding his tobacco and rolling himself another one. He examines me in silence for a time before gesturing at the monitor.

'Maybe you want to see more?'

'Sure,' I say. 'I'd love to.'

And so for the next twenty minutes or so I stare into the viewfinder while he runs the rough footage through the editing machine. He has a stack of film reels which do not appear to be in any kind of order. There is some confusion when I find myself in a canoe in what looks like a jungle.

'Wonderful,' he enthuses. 'I was looking for that.'

I see the mysterious landscapes through which he has travelled, and after a time I begin to see them as perhaps he did. It is like watching a man searching for something remarkable, and finding it in the ordinary, the everyday, the unremarkable. The last spool of film that he feeds into the machine is different. At first all I can see are unfocused flashes of light. The camera seems to move with less discipline. It takes me a moment to realise that I am looking at the room I am actually standing in. The big windows are open. The colours vanish in the fierce contrast between the dark room and the sunlight that floods in through the door at the far end. Gradually the bouncing rectangle of white light draws closer, expands to fill the screen, and then we are outside. I am about to look up and tell Lucien that this reel is obviously not what he thought it was when I see Dru. She is sitting in the shade on the terrace with her feet up on another chair, a book balanced on her knees, in almost the exact spot where I was sitting not so long ago. She looks up and smiles. It is a smile I know well. The screwed-up corners of her eyes, the way she tilts her head to one side, the wrinkle that appears on the bridge of her nose. But this time it is not meant for me. The impact of experiencing that intimacy again, now intended for someone else, feels wrong. I stiffen instinctively and lift my head. Lucien catches the look in my eye as I move out of the way. He looks into the viewfinder for a moment or two and then quietly reaches out for the switch and the whirring reels spin to a halt.

'I must have got them mixed up,' he says. 'It happens.'

'No harm done,' I say. There is silence for a moment, and then he takes a deep breath and repeats my words.

'No harm done.'

'I had better go and see how Leo is getting on.'

'Yes, of course.' And I leave him there, staring at the ceiling.

Later that morning, when Dru turns up on the terrace I tell her that I think that perhaps it is time for us to consider moving on. She sits down and pulls off her hat. She and Leo have been digging away in the patch of rough ground in front of the house. It was once a garden and she wants to restore it, and has some plan about growing herbal medicines in it. Crumbs of yellow soil drop to the table as she removes her gloves. Leo fetches a jug of water and some glasses from the kitchen.

'Where will you go then?' asks Dru.

'Well, looking at the map it doesn't seem that far to Spain. I sort of feel obliged to try and find Muk.' Dru watches me closely as I search around to find Muk's postcard.

She ruffles Leo's head. 'That sounds exciting, doesn't it? Off to Spain to find Uncle Muk!'

Leo's face is a picture of confusion. He looks at her, then at me and finally shrugs and goes back to examining his glass of water without saying a word. I slide the postcard across. Dru lifts it up and turns it over a couple of times. It is a simple picture of a sunny bay. Sand. A wooden fishing boat moored conveniently in the middle of placid blue sea. On the back are the famous lines, which Dru reads aloud:

'The Moving Finger writes . . .' She frowns at me. 'Very mysterious.'

'It's by Omar Khayyám,' I say.

'Well done, but what does it mean?' She tosses the card onto the table between us. 'What does it all mean? That postmark is dated almost a year ago. Why are you going there now?' Leo looks up at the change in her voice.

'Now seems as good a time as any,' I say as I tuck the card away. 'He's my brother,' I add finally, meeting her gaze. 'He's the only family I have left.'

'You don't even know he's still there. Why are you doing this, Yasin? Why don't you go back to Ellen and work out whatever it is you have to work out?' Dru looks at me for a moment, then she gets to her feet and says, 'Come on, Leo, let's go and see if we can't clear some more of that junk away.' She takes his hand and together they walk down to the garden. I watch them go. Leo doesn't look back.

A sombre mood hangs over lunch, and afterwards I am grateful when Lucien asks about the car.

'Any problems?'

'No. Well, now that you mention it there is a strange noise that comes when you put it in first gear.'

'A strange noise?'

'Yes, a grinding noise.'

'Maybe the clutch?'

'Is that good or bad?'

'Could be serious. Maybe we should take a look?'

'Well, I was meaning to take it down to the village one day. I saw a garage.'

'He's drunk most of the time. You would be lucky to get the same car back.'

'Right.'

Lucien shrugs. 'Why don't we take a look at it?' Within an hour most of the vital insides of my prized automobile are spread out on the ground like parts of a puzzle and I am not altogether sure how easy it will be to put them all back together in the right order. I watch all this with growing dismay.

'We're going for a walk,' Dru calls down from the terrace. Leo is standing beside her. He is in no hurry to leave this place.

'OK.'

'We'll go on to the market in the village. Maybe see you down there later.'

I watch them go. It would be easy to stay here, I realise, easy and comfortable, for both of us, except for the fact that we don't belong here, neither of us. This is not our house, not our life.

'I think you have a problem,' says Lucien from underneath

270

the car. He slides out to smile up at me. He is in his element. He is healing the world, repairing things. 'But we need to go down to the village to fetch a few things. Maybe we are lucky.'

'You think you can fix it?' I ask sceptically. I try to ignore the sense of panic this news instils in me. I can see myself being stranded here for weeks, months even.

'Oh, these cars can always be fixed.' He gets to his feet and searches his pockets for his tobacco. 'Don't look so worried.' He smiles. 'It can be sorted out. You'll soon be on your way.'

An hour or so later we climb into Lucien's car, a battered Ford Mustang that looks older than mine and is completely unwieldy on these narrow roads. From the outside it resembles an immovable wreck. It sounds like a tank. Lucien drives with one eye on the road and the other on the interior of the car as he explains the beauty of the sound system he has installed, with custom-made speakers concealed in the roof. When he slides a compact disc into the player to demonstrate, the sound fills the car like water rising up through the floor.

We reach the village in one piece and find the garage Lucien knows which has a room full of old parts stripped from cars just like mine. We collect the spares we need and retire to the café in the village square.

'You picked the right place to break down.' Lucien smiles as he holds the door for me. A faded poster of a youthful Maradona was slowly curling away from the toilet door and behind the bar, other trophies; a luminous green Statue of Liberty, a red kangaroo wearing boxing gloves. Lucien has lived in the jungles of Brazil, in the mountains of Papua New Guinea, in Vietnam, and Laos. I have no desire to go there, to see new places. That is not what this journey is about.

'The clutch would have gone sooner or later,' says Lucien. 'This is a good time to get it fixed.'

'I suppose you are right,' I agreed. 'I just don't want to overstay my welcome.' It is the wrong word to use. I can see that as I speak. I did not come here to see him, but to see Dru and we both know that. He picks a fleck of tobacco from his tongue and signals for another pastis.

'Tell me something – are you really going to drive to Spain?'

'Yes, of course.' I wonder what Dru has told him.

'And after that?'

'Well, I'm not sure.'

He nods as though this is all right. He looks right at home in this bar, as I imagine he would if we were sitting in a bar in Samoa. His sense of ease in the world derives from a confidence, a knowledge of precisely where he comes from. He is a country boy, despite his worldliness and his record collection. He grew up in Normandy, on a farm where his family has lived for eight generations. Despite the laid-back manner, the rolled-up cigarettes and unshaven chin, the long curls of unruly hair now flecked with grey, he exudes an air of belonging.

I feel the urge to explain. I would like him to understand. This seems important to me although it has never occurred to me before this moment. I feel that perhaps he, of all people, might understand. Before I can find the right words, however, he says, 'Here they come.'

I look over my shoulder to see Leo and Dru crossing the square in the sunshine. They pause to bend down and examine something on the ground together, deep in conversation. Leo is crouched down, pointing, as Dru tucks a lock of hair behind her ear.

'She is good with children,' I hear Lucien say quietly behind me. 'Sometimes I think perhaps it would have been better if she had stayed with you.'

I turn back to look at him. But he is already busy talking to the waiter.

24

The car, now miraculously cured thanks to Lucien's mechanical skills, is in need of a good wash, inside and out, to improve its appearance. Leo comes over while I am cleaning out the bits of old newspaper and cans, the surprising amount of junk that has accumulated, as though the car has just been dragged from a deep and murky lake.

He leans against the car with his hands in his pockets.

'Where exactly are we going to go?' he asks.

I look at him. He is not keen on leaving. For the last few days he has been cheerful, happy to run around, explore, ride the horse, walk in the hills. He has not asked to call his mother. Now, as we prepare to depart, his doubts are returning. He steps back, his eyes screwed up against the bright, mid-morning sunlight to peer in at me sprawled in the back seat. His hair is corkscrewing out of control in thick black curls. He looks like me, or how I remember myself from old photographs my mother used to keep in a biscuit tin. It is like looking back thirty years to see myself standing outside our old house.

'You don't remember my brother, do you? You were too small. You'll like it,' I say, straightening up. 'You've never been to Spain before.'

'What if I don't like it there?'

'Then we won't stay long.' I can see where this might be leading to. Where would we go from there? And just how long is this trip going to go on? I throw a piece of orange peel into the rubbish bag and turn to face him. 'When is your birthday, exactly?' I ask him with a frown which he throws back at me.

'Baba!' I know when his birthday is, surely?

'I've forgotten. Remind me again.'

'Next week. On Tuesday at four-fifteen in the afternoon.' He is precise about the time of day when he was born, which has fascinated him since he was five. He needs precision, accuracy, things to be in their place. 'And you know very well.'

'OK, I know very well. And what, more than anything, would you like to do that day?'

'I don't know. Go to the beach?'

'Exactly what I was thinking. There are no beaches in the world more beautiful than those of the Costa Brava, so we'd better get moving if we want to get there in time. We only have a week.' Leo adores swimming, although no signs yet that he is planning to take this up professionally. But I sense that this little manoeuvre of mine is not enough. He remains where he is, just standing there, looking at me. I notice how much taller he looks. He is growing fast, soon out of my hands, into the big wide world. In the blink of an eye. One of his expressions, picked up from a television documentary on dinosaurs, still one of his favourite subjects, a fascination that comforts me because it tells me he is still a little boy. At one stage the narrator, speaking in that grave tone assumed by television narrators, said, 'Compared to the millions of years when the dinosaurs ruled the earth, the timespan covered by man's presence on this planet would pass in just a blink of the eye.' The phrase stuck in his head for some reason and for months he would use it whenever an opportunity presented itself.

'How long is it going to take you to get your pyjamas on?'

'Just a blink of the eye.'

And that is how fast our time together is passing. All of this will soon be over and done with, distilled into a series of distorted memories that will colour his life, unresolved sentiments, doubts about who to blame. The sacred season of childhood, pierced by the black arrow of his parents' divorce.

He is looking back at the house.

'You're going to miss it here.'

He hesitates and then nods.

'Well, we can always come back.'

'Really, when?'

'When? I don't know. Any time. Some time.' His face sinks.

'That means we're not going to do it.'

'Of course we are. I wouldn't say we could come back if I didn't mean it.' I am a little distressed by this indictment; when have I ever let him down?

He looks at me. 'With Mum? Can we all come back together?'

'Let's wait and see, shall we? Before we start making all these plans.'

He leans down to pick up a stone to turn over in his hands. 'Baba, what's going to happen?'

'What do you mean?'

'You know, when it's all over. When we get there?'

'We'll find out then. Don't worry about that. It's an adventure. You never know how an adventure is going to end until you get to the last page, remember?'

He considers this. 'It'll be all right though, won't it? Not like Marcus?'

'Who is Marcus?'

'Marcus. You remember Marcus. In my class. His dad found himself a girlfriend and that was it. He had to go and live with the girlfriend and she was horrible. Always telling him to do this and do that.'

'Marcus had to go and live with the girlfriend?'

'Because she was his new mother. And she was really ugly.'

'Stepmother. She would be his stepmother, if they were married.'

'Well, that's what they're like, isn't it? Will I have to do that?'

Divorce has become everyday fare in his world. Who knows what kind of a libidinous cretin Marcus's father was, or what he was getting up to that made his wife demand a divorce? I am certain I have nothing in common with him. But you might have a hard time proving that if faced with a classroom full of worldly children. My son will have to endure the judgement of my morality by his classmates. How was he going to defend himself against that? Every divorce happens for reasons that are unique and specific to the couple involved. You could draw parallels, generalisations, based on all manner of statistical data, but how do you explain to a nearly eight-year-old boy that there was no other way out?

As I finish loading our bags into the boot I turn to find Dru standing beside the car, hip jutting out, one hand in the back pocket of her jeans and the other shielding her eyes from the sun.

'So, our two heroes sally forth into the world to do battle with the giants.'

'What?' demands Leo.

'Cervantes,' I explain. 'It's a book about two men who go in search of adventure.'

'Well, I'm not sure that's the accepted version, but I suppose it will have to do,' Dru smiles and puts her arms around Leo's shoulders. 'Now you know where we are you must come back. Napoleon will miss you.'

Leo looks up at her. 'Whatever you do, promise you won't sell him?'

'I promise,' laughs Dru, folding him to her for a big hug. They separate, awkwardly pulling apart. I turn and look towards the house. The terrace already looks far away. I catch sight of Lucien watching us from the doorway of his studio. He makes as though he is examining some object in his hands and then finally comes down to join us.

'So, you are really off then?' He digs a finger at Leo's ribs who giggles and fights him off. 'Which road are you going to take?' he asks, turning to me. Men discussing practical matters: cars and maps and what direction to go in. But I have no idea of the best route to the Costa Brava from here. I have felt the anxiety building up over the past few days, knowing it was time and not wanting to leave. Now, all I know is that we must make a start. I have only a vague plan and even that is improvised. In the meantime, however, we shall head for Arles.

'Arles, yes, of course.' I am aware of Dru watching us as Lucien stretches out his hand to squeeze Leo's shoulder. 'Well, take care of your baba, young man.'

Leo nods fiercely and says nothing.

'And you take care of him,' says Dru, giving me a quick hug. 'Drive carefully.' She waves as we get into the car.

It is a strange feeling, sitting behind the wheel. I have a sudden sense of foreboding. Nerves before the departure. A rising, asphyxiating feeling of having to let go and plunge in. I take a few deep breaths, push the key into the ignition, and with a silent prayer that Lucien has put all the bits back in the right places, I turn it. The dusty red light comes up on the dashboard. I stare at it until Leo leans over and puts his hand on my arm.

'It'll be all right, Dad, when we get there, when we get to the sea.'

The engine starts first time and then we are rolling through the gate and down the stony track we have walked up so many times, past the wall where Leo hunted for lizards in the cracks. A cloud of chalky dust rises up behind us. After a time he gives up waving to Dru and slumps down in the back seat out of sight. We are on our own again. The tyres grate as we bump down the uneven road to the village. We wave goodbye as we drive past the café. The dogs sleeping in the shade raise their heads and then drop them again. Then we are winding along the road to the next village and the next after that and so on, descending slowly down the side of the ridge of hills. We try to take in everything for the last time: the delivery vans, the barking dogs, a woman struggling along under a heavy load of firewood. The old men lifting faces like leather to watch us go by. A man on a green tractor raises a hand mistakenly in greeting. Two boys on scooters race by us to disappear round the next bend in a high-pitched whine, the wind in their hair, helmets dangling unconcerned from their elbows.

The world is rushing up to meet us. We gain speed as the road widens. The car soon becomes familiar again, the rattle of the engine, the flat beat of the tyres on the road. With every village we put behind us, slipping down the hillside to the flat plain, the long straight roads flanked by groves of fruit trees and banks of tall cane, I feel that this is right, this is where we belong. Moving. Always moving. In my love's house, wrote Hafiz, there is no peace in pleasure. At every breath, the caravan's bells cry: ride on!

25

After my mother died my father slumped into a daze, like a man in a trance. He could no longer fend for himself. He aged ten years overnight. He couldn't remain in London any longer and he couldn't go home. He was in a state of suspended animation, a voodoo limbo. Finally, it was decided that he should go and live with Yasmina and Umar, for a time at least.

'A fate worse than death,' he moaned. 'You condemn me to a life in the company of people who think that Disneyland is one of the Seven Wonders. I am lost.' But there was no alternative. Who else could he stay with?

The housing estate sat in the middle of a forest of billboards advertising its arrival in what had been an unremarkable field on the outskirts of Canterbury not so long ago. There were two types of housing unit on the estate, one faced to the right and the other to the left. The walls were the width of a thick cheese sandwich and roughly of the same consistency. Yasmina and Umar's faced right. If a door slammed their roof and windows would reverberate like the insides of a drum.

Inside they had created a hermetically sealed microcosm to deflect the dilemmas of post-national, post-industrial existence; how to have your Squeezy Cheez Rings and frozen Macaroni Surprise! without becoming part of the society that produced them. A society that gave rise to drugs and depravation, to racist attacks and senseless violence; eighty-year-old pensioners being raped and murdered in their lonely old flats; the obscenity, the drunks pissing on your lawn

279

while singing their way home from the pub, the pools of vomit, the joy-riding vagabonds, and so on and so forth. News of all of this horror poured into their comfortable existence through the letterbox, in the local paper. It was an awful world out there.

So they dug themselves in deep. They lived with the curtains drawn all day. They built a wall of Prawn Flavoured Puffs and Toastypops around them and, literally, began to pray. Like modern-day Puritans terrified of the freedom they found in the New World, they needed to compensate, to make up for the lack of boundaries by hardening their own peripheral delineations. They were building a fort. They needed a defence, they needed to rally together. They took an active part in the local Muslim community. Umar was elected to the board and Yasmina was running collections of old clothes for despatch to needy parts of the Islamic world: Chechnya, Kabul, Palestine. This was their atonement, for the comfort of their lives. And the ultimate act of expiation? Taking in the poor, the infirm, the aged and the widowed . . .

'There are more of them,' was my father's first remark, squinting through the windscreen of my car at the doorway where, flesh of his flesh, they stood eagerly awaiting us.

'No,' I said. 'They are just bigger.' The twins, on a high intake of carbohydrate and sugar-rich snacks had ballooned into blimps. They wore T-shirts the size of duvet covers. With their round shaven heads on top they looked like giant bobbins. He clutched the door but made no move to open it.

'I'm not sure about this. I mean they look like strangers to me.'

'We've been through this, Baba. You have no choice. This is the best place for you, for now. It's only temporary.'

'Only temporary,' he murmured. He made it sound like a death sentence, but they were all happy to see him. Umar respectfully made a long speech about how it was a great honour to have him staying with them, that he should consider the house as his own. My father stood through all of this looking older than I have ever seen him. His face folding inwards. The idea dawning, perhaps, that from now on he was to be dependent on his children. It was not a prospect that came easily to him. His eyes darted left and right and he seemed quite relieved when Umar stopped talking. He was tired, he said, from the journey, and would it be all right if he lay down for a while?

Yasmina showed him to his room and everyone else began whispering as though afraid of disturbing him. I fetched his bags. He was put at the back of the house, behind the kitchen, in a converted utility room which contained a washing machine that was to be moved any day now.

'What do you call those things they keep dogs in?' he asked as he surveyed it.

'It's not that bad. You're away from the rest of the house. Less noise.'

'Out of sight, out of mind.' Another gem from his list of English aphorisms.

It was a very simple house. The elongated wing projected into the garden. The single window, which for some reason had been placed at shoulder height, looked out on a sad little strip of lawn. It was a little like a prison, but I kept my mouth shut.

'This is it, then. The end of the line.'

'It's just for a while, until you feel stronger.'

'No.' He was staring at the grass. A magpie settled on the fence. He hardly seemed to notice I was in the room with him. 'This is the last stop.' He prodded the narrow bed with his fingers.

'I feel like those fish in one of his glass tanks.' The thin moustache was now entirely ash white, flecked only by the occasional dark hair – his eyes grew wide as though he had just been shaken awake. 'What am I going to do?'

'Get some sleep. You'll feel better later.'

'Don't tell me what to do, you son of a bitch.' Stunned by his vehemence, I stared at him in silence. He sat down suddenly on the bed and said, 'I'm scared.'

'It takes time. These things always do.'

'I don't want to lose my mind. I don't want to wind up one of those wretched creatures who can't even tell when they've wet themselves. You put a pillow over my head when that comes.'

I didn't know what to say. I had never heard him talk like this. The room was filled with evening shadows. With only the light from the window to see, all I could make out was the watery gleam of his eyes.

'Promise me.'

'I promise. Now get some rest. Just close your eyes. You'll feel much better. You're tired.' I got to my feet quickly, urging myself not to leave the room. He rolled onto his back.

'You won't be here when I wake up.'

'Baba!'

'OK. I have my eyes closed already. Look.'

I left him there despite his misgivings. After a time he recovered himself a little. He bought a typewriter, an old Remington portable that he picked up in a junk shop for fifteen pounds, which he set up on the table in front of the window in his room. There he settled himself to write long letters to Her Majesty's Government demanding they hurry up with his appeal for political asylum.

As a former employee of the British Government during my days as a junior clerk in Sudan Government Service, I feel that I have a patent right to remind you of your responsibility towards a former subject . . .

He would keep the house awake as he sat there tick-tacking away all night long. Then he set about advising human rights organisations:

What kind of work ethic do you call it when one of the most democratic countries in Africa is pulled back into the Dark Ages by religious fanatics and you mention not a word of it? In the bad old days, I can tell you, we would have looked carefully under your beds to see if there was a conspiracy afoot . . .

The idea of returning home had been postponed indefinitely: 'I shall not return, alive or dead, while those tyrants are in power.'

He received telephone calls from old friends, or relatives of theirs who had managed to get out, in tears with horror stories of who had been arrested and what had been done to them. He passed these accounts on to the House of Lords:

Innocent men and women are being threatened in going about their daily business. Journalists executed by government security officers who have the gall to deliver the cartridge shell which carried the fatal bullet into the hands of the grieving widow. Such callousness must not be allowed to go unopposed, My Lords, and so I beseech you . . .

Many of these missives were never actually posted. There were typing errors, places where the paper had slipped, or the line ran away, vanishing unchecked off the edge of the page, or the script turned from black to red in mid-sentence where an errant finger had switched the ribbon bands. There were illegible corrections in squiggly handwriting up and down the margins. The important thing was that it was work of a sort and it kept him busy. A local newspaper got wind of his endeavours (no doubt thanks to the number of letters he sent in: 'In order to make your publication more accessible, especially to elderly readers, allow me to give you a piece of professional advice: cut down the number of vertical columns on the page as these can be confusing and one tends to find oneself reading about lumbago cures or laxatives when deeply immersed in an entertaining account of the recent carnival . . .').

They sent someone around to interview him: 'Renowned Journalist Fights For Rights as Local Resident'.

'They understand nothing,' he reported back to me

dejectedly. 'Nobody really cares. They have to look me up in an atlas. I might as well be talking about another planet as far as they are concerned. People see no further than the ends of their noses. They are interested in the new shopping centre and how many types of Italian ice cream will be available for them to slurp up.' He stopped bothering to get dressed and took to wandering the house in a paisley dressing gown, a latter-day Citizen Kane lamenting the loss of his empire. He was driving his hosts crazy.

'What are we going to do with him?' Yasmina pleaded on the phone. 'He is becoming more and more impossible. He tyrannises the boys. He says they are ignoramuses because they prefer computer games to books. It's not that they don't read. Of course they read. They do their homework. They are top of their class. Umar is very strict with them. No playing until they have finished. But that is not good enough for him, oh no. He wants them to be reading something called *Ulysses*. Can you imagine? He brought home a copy and I looked at it and you know what, it is disgusting. People shitting and everything. How can he call that good for them?'

After a time his discontent began to channel itself into paranoia. He was not sleeping well, but he could not sit down and concentrate on anything either. He thought they were keeping him prisoner, monitoring his behaviour, even his telephone calls. He took to calling me from public telephones late at night. I would hear the click of a coin sinking through the machine and brace myself instinctively for what was coming.

'Ya Allah, save me, get me out of here.'

'What's wrong now? Where are you? Is that rain I can hear?'

'Rain? You want to see rain? Noah himself didn't see rain like this.'

'Tell me where you are.'

'In the street. I have fled to the streets. They are driving me mad with their pious manners, their snooty disapproval.

What did I do to deserve such children?' Eventually the reason for his distress would emerge. In this case one of the twins had come to him and said he was too tired to say his prayers. My father told him that it would be all right if he just said them in his head when he was in bed. Yasmina found out about this and went for him. She delivered a long lecture about how she had been let down as a child and how he had betrayed us by not bringing us up more strictly. She had had to fight to regain her Islamic roots.

'I failed her. I failed *her*? Did you starve, perhaps? Did you not eat as a child? Did I beat you as some fathers beat their children. No! *None of the above.*'

'Listen to me,' I managed to finally get in. 'You can't stay there in the dark and the rain. You will catch pneumonia.'

'Better I die here than suffer the humiliation of being told I am a failure as a father.' He broke off and there was the sound of squealing of brakes and then clattering and banging and over this the steady hiss of pouring rain. After a long time the receiver was lifted up from where it must have been left hanging and a vaguely familiar voice enquired, 'Who is this please?'

'Umar, is that you? It's Yasin. What is happening?'

'Nothing, don't worry about it. We have him now. I have got him into the car. I'll take him home now. He's a little tired, and of course, with this rain . . . Don't worry. It's all right now.' The line went dead. I felt awful. It was like committing him to a correctional institution.

I agreed to go up and spend a weekend there, to try and alleviate the tension. I arrived late one afternoon and found him asleep. Yasmina was in the kitchen.

'It's so strange to see him like this,' she said.

'Getting old, you mean? Yes, it is strange.'

'I have to think of where he is all the time, if he's all right, just like with the boys.' She reached for a Kleenex and turned to one side to wipe away the tear.

'It all seems to have happened so quickly.'

'I know, I know,' she said. 'Oh, I hate this. I feel as

though our parents should be around for longer. To see the children grow up.'

'I'm sure they'd want to be, if they had the choice.'

She sniffed and looked up. 'We worry about you.'

'We?'

'Dad, too. He cares about you.' She was scrutinising my face for traces of guilt. 'It's not easy for him, Yasin. The disappointment.'

Umar arrived before this conversation could go any further. After supper he and I sat in the living room together and tried to have a conversation while he flipped channels on the television.

'So, how is life treating you?' he asked. A classroom full of athletic-looking females appeared on the screen, engaged in strenuous callisthenics. Clad in combinations of stretch leotards and elastic tops, there was a good deal of bare midriff, thrust out chests and flexing buttocks. After some delay he found the button and switched channels. Television viewing was rife with hazard, potential *haram*, the shameful, the morally corrupting and explicitly forbidden might leap out at you at any moment. But I noticed that Umar's self-censorship instinct had a tendency to be delayed somewhat when Yasmina was not in the room. The television set encapsulated the dilemma of Muslim modernity; you never knew what was going to be beamed into your living room. Shampoo commercials, cleaning fluids, central heating; whatever the excuse there would be a woman in a shower spreading foaming lather over her naked body. Of course, the obvious solution was simply to get rid of it, but that was too much of a sacrifice – there were still the soaps to think about. Umar himself had a personal weakness for the science fiction channels. If he was ever in the room on his own you could be certain he would be engrossed in some florid tale of alien creatures intent on spreading an evil virus through the world. I had heard of people who devoted their lives to unravelling the mysteries of circles in cornfields and aircraft that vanished in mid-air, dazed victims wandering along a highway thousands of miles from home whose last recollection was being sucked into a whirling silver disc. I had heard of them but I had never met one before.

Umar surfed the Internet for specialist chat rooms and information sites. He pooled his knowledge with thickly bearded characters living in dog shacks in the Appalachians, on some hick farm in the boondocks of the American Midwest whose idea of a pleasant Sunday afternoon was sticking their hand into a box full of rattlesnakes to face the Old Testament trial by serpent. What would they say to *him*, I wondered, if he landed in person in Missouri, this son of the Sardine King, with his framed Koranic verses on the wall, and his striped tropical fish arrayed in the hall? Perhaps there was nothing odd about all this. Maybe it was just my warped way of looking at the world. Perhaps there was no link between his fascination with whirling lights in the sky and his religious faith. But any conversation with Umar invariably took place against a running background of spacecraft that looked as though they had been put together with a stapler and men covered in scales. Ray guns zapped and cars exploded into flames.

'So the business is going all right?'

A woman ran screaming down the street towards us, hands held to her head.

'Mmm, fine. Good month.' Munching cashews, he called to Yasmina in the next room and asked if I would like some tea.

'No, thanks.'

'Sure?' He reclined in a big winged armchair the colour of stale guacamole.

'Yes, really.' A creature in a silver helmet materialised on an empty road looking lost. Wondering, no doubt, why, after travelling zillions of light years he had forgotten to bring a road map of Kansas.

'I'm sorry that he's being so difficult.'

'It's not your fault,' Umar shrugged. 'He's getting old.'

I was curious about how all this came about. Perhaps it

was obvious; you grow up learning about the England of *David Copperfield* (the Dickens novel, not the illusionist), and what they don't tell you is that you might well be subject to insults, nasty looks and random searches. There are firebombs and stabbings, people have petrol and dog excrement pushed through their letterboxes, and even if it doesn't happen to you personally, you know it could. But there was something deeper at stake here and it was manifest in the general assumption that, by migrating physically, you also had to do so culturally; that every virtue, trait, or cultural value held over there, in your previous world, was now declared null and void. To eat the squeezy cheese pops and read the scandal sheets you had to renounce all previously held beliefs. To avoid the fate of banal indifference offered by secular, postmodern Britain they had turned sectarian.

I was befuddled by the fact that whenever the news came on they changed the channel, or the set, inexplicably, went off. On my last night, determined to find out whether California had fallen into the sea, or another war had broken out anywhere on the planet, I sneaked into the living room when no one was around. I got no further than the headlines when the screen went blank. I turned around to find Umar standing in the doorway behind me with another remote.

'I wanted to watch the news,' I explained, lamely, caught like a little boy engaged in something unspeakable.

He clicked his tongue impatiently. 'No point in that. What they tell you there is no use.' Umar slumped back in his armchair, his Garfield slippers coming up off the floor onto the footrest. 'You think they tell the truth? ITN? BBC? CNN?' Umar threw his head back and let out a long hearty chuckle. He was in stitches, the joke was on muggins here. I was the dunce. Yasmina joined us from the kitchen. I wondered when they were going to let me in on the joke. But there was no joke, they were both deadly serious.

'You're talking about what, some kind of conspiracy theory?'

'Yasin, everybody knows it is the Jews who run the media,

here and in the United States. They run the networks, the newspapers, television. They run Hollywood. Have you ever seen a movie with an Arab who is not an unshaven, illiterate terrorist? Name one.'

'That's Hollywood,' I objected. 'They play on prejudice and ignorance to increase their audience. There's nothing new about that.'

In unison they both shook their heads. Umar held out his hands, urging me to see the light. 'How did people get that ignorant? You think it is just coincidence? No, Yasin, my friend, my brother, wake up! They hate us. They want to see all Muslims wiped off the face of the earth.' Yasmina sat, quietly poised, hands in her lap. They had a point, I could not help thinking, about movies encouraging ignorance, reinforcing prejudice and stereotype, but there was still a long way to go from there to the conclusion they were offering.

'You, of all people, Yasin, ought to know better.'

'The media has its own way of compensating. Eventually the truth comes out.'

'You mean a column in the *Guardian* that no one ever reads? Those leftwing people are guilty of secular fascism. They disapprove of anyone who disagrees with them. Where is there a difference?'

There were no newspapers in the house, I realised, except in my father's room.

'There's bias out there, I know that. I've seen it first hand. There's ignorance, too, and prejudice, but we have to believe in a free press.'

'Why? Because it's more comfortable for you to believe that?'

'Because a free press is an essential part of any democracy. You can't fight prejudice with prejudice.' What was I talking about? Democracy? Free press? I knew how things worked. Why was I defending a system I had been fighting at the *Daily Crow*? I had seen how items were dropped or picked up according to the whims of an editor, but what choice did we have? What was the alternative?

Yasmina cleared her throat; 'There is something I've been meaning to say, Yasin.'

Had they been rehearsing this, I wondered? Umar held up a hand to correct her: 'We've *both* been meaning to say it.' I had a feeling I knew what was coming.

'About your book.' Yasmina turned the coffee mug around in her hands. A Disneyland mug, a memento of one of their many visits. They loved the place. They tried taking Dad along but he feigned appendicitis very convincingly and actually managed to get the doctor, a blustery Irish woman, to prescribe rest and no movement for at least a week.

'We feel we have to tell you this, Yasin. Don't take it the wrong way.' Yasmina took a deep breath. I waited. 'It was embarrassing,' she sighed.

'How you could say those things, about us? About our home?'

'The poverty.'

'The dirt. The misery.'

My head bobbed back and forth between them.

'Every prejudice they have in this country about us being backwards.'

'Underdeveloped.'

'Savages. At each other's throats.'

'The rubbish heaps.'

'The homeless children who sniff petrol. What did you call them?'

I tried to rally my forces. '*Tarzanis*, they call themselves, or *shamasis*. They exist. They live on the streets.'

'But what has that got to do with you?' Yasmina raised her face to me. Livid, her dismay complete. 'The shame of it. My own brother. How could you?'

'The sheikh.' Umar intoned, glaring fiercely at the ceiling, stroking his beard as new offences sprang eagerly to mind.

'The sheikh?'

'You don't even remember,' said Yasmina. 'The sheikh

who fondles the boys and drinks *merissa*. You made fun of us all. You must be proud of yourself.'

'It was considered a nutrional drink, not an alcoholic beverage. They used to have a bowl of *merissa* beside them when they gave lessons. Many societies . . .'

'There you go again, turning our lives into an anthropological thesis.'

This was clearly aimed below the belt. Me, the cultural traitor. I was, after all, married to one of those skull measurers. I was a willing dupe, a tacit accomplice in this conspiracy.

How to explain that if even a grain of righteousness entered that work it was triggered by outrage? I didn't write that book to appease the privileged classes, with their romantic vision of a country of whose existence they knew nothing. I didn't write it for jaded Westerners either, looking for evidence of barbaric decay and noble savages. I wrote it because I wanted to hold on to the world I remembered and to do that I had to write it down, plainly and without conceit. They were staring at me as though I were stark raving mad. They pitied me.

Yasmina said, 'Don't you realise what you have done? You have betrayed yourself. Where does that leave you?'

'I was trying to tell things as they are.'

'It's not only us.' Yasmina smiled sadly. 'You upset him, Yasin. You shamed your own father with this pathetic and vain attempt of yours.' Umar got to his feet and murmured something about prayers. Yasmina collected the mugs. She hesitated before turning away. 'I feel sorry for you, really I do. More than anger and shame, I feel pity. You have nothing to believe in. What can become of someone like that?'

I sat there for a long time after that. What if they were right, I wondered? What if there really were no such thing as honest, objective criteria, what if there were no universal human values, no moral absolutes? If they were right, then all we have left are relative truths, prejudice excused by counter-prejudice, sectarianism. Nothing will ever get any better and the development of civilisation is fated to remain stunted. The best we can hope for is a stand-off, a demarcation of limitations, whereby humanity is reduced to a series of teams, what used to be called tribes, either you are with us or you are against us. The values my father mourned the loss of had not vanished as a symptom of his age, but as the culmination of a failure to accommodate difference. It was lost for ever, for all of us. I realised now that I had written my book for him, hoping to carry his struggle for social justice to another level, trying to fulfil his ambitions for me as a nation builder.

We had never spoken about the book, he and I. The following afternoon I sat with him in his room. Dinner was in the microwave. The rest of the family were in the kitchen, munching away at snacks in anticipation. He held a finger to his lips and went over to close the door. 'They treat me like an idiot, with all their talk of religion. What do they know of Islam? I prayed. My mother prayed, my grandfather made the pilgrimage to Mecca by camel! That's devotion. To them it's just a fad. A fashionable addition to their attire. They want to be different. They want the English to step out of their way and bow their heads in reverence because they are so pious and holy.' He was pacing the floor. 'I did not bring my children up to feel morally superior to anybody, not even the English. Equal, yes, but never superior. Who are we to be superior? Do we not squat on the ground and move our bowels like ordinary people?'

'Calm down, you'll upset yourself.'

'What do you know? You are no better than they are. That novel you wrote? All that flowery language. Why not tell it how it is? Why not tell the world?' His face looked thin and bony. The veins stood out on his forehead. 'Poverty? High-level corruption? I worked for more than forty years trying to bring those issues to light in my own small way. And there you are, all the world looking, and what do you have to say? Hibiscus and pomegranates and the smell of dust when the rain comes!'

'Baba! Calm down, please.' But he was worked up into a fury and had obviously been building up to it for a long time.

'The obscenity of what we allowed the world to do to our country. The IMF, the World Bank. Don't try to shut me up. Let me finish! You didn't have time to mention that? The shame of it! My own son! Every time we had a chance they would block our way. Sanctions here, loan adjustments there. The debt! The debt! All those useless dams, canals unfinished, irrigation schemes that involved huge invest-ments in mechanisation. You could have said something about the civil war that nobody is interested in stopping. But no, you sold us like petty trinkets in a market.'

'Just take it easy, please. All this excitement is no good for you.'

Beads of sweat broke out on his forehead. He was tugging at his collar. 'All my life . . . I believed in . . . devoted . . . to building . . . something ah, I could be proud of and look what I have to show for it. Aah.'

'Just sit down. Catch your breath. Let me get you a glass of water. You don't look well.' Sweat was running down his face. He sat back down slowly on the bed.

'Ya Allah, I don't feel so good.' He was looking down at the floor. For a long time he didn't move, and then he bowed forwards and his tongue lolled out. I knelt down to look at him. He could not speak. I didn't know what to do. I had never seen a man having a heart attack before.

When he came out of hospital, the person I had known, loved, respected and feared all my life had been replaced by a shrunken, bowed figure, a docile old man. He denied that he was changed in any way, assured everyone that he had work to do. But the typewriter had to be moved to the high window-sill to make way for the plastic jars and bottles of medication. And it stayed up there with its cover on, perched like a silent black raven watching over him.

293

The anger had gone. The outrage at the world which had carried him through life was now turned down, reduced to a flickering, watery flame. By mid-morning he would be dozing in an armchair with a newspaper crumpled unread in his hands, a thread of saliva running like a spider's thread from the corner of his open mouth.

26

I wake up to find the world is still and utterly silent – nothing stirs. My watch says it's ten to five and I have a feeling this is all the sleep I am going to get tonight.

The narrow streets of Arles are dark and immobile. There is nowhere to go, nothing for me to do but wait for morning.

I stand up. It is difficult for me to walk with my knee strapped up. I hobble as quietly as I can. I lean over to check on Leo in the other bed. He is fast asleep. Kicked free of the blankets, he lies with his limbs stretched like a person caught in mid-flight, arms and legs half bent, head tilted back, mouth open. Boy running. He resembles one of those cartoon characters he is so fond of, flying through the air. I examine the bandage on his head to see if any blood has seeped through, whether the flow has been stemmed. I am worried about the effects of his concussion.

Everything has changed in the space of a few hours. The car is gone. All our things are in a heap at the back of an oily shed full of scrap metal on the other side of town. Tomorrow we shall have to go and sort through them, find out what we can carry and what has to be discarded.

I worked it all out in my head afterwards, sitting dazed under the white hospital light, waiting for them to come and put the stitches in Leo's head. A narrow groove in the road. Labourers laying telephone cables or pipes. They had cut a diagonal slash running from side to side and filled it in with sand and limestone chips but the tarmac had not been replaced. It was the weekend. They knocked off on Friday afternoon and said to themselves, 'It'll keep. Road's not going anywhere. All those fine people in their big cars will just have to hold onto their money as they go bumping over it.' It was raining, the road a black vein of flowing tar, slick with mineral perspiration. Was I driving too fast? I remember thinking about my mother and how she would have enjoyed being here in France. How little time we spent together seeing new places. Leo was singing to himself in the back seat, enjoying the thrill of being safe and dry inside a moving car in the middle of a storm. The Peugeot felt heavy and solid, muscular in the way of an ageing boxer, carrying more weight than he used to, but firm underneath.

Heavy turbulence toiled over the fields to the west of us, the shark-blue clouds tumbling over one another in vivid contrast to the golden-green sway of corn below. Silver threads slipped through the sky and rain the colour of mercury beads pressed down upon the glass.

The rain became more fierce and the sky was completely black when the wheel jumped in my hand as though startled. I felt as if someone had tried to wrench it from my grasp. There was a flat thump which I later learned was one of the tyres that I should have changed months ago but somehow had never got round to doing. My wrist was tingling. The burst tyre locked the wheel hard over to one side. I couldn't straighten it. I heard myself shout. Water was streaming left and right across the windscreen, headlights like candles floating towards us. My foot was locked down on the brakes but we were still moving, spinning, then dropping through blackness. It was all happening a long way off, just out of my reach.

I must have lost consciousness for a moment. It took me a long time to work out where the earth was, where the sky fitted, who I was, what I was doing here in this hard wet place. My head throbbed, the car was the wrong way up and the landscape had stopped moving. I heard voices far off. There was silence where Leo had been singing. I couldn't move at first and then found that my foot was jammed. I called his name. I found his foot first and frantically traced my way up his body, my hand fearing that at any moment it would meet emptiness. His face was wet. I touched my fingers to my mouth and they tasted metallic and earthy. I tried to shake him, gently at first and then more fiercely as the panic caved in. There were lights bobbing towards us and the weight on my chest made it difficult to breathe. People calling to one another off in the distance, but in a dislocated manner, as though they were having a casual conversation. Why couldn't they get over here? Didn't they realise we needed help?

The light fell on Leo's face and all I saw was blood. A veil of red drawn down from his temple. He was gone. I was sure of it. There was no life left in that little body. The little arms, the little legs were not moving. They were cold, not warm like when he was sleeping. A pair of hands was trying to pull me away. I fought. I didn't want to leave him in there on his own. I kicked. More shouting. They were running along the ditch. Red flashes of light. The rain had stopped and the air had that soft smell of damp dust that reminded me of when I was a child.

Later, when we were being patched up at the hospital, it was like awakening slowly from a deep sleep to find that the dream you were having was real. Leo had a cut on his head that needed four stitches, but other than that just bruises. I had a long gash on my left arm where a piece of the window had dug itself in. My left wrist was in plaster. The ligaments in my foot had been torn. I could walk, slowly, and with pain. We were lucky, the nurse said, looking me in the eye, very very lucky. People died in her arms. They went out of this world with the sight of her face fixed forever in their eyes. I didn't want to leave her. I wanted to stay by her side until all the bad things went away.

Instead we took a taxi to the garage where they had towed the remains of the car. It was a scrapyard on the outskirts of town. Leo had a headache. He lay down in the taxi while I went inside, my arm in a sling. It was as though someone had taken a hammer and brought it crashing down on the front of the car. It was folded and dented in a way that I had somehow never imagined possible. What had been straight and smooth was now crumpled, shattered. It had lost its form. No longer fluid and capable of flights of fancy and transporting you from here to there, it was now nothing more than a cumbersome piece of metal. It had lost the very thing which gave it sense. The mechanic had seen it all before. Mechanics and nurses, they are the gatekeepers between this world and the next. He shrugged a few times, wiped his hands with an oily rag, said he would have to move it but would get someone to empty everything out before he lifted it up on the forklift and rode it out to the field of crushed metal frames at the back.

There were acres of wrecked cars out there, every colour, shape, and fraction. They were balanced upon one another like warped building bricks, like rows of headstones. In the warehouse dismantled doors leaned against one wall. Wheels and bumpers were stacked against another. Engine parts were pored over and labelled and put on a shelf. People came from far and wide, they ordered parts by telephone: lights, generators, starter motors, fuel pumps, petrol tanks, gear-boxes. All marked according to model and age and then put on a shelf to wait for someone to claim them. It was like the pieces of people's lives being passed on. How many stories of death did that field hold? How many terminated lives were marked out there in crumpled metal and splintered glass?

I remembered the fields near Verdun where we stopped for lunch that time, and how the serenity of that place seemed at odds with the carnage that lay beneath our feet. Here in this yard I could feel a similar sense of reverence. Every dent, bump, spiderwebbed windscreen, sheared wing, each of these items was evidence of the passing hand of God. Providence. Fate. Call it whatever you like, here was the proof of that nameless power that could remove you from the world, tear off a limb, take the life of a loved one, all in the blink of an eye. I felt a sense of awe standing there in the middle of that windy field. Over by the perimeter fence a large dog was chained up, barking madly.

When I got back to the taxi I found Leo had vomited all over the back seat.

Night.

Nothing moves. I want to savour this moment; Leo's untroubled breathing, the contentment, the quiet joy of simply being alive. Tomorrow we will see about everything, about moving on, leaving things behind. But not now, not tonight.

27

If I have no firm beliefs left to sustain me, I do at least have a selection of temporary heroes. They seem to come and go, they wax and wane like everything else, but for a while they do lend some semblance of order to my world.

At the present time I have Joseph Roth for company. I came across him by accident in a bookshop by the river in Arles that sold books and aromatic candles. Leo and I, the walking wounded, went in to have a look. We had spent the morning wandering the streets. At the amphitheatre we sat in the sun and closed our eyes, trying to ignore the delirious babble of tourists (Americans gasping in wonder, 'How old did you say it wuz?', and Italians yelling to one another about lunch) and imagine instead lions and gladiators. We visited the hospital where Van Gogh was treated and I was reminded again of film memories. I found myself trying to exorcise the ghost of Kirk Douglas furiously painting the courtyard and raving about being driven out of his mind by the mistral wind banging the town's window shutters. The film was memorable for Anthony Quinn's Oscar-winning performance as Paul Gauguin (we were, as it happened, staying at the P. Gauguin Hotel, complete with framed scenes from Tahiti on every available surface). Leo nodded as I imparted this vital piece of information. Secretly I hoped that he learnt about Van Gogh before he saw the film. Sometimes films are too concise, too clear, they get in the way of our imaginings.

Leo wanted to buy a present for his mother, which I said was a good idea. He hadn't asked to call her again, not even after the accident, as though he fears that by insisting he would not be being loyal to me. Wanting to buy a gift for her was a reminder to me that he had not forgotten her. And so we entered the shop. I left him to the difficult, and very personal, decision of whether his mother was more a Vanilla Fudge-type person than Honeysuckle Rose – these aromatic candles were imported from somewhere in California. As he sniffed away I ran my eye over the bookshelves. Reading in French, I told myself, would help to improve my grasp of this language – a language that is forever bound up in my head with the sight of Mrs Hagopyjanian, who resembled a Turkish wrestler but was in fact Armenian, as she came striding across the schoolyard in a dress that was invariably too short and tight, her powerful thighs bulging as her stocky torso bore down on us, bare, fleshy biceps slick with perspiration and cheap perfume. We were terrified of her in the way that only a school full of men and boys could be scared of the only woman there. We were unable to understand her potential fury, her terrifying silences and sudden outbursts, her intense disgust at the sight of us all, a dusty band of vagabond adolescents who exuded an odour of unwashed crevices, stale urine and feverish ejaculations. We were smelly and nasty, dark with mistrust and pride at our swelling male athleticism, the growing awareness of our capacity for violence.

In the classroom she held a handkerchief laced with harsh scent to her face as she settled herself behind the raised desk and removed her sunglasses to begin the task of polishing them, commanding the first person her eye fell upon to begin reading the next chapter: 'M. et Mme. Vincent dans la salle de bain.'

Sometimes, finding a particular book at a particular time can seem to form an arc that travels through the unlit void, connecting your life with that of the author, with another past, that other past which is not yours. This is one such book, which contains an essay originally written in German, 'Die weissen Städte' – 'The White Towns'. Joseph Roth the eternal wanderer, born in Austria in the dying days of the Habsburgs, passed through this region in the thirties looking for the harmony he had known as a child in the eastern province of Galicia. The Great War of 1914–18 had marked the end of the world as he knew it. The end of an empire that spanned a dozen nationalities, sixteen languages and five major religious faiths. Out of the ashes of a defeated Germany rose the Third Reich. Uniformity replaced diversity. Convinced that Europe was doomed he fled Germany in 1933 and remained on the move for the rest of his life, wandering in solitary exile from café to hotel, from city to city, sustained, one imagines, only by his constant writing – as though hoping to turn the tide of history with words.

His flight led him to the south of France in search of the whitewashed and timeless villages of his dreams. In the scene of a group of silk workers relaxing by the banks of the Rhône in Lyon, he saw a reflection of Europe's long history made flesh. In the faces of the slim, dark women working in the factories he saw the features of the Roman legionaries who had arrived in these parts two thousand years earlier. He saw the living, breathing perpetuation of something he had imagined lost for ever. Evidence of a continuity to which he felt he belonged, in which there was no distinction made, there were no exclusions, banishments, exiles. A continuity from which, as a Jew, he was being expelled. He found solace in the intimate silences of the afternoons when everyone was sleeping; the motionless typewriters silent in the offices, the thousands of fine silk threads stretched gleaming across the looms, waiting. He managed to complete six novels in as many years. It wasn't enough: he died in poverty in Paris in 1939 just as the Nazis began their dark march across the map.

Everything now seems intricately connected. I occupy the centre of a complex maze, a mystery to which my existence is the key. I see clues everywhere: in this darkened road; in the words of Joseph Roth whose world fell apart at the exact same time as mine was forming, like an origami paper puzzle, closing one way as it opens the other. World War II effectively marked the beginning of the end of the British Empire. Eleven years after it was over, my father and his generation achieved their dreams of independence.

And there are other ghosts travelling with us, other djinns.

'I am helpless and unhappy and I can find nothing, any dog in the street can tell you that,' wrote Arthur Rimbaud, one leg already amputated, bound for Marseilles. On 9 November 1891 he was eager to ensure that plans were in hand for his departure. 'Please let me know the cost of passage from Aphinar to Suez. I am completely paralysed, and so am anxious to be on board early. Please tell me what time I can be carried on board . . .' He died in hospital in Marseilles the following day.

Rimbaud was thirty-seven, exactly the same age as I am now. He stopped writing poetry at the age of nineteen, left Europe in search of 'lost climates' to turn his 'skin to leather'. 'If only I had a link to some point in the history of France,' he wrote. He did not feel he belonged to reason, nation or state, and yet the only way out from the shadow of Catholic France was through poetry and when that failed him he turned his back on it and departed, bound for Aden and Ethiopia. He bought ancient percussion rifles, forty years or so old, from second-hand dealers in Liège or France for eight francs each and sold them to King Menelik II of Ethiopia for forty francs each. A mark up of five hundred per cent.

On 3 March 1896, five years after the poet's death and two days after the Italians had been defeated by King Menelik's forces – with a little help, no doubt, from Rimbaud's guns – Kaiser Wilhelm II, grandson of Queen Victoria (and emperor of Joseph Roth's Habsburg childhood) advised the British ambassador in Berlin, Sir Frank Lascelles, that the British should go to the aid of the Italians in Ethiopia. They needed no encouragement. For more than a decade the British had been waiting impatiently in Cairo for an opportunity to go back to the Sudan and finish the job, to appease the headless spirit of General Gordon which still roamed the battlements of Khartoum awaiting the rescue which never came eleven years earlier. And so the British Reconquest headed up the Nile for a rendevous on the plains of Kerreri in September 1898 with my great-grandfather, Zahir, and the remains of the faithful and rather dilapidated *Ansar*, the Mahdi's Dervish army.

We decide to take a coach to Spain. We shall carry on, continue our journey to its designated end. For the moment it seems to me there is no other choice, no available option which makes any more sense.

The pale orange lights sweep over the darkened interior of the coach like bars. Leo is curled on his side, sleeping on an empty double seat across the aisle from me. I see his face turned upwards in the waves of light as I pull my jacket up to his shoulders to keep him warm. The bandage has come off and there are no signs of any lasting damage. Now he sleeps the sleep of the innocent, with the faith that we shall arrive by morning, that everything will take care of itself.

The border is, of course, supposed to be open. But I have discovered on our little odyssey that in effect this is often not the case. There is an eerie moment when two police officers step on board and walk up the aisle flashing a torch into the faces of the sleeping passengers. They know where the bus has come from and we all had to register our passports with the driver before we set off from Arles. They are looking for strays who should not be flitting about the continent at this or any other hour. I am the only one on board they bother to check. As they examine my passport I look out to see a couple of figures sitting in a room.

There are two lit windows in what looks like a temporary arrangement of facilities. A Portakabin raised off the ground on blocks stands in for the border post. The first window is an office for the guards. There is a light on over a desk and the blue glow of a computer screen. Someone has left a cigarette smoking in an ashtray. The room next door is utterly bare. Four men are stretched out on narrow benches along the walls, uncomfortably trying to sleep. Europe is again under siege. The new enemy comes without a uniform or a weapon, risking life and liberty for more even odds. An army whose only strength is its weight in numbers. The guards hand me my passport and step down, waving the driver on.

I am reminded of another illegal immigrant as we curl down the dark hillside to Port Bou. This is the place where Walter Benjamin fumbled his way from this world. He was detained by Spanish border guards and in a moment of desperation, envisaging the cruel prospect of a train journey back to Germany, to Buchenwald, or Auschwitz, he took an overdose of morphine.

In photographs, Benjamin resembles a species of cardigan: doubleknit, chubby and bespectacled, the sort of fellow who has spent his entire life worrying about one thing or another. He is a curious character, admired as a kind of intellectual Quixote, tilting his umbrella at projects of such audacious scope as to be quite remarkable. He is admired for taking chances, having ambitions and ultimately failing, which makes him human. He wrote an essay once about his library. As he unpacks his books they remind him of the cities where he collected them: Florence, Basel, Riga, Munich and others. The collector is possessed by a kind of djinn (a spirit according to him) which makes him believe that ownership is the most intimate relationship one can have to objects. Benjamin, the djinn, constructed his own labyrinth out of his collection of books, and then, like an illusionist, he turned and vanished inside.

At dawn we wake up to find ourselves in a bus depot below ground in a kind of concrete trench. Our first view of Barcelona is the red brick of the Arc del Triomf, built for the Universal Expo of 1888. The air is balmy and warm and the traffic furious and urgent. I am excited. This is where Orwell came to fight for liberty. Malraux was here. I feel assailed by history, the lies and legends that roll back to the days when this was briefly part of Al Andalus, home to Ibn Arabi. A flight of three green parrots flash by, squawking excitedly. Leo rubs his eyes.

'Did you see that? Parrots! Real ones.'

He calms down long enough to let me drag him to a nearby terrace where we order breakfast. He finds a new pleasure in dipping deep-fried fingers of dough, *churros*, into hot chocolate and waves me off to do whatever I want. He slept for most of the journey and looks much better. The headache is gone and he has not thrown up again, which is reassuring. The waitress fusses over the large plaster on the back of his head, but I can only gesture and smile. I leave him in her capable hands and cross to a newspaper stand where I buy a map and ask the man how to get to the place we were going. I have no Spanish and he no English. A third person stops to buy a newspaper and he gets involved. Now I have the two men talking to one another in an animated fashion and both appear to have forgotten about me. Then a slim girl arrives in a brown suit wearing a neat little knapsack on her back. She speaks enough English to tell me which railway station I need and how to get there. I thank everybody and go back to Leo who hasn't missed me and now has chocolate all over his face.

It is early afternoon by the time we are aboard a train that is running us smoothly back up the coast. We could have waited, I realise, taken a day to see the city, but I feel that we are in danger of being overtaken by time, which seems to be speeding up. I am afraid, too, that now we are so close all of this will come to nothing, that Muk will be gone, vanished like a whisp of smoke from an oil lamp.

The train delivers us to Blanes and from there we have a choice between a bus and a ferry to take us around to Tossa de Mar. Leo suggests it is time to take to the sea. So we lug our bags up the gangway with some difficulty. Between us we are carrying a fair amount of luggage. As well as my old canvas holdall and Leo's rucksack, we also have two large new nylon bags. These are cumbersome and heavy, filled with hiking boots, cassette tapes, Thermos flasks, books, even my father's old typewriter which had been lying undisturbed in the boot of the car since he died, along with all manner of odds and ends that used to sit there quietly and unnoticed. We draw a few curious stares and are clearly out of step with our fellow passengers, many of whom are tourists, day trippers unencumbered by anything more demanding than digital cameras and sunglasses. We resemble stowaways or, well, immigrants come to stay.

The ship bobs along contentedly while we sit up on deck and Leo scans the horizon for submarines, using his cupped hands for binoculars. It feels as though we are on holiday, but I am thinking about how Muk will greet us. It is entirely possible that, by sending me the card, he didn't mean that I should actually come and find him. The last time I saw him he wanted to kill me. And supposing he had posted the card and left by the next ferry? I work out that it is over a year and a half now since I last saw him. The card is nine months old. There is every chance that he is no longer living here.

But such worries fade for some reason, and the sound of seagulls whipping overhead and waves slapping against the hull bring a sense of calm and resignation. I feel as though I am floating freely through the world unhindered by anything or anyone. I am resigned to my fate. Somehow we will find a way out of this. Four days ago I thought I was dead. Worse than that, I thought the unthinkable, I thought my son was dead. Now I feel I am prepared to meet whatever the world has to throw at me.

The town nestles in the embrace of a circular bay, hemmed in at either end by the curve of rocky bluffs. It used to be a smuggler's haven; a ridge of hills helped to keep the inlanders away, and their noses out of what was going on down here. On the southern side, to the left when approaching from the sea, a high stone wall can be seen curling up the promontory at the southern end of the town. In the tenth century these fortifications of rust-coloured sandstone, along with the watchtower that can be glimpsed further inland, were built to keep the marauding Arabs out.

Today they are crawling with tourists taking pictures of one another, leaning against the railings above the sea. Moorish Spain is now little more than an exotic, and very brief, footnote in their guidebooks.

Most visitors scratch their heads when they come across the lines from the *Rubáiyát* of Omar Khayyám which are carved into a piece of stone on the clifftop overlooking the town. The same cryptic lines that Muk wrote on the postcard he sent me. The poet of Nieshapour's presence has less to do with the Moors who once lived here than with the movies. Beside the stone tablet is a statue of Ava Gardner who came here with James Mason in 1950 to film *Pandora and the Flying Dutchman*. There are pictures posted in shop windows all over town, black-and-white stills taken by a local photographer: Ava Gardner reclining on the beach, surrounded by adoring fans; the two stars posed on the same clifftop which now resounds to the snap of pocket disposables and the whirr of digital movie cameras. The lines of poetry appear over the credits as the film opens.

> The Moving Finger writes; and, having writ,
> Moves on: nor all your Piety nor Wit
> Shall lure it back to cancel half a Line,
> Nor all your Tears wash out a Word of it.

The film tells the story of a ghost ship and her captain, condemned to sail the seas for ever for having killed his wife in a fit of jealous rage. Moored outside the town he meets the beautiful Pandora, desired by all. She falls in love with the one man she can't have – the phantom Dutchman. His only chance for redemption is to find a woman who is so in love with him that she is prepared to die for him.

The romantic intrigues of the story were reflected in the goings-on surrounding the shooting of the actual film. The other character who appears regularly in shop windows, and on the walls of almost any restaurant you might care to walk into, is Frank Sinatra, as thin as a fish hook in a light three-piece-suit. Sinatra, the story goes, was deeply jealous of the affair Gardner was allegedly having with a local *torero*, a bullfighter named Mario Cabré who also had a part in the film. Gardner denied all and she and Sinatra were married the following year. When they divorced five years later, Sinatra went into the studio to record what is purportedly one of the saddest records of all time, *Only the Lonely*.

I have no idea of any of this as we rock slowly towards the sandy beach. I am to learn much of it later, from Inés, who visited the town for the first time because of the film, leaving her family far behind in Andalusia. This was her idea of Mecca. In the film the town is renamed Esperanza, which means hope.

There is no quay to speak of in the bay. The ferry simply discharges its passengers directly onto the beach by means of a narrow gangway that is extended from the bow. The sea floor drops away steeply enough for us to come right in to the shore. As we approach, the ferry swings around in a braking manoeuvre, turning broadside to the beach as the captain cuts the engines. A wave follows in our wake. When it hits us side-on the boat begins to rock wildly from side to side. Alarmed shrieks and cries come from the passengers as hands shoot out to grab hold of seats and railings. But it is all part of the adventure, a little more dramatic than intended, perhaps, but nothing of consequence. For a few moments it is like being on a roller coaster as we pendulum from side to side. As we gain momentum the deck tilts to a good thirty degrees. That is when our bags begin to slide. I reach out quickly and manage to catch the one nearest to me, but one of them, the one furthest away, slips by my outstretched fingers. Leo throws himself onto his rucksack as I go for the other one. I am sure it will stop. It will slow down, reach a certain point and then swing back to me as the deck rights itself. When I realise it is not stopping I hurl myself after it and nearly go over the side myself. I watch the bag slide smoothly and neatly underneath the safety chain and fly out into the air. For a moment it is poised in mid-air, then it plunges downwards to a watery grave. A slight splash and it is gone. I sit on the deck staring at the empty space, the swaying chain links, not quite believing what has happened. Leo runs to the rail frantically.

'It's gone, Baba! It's sunk. How are we going to get it back?'

A commotion descends upon us in a variety of languages, none of which make much sense to me. A few men shake their heads at such foolhardy behaviour. Several people step up to the rail to have a look. A woman with crooked teeth makes a poor try at stifling a laugh. By now the deck is in balance and we have reached the shore. People turn their attention to disembarking. A crewman is summoned by a Polish tourist in a white shirt and checkered trousers. He seems quite good at taking charge. A policeman, perhaps, when he isn't wandering the world with a camera around his neck. But the crewman is not particularly concerned. He shrugs. We should have held onto our bags more carefully. The risks of sea travel. All baggage should be stowed safely.

'You must tell the coastguard,' a stern woman says to me in English. She is tall and thin, with an angular face. German perhaps, or Dutch. She studies the plaster on Leo's head and gives me a strange look. 'Tell the police. Tell somebody.' Then she turns and is gone, chasing after her group before they leave her behind. Leo is close to tears. His face is grimy with dirt and sweat and the dressing on his head definitely needs changing. I squeeze his shoulder and together we stagger down the shaky ramp with the remainder of our bags and bundles. I dump everything on the sand and slump down to consider the significance of this in the overall scheme of things. Leo joins me, his gaze on the same spot of dull blue into which our bag vanished.

'What are we going to do?' The ferry is already on its way, the gangway folding up as she chugs back away from the beach. Soon there is no trace of our landing, except for the little crowd of onlookers turning to stare in our direction.

'Nothing we can do.'

Two crewmen are leaning over the side of the ferry, looking down into the water.

'But we have to get it back.'

'We can't,' I snap. 'It's at the bottom of the sea.'

'What was in it?' he asks gently, after a time.

'Books, just some old books that needed clearing out anyway. I feel lighter already. Who needs to cart all those heavy things about?'

'Baba,' he smiles at me. 'Sometimes you really are crazy.'

'You'd better be careful then, because it probably runs in the family.'

Among the people standing and pointing first at the water and then at us are a couple of waiters from one of the seafront restaurants. I walk over and show them the address on the card and they direct us towards the walls of the old city.

With our burden now lightened considerably we move slowly to the far end of the bay and pass through a gateway in the high stone wall we saw from the sea. My brother lives in the old town, it seems. Leo cheers up considerably at the thought of staying in a medieval fortress. We find ourselves within a maze of cobbled streets that zig-zag back and forth around the promontory. We follow a narrow passageway leading between two rows of houses jammed together. In a little terraced square at the foot of a set of stairs we put our bags down and try to trace the numbers on the houses. The air is rich with the scent of jasmine coming from the trees that loom over us, and far above the little cottages three seagulls hang in a line, suspended in mid-air, greedily yapping at one another. We find what we are looking for eventually – a small green door set into a wall thick with vines that snake like powerful sinews up the stone. The leaves tremble in the sea breeze as we knock and wait.

'Are you sure this is right?' Leo whispers. Whether it is or not no one appears to be home. I raise my hand to knock again when I hear footsteps coming from within, a muffle of voices. The door opens and we find ourselves looking at a woman neither of us has ever set eyes on before. She is in her late twenties with a head of dark thick braids that are straining to break free from the blue ribbon that holds them behind her head. All three of us are a little perplexed. I am holding the postcard in my hand, now so badly worn it looks as if it had been recovered from a trouser pocket that has just come out of the washing machine. The girl turns the card slowly over in her hands trying to work out what we are asking from her. A man's voice echoes from within: '¿Quién es?' She doesn't answer, she is still examining the card. Then she turns abruptly away and the door slams in our face. Leo and I look at one another.

'Now what?'

'Are you sure this is the right place?' he demands urgently. 'Now she's got our postcard.' Which is a good point. We ought to get that back. I raise my hand to knock when the door opens again and this time it is a large bearded man. We stare at one another.

'Muk?'

'Yasin? I don't believe it!' He looks bigger all round, plumper, his rounded face enhanced by the wild beard and the bush of hair which has bits of what might be clay in it. He looks past me. 'Who's this, then?' He has not seen Leo since he was a toddler. The frown clears slowly. 'Of course. Hey!' He reaches out to shake Leo by the hand. 'You know who I am? I'm your uncle. That's right. You're my nephew.'

Leo looks to me for help. Muk steps back for a moment. He is still standing inside the doorway. 'I don't believe it,' he keeps repeating. The door widens behind him and the girl reappears. 'Yeah,' he shrugs, as though trying to work out how to put it: 'This is . . . mi hermano,' he says gesturing. 'This is my brother, Yasin. And this is . . . Hamdi?'

'Leo,' says Leo.

'Right, Leo. Leo the Lion.' Muk smiles. He puts out a hand to squeeze my shoulder awkwardly. We all stand there looking at one another as though not quite sure what is supposed to come next.

28

My brother is a changed man it appears. I always thought it would be religion that saved him. I wasn't sure what faith exactly, just one of the many on offer. Not necessarily Islam, or Christianity, but perhaps something entirely different. I expected he might find salvation in one of those sects of lost souls living in reclusive splendour on a mountainside in Switzerland, say, or a ranch in Texas, waiting for the mothership to swoop down and gather them all up. It seemed logical that he would choose that direction, a combination of spiritual guidance and quirky fascination. Now here he is looking like Cat Stevens and living in a fisherman's cottage with just enough room for two romantic people and a small cat. No guitars, no strange robes or rituals. He takes whatever employment he can find. There is plenty of building work about. New hotels, luxury flats. Already it is difficult to pick out the little fishing village that is being slowly buried beneath the weight of all that concrete and glass. The small streets are jammed with restaurant terraces and waiters who wave menus at you in six different languages. A few elderly women dressed in black stand about on the steps and watch the parade of energetic tourists flocking by. Some of them can probably tell you stories about the civil war and when they are gone it will all be lost. Most of the inhabitants are transitory; new arrivals from other parts of the country, other parts of the world, come to find their own personal El Dorado.

Muk is currently employed by a pair of hard-looking nails who hail from somewhere in the Ukraine. They came with suitcases full of cash and Black Sea caviar and swept about in BMWs complete with smoked windows and blonde wives. They have bought an old building on the seafront, whose arched verandas, leached khaki walls and battered shutters have lent it a crumbling, colonial air. They are turning it into a hotel. Tourism is like a relentless fever and it shows no signs of relinquishing its grip until it has squeezed the last drop out of the place. The season is now coming to a close. Many of the hotels and restaurants are shutting down for the winter. In the quiet months it is different here, says Muk, deserted and tranquil. He prefers it that way. So does Inés. She is quiet and pensive and at first I assume this is because she is not too confident about speaking English. Later I realise that she simply keeps her thoughts to herself.

Right from the start there is a mutual unspoken agreement between Muk and me to restrict ourselves to the present. There is enough to occupy us here; settling into the house and exploring our new surroundings. Neither of us wants to break the spell which this town seems to cast over our meeting again. Both of us would rather postpone the inevitable, avoid dealing with the memory of what has passed between us. For a moment I catch a glimpse of the little brother I used to know, long ago and under different circumstances.

And Leo gets his birthday swim in the sea. He wanders up and down, lost in exploration, a child again, doing what children do. He splashes in the water, digs holes in the sand. He rushes over to show me a shell he has found. Water drips in luminous beads from his hair. It is a big shell, almost the size of his palm, and perfectly round. It is worn smooth as porcelain and has a concentric pattern of sepia-coloured ripples arched across it. He is breathless with excitement.

'It almost looks like writing, you know, on a piece of paper.'

We stare at the shell together as he tries to show me what he sees.

There is a cool breeze and the beach is almost deserted but

for us and a few hardy tourists. I sleep, try to read a Spanish newspaper without success and sleep some more.

We get back to the house to find Inés and Muk busy in the kitchen. Muk seems large and clumsy in these surroundings, but he is making an effort. I offer to help chop the vegetables, but he shoos me out onto the patio at the back of the house. The stone garden wall holds the sun's warmth and it feels pleasant and still. They are chattering away in Spanish and I wonder how Muk has picked the language up so quickly. I close my eyes and enjoy the sound and smell of food being prepared. I don't want to think about the past or the future.

The meal turns out to be a lavish affair. Two different salads and a selection of pastries with savoury fillings in them, then sardines roasted in the oven, followed by an enormous rice dish which Inés has prepared. A cake has been ordered from the bakery with Leo's name on it.

'Quick, light the candles!' Muk is fumbling with a box of matches. I put my arm around Leo's shoulders.

'Happy birthday, Eight-year-old.'

'Pretty old for a dog,' he says. We sing 'Happy Birthday' in English, Arabic and Spanish and he blows the candles out.

'Careful! Don't sit down on your present.' It is a pair of binoculars I managed to buy without him noticing. I know he has been dreaming about them for some time. Muk has bought a football and Inés a pen for sketching with. Leo thanks everyone and then settles down, emitting a gasp of glee as he studies a seagull floating over the house.

After that Muk talks for a while about the problems he is having at work. None of them speak the same language, it seems. His fellow labourers come from Ecuador, Morocco and Senegal. And then there are the Russians. They treat him as though he had just climbed out of a tree, he says. He could teach them a thing or two about building. The same old Muk. When he becomes animated it reminds me of the unresolved tension between us and I think it best to let him just talk.

I notice Inés trying to draw my attention. She is nodding towards Leo. He is sitting very still, clutching the binoculars in his hands. I can see the little splatters his tears make where they strike the rubber casing. When I put my hand out to him he jerks away and runs inside the house.

'He misses his mother,' says Inés. I say nothing. I don't need people to tell me what my son needs. Then Muk decides to throw in his penny's worth.

'Look, Yasin, it's none of my business, but maybe he'd like to talk to his mother? It is his birthday, after all.'

'He's all right,' I say. 'He just needs a little time by himself. He'll be fine.' I stare at them. They don't look entirely convinced. 'Believe me, he'll be fine. Maybe we should clear these things away.'

But when I go upstairs I find that Leo is not there. We search the house from top to bottom, but he's nowhere to be found.

'He must have gone out,' suggests Muk.

'But where? Where would he go?'

I leave them there and step out into the street. I try to imagine what Leo would have done. Would he go up or down? Up, I decide. So I start jogging up the steps towards the fortifications on top of the promontory.

I emerge to find the place deserted but for a few solitary couples and a guided tour making their way along the castle walls. I pass the statue of Ava Gardner looking out to sea for her phantom lover. The wind is blowing through the pines and there is no sign of an eight-year-old boy alone anywhere. I walk quickly along the cliff path, trying not to look down at the long drop to the crashing sea. It makes sense, I decide, to go up as far as I can and then work my way down. When I reach the artillery breech at the highest point in the wall I find him. He is sitting there with his side against the iron railing, both feet up on the low rampart.

'You scared me,' I say. 'I thought I'd lost you.'

'It doesn't matter,' he replies.

'What do you mean?' I sit down beside him.

'It doesn't matter to you if I am lost or not.' He is tossing small stones over the side. It is a long way down to the rocky shore. 'Nothing matters to you,' he says as he grinds an ant into the dust.

'How can you say that?'

'Because it's true!' he shouts at me. 'This is not for me. None of it is. You say it's an adventure. It doesn't seem like much of an adventure to me!'

'I thought you were enjoying yourself.'

'OK, just tell me one thing. What are we going to do now?'

'We'll go back to the house. We can read.'

'No! I mean, what are we going to do now!' He flings his arm out towards the horizon and a stone curves downwards through the air. 'Where are we going to go next?'

'Where would you like to go?'

'Baba!' he implores. 'You are the adult. You are supposed to know. You have to decide.'

It is plain that I have no answers for him. Turning away in disgust he hugs his knees to his chest and gazes at the sea.

'Look,' I say, finally. 'I have an idea. Why don't we try to find a phone and call your mother? I'm sure she'd like to say happy birthday.' He doesn't answer, but I stand up and take a few paces and wait. After a time he gets to his feet. He follows behind me all the way down into town, slowly, keeping his distance as if waiting to see if I intend doing what I say. It is like a game, except that he is deadly serious.

Eventually we find a place, a telephone exchange for overseas calls, brightly lit and full of cigarette smoke. We crowd into a booth and I dial the number and wait. Leo holds the receiver to his ear and listens for a long time. Then he hands it to me and walks out without saying a word. The answerphone machine. Nobody is home. I listen to Ellen's voice and after a while I start to speak.

Later that evening, when the others have turned in, Inés and I go for a walk along the beach together. Muk has to get

317

up before dawn and Leo has gone to bed early. He is still not speaking to me. I need to get out and get some air.

The night is remarkably quiet and still. The moon a perfect brushstroke of white silver that stretches over the gleaming dark sea to our feet. The air is balmy and warm and the only sounds come from the sea and the gentle tapping of a sail line against a mast just across the cove where a handful of yachts are moored.

We talk about this and that. She tells me she once toyed with the idea of opening a restaurant, but her cooking wasn't good enough, and as for Muk, well, she laughs, she would have to hire a professional. She seems quite devoted to him.

We sit in the sand and watch the way the sea plays with the moonlight. I am glad of her company. She tells me about the film that brought her here to begin with.

The tale of the ghost ship, the *Flying Dutchman*, was apparently based on a true story. The Dutch East India Company records show that a ship captained by a man named Hendrik van der Decken disappeared off the Cape of Good Hope around 1641. Van der Decken apparently made a pact with the Devil, swearing that he would round the Cape with or without God's help. For that he was condemned to sail the seas until Judgement Day. The legend of a phantom schooner developed over centuries and there were numerous accounts of sightings right up until the 1940s. Inés saw the film on television and it stuck in her memory.

Inés was born on the great plains south of Cordoba. She came from a wealthy family of landowners. They produced their own wine, they raised horses. After a couple of years at university she dropped out of her philosophy classes and went to Guatamala with a group of like-minded wanderers. Then she and another girl went on to India where they joined an ashram in Darjeeling and spent three months weaving cloth and boiling lentils. They went on to Nepal and walked up to Anapurna base camp only to find it overcrowded and filthy. Everybody went to these places in search of the sacred and the sublime, she said, only to arrive there and find hundreds of other people with exactly the same idea. She fell sick with dysentery and had to make a harrowing bus trip down to Delhi where her friend decided she had had enough. So Inés went on to Thailand alone, first to Bangkok and then north to Chiang Mai where she was raped in a boarding house by two Australian backpackers. 'I was feeling reckless. I was on my own, and we had too much to drink and smoke and when I said no they just went a little wild.' She tried reporting the two men but the local authorities took the attitude that anything the tourists got up to was their own business. She broke down then, and spent three weeks locked up alone in a room in a boarding house unable to speak to anyone, barely able to summon the energy to get out of bed. When she got back to Spain, she couldn't face going home. Instead, she came here, to a town she didn't know, a town she remembered as being called Hope.

'Your brother has told me so much about you, I feel that I know you already for a long time.'

'I can't imagine he had anything very complimentary to say. We didn't get on all that well.'

'Your brother,' she says, 'went through a very bad time and now he wants to do good.'

'Good?'

'He's like me. The world hurt him and now he wants to make it better.'

This is what they have in common, then. But I am still not sure what she is talking about. 'Make it better how?'

'He didn't tell you?' She turns to examine my face. 'We are going together to Sudan.'

Muk is going home? 'You mean travelling?'

'No,' she laughs. 'To work in the south. In a camp for refugees. It's an organisation, you know? Not the government? ONG?'

'NGO – non-governmental organisation.'

'He didn't tell you?'

I shake my head. He didn't tell me. Perhaps this is it, he

319

has found his cause. He was going to save people, put the world right.

'He's a funny person, your brother. He makes me laugh. But he's like me. He lost his self-esteem. Everyone has two sides, good and bad. He did something bad and now he is going to do something good.'

I listen to her, and try to think of something good that I had ever done.

They are leaving at the end of the month and have no idea when they will be back. They are to become volunteers. We have too much in the West, says Inés. Too much food. Too many cars. Too much everything. The planet can't sustain it. This is the revolution of our age. In generations people will look back. We have to go back to the earth with our hands and beg for forgiveness.

'I think that's why he came here, to make a new start. What about you?' she asks, turning to me finally. 'What made you come here?'

29

My father's second heart attack came with as little warning as the first. Yasmina told me that she only began to get worried that morning after she had sent the children off to school and he still had not made an appearance. He was usually up before them all, wandering about the kitchen, going back to bed with a piece of toast to read his newspapers only to reappear, dressed and ready to go out, around ten. But there was no evidence of his usual pre-dawn wanderings to be found in the kitchen, no crumbs of burnt toast scraped into the sink, no carton of milk left out. At eleven o'clock she knocked on his door. When there was no answer she still waited half an hour before going in.

He was lying half out of bed, arms and head hanging down to the floor, legs twisted in the sheets, like a parachutist caught in a tree, a horseman dead in his saddle.

It took me a long time to understand what his death meant exactly. What about all those unfinished conversations, arguments, matters that were one day to be resolved? All suddenly anulled, rendered meaningless. And I was no closer to knowing what I wanted out of life than I had been when I was twelve and he tried to dissuade me from a career as a swimmer. He had won. He got his own way as he always did, the last word. And he had got away cleanly. No fuss. There one minute and the next minute, gone. He lay there in the undertaker's back room. His eyes closed, his mouth open. There was a gap at the front where his denture was missing. He never wore it at night and no one had bothered to put it back in. His arms by his sides, the neck craned back, hands splayed out, straining to hold on. Gone. That was the way of it. Leo and Yasmina's twins, the next generation, were all too young to remember much. His memory would die with us, Muk, Yasmina and I. A part of me had gone with him, I realised, vanished from the world. The childhood years, the baby years, the other side of me which he had witnessed. Things I would never know about his life, things I had not managed to get out of him, they went with him too.

What he left behind: a pile of clothes that didn't fit anyone in the family, to our great relief. There were cardboard boxes full of newspaper cuttings. Boxes that once held oranges from Valencia spilled over with heaps of inky newsprint. Clippings snipped with a pair of nail scissors; little half-moons snaking up the edges; articles about everything under the sun. Train crashes. Hijackings. Outbreaks of salmonella. A miner's strike in Bolivia. A riot in Manila. Thickly underlined sentences. Luminous highlights. Exclamation marks. But where was the common axis? How did all of this make sense to anyone? I spent hours trying to piece together the state of mind of a person who could see a tangible centre to all of it, to understand the struggle into which all this information fitted. Tracing the squiggles of his notes in the margins I felt closer to him than I had in years, but by the end I realised I was no wiser. His mind was like a magpie, collecting little nuggets that glittered here and there. Perhaps there was no centre. Perhaps he himself was looking for some way of making sense of the world. Whatever it was, the real mystery of what he might have done with those clippings evaded me. But the absence of an answer lingered, hinting at the existence of a part of him I had never known.

Then there were the letters. Box files full of them, all with carbon copies. The ones he had sent off, the ones he hadn't sent. There were folders and files and all of it a chaotic mess. Reams of typewritten pages, outrage fuelled into ink. This was the sum total of his final will and testament; a pile of angry missives, copies of letters which had probably already been pushed into a bin along with thousands of other letters that newspaper editors and the Home Secretary's office receive every year. This is what we do with our lives, exchange the ethereal substance of our souls for paper covered in signs, even though we know they will probably never do justice to the latent promise of inspiration that triggered them.

Yasmina didn't want a shred left in the house, so I packed the boxes and the typewriter into the car to take home with me. I didn't know what I was going to do with it all, I just couldn't bring myself to throw it away. This was what he had left in the world. Whatever it was, it meant something to him.

The funeral was organised by Umar with his usual managerial flair. It was to take place in the same windy Muslim cemetery in North-East London where my mother had been buried. Umar had arranged it long ago, because he was ahead of us all on this. He had bought the plot right next to her. It even had my father's name on it. Of course Umar hadn't told anyone about this, not me, not Yasmina.

'What about Muk?'

'What about him?' I asked.

'We have to find him, wherever he is.'

She was right, of course. Whether he wanted to see us or not, one of us was going to have to go and find him. There was no choice, I had to do it. Yasmina was not going to venture in the direction of Soho, so I went. There was a girl with a bad case of congestion living in the flat now and she knew nothing about anyone. She told me to get lost or she would call the police. I left and went to sit in the sad little café in Berwick Street, not in hope so much as in need of time to think. The coffee had not improved.

'He's a grown man,' I said to Yasmina later. 'If he doesn't want to be found, he won't be found. Unless he's dead or something,' I ventured.

'If he had had an accident then they would have contacted us, next of kin and all that,' she said with patient logic.

'And if he was in prison?' I aired my second worst-case scenario.

'Prison? Muk?' She was standing with the kettle in one hand, the lid in another. We were in her kitchen, two black plastic bin-liners of clothes stood by the door behind me waiting to be taken down to the Islamic charity office at the mosque. They would send them off into the world and someone somewhere would step gratefully into them. They bore too much significance to us, out there they were just old worn shirts and corduroys. Yasmina gave a laugh, as if I were trying to be funny, and then abruptly stopped herself as though remembering that this wasn't appropriate. She gave me a hook-nosed frown. 'Always joking, even at a time like this.' But she could see that I wasn't trying to be funny. She put the kettle down.

'You know something that I don't. He's in some sort of trouble.'

'I don't *know* anything. I just think we can't rule it out.'

'Ya Allah.' Yasmina sat down slowly at the table, one hand on the formica, a finger traced the lines where the skin bunched around her knuckles. She didn't look up. 'If he was in prison he wouldn't have to tell us, would he?'

'Look, I might be wrong. I . . .'

'You're not wrong, Yasin. You are never wrong.' She was on her feet again. 'When it comes to the downfall of this family you are always there, right on the spot. You enjoy misery and shame. You wallow in it.'

'We have to face the facts.'

'Just go and find him.' She turned away from me. 'That's all. Just do it. But I don't want to hear anything about it.'

So I went. I contacted the police and the hospitals and, as we had suspected, there was no record of him being either dead or in treatment. To locate someone you suspect might be in prison you have to write to a post-office box in Birmingham. If the person is on their books they pass your message on and then it is up to the person involved if they want to contact you. In the meantime the funeral happened.

The odd little convoy made its way across London after prayers were said at the mosque in Regent's Park. The cemetery was penned in between a reservoir and a busy road, and dotted with pylons that buzzed ominously. The wind blew hard across the bare ground which not so long ago had been trodden only by the slow plod of bovine hooves. There was evidence of some effort being made to improve the look of the place and the neatly ordered plots separated by lines of whitewashed bricks and chips of stone at the top end of the field contrasted with the bare overturned mounds of soil where we were standing. The clods of sticky earth were still redolent of cattle. Events were overseen by a pale-skinned man who spoke with a thick Yorkshire accent. He was dressed in a fine outfit with an embroidered silk ibaya and imma and a rather stylish beard. He also doubled as driver of the hearse, I noted. The helpers had all arrived from Umar's mosque in Canterbury driving a battered green Transit van circa 1979, and dressed in a variety of outfits. These were not the well-heeled lot Dad had known in Bayswater and Edgware Road, the exiled journalists from Baghdad and Damascus, the poets from Lebanon. These were the common men, the hordes, the salt of the Muslim earth, bulky and well fed, with curly beards and woolly glares, their peasant simpleness part of their essential credentials. The world had changed from those days when my father used to dress himself up in his Jermyn Street ties and stroll down Queensway to discuss politics over jebena coffee and the Arabic newspapers.

The old guard were thus shunted to one side, shaky with age, shrunken, withered, a group of old men for whom funerals were becoming one of the only regular fixtures on their social calendar. They chatted no more about revolution and ideals. Nowadays their preoccupations were blood sugar, cholesterol and prostate glands. They stood by and watched as the gang of well-padded men in Doc Marten boots and turbans struck a hearty path across the uneven ground with mud clinging to the tails of their kurtas.

I, too, found myself pressed back to the sidelines. The simple box in which my father was now laid out (on his side so as to face Mecca) was pulled from the hearse with as much ceremony as a jackhammer, and shouldered hastily. Everything was happening at breakneck speed for some reason, as though they all had an appointment pending or another mission lined up. They jogged across the field like mujahidin guerrillas heading for an artillery emplacement. I raised a hand towards Umar who was in the thick of the crowd, but he didn't seem to notice. There was much shouting and angry gesticulation around the grave as the coffin slipped from the straps and bumped hard against the earth. I heard a nauseating crack of thin pine. It seemed as though it wouldn't quite fit into the hole. Stubborn to the end, Dad refused to go in. They set the coffin to one side and the gang of men buzzed about trying to decide what to do. Shovels were raised and stabbed down into the thick marl. No one seemed to be in charge. It was burial by mass confusion. When he finally made it into the ground it was with all the grace and ceremony of a badly fitting door being knocked into place.

Then a real commotion broke out. Some of Umar's friends objected to the behaviour of one of the old fellows, whom I then recognised as being Abdelsalam al Hadi, a professor of Arabic literature who had written a racy novel in the fifties that was immediately banned everywhere and thus transformed the author into a luminary figure on the Arab literary horizon. He had written nothing much since then but was still picking up awards for that novel. He had stepped up to the grave and, holding up his hands in the prescribed manner as though reading from the sacred book, had started to recite the *fatihah*, the opening sura of the Koran. There was a lot of gesticulation and shouting. The objection, it transpired, was theological: the Koran, they shouted angrily, was not meant for the dead, but for the living. Nobody else had ever heard this before. People always recited at the graveside, didn't they? No longer it seemed. They roughly pushed the stunned and confused old man aside. I stepped in to intervene, or rather to encourage my brother-in-law to do so.

'Umar, tell them to behave themselves!'

'Please, Yasin, they only mean well. They only mean it out of respect.'

'Respect for whom?'

Umar frowned at me. 'A member of the community has died. We must all show our respect for his passing.'

'How about showing respect for his friends?'

His look betrayed the kind of undisguised contempt I was growing familiar with. In his eyes I had no business being here. I was too lax, too much of a lapsed case to be worthy of this honour. He turned and began talking quickly to the others, while I helped al Hadi out of the way.

'I don't understand anything any more. Nothing. I understand nothing,' he kept repeating. Turning the phrase back and forth as though unable to decide which way round it ought to be. We stopped at a safe distance to watch them filling in the grave, taking turns with the shovel. It really didn't feel like it was actually happening.

'By the way,' he said, 'I hear you have written a fine novel. Why? What for? The age of novels is dead. If I was your age I would be in the cinema, chasing all those actresses.' He winked.

'Perhaps you are right. People seem to either hate it or love it.'

'A good sign! It means there is something worthwhile there. Look at me. Only the best get that treatment.' He touched my arm. 'Your father was a good man. We shall all miss him. He must have been very proud of you.'

I didn't have the heart to tell him what my father really thought.

*

327

A week later I discovered that in Britain prisons don't have wardens, they have governors. I had a feeling that Muk's ability to charm the warden at school was not going to help him now. I had received word that he was indeed 'inside', and that there would be no objection to my visiting him if I so wished, even though Muk had not sent me a visitor's pass. I called the governor, who was very civil and sounded so concerned and understanding that it made me think that perhaps he had just returned from a course in public relations. He said that considering the circumstances I should just come down the following day. He would inform Muk that I would be there during visiting hours and it would be up to him, but in light of the situation, etc. etc.

As it turned out, my brother and I were virtually neighbours, had been for over a year. It took me no more than twenty minutes to drive to the place on the border with Hertfordshire. It took longer to get through the checks and into the visiting room. The prison was set behind a row of tall poplars and pines in a charming secluded area surrounded by golf courses. The roads were thick with Daimlers and Jaguars heading for a quick round on a sunny Saturday morning.

They patted down your pockets before letting you in: no guns, knives, razor blades, or hacksaws hidden in cakes. Anything you brought for the inmate went through a separate door. Then you were led inside a big hall. The other visitors looked excited, as though this were the high point of their week, a day out. Some, I noticed, were on first-name terms with the guards. A little girl with a plump midriff poking out of her tracksuit bobbed up and down for a glimpse of her father. An older couple, the man in an old-fashioned brown suit and the mother in a tweed skirt and jacket sat in silence, not even looking at one another as they waited for their son. The inmates came in one by one through a door on the other side of the room. You could see them through the glass as they stood in the interim space waiting to be let through.

I barely recognised him at first as he came towards me. He was thin and jowly and his hair had been shaved to a stubble. It was the way he moved that gave him away because from a distance, across that enormous hall the size of a basketball court, he walked just like my father, his feet splayed out to one side, his knees flexing, shoulders forward. He was accompanied by a warder who led him to where he was to sit and told him to 'mind your manners now', giving me a wink as he carried on. Perhaps this cheerful tone was part of the same public relations drive as the governor's charm. They would be offering me share options on the way out.

The numbered seating areas each comprised four moulded plastic seats bolted to a metal frame that was fixed to the floor. Three chairs were white and one was orange; the inmate sat on the orange one and had to stay there the entire duration of the visit. Through an observation window above and behind me a couple of guards were able to keep an eye on us. All around us people were hugging one another and getting down to the business of finding out how the world was getting on in their absence. The little family alongside us were chattering away cheerily as though this were any Saturday afternoon and we were sitting in a shopping centre.

The room filled up with sound. The pale man in the brown suit shook hands with his son and lit a cigarette, leaning forward, his elbows on his knees, a red and blue tattoo on his wrist shaking itself out of his shirt cuff like a playing card. The little girl bounced up and down on her father's lap while the mother recounted what she had to tell. Who was seeing whom and who was up the spout again and whatforeedjit was in trouble again and how when the doctor said her mother had high blood pressure she knew instantly why the cow was so bloody nervy all the time.

And we just sat there in silence, the two of us, Muk in his blue denim outfit (no arrows), until finally I said, 'He's gone.' He looked up at me and snapped, 'I worked that out for myself. Why else would you be here?' and I realised then that I didn't have anything else to say to him, not really. He was inside for four years for selling hard drugs but they might let him out in half that time if he behaved himself. They found bags and weights and syringes and all kinds of incriminating things in his flat. They caught him quite easily as it turned out, followed him home, watched him for a couple of days and then two plainclothes men jumped him in an alleyway in the middle of a deal. He struggled to fight them off and then tried to swallow what he had on him which would have killed him instantly, except they put a necklock on him and forced him to choke the packet up.

We were locked there, in that room together, poised opposite one another. Issue of the same womb, the same genetic patterns in our helical DNA spirals, winding round one another. Intertwined. But we still had nothing to say to one another. This wasn't the end of the world. It was bad, but people survived. The voices around us spoke of the ways in which lives could be improvised around the intrusion of the law. The incorporation of criminal offence into the ordinariness of daily routine; take the kid to school, do the shopping, rob a post office, go to prison. Everyone around us seemed to have attained some degree of ease, some coming to terms with the reality of their situation. The plump little girl in the grey sweatshirt and pants, crawling up and down off her father's knees trying to get his attention. Her mother batting smoke away from her eyes, still talking in an unbroken litany of complaint. The man seemed bemused by the whole thing. He looked incapable of anything nasty. I wondered what he had done, what crime he had committed to make society decide to lock him up. He seemed relaxed, comfortable, as though he might even be looking forward to saying goodbye and going back to the simple life of his cell. Beyond him the man with the tattoo looked resigned to his lot. He had no more expectations from life, or from the bullet-headed lunk of a son who was chatting away to the warders as though he were sitting on a park bench. The boy was already at home here. This was to be his life. He had already learned to talk himself out of here.

We sat in silence. Perhaps we were both trying to work out how we had ended up here in this place together. An old-fashioned idea of fate surfaced in my mind. That was where Haboba would have pointed. There was no explanation. What could you learn from examining the course of this little family history, the trajectory which led Muk into those shapeless denims, and Yasmina to a semi in Canterbury with her head covered in pious deference, to her husband, to her dead father, to God. On her knees praying for all of us to be saved, even me? Did any of it make sense? Was it meant to make sense?

We had a good start in life: clean clothes, three square meals a day, a home to live in, a school to go to. We had liberal-minded parents who taught us to read and write and think for ourselves, who did not abuse us, or beat us with a stick and lock us in the chicken shed. They did not drink themselves into oblivion every night, nor send us out begging on the streets for a crust of bread. We played in the sunshine and dreamed of doing good things when we were grown. Where did it all go wrong? Where does it go wrong with anyone?

'Why don't you come out and say it?' he asked, sitting upright in his chair suddenly, examining me morosely through half-closed lids. 'You're thinking what a shame all of this is; your own brother locked up, wasting his life. You're thinking that what I did was wrong, that I deserve everything I got.' He smiled now, getting into his stride, letting all the bile ooze out. 'Well, it wasn't wrong, everyone is at it. I just happened to cross the wrong people and they paid me back by snitching, that's all it is. There is no right and wrong any more. That was the old way of the world. Look around you. Do these people look bad, or evil? No, they just got caught, that's all. No different from some executive who fiddles his taxes. What do you think people get up to on the stock market all day? Ripping people off is what. Let me tell you, those people in their expensive suits and sports cars are no better than I am. Who do you think imports the stuff?

Where do they stay when they come to town? The Ritz, that's where, the Four Seasons. Not some poxy little place where the toilet leaks onto the carpet and the television only has three channels. They travel in style and they are treated with respect because that's all there is now, the money. Respect is money. All that stuff about learning and education and values? Well that was fine for people forty years ago. That was the way the world was in those days. But you know what? You could never get anywhere because there was always something in your way. You couldn't get into places because your skin was too dark. You couldn't buy a house on certain streets. You couldn't get promoted beyond a certain point. The glass ceiling they call that. The world was ruled by *them*, and they wanted to keep *us* out. You can try as hard as you want but you never get anywhere. You know why? Because you're playing by their rules. They run the game. You can't win. And that is what has changed. We stopped respecting the rules. And that is a change for the better, believe you me. No matter which way things go, they will never go back to how they were before. So what matters now is who has the money. That guy who bought Harrods. What's his name? Look at him. They were scared of him because he was actually buying them out. Imagine, their precious democracy being bought and sold by a greasy gyppo. That's what he did, and then he went for the royals and they put a stop to him. You think that was an accident in that underpass in Paris? No way. They went for him and they went down hard. People make the best of what they start out with in life, and I didn't have all that much going for me. I had to do the best I could. Well, this is what happened. It's a setback, but don't despair. I shall be out of here and on my way again. You'll see.'

He sat back, breathing heavily, and lit another cigarette. The ends of his fingers were stained yellow with about an inch of nicotine. This was how it was, and now I knew. I looked at the clock on the wall. Less than fifteen minutes had gone by.

'You missed the funeral. I suppose that if we had known you were here we could have tried to get you out. I don't know if they do that kind of thing?' I was thankful that we had not had to go through that. I imagined to myself what people would have made of him turning up in handcuffs, or with a police escort. 'At least Mum never had the chance to see you in this situation,' I said. 'That is at least some kind of blessing.'

He let out a kind of strangled wail and threw himself across the space between us. His fingers locked themselves around my throat and we both fell heavily to the hard concrete floor. There were whistles blowing somewhere and he was on top of me. His eyes were bulging and I had bruises on my neck for nearly three weeks. They grabbed us and sort of tore us apart. I felt the sleeve of my jacket pop and the cloth of my shirt give way. Then I was pinned to the ground with two guards kneeling on me while four others were dragging Muk backwards towards the door he had come through, still spluttering and swearing as though in the throes of a fit. They had batons twisting his arms behind him. The buzzer sounding for the inner door seemed to send a signal through him and his heaving, thrashing body instantly went limp. His heels scraped along the ground and his face went blank as the electric door slid open behind him. With a long moan he vanished from sight.

The guards helped me to my feet and I straightened my clothes as they waited. I would have to leave. I had no objections. No, I would not be buying any shares. Together they walked me towards the exit. I was aware of everyone looking at me. The wooden-faced man with the tattoo was grinning, the first sign of cheer from him, so the day had not been an entire waste. His thick-necked son sniggered to himself. The little girl clung to her father. The mother shook her head in disgust at the kind of degenerates they let into these places nowadays. All across the room people were shrugging and asking one another what on earth was going on over there.

That had been the last time I saw Muk. Later, when I went through all of my father's papers I discovered that he had actually known where Muk was. There was a letter from him stamped HM Prisons in among the heap of correspondence he left behind. He had kept it a secret from us all, took it to the grave with him rather than admit his son was a convicted criminal.

30

The following morning Leo has recovered his humour and we go down to the beach. I am determined to make it a good day. We will do everything he wants to. And no limit on the amount of ice cream he can have. So we swim and build moats and more fortresses in the sand. I tell him that the watchtower behind the town was used to keep a lookout for pirates from the Barbary coast. He scans the horizon with his new binoculars.

'We have to be careful,' I say. 'This life of leisure might grow on us.'

'What's a life of leisure?'

'One in which you don't have to do any work.'

'Uncle Muk is working.' He trains his glasses inland.

'Can you see him?' I sit up.

'He's coming this way.'

And so he is, bearing sandwiches and cans of soft drink. There are smears of plaster on his face and arms and he has a kind of scarf tied around his head which makes him look a little like a pirate according to Leo. He throws himself down and I can see that despite the hard physical work, he was actually putting on weight. Perhaps it is age, I think, deciding that this might be a good moment to set a few things straight.

'Did you skip parole,' I ask as casually as I can, 'or were you allowed to leave the country?'

Muk gives a snort of laughter and shakes his head. 'You think I would stay there any longer than I had to?'

'That's an answer?'

He looks at me out of the corner of his eye as he takes a swig of lemonade.

'I'm never going back, that country nearly killed me.' He gestures out towards the sea. 'This is where I belong now, out in the open air, not in prison.' He still hasn't told me about their plans to leave here.

Leo squints up at him. 'Did you really go to prison for being a pirate?'

'That's right,' Muk gives a mock growl and flexes his muscles. Then he laughs and ruffles Leo's wet head. He is awkward around Leo, perhaps around all children. There is a part of him which I suspect will never quite grow out of the teenage sentimentality that passes for emotion with him. He has missed out a lot of important years, years he spent looking for a way out of reality, convincing himself that he was born to stand on a stage with thousands of adoring fans cheering wildly at his feet. Years that disappeared down a hazy drugged road of scoring, fixing and dealing. There is a gap, like a long lost weekend, in his development and he will probably never get it back. A part of him will always be that overgrown boy who thinks he deserves more attention than he is getting. If I rub him the wrong way he will turn on me, livid with fury. At the same time he is like a gentle giant with Leo, worried that he might break a bone if he touches him.

We finish eating and walk down to the water's edge. Leo kicks off his sandals and goes exploring the rocky shallows, stepping cautiously over the green algae, stopping to peer through the binoculars at crabs scuttling between his feet.

'So,' Muk says, 'your turn now. When are you going to tell me?'

'About what?' I ask.

'Well, everything, why you decided to come. How you got that.' He taps the plaster cast on my left wrist.

'I told you, we had a little accident with the car.'

'How little is little?' He studies me for a moment, and then he shrugs and looks away. 'You've always been lucky.' There is a yacht crossing the mouth of the bay, the billowing sail a brilliant white crescent in the sun. 'You never knew how lucky you were. You never believed in anything, always distrusted everyone. You didn't want to be on that side, or this side. Do things your own way. Always so sure of yourself. Always the independent one. There was always a mystery about you, as though you had a secret, something that nobody else knew. Yasmina was Miss Conventional. Did everything she was told, perfectly. I was the joker. I could make people laugh. I needed to make them laugh. I needed their approval, admiration, love. But not you. You went off alone and nobody could believe it. You seemed to forget about us from one day to the next. You hardly ever wrote. Oh, you would call once in a while, but we never heard very much of anything. Mum used to cry. Did you know that? She used to sit there with your letters in her hand and cry. I asked her why once and she said it was as though you had spent your life just waiting for a chance to get away from us. She knew you were gone for ever. You would never be coming back. And I remember thinking, if he is not coming back, what am I doing here? Of course, then I went and got carried away with it all. I have no talent, I know that now, and besides, even musicians have to do some work. I thought it would come to me easily, the way everything seemed to come to you.'

He faces the sea as he talks, speaking with the detachment of one who has come to terms with a lot of things about himself. 'I felt abandoned. I thought I could better you, achieve something that would knock you all off your feet. That's what we all want, isn't it? To be above it all, to be free.'

He stretches his arms. It is almost the end of his lunchbreak. He has to get back to work, reconstructing the 'El Dodi' as he has nicknamed it, on account of the fact that it is next door to the Hotel Diana. The Russians don't get his rather obscure brand of humour. They never laugh with you, Muk says, only at you.

'I'm happy, for the first time since I was a child. I'm out in

337

empty space. I don't have to please anyone. I don't need the drugs. Oh, we smoke a little hash once in a while, but that's all. I watch the sunrise and I watch it set and I know there is nothing more beautiful and nowhere I would rather be.' He turns to face me. 'You're wondering why I'm telling you this?' He takes a deep breath. 'I don't want you messing things up for me. You're my brother and I love you, but you need to stay away from me. You're bad luck to me.'

This is why he has not told me about their plans. I look down at Leo. He is out of earshot, crouching down in the water. In a few days we will have to find a doctor to take the stitches out. What are Spanish doctors like? He looks up and sees me watching him. He holds up something in his hands that jumps and plops back into the water around his ankles.

'Not everyone is like you, Yasin. We can't all live on a diet of pure air. That boy of yours needs a mother. He needs people around him, order, something to make sense of it all. Don't mistake him for you, no matter how much he resembles you. Nobody is like you.'

I watch Muk walking away for a minute or two, trying to think what to do.

'Don't go anywhere,' I call down to Leo. 'Not out in the deep water.'

'Where are you going?'

'I'll be right back.'

At first I can't see where Muk has gone. He has got further than I thought and almost reached the road. I begin to jog along the sand but it is slow going. I am not exactly sure what I want to say to him, but I need to say something. I pause to catch my breath and turn back to check on Leo. I can't see him for a moment, and then he straightens up and I can see him watching me in a curious way. He turns and wades deeper into the water. The road is not far away now. I run until my lungs hurt. If Leo falls over in the water I will not be able to get back to him in time to pull him out. My lungs ache and I am sweating quite profusely. None of it

338

matters any more, I realise. All that I care about, all that I have, is here and now. And Muk is about to run away from me because he thinks I am going to ruin things for him. There is nothing else to hold on to. I am tired of hurting people. I want to stop and rest.

I call out to him once or twice, but by the time I reach the road he is already on the other side picking up a wheelbarrow and heading in through a gate to the yard of the building site. I call his name again, and this time he hears me. He stops and I see him turn towards me. A cement mixer starts up with a clatter. He is saying something, but I can't hear what it is. I see him raise his hand as I step into the road, and then I feel myself lifted up into the air very quickly. A shadow comes down towards me and I know it is going to hit me and that there is nothing I can do. It strikes me right between the eyes. Hard. And then there is nothing.

31

I ought to have been expecting it. Accidents always happen in threes. I didn't even hear it coming. It was a light two-stroke machine, which was lucky, and it hit me just by a bend in the road which meant it was not travelling so fast, which was also lucky. Not so lucky was the fact that when I fell I hit my head. I was out for a week. Just like my father when he was struck by that golf ball all those years ago. When I woke up I found Ellen standing over me.

'Is this the scene where the doctor tells me I only have three months to live?'

She smiled and shook her head. I looked around the room. We were alone. It seemed very quiet and still. The sun was shining brightly outside. There was a yellow shade to keep the light out of the room.

'Where is he?'

'Don't worry, he's fine. He's down at the seaside with your brother and the girl, what is her name?'

'Inés.' My hearing was a little fuzzy, and there was a kind of ringing sound. My back hurt when I breathed.

'That's the one.' Ellen was looking well, confident, strong. She was wearing a pair of light-coloured linen trousers and a striped blouse. There was a jacket over the back of a chair by the window. There was something ordered and together about her, which I had not seen for a long time.

'Everyone has been making a fuss of him. He has been standing guard over you night and day.'

'He's a good boy.'

'He loves you very much.'

340

'I know.'

She looked at me for a while, and then she sighed and shook her head. She unfolded her arms and pulled up the chair. 'I was worried about both of you. You had no right to go off like that. Leo told me about the accident with the car. You were lucky.'

'Everybody says that.'

'I'm taking him back with me. He's supposed to be in school.'

I nodded, but said nothing. She was right, school was where he belonged. She stood up and went over to the window.

'I have a new job,' she said.

'Wonderful.'

'It's just a teaching post. The letter was waiting for me when I got home.' She came back to the chair and sat down, leaning towards me, elbows on her knees. There was a pain in my neck I discovered, when I turned my head. 'You never even tried to apologise,' she said softly. 'You owed that to me, after all the years together. But you didn't do it. You never said sorry.'

'What happens now?' I asked.

'Things have to be different, for Leo's sake if for nothing else.'

'Then you're still determined to go ahead with the divorce?'

'We can't go back. Too much damage has been done. I need to hold on to the order I have in my life. I can't deal with you, Yasin. And besides, it's been over for a long time. I don't have time for that destructive element in you. People change. Sometimes they become incompatible. Our lives no longer fit together.'

'Have you told Leo yet?'

'I think he knows how bad things are without anyone telling him, don't you?'

'We tried to phone you.'

'Not very hard. I was worried. You scared me.'

'I scared all of us.' I wasn't sure I could go through with this. A new life. Ellen seemed to know what I was thinking.

'You won't lose him. Even if I wanted to cut you out of his life completely, he wouldn't let me do it.'

'I need him around me. I'm not sure I can manage without him.'

'Of course you can. You've done it before. You're the same person you've always been, Yasin. You haven't changed at all. This is who you are. There are no more answers than that. It's not the end of the world, but I think we both owe it to ourselves to make a fresh start.'

'I don't know where to start.'

'You still have a job, don't you? Start there.'

'I'm not sure you can work in radio if you have deficient hearing.'

'Don't feel so sorry for yourself,' she said, then she put a hand on my arm. It was the first time in a long while that I had known her to be comforting, caring. 'It will take time.' She stood up. 'I'll go and fetch Leo now. He's dying to see you. He's been very worried.'

I watched her go, out of the door, to her new life, her life without me, striding away with new-found purpose. I sighed and stared at the ceiling.

There was a moment's pause and then the sound of Leo's whoop came from somewhere not far away. I could just picture him jumping and punching the air. Yes! I heard his footsteps coming along the corridor and his mother telling him not to run.

Epilogue

We sit down and I feel a great constriction in my chest, as
though the place where my heart normally sits has been
invaded by an enormous bird. The station is almost empty.
There is an old couple trying to decide where to stand, the
woman licks her lips and the man looks at his watch. Leo sits
by my side.

'It'll be all right,' he says, putting his hand on my arm.
'You'll see.'

I am not sure how long we sit there, perhaps half an hour,
perhaps as little as ten minutes, but then suddenly there it is, a
ray of sunlight gleaming along its flank as it curves up the
track towards the station. Everything then happens very
quickly. The platform suddenly swells with people, pouring
out from inside the waiting room, or down from the train.
There is an air of hectic urgency. Suitcases, large, hard shells
on wheels, are dropped unceremoniously to the ground,
handed up, down, trundled away. There are shouts of
greeting and exclamations of surprise and joy as all around us
people greet one another, embrace, weep, and part. As easy
as that. Grandparents stand waving at the carriage window,
young people leap up and down hugging one another
ecstatically, dancing in a circle. Coming or going, it makes
no difference. It is as though this is a celebration, of motion,
of travel, of human endeavour, of the aching need to be in
two places at once; one for the heart, one for the head. The
platform, which a few moments ago had been bare and still,
is now awash with human emotions, frothing back and forth
between the faded brick walls and the steely white of the

carriages. I cling to the past because it is all I have. I do not exist without it, or at least, that is what I have always believed. I am afraid of letting go. As though he reads my mind, Leo turns and looks up at me.

Ellen is over by the train with the suitcases, showing her tickets to a man in a uniform who is pointing. She waves to us indicating that it is the next carriage down. Already the engine is revving up, but no one seems to be in any hurry.

'Baba?'

'Yes?'

'It won't be so long, will it?'

'No,' I kneel down and he puts his arms around me. 'It won't be so long.'

'Here.' He reaches into his pocket and holds out the shell from the beach. 'You keep this. Then, next time we meet you can give it to me and . . .' We haven't got the heart to play this one out. He puts his arms back around my neck and neither of us says anything.

'Go on, run, or you'll miss the train.' I stand up.

He walks backwards. 'I miss you already,' he says.

'I know. I miss you. Watch where you're going.'

He smiles, full of confidence, and then turns to vanish into the crowd.

For a moment I feel like a diver who has gone down into the water too fast, unable to get back to the surface. I see nothing around me but a blur of unfamiliar faces. People whom I have never seen before in my life and in all likelihood never shall again. The sudden unbearable sensation of being swamped by this mass of nobodies. But that is the thing, they are all somebody. They belong to other people. They have sons too, and daughters and parents and even grandparents. It all fits together. It all makes sense, because we give it meaning. Even me.

I hear the sound of the announcer coming over the loud-hailer. I can't see Leo. Then he is up there in the doorway, by Ellen's side. They say something to one another and Ellen steps back out of sight. Leo raises his arm and waves. I wave back. Then there is a beeping sound as the doors slide closed and his face is replaced by a shining glass reflection of the sky above my head.

The train begins to roll away, wheels clicking over the points, the shiny white carriages curving out of the station, like beads of white amethyst clicking through my fingers in a steady purl, out into the sunlight. It keeps going, increasing the distance, a reel of celluloid ticking through the sprockets. I see myself from far away, a tiny figure on the platform, growing smaller, the world expanding around me.

The sun is about to set behind the hills by the time the bus deposits me back on the corner of the seafront. I walk along towards where Muk will be finishing his work for the day and find him sitting there on the low wall, staring at the sea.

'Everything go all right?'

I nod. It is done. Everything appears slightly changed to me. The beach, the sky. I can hear the sea as though I were right next to it. There is a crowd down by the water's edge and I ask Muk what is going on.

'I think they found something. Something washed up on the beach.'

We wander over. A group of adolescent boys, damp from the sea, are crouched down. Others scamper up from the waterline to drop objects in the growing pile. Muk and I push forwards to crane our necks over their shoulders. There, at the centre of the circle of curious onlookers, is a ripped strip of nylon. A bag, its contents strewn like the disconnected parts of a puzzle all the way back along the beach.

'It looks like books,' laughs Muk, 'and what is that thing?'

'A typewriter,' I say. 'A Remington portable. Circa 1964, bought second-hand in an Oxfam shop in Canterbury. The A key is loose and the Y sticks a little.' Muk stares at me as though I have gone mad. Then he frowns and pushes his way through the crowd, shouting and gesticulating. He picks up a book from the pile and the pages, pulpy and heavy with

345

water, unfurl like a sea polyp. He flips to the front where you might find the name of an owner, or the price stamped in a dusty bookshop several thousand miles and more than twenty years away, and gives a cry of recognition.

He throws it into my arms for me to catch and stoops to pluck up another one, and then another. Then he is off, bobbing down the beach, clutching the books to his chest, waving when he finds something of particular interest. Soon he is out of earshot and all I see is this hairy creature silhouetted against the deepening purple of the sky over the distant rocks, the lights coming up along the road. People have already begun to disperse.

The length of the beach is almost deserted now. A simple stretch of water and sand meeting in a fluorescent hiss. It has not changed in a million years and it will remain that way long after we are gone. My brother, a solitary figure jogging along the empty beach plucking sunken objects from the surf. I look down at the one in my hand, barely recognisable, the pages already drying in the breeze.

Something rough is grating in the spine, working itself back and forth. I look more carefully and see the timelessness of those grains of sand, hard and minuscule, trapped between the pages. In the pale evening light they seem to burn with the warm glow of fallen stars, just waiting for someone to catch them.